FABLES

OF

ÆSOP

AND

OTHERS:

TRANSLATED INTO ENGLISH.

WITH

INSTRUCTIVE APPLICATIONS;

And a PRINT before each FABLE.

By SAMUEL CROXALL, D.D.

LATE ARCHDEACON OF HEREFORD.

ISBN 978-1-4357-4935-1

TO THE RIGHT HONOURABLE

GEORGE,

Lord Viſcount Sunbury, Baron Halifax.

My Lord,

YOU muſt not be ſurprized at my begging Your Protection for this little Book, when I aſſure You it was principally intended for Your Peruſal. I had often wiſhed to ſee ſomething of this Kind publiſhed by an able Hand:

A 3

And,

And, for want of that, have fometimes had an Inclination to do it myfelf: But never came to any Refolution in that Point, till very lately; when, at *Horton*, I had the Pleafure to find Your Lordfhip, tho' but in your fifth Year, capable of reading any Thing in the *Englifh* Tongue, without the leaft Hefitation.

Thefe Fables, My LORD, abound in Variety of Inftruction, Moral and Political. They furnifh us with Rules for every Station of Life: They mark out a proper Behaviour for us, both in refpect of ourfelves and others; and demonftrate to us, by a Kind of Example, every Virtue which claims our beft Regards, and every Vice which we are moft concerned to avoid. Confidering them in this View, I could not think of any Thing more proper, to be put fo early into Your Lordfhip's Hands, as well for Your own Sake, as that of the Public. As I wifh You all the Happinefs which Man can enjoy, I know of nothing more likely to procure

it,

it, than Your imbibing, in Your Childhood, such Seeds of Reason and Philosophy, as may rectify and sweeten every Part of Your future Life. And as You are by Birth intitled to a Share in the Administration of the Government, I flatter myself that your Country will feel the Benefit of these Lectures of Morality; when hereafter it beholds Your Lordship, steadily pursuing those Principles of Honesty and Benevolence, which, by such Instructions in Your Infancy, You will be taught to love.

I am happy, upon several Accounts, in the Opportunity I take in addressing myself to Your Lordship, in this early Time of Your Life. Without any Reflexion upon Your Parts, My LORD, I comfort myself with the Consideration, that You are not yet able to discern all the Imperfections of my Performance. Nay, when you are a little older, and Your Judgment is strong enough to discover every Weakness in the following Sheets, You will yet remember for what

DEDICATION.

a young Capacity they were intended; and whatever You may think of the Style and Language, the honeſt Purpoſe of the Whole cannot fail of Your Approbation.

Another Advantage, My LORD, is, That when I tell the World You are the moſt lovely and the moſt engaging Child that ever was born, I cannot be charged with offending in Point of Flattery. No one ever ſaw You but thought the ſame.

And this puts me in Mind, that You are deſcended from a Race of Patrons. Arts and Learning did not owe more to the Influence of *Mecenas* at *Rome*, than they have done to that of *Montagu* at *London*. Perhaps, young as You are, You may think it ſtrange to find Yourſelf at the Head of a Dedication: But, My LORD, nobody elſe will wonder at it. You are born to protect and encourage all Endeavours at the Public Good. We cannot help telling You, that we expect it from you: and we beg Leave to put You in Mind to affert Your native Right.

If it is true, that Virtue may be conveyed by Blood, and communicated by Example, I have all the Prefumption imaginable for what I affert. My LORD, Your Father, the EARL of HALIFAX, poffeffes every agreeable Quality in Life: Whether natural or acquired, I will not pretend to determine. They are fo eafy and habitual to Him, one would think them born with Him; but at the fame Time fo accomplifh-ed, that we cannot but difcover they have had the Advantage of a finifhed Education.

If I durft follow the Suggeftions of a Heart truly fenfible of them, I could dwell with Pleafure upon every Particular of his Worth. But nobody who deferves Applaufe fo much, declines it more than he does. Indeed, My LORD, his Merit is fo great, that we cannot do him Juftice in that Refpect, without offending him.

That,

DEDICATION.

That, upon all Occasions, you may imitate the Example he sets, and copy out his Virtues, for your own and the Welfare of Mankind, is the sincere Wish of,

My LORD,

Your Lordship's

most obedient, and

most humble Servant,

Hampton-Court,
May 1, 1722.

S. CROXALL.

PREFACE.

SO much has been already said concerning *Æsop* and his Writings, both by ancient and modern Authors, that the Subject seems to be quite exhausted. The different Conjectures, Opinions, Traditions, and Forgeries, which from Time to Time we have had given to us of him, would fill a large Volume: But they are, for the most Part, so inconsistent and absurd, that it would be but a dull Amusement for the Reader to be led into such a Maze of Uncertainty: Since *Herodotus*, the most ancient *Greek* Historian, did not flourish till near an hundred Years after *Æsop*.

As for his Life, with which we are entertained in so complete a Manner, before most of the Editions of his Fables, it was invented by one *Maximus Planudes*, a *Greek* Monk; and, if we may judge of him from that Composition, just as judicious and learned a Person, as the rest of his Fraternity are at this Day observed to be. Sure there never were so many Blunders and childish Dreams mixed up together, as are to be met with in the short Compass

A 6   of

of that Piece. For a Monk, he might be very good and wife, but in Point of Hiftory and Chronology, he fhews himfelf to be very ignorant. He brings *Æfop* to *Babylon*, in the Reign of King *Lycerus*, a King of his own making; for his Name is not to be found in any Catalogue, from *Nabonaffar* to *Alexander the Great*; *Nabonadius*, moft probably, reigning in *Babylon* about that Time. He fends him into *Egypt* in the Days of *Nectanebo*, who was not in being till two Hundred Years afterwards; with fome other grofs Miftakes of that Kind, which fufficiently fhew us that this Life was a Work of Invention, and that the Inventor was a bungling poor Creature. He never mentions *Æfop's* being at *Athens*; though *Phædrus* fpeaks of him as one that lived the greateft Part of his Time there; and it appears that he had a Statue erected in that City to his Memory, done by the Hand of the famed *Lyfippus*. He writes of him as living at *Samos*, and interefting himfelf in a public Capacity in the Adminiftration of the Affairs of that Place; yet, takes not the leaft Notice of the Fable which * *Ariftotle* tells us he fpoke in Behalf of a famous Demagogue there, when he was impeached for imbezzling the public Money; nor does he indeed give us the leaft Hint of fuch a Circumftance. An ingenious Man might have laid together all the Materials of this Kind that are to be found in good old Authors, and, by the Help of a bright Invention, connected and worked them up with Succefs; we might have fwallowed fuch an Impofition well enough, becaufe we fhould not have known how to contradict it: But in *Planudes's* Cafe, the Impofture is doubly difcovered; firft, as he has the unqueftioned Authority of Antiquity againft him; fecondly, (and if the other did not condemn him) as he has

* *Arift. Rhet.* Lib. 2. Cap. 21.

intro-

introduced the witty, difcreet, judicious *Æfop*, quibbling in a Strain of low Monaftic Waggery, and as archly dull as a Mountebank's Jefter.

That there was a Life of *Æfop*, either written or traditionary, before *Ariftotle*'s Time, is pretty plain; and that there was fomething of that Kind extant in *Auguftus*'s Reign, is, I think, as undoubted; fince *Phædrus* mentions many Tranfactions of his, during his Abode at *Athens*. But it is as certain, that *Planudes* met with nothing of this Kind; or, at leaft, that he met not with the Accounts with which they were furnifhed, becaufe of the Omiffions before-mentioned; and confequently with none fo authentic and good. He feems to have thrown together fome merry Conceits which occurred to him in the Courfe of his Reading, fuch as he thought were worthy of *Æfop*, and very confidently obtrudes them upon us for his. But, when at laft he brings him to *Delphos* (where he was put to Death by being thrown down from a Precipice) that the *Delphians* might have fome Colour of Juftice for what they intended to do, he favours them with the fame Stratagem which *Jofeph* made ufe of to bring back his Brother *Benjamin*; they clandeftinely convey a Cup into his Baggage, overtake him upon the Road, after a ftrict Search find him guilty; upon that Pretence carry him back to the City, condemn and execute him.

As I would neither impofe upon others, nor be impofed upon, I cannot, as fome have done, let fuch Stuff as this pafs for the Life of the great *Æfop*. *Planudes* has little Authority for any Thing he has delivered concerning him; nay, as far as I can find, his whole Account, from the Beginning to the End, is mere Invention, excepting fome few Circumftances; fuch as the Place of his Birth, and of his Death; for in refpect of the Time in which he lived, he has blundered egregioufly, giouſly, by mentioning ſome Incidents as contemporary with *Æſop*, which were far enough from being ſo. *Xanthus*, his ſuppoſed Maſter, puts his Wife into a Paſſion, by bringing ſuch a Piece of Deformity into her Houſe, as our Author is deſcribed to be. Upon this, the Maſter reproaches his Slave for not uttering ſomething witty, at a Time that ſeemed to require it ſo much: And then *Æſop* comes out, ſlap daſh, with a ſatirical Reflexion upon Women, taken from *Euripides*, the famous *Greek* Tragedian. Now *Euripides* happened not to be born till about fourſcore Years after *Æſop*'s Death. What Credit therefore can be given to any Thing *Planudes* ſays of him?

As to the Place of his Birth, I will allow, with the Generality of thoſe who have written about him, that it might have been ſome Town in *Phrygia Major*. *Lucian* calls him Αἴσωπος ὁ Φρὶξ: In *Phædrus* he is ſtyled *Phryx Æſopus*; and *A. Gellius*, making mention of him, ſays, *Æſopus ille, è Phrygia, Fabulator*. That he was alſo by Condition a Slave, we may conclude from what *Phædrus* † relates of him. But whether at both *Samos* and *Athens*, he does not particularly mention: Tho' I am inclined to think it was at the latter only; becauſe he often ſpeaks of him as living at that Place; and never at any other. Which looks as if *Phædrus* believed that he had never lived any where elſe. Nor do I ſee how he could help being of that Opinion, if others of the Ancients, whoſe Credit is equally good, did not carry him into other Places. *Ariſtotle* introduces him (as I mentioned before) ſpeaking in public to the *Samians*, upon the Occaſion of their Demagogue, or Prime Mi‑ niſter, being impeached for plundering the Common‑ wealth: In which Oration he makes him inſert the ‡

† Lib. 2. Fab. 9. & Lib. 3. Fab. 19.
‡ CXCV. of this Collection.

Fable

PREFACE.

Fable of the Fox who was peſtered with Flies; and who, upon an Hedgehog's offering to drive them away, would not conſent to it, upon Suſpicion that a new Swarm would come in their room, and drain him of all the reſt of the Blood in his Body. Which *Æſop* applies thus: *Ye Men of* Samos, *let me intreat you to do as the Fox did; for this Man having got Money enough, can have no farther Occaſion to rob you; but if you put him to Death, ſome needy Perſon will fill his Place, whoſe Wants muſt be ſupplied out of your Property.*

I cannot but think *Æſop* was ſomething above the Degree of a Slave, when he made ſuch a Figure as an eminent Speaker in the *Samian* State. Perhaps he might have been in that low Condition in the former Part of his Life; and therefore *Phædrus*, who had been of the ſame Rank himſelf, might love to inlarge upon this Circumſtance, ſince he does not chuſe to repreſent him in any higher Sphere. Unleſs we allow him to be ‡ ſpeaking in as public a Capacity to the *Athenians*, upon the Occaſion of *Piſiſtratus*'s ſeizing their Liberties, as we have before ſuppoſed he did to the *Samians*. But however, granting that he was once a Slave, we have great Authority that he was afterwards not only free, but in high Veneration and Eſteem with all that knew him; eſpecially all that were eminent for Wiſdom and Virtue. *Plutarch*, in his *Banquet of the Seven Wiſe Men*, among ſeveral other illuſtrious Perſons, celebrated for their Wit and Knowledge, introduces *Æſop*. And, tho' in one Place he ſeems to be ridiculed by one of the Company for being of a clumſy mongrel Shape, yet in general he is repreſented as very courtly and polite in his Behaviour. He rallies *Solon* and the reſt for taking too much Liberty in preſcribing Rules for the Conduct of Sovereign Princes; putting them in Mind, that thoſe who

‡ *Phæd.* Lib. 1. Fab. 2.

aſpire

PREFACE.

afpire to be the Friends and Counfellors of fuch, lofe that
Character, and carry Matters too far when they proceed
to cenfure and find Fault with them. Upon the Credit
of *Plutarch*, likewife, we fix the Life of *Æfop* in the
Time of *Cræfus*, King of *Lydia* ; with whom he was in
fuch Efteem, as to be deputed by him to confult the
Oracle at *Delphos*, and be fent as his Envoy to *Periander*
King of *Corinth* ; which was about three Hundred and
twenty Years after the Time in which *Homer* lived, and
five Hundred and Fifty before *Chrift*.

Now, though this imaginary Banquet of *Plutarch* does
not carry with it the Weight of a ferious Hiftory, yet
we may take it for granted, that he introduced nothing
in his fictitious Scene, which might contradict either the
written or traditionary Life of *Æfop* ; but rather chofe to
make every Thing agree with it. Be that as it will, this
is the Sum of the Account which we have to give of
him. Nor, indeed, is it material for us to know the little
trifling Circumftances of his Life ; as whether he lived
at *Samos* or *Athens*, whether he was a Slave or a Free-
man, whether handfome or ugly. He has left us a Legacy in his Writings that will preferve his Memory dear
and perpetual among us : What we have to do, therefore, is to fhew ourfelves worthy of fo valuable a Prefent, and to act, in all Refpects, as near as we can to
the Will and Intention of the Donor. They who are
governed by Reafon, need no other Motive than the
mere Goodnefs of a Thing to incite them to the Practice of it. But Men, for the moft Part, are fo fuperfi-
cial in their Enquiries, that they take all upon Truft ;
and have no Tafte for any Thing but what is fupported
by the Vogue of others, and which it is inconfiftent with
the Fafhion of the World not to admire.

As an Inducement, therefore, to fuch as thefe to like
the Perfon and Converfation of *Æfop*, I muft affure them
that

PREFACE.

that he was held in great Esteem by most of the great Wits of old. There is scarce an Author among the Ancient *Greeks*, who mixed any Thing of Morality in his Writings, but either quotes or mentions him. *Socrates* is described by * *Plato* as turning some of his Fables into Verse; and that in some of those serious Hours which he spent in Prison, a little before his Death. *Aristophanes* not only takes Hints from him, but mentions him much to his Honour, as one whose Works were, or ought to be read before any other. He brings in one Man upbraiding another with Ignorance and Illiterateness in these Words, ἐδ' Αἴσωπον πεπάτικας, *You have not so much as read Æsop*; it being, as *Suidas* observes, a proverbial Expression. *Aristotle* (as you have seen) speaks of him to his Advantage. *Laertius* tells us, *Demetrius Phalereus* wrote a Book intituled Αἰσωπεια, & Αἰσωπείων Λόγων Συναλογαὶ; being a Collection of Fables, so many of which were *Æsop*'s, or done in his Manner, that he thought fit to call the whole by his Name. *Ennius* and *Horace* have embellished their Poetry with him. *Phædrus* gives him abundant Applause. And *A. Gellius* delivers his Opinion of him in a Manner too particular to be omitted. *Æsop the* Phrygian (says he) *the famous Fabulist, has justly acquired a Reputation for his Wisdom; for, as to those Things which are beneficial and adviseable for us to do, he does not dictate and prescribe them in that haughty dogmatical Way, so much used by some other Philosophers; but dresses up a Parcel of agreeable entertaining Stories, and by them conveys to the Mind the most wholesome and seasonable Doctrine, in the most acceptable and pleasant Manner. As that* † *Fable of his, for Example, of the* Lark *and her* Young Ones, *warns us, in the prettiest Way imaginable, never to lay any Stress upon the Assistance of others, in regard to any*

* *In* Phædone.   † Fab. XXXVIII.

Affair

PREFACE.

Affair which we are ourselves able to manage without them. Then he proceeds to give us a fine Version of the Fable itself; and, having finished it, *This Fable of Æsop*, says he, *is a Lecture to us concerning the little Reliance we ought to have upon Friends and Relations, and what now do the grave Books of Philosophers teach us more, than that we should depend upon ourselves only ; and not look upon those Things which are beyond our Reach, as any Concern of ours.*

Thus we see, whatever his Person was, the Beauties of his Mind were very charming and engaging; that the most celebrated among the Ancients were his Admirers ; that they speak of him with Raptures, and pay as great a Respect to him, as to any of the other wise Men who lived in the same Age. Nor can I perceive, from any Author of Antiquity, that he was so deformed as the Monk has represented him. If he had, he must have been so monstrous and shocking to the Eye, as not only to be a very improper Envoy for a great King, but scarce fit to be admitted as a Slave in any private Family. Indeed, from what *Plutarch* hints of him, I suspect he had something particular in his Mien, but rather Odd than Ugly, and more apt to excite Mirth than Disgust, in those that conversed with him. Perhaps something humorous displayed itself in his Countenance as well as his Writings; and it might be upon Account of both, that he got the Name of Γελωτόποιὸς, as *Lucian* calls him, and his Works that of Γελοῖα. However, we will go a middle Way; and without insisting upon his Beauty, or giving into his Deformity, allow him to have made a merry comical Figure; at least as handsome as *Socrates*; but at the same Time conclude, that this Particularity in the Frame of his Body was so far from being of any Disadvantage to him, that it gave a

mirthful

PREFACE.

mirthful Caſt to every Thing he ſaid, and added a Kind of Poignancy to his Converſation.

We have ſeen what Opinion the Ancients had of our Author, and his Writings. Now, as to the Manner of conveying Inſtruction by Fables in general, tho' many good Vouchers of Antiquity ſufficiently recommend it, yet, to avoid tiring the Reader's Patience, I ſhall wave all Quotations from thence, and lay before him the Teſtimony of a Modern; whoſe Authority, in Point of Judgement, and conſequently in the preſent Caſe, may be as readily acknowledged as that of any Ancient of them all. ‡ *Fables, ſays Mr. Addiſon, were the firſt Pieces of Wit that made their Appearance in the World; and have been ſtill highly valued, not only in Times of the greateſt Simplicity, but among the moſt polite Ages of Mankind. Jotham's Fable of the Trees is the oldeſt that is extant, and as beautiful as any which have been made ſince that Time. Nathan's Fable of the poor Man and his Lamb, is likewiſe more ancient than any that is extant, beſides the above-mentioned, and had ſo good an Effect, as to convey Inſtruction to the Ear of a King, without offending it, and to bring the Man after God's own Heart to a right Senſe of his Guilt, and his Duty. We find Æſop in the moſt diſtant Ages of Greece. And, if we look into the very Beginning of the Commonwealth of Rome, we ſee a Mutiny among the common People appeaſed by the Fable of § the Belly and the Limbs; which was indeed very proper to gain the Attention of an incenſed Rabble, at a Time, when, perhaps, they would have torn to Pieces any Man who had preached the ſame Doctrine to them, in an open and direct Manner. As Fables took their Birth in the very Infancy of Learning, they never flouriſhed more than when Learning was at its greateſt Height. To juſtify this Aſſertion, I ſhall put my Reader in Mind of* Horace, *the greateſt Wit and Critic in*

‡ Spect. No. 183. § Fab. XXXVII.

the

PREFACE.

the Auguftan *Age*; *and of* Boileau, *the moft correct Poet among the Moderns*; *not to mention* la Fontaine, *who by this Way of Writing, is come more into Vogue than any other Author of our Times.* After this, he proceeds to give fome Account of that Kind of Fable, in which the Paffions, and other imaginary Beings, are Actors; and concludes with a moft beautiful one of that Sort, of his own contriving. In another Place, he gives us a Tranflation from *Homer* of that inimitable Fable comprifed in the Interview betwixt *Jupiter* and *Juno*, when the latter made Ufe of the Girdle of *Venus*, to recal the Affection of her Hufband; a Piece never fufficiently to be recommended to the Perufal of fuch of the Fair Sex, as are ambitious of acquitting themfelves handfomely in Point of conjugal Complacence. But I muft not omit the excellent Preface, by which the Fable is introduced. † *Reading is to the Mind, fays he, what Exercife is to the Body: As by the one, Health is preferved, ftrengthened, and invigorated; by the other Virtue (which is the Health of the Mind) is kept alive, cherifhed, and confirmed. But, as Exercife becomes tedious and painful when we make Ufe of it only as the Means of Health, fo Reading is too apt to grow uneafy and burthenfome, when we apply ourfelves to it only for our Improvement in Virtue. For this Reafon, the Virtue which we gather from a Fable, or an Allegory, is like the Health we get by Hunting, as we are engaged in an agreeable Purfuit that draws us on with Pleafure, and makes us infenfible of the Fatigues that accompany it.*

Having given my Reader the Opinion of this great Man, who has fpoken fo much and fo well in Favour of the Subject I am concerned in, there is no Room for me to enlarge farther upon that Head. His Argument demonftrates the Ufefulnefs and Advantage of this Kind of

† Tatler, No. 147.

Writing,

PREFACE.

Writing, beyond Contradiction: It therefore only remains that I make some Apology for troubling the Public with a new Edition, of what they have had so often, and in so many different Forms already.

Nothing of this Nature has been done, since *Leftrange*'s Time, worth mentioning; and we had nothing before, but what (as he † observes) was so *insipid and flat in the Moral, and so coarse and uncouth in the Style and Diction, that they were rather dangerous than profitable, as to the Purpose for which they were principally intended; and likely to do forty Times more Harm than Good.* I shall therefore only observe to my Reader, the Insufficiency of *Leftrange*'s own Performance as to the Purpose for which he professes to have principally intended it; with some other Circumstances, which will help to excuse, if not justify, what I have enterprized upon the same Subject.

Now the Purpose for which he principally intended his Book, as in his Preface he expends a great many Words to inform us, was for the Use and Instruction of Children; who being, as it were, mere blank Paper, *are ready indifferently for any Opinion, good or bad, taking all upon Credit; and that it is in the Power of the first Comer to write Saint or Devil upon them, which he pleases.* This being truly and certainly the Case, what poor Devils would *Leftrange* make of those Children, who should be so unfortunate as to read his Book, and imbibe his pernicious Principles! Principles coined and suited to promote the Growth, and serve the Ends of Popery and Arbitrary Power. Tho' we had never been told he was a Pensioner to a Popish Prince, and that he himself professed the same Religion, yet his Reflections upon *Æsop* would discover it to us: In every political Touch, he shews himself to be the Tool and Hireling of

† Pref. to Part I.

the

the Popiſh Faction; ſince even a Slave, without ſome mercenary View, would not bring Arguments to juſtify Slavery, nor endeavour to eſtabliſh Arbitrary Power upon the Baſis of Right Reaſon. What Sort of Children therefore are the *Blank Paper*, upon which ſuch Morality as this ought to be written? Not the Children of *Britain*, I hope, for they are born with free Blood in their Veins, and ſuck in Liberty with their very Milk. 'This they ſhould be taught to love and cheriſh above all Things, and, upon Occaſion, to defend and vindicate it; as it is the Glory of their Country, the greateſt Bleſſing of their Lives, and the peculiar happy Privilege in which they excel all the World beſides. Let therefore the Children of *Italy*, *France*, *Spain*, and the reſt of the Popiſh Countries furniſh him with Blank Paper for Principles, of which free-born *Britons* are not capable. The earlier ſuch Notions are inſtilled in ſuch Minds as theirs indeed, the better it will be for them, as it will keep them from thinking of any other than the abject ſervile Condition to which they are born. But let the Minds of our *Britiſh* Youth be for ever educated and improved in that Spirit of Truth and Liberty, for the Support of which their Anceſtors have often bravely exhauſted ſo much Blood and Treaſure.

Had any Thing tending to debaſe and inſlave the Minds of Men been implied, either in the Fables or Morals of *Æſop*, upon which *Leſtrange* was to make juſt and fair Reflections, he might have pleaded that for an Excuſe. But *Æſop*, though it was his own accidental Misfortune to be a Slave, yet paſſed the Time of his Servitude among the free States of *Greece*, where he ſaw the high Eſteem in which Liberty was held, and poſſibly learned to value it accordingly. He has not one Fable, or ſo much as a Hint, to favour *Leſtrange's* Inſinuations;

finuations; but, on the contrary, takes all Occasions to recommend a Love for Liberty, and an Abhorrence of Tyranny, and all arbitrary Proceedings. Yet *Leftrange* (though in the Preface to his Second Part, he ufes thefe Words, *I have confulted the beft Authorities I could meet withal, in the Choice of the Collection, without ftraining any Thing, all this while, beyond the ftricteft Equity of a fair and an innocent Meaning*) notorioufly perverts both the Senfe and Meaning of feveral Fables; particularly when any political Inftruction is couched in the Application. For Example, in the famous Fable of *The Dog and the Wolf*. After a long tedious amufing Reflection, without one Word to the Purpofe, he tells us at laft, *That the Freedom which Æfop is fo tender of here, is to be underftood of the Freedom of the Mind*. No Body ever underftood it fo, I dare fay, that knew what the other Freedom was. As for what he mentions, it is not in the Power of the greateft Tyrant that lives, to deprive us of it. If the *Wolf* was only fenfible how fweet the Freedom of Mind was, and had no Concern for the Liberty of his Perfon, he might have ventured to have gone with the *Dog* well enough: But then he would have faved *Leftrange* the fpoiling of one of the beft Fables in the whole Collection. However, this may ferve as a Pattern of that Gentleman's Candor and Ingenuity in the Manner of drawing his Reflections. *Æfop* breathed Liberty in a political Senfe, whenever he thought fit to hint any Thing about that happy State. And *Phædrus*, whofe hard Lot it was once to have been a domeftic Slave, had yet fo great a Veneration for the Liberty I am fpeaking of, that he made no Scruple to write in Favour of it, even under the Ufurpation of a Tyrant, and at a Time when the once glorious free People of *Rome* had nothing but the Form and Shadow of their

ancient

P R E F A C E.

ancient Conftitution left. This he did particularly in
the Fable of *The Frogs defiring a* * *King*; as I have obferved in the Application to it. After which I leave it
to the Decifion of any indifferent Perfon, whether *Leftrange,* in the Tenor of his Refleftions, has proceeded
without ftraining moft Things, in Point of Politics, *beyond the ftriateft Equity of a fair and an innocent Meaning.*

  Whether I have mended the Faults I find with him,
in this or any other Refpeft, I muft leave to the Judgment of the Reader ; profeffing (according to the Principle on which the following Applications are built) that
I am a Lover of Liberty and Truth ; an Enemy to Tyranny, either in Church or State ; and one who detefts
Party Animofities, and factious Divifions, as much as I
wifh the Peace and Profperity of my Country.

* **Fab. III.**

T H E

THE

TABLE of CONTENTS.

A.

The CONTENTS.

2   88 *The*

The CONTENTS.

D.

a 2

The CONTENTS.

The CONTENTS.

The CONTENTS.

G.

H.

4 *The*

The CONTENTS.

I.

K.

L.

82 *The*

The CONTENTS.

39 *The*

The CONTENTS.

N.

O.

P.

The CONTENTS.

R.

S.

T.

The CONTENTS.

70 *The*

The CONTENTS.

Y.

ÆSOP's

ÆSOP's FABLES.

FAB. I. *The* Cock *and the* Jewel.

A BRISK young Cock, in Company with two
or three Pullets, his Miſtreſſes, raking upon
a Dunghill for ſomething to entertain them
with, happened to ſcratch up a Jewel; he knew
what it was well enough, for it ſparkled with an
exceeding bright Luſtre; but, not knowing what to
do with it, endeavoured to cover his Ignorance under a gay Contempt. So, ſhrugging up his Wings,
ſhaking his Head, and putting on a Grimace, he

B   expreſſed

expreſſed himſelf to this Purpoſe: Indeed, you are a very fine Thing; but I know not any Buſineſs you have here. I make no Scruple of declaring that my Taſte lies quite another Way; and I had rather have one Grain of dear, delicious Barley, than all the Jewels under the Sun.

The APPLICATION.

There are ſeveral People in the World, that paſs, with ſome, for well-accompliſhed Gentlemen, and very pretty Fellows, tho' they are as great Strangers to the true Uſes of Virtue and Knowledge, as the Cock upon the Dung-hill is to the real Value of the Jewel. He palliates his Ignorance by pretending that his Taſte lies another Way: But whatever gallant Airs People may give themſelves upon theſe Occaſions, without Diſpute, the ſolid Advantages of Virtue, and the durable Pleaſures of Learning, are as much to be preferred before other Objects of the Senſes, as the fineſt brilliant Diamond is above a Barley-Corn. The greateſt Blockheads would appear to underſtand, what at the ſame Time they affect to deſpiſe; and nobody yet was ever ſo vicious, as to have the Impudence to declare in public, that Virtue was not a fine Thing.

But ſtill, among the idle, ſauntering, young Fellows of the Age, who have Leiſure, as well to cultivate and improve the Faculties of the Mind, as to dreſs and embelliſh the Body; how many are there, who ſpend their Days in raking after new Scenes of Debauchery, in Compariſon of thoſe few who know how to reliſh more reaſonable Entertainments! Honeſt, undeſigning good Senſe is ſo unfaſhionable, that he muſt be a bold Man, who at this Time of Day attempts to bring it into Eſteem.

How diſappointed is the Youth, who, in the Midſt of his amorous Purſuits, endeavouring to plunder an Outſide of Bloom and Beauty, finds a Treaſure of impenetrable Virtue concealed within! And why may it not be ſaid, how delighted are the Fair Sex, when, from among a Crowd of empty, frolic, conceited Admirers, they find out and diſtinguiſh with their good Opinion, a Man of Senſe, with a plain, unaffected Perſon, which, at firſt Sight, they did not like!　　　　　FAB.

F A B. II. *The* Wolf *and the* Lamb.

ONE hot, fultry Day, a Wolf and a Lamb happened to come, juft at the fame Time, to quench
their Thirft in the Stream of a clear Silver Brook,
that ran tumbling down the Side of a rocky Mountain. The Wolf ftood upon the higher Ground;
and the Lamb at fome Diftance from him down the
Current. However, the Wolf, having a Mind to
pick a Quarrel with him, afked him, What he meant
by difturbing the Water, and making it fo muddy
that he could not drink; and at the fame Time, demanded Satisfaction. The Lamb, frightened at this
threatening Charge, told him, in a Tone as mild as
poffible, That, with humble Submiffion, he could not
conceive how that could be; fince the Water which
he drank, ran down from the Wolf to him, and
therefore it could not be difturbed fo far up the
Stream. Be that as it will, replies the Wolf, you
are a Rafcal, and I have been told that you treated
me

me with ill Language behind my Back, about half a Year ago. Upon my Word, says the Lamb, the Time you mention was before I was born. The Wolf, finding it to no Purpose to argue any longer against Truth, fell into a great Passion, snarling and foaming at the Mouth, as if he had been mad ; and drawing nearer to the Lamb, Sirrah, says he, if it was not you, it was your Father, and that's all one. ——So he seiz'd the poor, innocent, helpless Thing, tore it to Pieces, and made a Meal of it.

The APPLICATION.

The Thing which is pointed at in this Fable is so obvious, that it will be impertinent to multiply Words about it. When a cruel, ill-natured Man has a Mind to abuse one inferior to himself, either in Power or Courage, though he has not given the least Occasion for it, how does he resemble the Wolf! whose envious, rapacious Temper could not bear to see Innocence live quietly in its Neighbourhood. In short, wherever ill People are in Power, Innocence and Integrity are sure to be persecuted ; the more vicious the Community is, the better Countenance they have for their own villainous Measures : To practise Honesty in bad Times, is being liable to Suspicion enough ; but if any one should dare to prescribe it, it is ten to one but he would be impeached of high Crimes and Misdemeanors : For to stand up for Justice in a degenerate and corrupt State, is tacitly to upbraid the Government ; and seldom fails of pulling down Vengeance upon the Head of him that offers to stir in its Defence. Where Cruelty and Malice are in Combination with Power, nothing is so easy as for them to find a Pretence to tyrannize over Innocence, and exercise all Manner of Injustice.

FAB.

FAB. III. *The* Frogs *defiring a* King.

THE Frogs, living an eafy free Life every where among the Lakes and Ponds, affembled together, one Day, in a very tumultuous Manner, and petitioned *Jupiter* to let them have a King, who might infpect their Morals, and make them live a little honefter. *Jupiter*, being at that Time in pretty good Humour, was pleafed to laugh heartily at their ridiculous Requeft; and throwing a little Log down into the Pool, cried, There is a King for you. The fudden Splafh which this made by its Fall into the Water, at firft terrified them fo exceedingly, that they were afraid to come near it. But in a little Time, feeing it lay ftill without moving, they ventured, by Degrees, to approach it; and at laft, finding there was no Danger, they leaped upon it; and, in fhort, treated it as familiarly as they pleafed. But not contented with fo infipid a King as this was, they fent their Deputies to petition again for another

Sort

Sort of one; for This they neither did nor could like. Upon that, he sent them a Stork; who, without any Ceremony, fell a devouring and eating them up, one after another, as fast as he could. Then they applied themselves privately to *Mercury*, and got him to speak to *Jupiter* in their Behalf, That he would be so good as to bless them again with another King, or restore them to their form er State:—No, says he, since it was their own Choice, let the obstinate Wretches suffer the Punishment due to their Folly.

The APPLICATION.

It is pretty extraordinary to find a Fable of this Kind, finished with so bold and yet polite a Turn by *Phædrus:* One, who attained his Freedom by the Favour of *Augustus*, and wrote it in the Time of *Tiberius*; who were, successively, tyrannical Usurpers of the *Roman* Government. If we may take his Word for it, *Æsop* spoke it upon this Occasion. When the Commonwealth of *Athens* flourished under good wholesome Laws of its own enacting, they relied so much upon the Security of their Liberty, that they negligently suffered it to run out into Licentiousness. And Factions happening to be fomented among them by designing People, much about the same Time, *Pisistratus* took that Opportunity to make himself Master of their Citadel and Liberties both together. The *Athenians* finding themselves in a State of Slavery, tho' their Tyrant happened to be a very merciful one, yet could not bear the Thoughts of it; so that *Æsop*, where there was no Remedy, prescribes them to Patience, by the Example of the foregoing Fable; and adds, at last, *Wherefore*, my dear Countrymen, *be contented with your present Condition, bad as it is, for fear a Change should be worse.*

FAB. IV. *The vain* Jack-Daw.

A Certain Jack-Daw was fo proud and ambitious, that not contented to live within his own Sphere, he picked up the Feathers which fell from the Peacocks, ſtuck them in among his own, and very confidently introduced himſelf into an Aſſembly of thoſe beautiful Birds. They ſoon found him out, ſtripp'd him of his borrow'd Plumes, and falling upon him with their ſharp Bills, puniſh'd him as his Preſumption deſerv'd. Upon this, full of Grief and Afflcition, he return'd to his old Companions, and would have flock'd with them again; but they, knowing his late Life and Converſation, induſtriouſly avoided him, and refus'd to admit him into their Company : And one of them, at the ſame Time, gave him this ſerious Reproof. If, Friend, you could have been contented with our Station, and had not diſdain'd the Rank in which Nature had placed you, you had not been us'd ſo ſcurvily by thoſe upon whom you intruded yourſelf, nor ſuffer'd the notorious Slight which now we think ourſelves obliged to put upon you.

The

The APPLICATION.

What we may learn from this Fable, is, in the main, to live contentedly in our own Condition, whatever it be, without affecting to look bigger than we are, by a false or borrowed Light. To be barely pleased with appear. ing above what a Man really is, is bad enough; and what may justly render him contemptible in the Eyes of his Equals: But if, to enable him to do this with some. thing of a better Grace, he has clandestinely feathered his Nest with his Neighbour's Goods, when found out, he has nothing to expect but to be stripped of his Plunder, and used like a felonious Rogue into the Bargain.

FAB. V. *The* Dog *and the* Shadow.

A DOG, crossing a little Rivulet with a Piece of Flesh in his Mouth, saw his own Shadow represented in the clear Mirrour of the limpid Stream; and believing it to be another Dog, who was carrying another Piece of Flesh, he could not forbear catching at it; but was so far from getting any
Thing

Thing by his greedy Defign, that he dropt the Piece he had in his Mouth, which immediately funk to the Bottom, and was irrecoverably loft.

The APPLICATION.

He that catches at more than belongs to him, juftly deferves to lofe what he has. Yet nothing is more common, and, at the fame Time, more pernicious, than this felfifh Principle. It prevails, from the King to the Peafant; and all Orders and Degrees of Men are, more or lefs, infected with it. Great Monarchs have been drawn in, by this greedy Humour, to grafp at the Dominions of their Neighbours; not that they wanted any Thing more to feed their Luxury, but to gratify their infatiable Appetite for Vain-Glory. If the Kings of *Perfia* could have been contented with their own vaft Territories, they had not loft all *Afia* for the Sake of a little petty State of *Greece*. And *France*, with all its Glory, has, ere now, been reduced to the laft Extremity by the fame unjuft Encroachments.

He that thinks he fees another's Eftate in a Pack of Cards, or a Box and Dice, and ventures his own in the Purfuit of it, fhould not repine, if he finds himfelf a Beggar in the End.

Blackman FAB.

FAB. VI. *The Lion and other* Beaſts.

THE Lion and ſeveral other Beaſts, entered into
an Alliance offenſive and defenſive, and were to
live very ſociably together in the Foreſt ; one Day,
having made a ſort of an Excurſion by way of
Hunting, they took a very fine, large, fat Deer,
which was divided into four Parts ; there happening
to be then preſent, his Majeſty the Lion, and only
three others. After the Diviſion was made, and the
Parts were ſet out, his Majeſty advancing forward
ſome Steps, and pointing to one of the Shares, was
pleaſed to declare himſelf after the following Manner: This I ſeize and take Poſſeſſion of as my
Right, which devolves to me, as I am deſcended
by a true, lineal, hereditary Succeſſion from the
Royal Family of *Lion :* That (pointing to the ſecond) I claim by, I think, no unreaſonable Demand ; conſidering that all the Engagements you
have with the Enemy turn chiefly upon my Courage

rage and Conduct: And you very well know, that Wars are too expensive to be carried on without proper Supplies. Then (nodding his Head towards the Third) That I shall take by Virtue of my Prerogative; to which, I make no Question, but so dutiful and loyal a People will pay all the Deference and Regard that I can desire. Now, as for the remaining Part, the Necessity of our present Affairs is so very urgent, our Stock so low, and our Credit so impaired and weakened, that I must insist upon your granting That without any Hesitation or Demur; and hereof fail not at your Peril.

The APPLICATION.

No Alliance is safe which is made with those that are superior to us in Power. Tho' they lay themselves under the most strict and solemn Ties at the Opening of the Congress, yet the first advantageous Opportunity will tempt them to break the Treaty; and they will never want specious Pretences to furnish out their Declarations of War. It is not easy to determine, whether it is more stupid and ridiculous for a Community, to trust itself first in the Hands of those that are more powerful than themselves, or to wonder afterwards that their Confidence and Credulity are abused, and their Properties invaded.

FAB. VII. *The* Wolf *and the* Crane.

A WOLF, after devouring his Prey, happened to have a Bone ſtick in his Throat, which gave him ſo much Pain, that he went howling up and down, and importuning every Creature he met, to lend him a kind Hand in order to his Relief; nay, he promiſed a reaſonable Reward to any one that ſhould undertake the Operation with Succeſs. At laſt the Crane, tempted with the Lucre of the Reward, and having firſt procured him to confirm his Promiſe with an Oath, undertook the Buſineſs, and ventured his long Neck into the rapacious Felon's Throat. In ſhort, he plucked out the Bone, and expected the promiſed Gratuity. When the Wolf, turning his Eyes diſdainfully towards him, ſaid, I did not think you had been ſo unconſcionable; I had your Head in my Mouth, and could have bit it off whenever I pleaſed, but ſuffered you to take it away without any Damage, and yet you are not contented.

The

The APPLICATION.

There is a fort of People in the World, to whom a Man may be in the wrong for doing Services, upon a double Score; firſt, becauſe they never deſerved to have a good Office done them; and ſecondly, becauſe, when once engaged, 'tis ſo hard a matter to get well rid of their Acquaintance.

This Fable is not an Example of Ingratitude, as at firſt Sight it ſeems to be, and as ſome of the Mythologiſts have underſtood it; to make it a Parallel in that Caſe, the Crane ought to have been under ſome Difficulties in his Turn, and the Wolf have refuſed to aſſiſt him when it was in his Power. The whole Streſs of it lies in this, That we ought to conſider what Kind of People they are to whom we are deſired to do good Offices, before we do them; for that he grants a Favour, or even confides in a Perſon of no Honour, inſtead of finding his Account in it, comes off well if he is no Sufferer.

F A B. VIII. *The* Stag *looking into the* Water.

A STAG that had been drinking at a clear Spring, ſaw himſelf in the Water; and, pleaſed with the Proſpect, ſtood afterwards for ſome Time contemplating and surveying his Shape and Features, from Head to Foot. Ah! says he, what a glorious Pair of branching Horns are there! how gracefully do those Antlers hang over my Forehead, and give an agreeable Turn to my whole Face! If some other Parts of my Body were but proportionable to them, I would turn my Back to nobody; but I have a Set of such Legs, as really makes me ashamed to see them. People may talk what they please of their Conveniencies, and what great Need we stand in of them, upon several Occasions; but for my Part, I find them so very slender and unsightly, that I had as lief have none at all. While he was giving himself these Airs, he was alarmed with the Noise of some Huntsmen and a Pack of Hounds, that had been just laid on upon the Scent, and were making towards him. Away he flies in some Consternation, and, bounding nimbly over the Plain, threw Dogs and Men at a vast Distance behind him. After which, taking a very thick Copse, he had the Ill-fortune to be entangled by his Horns in a Thicket; where he was held fast, till the Hounds came in and pulled him down. Finding now how it was like to go with him, in the Pangs of Death, he is said to have uttered these Words: Unhappy Creature that I am! I am too late convinced, that, what I prided myself in, has been the Cause of my Undoing; and what I so much disliked, was the only Thing that could have saved me.

The APPLICATION.

Perhaps we cannot apply this better, than by supposing the Fable to be a Parable; which may be thus explained. The Deer, viewing itself in the Water, is a beautiful young Lady at her Looking-glass. She cannot help being sensible of the Charms which lie blooming in every Feature of her Face. She moistens her Lips,

languishes

languifhes with her Eyes, adjufts every Lock of her Hair
with the niceft Exactnefs, gives an agreeable Attitude to
her whole Body : And then, with a foft Sigh, fays to
herfelf, Ah! how happy might I be, in a daily Crowd
of Admirers, if it were not for the Cenforioufnefs of the
Age! When I view that Face, where Nature, to give
her her Due, has been liberal enough of Charms, how
eafy fhould I be, if it were not for that flender Particular, my Honour. The odious Idea of that comes acrofs
all my happy Moments, and brings a Mortification with
it that damps my moft flattering tender Hopes. Oh!
that there were no fuch Thing in the World! In the
Midft of thefe Soliloquies, fhe is interrupted by the Voice
of her Lover, who enters her Chamber finging a Riga-
doon Air; and, introducing his Difcourfe in a familiar
eafy Manner, takes Occafion to launch out in Praife of
her Beauty, fees fhe is pleafed with it, fnatches her Hand,
kiffes it in a Tranfport; and in fhort, purfues his Point
fo clofe, that fhe is not able to difengage herfelf from
him. But, when the confequence of all this approaches,
in an Agony of Grief and Shame, fhe fetches a deep
Sigh, and fays, Ah! how miftaken have I been! the
Virtue I flighted might have faved me; but the Beauty
I prized fo much has been my Undoing.

FAB.

FAB. IX. *The* Fox *and the* Crow.

A CROW having taken a Piece of Cheefe out of a Cottage Window, flew up into a high Tree with it, in order to eat it. Which a Fox obferving, came and fat underneath, and began to compliment the Crow upon the Subject of her Beauty. I protest, fays he, I never obferved it before, but your Feathers are of a more delicate White than any that ever I faw in my Life! Ah! what a fine Shape and graceful Turn of Body is there! And I make no Queftion but you have a tolerable Voice. If it is but as fine as your Complexion, I do not know a Bird that can pretend to ftand in Competition with you. The Crow, tickled with this very civil Language, neftled and riggled about, and hardly knew where fhe was; but thinking the Fox a little dubious as to the Particular of her Voice, and having a Mind to fet him right in that Matter, began to fing, and, in the fame Inftant, let the Cheefe drop out of her Mouth. This being what the Fox wanted, he chopped it up in a Moment; and trotted away, laughing to himfelf at the eafy Credulity of the Crow. *The*

The APPLICATION.

They that love Flattery (as, it is to be feared, too many do) are in a fair Way to repent of their Foible at the long Run. And yet how few are there among the whole Race of Mankind, who may be said to be full Proofs against its Attacks! The grofs Way by which it is managed by some silly Practitioners, is enough to alarm the dulleft Apprehenfion, and make it to value itfelf upon the Quicknefs of its Infight into the little Plots of this Nature. But, let the Ambufcade be difpofed with due Judgment, and it will fcarce fail of feizing the moft guarded Heart. How many are tickled to the laft Degree with the Pleafure of Flattery, even while they are applauded for their honeft Deteftation of it! There is no Way to baffle the Force of this Engine, but by every one's examining impartially for himfelf, the true Eftimate of his own Qualities: If he deals fincerely in the Matter, nobody can tell fo well as himfelf, what Degree of Efteem ought to attend any of his Actions; and therefore he fhould be entirely eafy, as to the Opinion Men are like to have of them in the World. If they attribute more to him than is his Due, they are either defigning or miftaken; if they allow him lefs, they are envious, or, poffibly, ftill miftaken; and, in either Cafe, are to be defpifed, or difregarded. For he that flatters without defigning to make Advantage of it, is a Fool: And whoever encourages that Flattery which he has Senfe enough to fee through, is a vain Coxcomb.

FAB.

FAB. X. *The Two* Bitches.

A BITCH, who was juſt ready to whelp, intreated another Bitch to lend her her Kennel, only
till her Month was up, and aſſured her that, then
ſhe ſhould have it again.   The other very readily
conſented, and, with a great deal of Civility, re-
ſigned it to her immediately.   However, when the
Time was elapſed, ſhe came and made her a Viſit,
and very modeſtly intimated, that now ſhe was up
and well, ſhe hoped ſhe ſhould ſee her abroad again;
for that, really, it would be inconvenient for her to
be without her Kennel any longer, and therefore ſhe
told her ſhe muſt be ſo free as to deſire her to provide herſelf with other Lodgings as ſoon as ſhe could.
The lying-in Bitch replied, That truly ſhe was
aſhamed for having kept her ſo long out of her own
Houſe; but it was not upon her own Account, (for
indeed ſhe was well enough to go any where) ſo much
as that of her Puppies, who were yet ſo weak, that
ſhe

she was afraid they would not be able to follow her; and, if she would but be so good as to let her stay a Fortnight longer, she should take it for the greatest Obligation in the World. The other Bitch was so good-natured and compassionate as to comply with this Request too; but at the Expiration of the Term, came and told her positively that she must turn out, for she could not possibly let her be there a Day longer. Must turn out—says the other; we will see that; for I promise you, unless you can beat me, and my whole Litter of Whelps, you are never like to have any Thing more to do here.

The APPLICATION.

Possession is eleven Points of the Law; and though, where Equity flourishes, and Property is duly secured, the twelfth Point, I mean that of Right, is better than the other eleven; yet this Fable may serve as a very good Lesson of Caution to us, never to let any Thing we value go out of our Possession, without very good Security. Wise and good-natured Men will give liberally and judiciously what they can spare; but to lend, where there is a Probability of our being defrauded by the Borrower, is the Part of a too easy and blameable Credulity.

FAB.

FAB. XI. *The Proud* Frog.

AN Ox, grazing in a Meadow, chanced to set his Foot among a Parcel of young Frogs, and trod one of them to Death. The rest informed their Mother, when she came Home, what had happened; telling her, that the Beast which did it was the hugest Creature that they ever saw in their Lives. What, was it so big? says the old Frog, swelling and blowing up her speckled Belly to a great Degree. Oh! bigger by a vast deal, say they. And so big? says she, straining herself yet more. Indeed, Mamma, say they, if you were to burst yourself, you would never be so big. She strove yet again, and burst herself indeed.

The APPLICATION.

Whenever a Man endeavours to live equal with one of a greater Fortune than himself, he is sure to share a like Fate with the Frog in the Fable. How many vain
People,

People of moderate eafy Circumftances, burft and come to nothing, by vying with thofe, whofe Eftates are more ample than their own! Sir *Changeling Plumftock* was poffeffed of a very confiderable Eftate, devolved to him by the Death of an old Uncle, who had adopted him his Heir. He had a falfe Tafte of Happinefs; and, without the leaft Oeconomy, trufting to the Sufficiency of his vaft Revenue, was refolved to be out-done by nobody, in fhewifh Grandeur and expenfive Living. He gave five thoufand Pounds for a Piece of Ground in the Country, to fet a Houfe upon; the Building and Furniture of which coft fifty thoufand more; and his Gardens were proportionably magnificent. Befides which, he thought himfelf under a Neceffity of buying out two or three Tenements which ftood in his Neighbourhood, that he might have Elbow-room enough. All this he could very well bear; and ftill might have been happy, had it not been for an unfortunate View which he one Day happened to take of my Lord *Caftlebuilder*'s Gardens, which confift of twenty Acres, whereas his own were not above twelve. From that Time he grew penfive; and before the enfuing Winter gave five and thirty Years Purchafe for a dozen Acres more to enlarge his Gardens, built a Couple of exorbitant Green-Houfes, and a large Pavilion at the farther End of a Terrace-Walk. The bare Repairs and Superintendencies of all which, call for the remaining Part of his Income. He is mortgaged pretty deep, and pays nobody: But being a privileged Perfon, refides altogether at a private cheap Lodging in the City of *Weftminfter*.

FAB.

FAB. XII. *The* Fox *and the* Stork.

THE Fox invited the Stork to Dinner; and, being
disposed to divert himself at the Expence of his
Guest, provided nothing for the Entertainment, but
a Soup, in a wide shallow Dish. This himself could
lap up with a great deal of Ease; but the Stork, who
could but just dip in the Point of his Bill, was not
a Bit the better all the while: However, in a few
Days after, he returned the Compliment, and invited
the Fox; but suffered nothing to be brought to Table but some minced Meat in a Glass Jar; the Neck
of which was so deep, and so narrow, that, though
the Stork with his long Bill made a Shift to fill his
Belly, all that the Fox, who was very hungry, could
do, was to lick the Brims, as the Stork slabbered
them with his eating. *Reynard* was heartily vexed
at first; but when he came to take his Leave, owned
ingenuously, that he had been used as he deserved;
and that he had no Reason to take any Treatment
ill, of which himself had set the Example.

I   *The*

The APPLICATION.

It is mighty imprudent, as well as inhuman and uncivil, to affront any body; and whoever takes the Liberty to exercise his witty Talent that Way, muſt not think much of it, if he meets with Repriſals. Indeed, if all thoſe who are thus paid in their own Coin, would take it with the ſame Franknefs the Fox did, the Matter would not be much; but we are too apt, when the Jeſt comes to be turned home upon ourſelves, to think that inſufferable in another, which we looked upon as pretty and facetious, when the Humour was our own.   The Rule of doing as we would be done by, ſo proper to be our Model in every Tranſaction of Life, may more par.icularly be of Uſe in this Reſpect: Becauſe People ſeldom or never receive any Advantage by theſe little ludicrous Impoſitions; and yet, if they were to afk themſelves the Queſtion, would find, that another's uſing them in the ſame Manner, would be very diſpleaſing.

F A B. XIII.   *The* Eagle *and the* Fox.

AN Eagle that had young ones, looking out for ſomething to feed them with, happened to ſpy a Fox's **Cub**, that lay bafking itſelf abroad in the Sun.

She

She made a Stoop, and truffed it immediately; but before she had carried it quite off, the old Fox coming Home, implored her, with Tears in her Eyes, to spare her Cub, and pity the Distress of a poor fond Mother, who should think no Affliction so great as that of losing her Child. The Eagle, whose Nest was up in a very high Tree, thought herself secure enough from all Projects of Revenge, and so bore away the Cub to her young ones, without shewing any Regard to the Supplications of the Fox. But that subtle Creature, highly incensed at this outrageous Barbarity, ran to an Altar, where some Country People had been sacrificing a Kid in the open Fields, and catching up a Firebrand in her Mouth, made towards the Tree where the Eagle's Nest was, with a Resolution of Revenge. She had scarce ascended the first Branches, when the Eagle, terrified with the approaching Ruin of herself and Family, begged of the Fox to desist, and, with much Submission, returned her the Cub again safe and sound.

The APPLICATION.

This Fable is a Warning to us not to deal hardly or injuriously by any body. The Consideration of our being in a high Condition of Life, and those we hurt, far below us, will plead little or no Excuse for us in this Case. For there is scarce a Creature of so despicable a Rank, but is capable of avenging itself some Way and at some Time or other. When great Men happen to be wicked, how little Scruple do they make of oppressing their poor Neighbours! They are perched upon a lofty Station, and have built their Nest on high; and, having outgrown all Feelings of Humanity, are insensible of any Pangs of Remorse. The Widow's Tears, the Orphan's Cries, and the Curses of the Miserable, like Javelins thrown by the Hand of a feeble old Man, fall by the Way, and never reach their Heart. But let such a one, in the Midst of his flagrant Injustice, remember, how easy a Matter it is, notwithstanding his superior Distance, for

the

the meaneſt Vaſſal to be revenged of him.   The Bitter-
neſs of an Affliction, even where Cunning is wanting,
may animate the pooreſt Spirit with Reſolutions of Vengeance; and when once that Fury is thoroughly awak-
ened, we know not what ſhe will require before ſhe is
lulled to Reſt again.   The moſt powerful Tyrants cannot prevent a reſolved Aſſaſſination; there are a thouſand different Ways for any private Man to do the Buſineſs, who is heartily diſpoſed to it, and willing to ſatisfy
his Appetite for Revenge, at the Expence of his Life.
An old Woman may clap a Firebrand in the Palace of a
Prince, and it is in the Power of a poor weak Fool to
deſtroy the Children of the Mighty.

F A B. XIV.   *The* Boar *and the* Aſs.

A Little Scoundrel of an Aſs, happening to meet
with a Boar, had a Mind to be arch upon him;
And ſo, Brother, ſays he, your humble Servant.
The Boar, ſomewhat nettled at his Familiarity,
briſtled up to him and told him, he was ſurpriſed to
hear him utter ſo impudent an Untruth, and was

                              C   juſt

juſt going to ſhew his noble Reſentment, by giving him a Rip in the Flank; but wiſely ſtifling his Paſſion, he contented himſelf with only ſaying, Go, you ſorry Beaſt! I could be amply and eaſily revenged of you, but I don't care to foul my Tuſks with the Blood of ſo baſe a Creature.

The APPLICATION.

Fools are ſometimes ſo ambitious of being thought Wits, that they run great Hazards in attempting to ſhew themſelves ſuch. This is not the firſt Aſs, who, after a handſome Rebuke from one ſuperior to himſelf, both in Courage and Merit, has continued his aukward Raillery even to the laſt Degree of Offence. But ſuch a dull Creature is ſo far from raiſing himſelf the leaſt Eſteem by his ludicrous Vein, that he has very good Luck if he eſcapes with a whole Skin. Buffoons, like Dwarfs, ſhould be matched with thoſe of their own Level; a Man, in Senſe or Stature, would be aſhamed to encounter either of them. But, notwithſtanding all this; and tho' the Boar in the Fable is a very good Example to Men of generous brave Spirits, not to give themſelves up to Paſſion, nor to be diſtempered with Thoughts of Revenge upon the inſolent Behaviour of every Aſs that offends them, becauſe their Hands would be diſhonoured by the Tincture of a baſe Man's Blood; yet, among human Creatures, the Correction of an Aſs that would be unſeaſonably witty, may be performed with Juſtneſs and Propriety enough, provided it be done in good Humour. The Blood of a Coward, literally ſpeaking, would ſtain the Character of a Man of Honour; when we chaſtiſe ſuch Wretches, it ſhould be done, if poſſible, in the utmoſt Calmneſs of Temper. It takes off ſomething from the Reputation of a great Soul, when we ſee it is in the Power of a Fool to ruffle and unſettle it.

FAB.

FAB. XV. *The* Frogs *and the fighting* Bulls.

A FROG, one Day, peeping out of the Lake, and
looking about him, faw two Bulls fighting at
fome-Diftance off in the Meadow, and calling to one
of his Acquaintance, Look, fays he, what dreadful
Work is yonder! Dear Sirs, what will become of
us! Why, pray thee, fays the other, do not frighten
yourfelf fo about nothing; how can their Quarrels
affect us? They are of a different Kind and Way of
living, and are at prefent only contending which fhall
be Mafter of the Herd. That is true, replies the firft,
their Quality and Station in Life, is, to all Appearance,
different enough from ours: But, as one of them will
certainly get the better, he that is worfted, being beat
out of the Meadow, will take Refuge here in the
Marfhes, and may poffibly tread out the Guts of fome
of us: So, you fee, we are more nearly concerned in
this Difpute of theirs, than at firft you were aware of.

The APPLICATION.

This poor timorous Frog had juſt Reaſon for its Fears and Suſpicions; it being hardly poſſible for great People to fall out, without involving many below them in the ſame Fate: Nay, whatever becomes of the former, the latter are ſure to ſuffer; thoſe may be only playing the Fool, while theſe really ſmart for it.

It is of no ſmall Importance to the honeſt, quiet Part of Mankind, who deſire nothing ſo much as to ſee Peace and Virtue flouriſh, to enter ſeriouſly and impartially into the Conſideration of this Point: For, as ſignificant as the Quarrels of the Great may ſometimes be, yet they are nothing without their eſpouſing and ſupporting them, one Way or other. What is it that occaſions Parties, but the ambitious or avaritious Spirit of Men in eminent Stations, who want to engroſs all Power in their own Hands? Upon this they foment Diviſions, and form Factions, and excite Animoſities between well-meaning, but undiſcerning People, who little think that the great Aim of their Leaders is no more than the Advancement of their own private Self-intereſt. The Good of the Public is always pretended upon ſuch Occaſions, and may ſometimes happen to be tacked to their own; but then it is purely accidental, and never was originally intended. One knows not what Remedy to preſcribe againſt ſo epidemical and frequent a Malady, but only, that every Man who has Senſe enough to diſcern the pitiful private Views that attend moſt of the Differences between the great Ones, inſtead of aiding or abetting either Party, would, with an honeſt Courage, heartily and openly oppoſe both.

FAB. XVI. *The* Kite *and the* Pigeons.

A KITE, who had kept failing in the Air for many Days near a Dove-Houfe, and made a Stoop at feveral Pigeons, but all to no Purpofe, (for they were too nimble for him) at laft had Recourfe to Stratagem, and took his Opportunity one Day, to make a Declaration to them, in which he fet forth his own juft and good Intentions, who had nothing more at Heart than the Defence and Protection of the Pigeons in their ancient Rights and Liberties; and how concerned he was at their Fears and Jealoufies of a foreign Invafion, efpecially their unjuft and unreafonable Sufpicions of himfelf, as if he intended, by Force of Arms, to break in upon their Conftitution, and erect a tyrannical Government over them. To prevent all which, and thoroughly to quiet their Minds, he thought proper to propofe to them fuch Terms of Alliance and Articles of Peace, as might for ever cement a good Underftand-

ing

ing betwixt them: The principal of which was, That they fhould accept of him for their King, and inveft him with all kindly Privilege and Prerogative over them. The poor fimple Pigeons confented: The Kite took the Coronation Oath after a very folemn Manner, on his Part, and the Doves, the Oaths of Allegiance and Fidelity, on theirs. But much Time had not paffed over their Heads, before the good Kite pretended that it was Part of his Prerogative to devour a Pigeon whenever he pleafed. And this, he was not contented to do himfelf only, but inftructed the reft of the Royal Family in the fame kingly Arts of Government. The Pigeons, reduced to this miferable Condition, faid one to the other, Ah! we deferve no better! Why did we let him come in?

The APPLICATION.

What can this Fable be applied to, but the exceeding Blindnefs and Stupidity of that Part of Mankind, who wantonly and foolifhly truft their native Rights of Liberty without good Security? Who often chufe for Guardians of their Lives and Fortunes, Perfons abandoned to the moft unfociable Vices; and feldom have any better Excufe for fuch an Error in Politics, than, That they were deceived in their Expectation; or never thoroughly knew the Manners of their King, till he had got them intirely in his Power. Which however is notorioufly falfe; for many, with the Doves in the Fable, are fo filly, that they would admit of a Kite, rather than be without a King. The Truth is, we ought not to incur the Poffibility of being deceived in fo important a Matter as this; an unlimited Power fhould not be trufted in the Hands of any one, who is not endued with a Perfection more than human.

FAB.

FAB. XVII. *The* Man *and his two* Wives.

A MAN, in Times when Polygamy was allowed,
had two Wives: One of which, like himself,
had seen her best Days, and was just as it were entering upon the Declivity of Life; but this, being
an artful Woman, she entirely concealed by her
Dress; by which, and some other elegant Qualities,
she made a shift sometimes to engage her Husband's
Heart. The other was a beautiful young Creature
of Seventeen, whose Charms, as yet in the Height
of Bloom, and secure of their own Power, had no
Occasion to call in any Artifice to their Assistance.
She made the good Man as happy as he was capable
of being, but was not, it seems, completely so herself: The grey Hairs, mixed among the black, upon
her Husband's Head, gave her some Uneasiness, by
proclaiming the great Disparity of their Years;
wherefore, under Colour of adjusting and combing
his Head, she would every now and then be twitch-

C 4   ing

ing the silver Hairs with her Nippers; that, however Matters were, he might still have as few visible Signs of an advanced Age as possible: The Dame, whose Years were nearer to an Equality with his own, esteemed those grey Locks as the Honours of his Head, and could have wished they had all been such; she thought it gave him a venerable Look; at least, that it made her appear something younger than him: So that every Time the honest Man's Head fell into her Hands, she took as much Pains to extirpate the black Hairs, as the other had done to demolish the grey. They neither of them knew of the other's Design; but each continuing her Project with repeated Industry, the poor Man, who thought their Desire to oblige put them upon this extraordinary Officiousness in dressing his Head, found himself, in a short Time, without any Hair at all.

The APPLICATION.

Phædrus, whose Sense I have generally followed in every Fable of which he has made a Version, in his Application of this, is a little severe upon the Ladies; and tells us, that by this Example we may see, the Men are sure to be Losers by the Women; as well, when they are the Objects of their Love, as while they lie under their Displeasure. All that I shall add to what he has said, is to observe, that many Women may unfortunately, out of a pure Effect of Complaisance, do a thousand disagreeable Things to their Husbands. They, whose Love is tempered with a tolerable Share of good Sense, will be sure to have no separate Views of their own, nor do any Thing more immediately relating to their Husband, without consulting him first. In a married State, one Party should inform themselves certainly, and not be guessing and presuming what will please the other; and if a Wife uses her Husband like a Friend only, the least she can do, is first to communicate to him all the important Enterprises she undertakes; and especially those which she intends should be for his Honour and Advantage.

FAB.

FAB. XVIII. *The* Stag *in the* Ox-Stall.

A STAG, roufed out of his thick Cover in the
Midft of the Foreft, and driven hard by the
Hounds, made towards a Farm-Houfe, and feeing
the Door of an Ox-Stall open, entered therein, and
hid himfelf under a Heap of Straw. One of the
Oxen, turning his Head about, afked him what he
meant by venturing himfelf in fuch a Place as that
was, where he was fure to meet with his Doom! Ah!
fays the Stag, if you will but be fo good as to favour
me with your Concealment, I hope I fhall do well
enough; I intend to make off again the firft Opportunity. Well, he ftaid there till towards Night; in
came the Ox-Man with a Bundle of Fodder, and
never faw him. In fhort, all the Servants of the
Farm came and went, and not a Soul of them fmelt
any Thing of the Matter. Nay, the Bailiff himfelf
came, according to Form, and looked in, but walked
away, no wifer than the reft. Upon this, the Stag,

ready

ready to jump out of his Skin for Joy, began to return Thanks to the good-natured Oxen, protesting that they were the most obliging People he had ever met with in his Life. After he had done his Compliments, one of them answered him gravely; Inded we desire nothing more, than to have it in our Power to contribute to your Escape; but, there is a certain Person, you little think of, who has a hundred Eyes; if he should happen to come, I would not give this Straw for your Life. In the Interim, Home comes the Master himself, from a Neighbour's where he had been invited to Dinner; and because he had observed the Cattle to look but scurvily of late, he went up to the Rack, and asked, why they did not give them more Fodder? then, casting his Eyes downward, Hey-dey! says he, why so sparing of your Litter? pray scatter a little more here. And these Cobwebs—But I have spoke so often, that unless I do it myself—Thus, as he went on, prying into every Thing, he chanced to look where the Stag's Horns lay sticking out of the Straw; upon which he raised a Hue-and-Cry, called all his People about him, killed the poor Stag, and made a Prize of him.

The APPLICATION.

The Moral of this Fable is, That nobody looks after a Man's Affairs so well as he himself. Servants being but Hirelings, seldom have the true Interest of their Master at Heart, but let Things run on in a negligent constant Disorder; and this, generally, not so much for want of Capacity as Honesty. Their Heads are taken up with the Cultivation of their own private Interest; for the Service and Promotion of which, that of their Master is postponed, and often entirely neglected.

Few Families are reduced to Poverty and Distress merely by their own Extravagance and Indulgence in Luxury: The Inattention of Servants swells every Ar-

ticle

ticle of Expence in domeftic Oeconomy; and the Reti-
nue of great Men, inftead of exerting their Induftry to
conduce as far as poffible to the Increafe of their Mafter's Wealth, commonly exercife no other Office, than
that of Locufts and Caterpillars, to confume and devour it.

FAB. XIX. *The* Dog *and the* Wolf.

A Lean, hungry, half-ftarved Wolf, happened,
one Moon-fhiny Night, to meet with a jolly,
plump, well-fed Maftiff; and, after the firft Compliments were paffed, fays the Wolf, you look extremely well; I proteft, I think I never faw a more
graceful, comely Perfon; but how comes it about,
I befeech you, that you fhould live fo much better
than I? I may fay, without Vanity, that I venture
fifty Times more than you do; and yet I am almoft
ready to perifh with Hunger. The Dog anfwered
very bluntly, Why, you may live as well, if you
will do the fame for it that I do. Indeed! What is
that? fays he: Why, fays the Dog, only to guard

the

the Houfe a-Nights, and keep it from Thieves. With all my Heart, replies the Wolf; for at prefent I have but a forry Time of it; and I think to change my hard Lodging in the Woods, where I endure Rain, Froft, and Snow; for a warm Roof over my Head, and a Belly-full of good Victuals, will be no bad Bargain. True, fays the Dog; therefore you have nothing more to do but to follow me. Now, as they were jogging on together, the Wolf fpied a Creafe in the Dog's Neck, and, having a ftrange Curiofity, could not forbear afking him what it meant! Pugh! nothing, fays the Dog. Nay, but pray, fays the Wolf. Why, fays the Dog, if you muft know, I am tied up in the Day-time, becaufe I am a little fierce, for fear I fhould bite People, and am only let loofe a-Nights. But this is done with Defign to make me fleep a-Days, more than any Thing elfe, and that I may watch the better in the Night-time; for, as foon as ever the Twilight appears, out I am turned, and may go where I pleafe. Then, my Mafter brings me Plates of Bones from the Table with his own Hands; and whatever Scraps are left by any of the Family, all fall to my Share; for you muft know I am a Favourite with every Body. So you fee how you are to live.—Come, come along; what is the Matter with you? No, replied the Wolf, I beg your Pardon; keep your Happinefs all to yourfelf. Liberty is the Word with me; and I would not be a King upon the Terms you mention.

The APPLICATION.

The loweft Condition of Life, with Freedom attending it, is better than the moft exalted Station under a Reftraint. Æfop and Phædrus, who had both felt the bitter Effects of Slavery, though the latter of them had the good Fortune to have the mildeft Princes that ever was, for his Mafter, cannot forbear taking all Opportunities

tunities to exprefs their great Abhorrence of Servitude, and their Paffion for Liberty, upon any Terms whatfoever. Indeed, a State of Slavery, with whatever feeming Grandeur and Happinefs it may be attended, is yet fo precarious a Thing, that he muft want Senfe, Honour, Courage, and all Manner of Virtue, who can endure to prefer it in his Choice. A Man who has fo little Honour as to bear to be a Slave, when it is in his Power to prevent or redrefs it, would make no Scruple to cut the Throats of his Fellow-Creatures, or to do any Wickednefs that the wanton unbridled Will of his tyrannical Mafter could fuggeft.

FAB. XX. *The* Lamb *brought up by a* Goat.

A WOLF meeting a Lamb, one Day, in Company with a Goat, Child, fays he, you are miftaken, this is none of your Mother, fhe is yonder, (pointing to a Flock of Sheep at a Diftance.) It may be fo, fays the Lamb; the Perfon that happened to conceive me, and afterwards bore me a few Months in her Belly becaufe fhe could not help it, and then

dropt

dropt me, fhe did not care where, and left me to the
wide World, is, I fuppofe, what you call my Mother; but I look upon this charitable Goat as fuch,
that took Compaffion on me in my poor, helplefs,
deftitute Condition, and gave me Suck; fparing it
out of the Mouths of her own Kids, rather than I
fhould want it. But fure, fays he, you have a greater
Regard for her that gave you Life, than for any
body elfe. She gave me Life? I deny that. She
that could not fo much as tell whether I fhould be
black or white, had a great Hand in giving me Life,
to be fure! But, fuppofing it were fo, I am mightily obliged to her truly for contriving to let me be
of the Male-kind, fo that I go every Day in Danger of the Butcher. What Reafon then have I to
have a greater Regard for one to whom I am fo little indebted for any Part of my Being, than for
thofe from whom, I have received all the Benevolence and Kindnefs which have hitherto fupported
me in Life.

The APPLICATION.

It is they whofe Goodnefs makes them our Parents,
that properly claim our filial Refpect from us, and not
thofe who are fuch only out of Neceffity. The Duties
between Parents and their Children are relative and reciprocal. By all Laws, natural as well as civil, it is expected that the Parents fhould cherifh and provide for
the Child, till it is able to fhift for itfelf; and that the
Child with a mutual Tendernefs, fhould depend upon
the Parent for its Suftenance, and yield it a reafonable
Obedience. Yet, through the Depravity of human
Nature, we very often fee thefe Laws violated, and the
Relations before-mentioned treating one another with
as much Virulence as Enemies of different Countries are
capable of. Through the natural Impatience and Pro-
tervity of Youth, we obferve the firft Occafion for any
Animofity moft frequently arifing from their Side; but,
however,

however, there are not wanting Examples of undutiful
Parents: And, when a Father, by ufing a Son ill, and
denying him fuch an Education and fuch an Allowance
as his Circumftances can well afford, gives him Occafion to withdraw his Refpect from him, to urge his Be-
getting of him as the fole Obligation to Duty, is talking like a filly, unthinking Dotard. Mutual Benevolence muft be kept up between Relations, as well as
Friends; for, without this Cement, whatever you pleafe
to call the Building, it is only a Caftle in the Air, a
Thing to be talked of, without the leaft Reality.

FAB. XXI. *The* Peacock's *Complaint.*

THE Peacock prefented a Memorial to *Juno,* im-
porting, how hardly he thought he was ufed in
not having fo good a Voice as the Nightingale;
how that pretty Animal was agreeable to every Ear
that heard it, while he was laughed at for his ugly
fcreaming Noife, if he did but open his Mouth.
The Goddefs, concerned at the Uneafinefs of her
favourite Bird, anfwered him very kindly to this
Purpofe:

Purpofe : If the Nightingale is bleft with a fine Voice, you have the Advantage in Point of Beauty and Largenefs of Perfon.   Ah ! fays he, but what avails my filent unmeaning Beauty, when I am fo far excelled in Voice ! The Goddefs difmiffed him, bidding him confider, that the Properties of every Creature were appointed by the Decree of Fate ; to him Beauty ; Strength to the Eagle ; to the Night-ingale a Voice of Melody ; the Faculty of Speech to the Parrot ; and to the Dove Innocence.   That each of thefe was contented with his own peculiar Quality ; and unlefs he had a Mind to be mifera-ble, he muft learn to be fo too.

The APPLICATION.

Since all Things (as *Juno* fays) are fixed by the eter-nal and unalterable Decree of Fate, how abfurd it is to hear People complaining and tormenting themfelves for that which it is impoffible ever to obtain ! They who are ambitious of having more good Qualities, fince that is impracticable, fhould fpare for no Pains to cultivate and recommend thofe they have ; which, a Sournefs and Peevifhnefs of Temper, inftead of improving, will certainly leffen and impair, whether they are of the Mind or Body.   If we had all the defirable Properties in the World, we could be no more than eafy and con-tented with them ; and, if a Man, by a right Way of thinking, can reconcile himfelf to his own Condition, whatever it be, he will fall little fhort of the moft com-plete State that Mortals ever enjoyed.

FAB.

F A B. XXII. *The* Fox *and the* Grapes.

A FOX, very hungry, chanced to come into a
Vineyard, where there hung Branches of charming ripe Grapes; but nailed up to a Trellis fo high,
that he leaped till he quite tired himfelf without
being able to reach one of them.   At laft, Let who
will take them! fays he; they are but green and
four; fo I'll even let them alone.

The APPLICATION.

This Fable is a good Reprimand to a Parcel of vain
Coxcombs in the World, who becaufe they would never be thought to be difappointed in any of their Purfuits, pretend a Diflike to every Thing which they cannot obtain.   There is a ftrange Propenfity in Mankind
to this Temper, and there are Numbers of grumbling
Malecontents in every different Faculty and Sect in
Life.   The difcarded Statefman, confidering the Cor-
ruption of the Times, would not have any Hand in the
Adminiftration of Affairs for all the World. The Country

try 'Squire damns a Court Life, and would not go cring-
ing and creeping to a Drawing-Room for the beſt Place
the King has in his Diſpoſal.   A young Fellow, being
aſked how he liked a celebrated Beauty, by whom all
the World knew he was deſpiſed, anſwered, She had a
ſtinking Breath.   How inſufferable is the Pride of this
poor Creature Man ! who would ſtoop to the baſeſt,
vileſt Actions, rather than be thought not able to do any
Thing.   For what is more baſe and vile than Lying?
And when do we lye more notoriouſly, than when we
diſparage and find Fault with a Thing for no other
Reaſon but becauſe it is out of our Power?

F A B. XXIII. *The* Viper *and the* File.

A VIPER entering a Smith's Shop, looked up
and down for ſomething to eat ; and ſeeing a
File, fell to gnawing it as greedily as could be.
The File told him, very gruffly, that he had beſt be
quiet and let him alone ; for he would get very little by nibbling at one, who, upon Occaſion, could
bite Iron and Steel.

The

The APPLICATION.

By this Fable we are cautioned to confider what any Perfon is, before we make an Attack upon him after any Manner whatfoever : Particularly how we let our Tongues flip in cenfuring the Actions of thofe who are, in the Opinion of the World, not only of an unquef-tioned Reputation, fo that nobody will believe what we infinuate againft them ; but of fuch an Influence, upon account of their own Veracity, that the leaft Word from them would ruin our Credit to all Intents and Pur-pofes. If Wit be the Cafe, and we have a fatirical Vein, which at certain Periods muft have a Flow, let us be caucious at whom we level it ; for if the Perfon's Un-derftanding be of better Proof than our own, all our in-genious Sallies, like Liquor fquirted againft the Wind, will recoil back upon our own Faces, and make us the Ridicule of every Spectator. This Fable, befides, is not an improper Emblem of Envy ; which, rather than not bite at all, will fall foul where it can hurt nothing but itfelf.

FAB. XXIV. *The* Fox *and the* Goat.

A FOX having tumbled, by Chance, into a Well,
had been casting about a long while, to no Purpose, how he should get out again; when, at last, a
Goat came to the Place, and wanting to drink, asked
Reynard, whether the Water was good? Good! says
he; ay, so sweet, that I am afraid I have surfeited myself, I have drank so abundantly. The Goat, upon
this, without any more ado, leapt in; and the Fox,
taking the Advantage of his Horns, by the Assistance
of them, as nimbly leapt out, leaving the poor Goat
at the Bottom of the Well, to shift for himself.

The APPLICATION.

The Doctrine taught us by this Fable is no more than
this, That we ought to consider who it is that advises
us, before we follow the Advice. For, however plau-
sible the Counsel may seem, if the Person that gives it
is a crafty Knave, we may be assured that he intends to
serve himself in it, more than us, if not to erect something to his own Advantage out of our Ruin.

The

The little, poor, Country Attorney, ready to perish, and sunk to the lowest Depth of Poverty, for Want of Employment, by such Arts as these, draws the 'Squire his Neighbour into the Gulph of the Law; till, laying hold on the Branches of his Revenue, he lifts himself out of Obscurity, and leaves the other immured in the Bottom of a Mortgage.

FAB. XXV. *The* Countryman *and the* Snake.

A Villager, in a frosty, snowy Winter, found a Snake under a Hedge, almost dead with Cold. He could not help having a Compassion for the poor Creature, so brought it Home, and laid it upon the Hearth near the Fire; but it had not lain there long, before (being revived with the Heat) it began to erect itself, and fly at his Wife and Children, filling the whole Cottage with dreadful Hissings. The Countryman hearing an Outcry, and perceiving what the Matter was, catched up a Mattock, and soon dispatched him; upbraiding him at the same Time in

these

thefe Words: Is this, vile Wretch, the Reward you make to him that faved your Life? Die, as you deferve; but a fingle Death is too good for you.

The APPLICATION.

'Tis the Nature of Ingrates to return Evil for Good: And the Moralifts in all Ages have inceffantly declaimed againft the Enormity of this Crime, concluding that they who are capable of hurting their Benefactors, are not fit to live in a Community; being fuch, as the natural Ties of Parent, Friend, or Country, are too weak to reftrain within the Bounds of Society. Indeed, the Sin of Ingratitude is fo deteftable, that, as none but the moft inhuman Temper can be guilty of it, fo, in writing to Men, there is no Occafion to ufe many Words, either in expofing the Vice itfelf, or diffuading People from the Commiffion of it. Therefore it is not likely that a Perfon of Æfop's Sagacity would have compiled this Fable, without having fomething elfe in view, befides this trite and obvious Subject. He certainly intended to put us in mind, That, as none but a poor filly Clown would go to take up a Snake and cherifh it, fo, we fhall be very negligent and ill-advifed, if, in doing good Offices, we do not take Care to beftow our Benevolence upon proper Objects. It was not at all unnatural in the Snake to hifs, and brandifh his Tongue, and fly at the firft that came near him; as foon as the Perfon that faved his Life as any other; indeed more likely, becaufe nobody elfe had fo much to do with him. Nor is it ftrange at any Time to fee a reprobate Fool throwing his poifonous Language about, and committing his Extravagancies againft thofe, more efpecially, who are fo inadvertent as to concern themfelves with him. The Snake and the Reprobate will not appear extraordinary in their Malevolence: But the fenfible Part of Mankind cannot help thinking thofe guilty of great Indifcretion, who receive either of them into their Protection.

FAB.

FAB. XXVI. *The* Mountains *in* Labour.

THE Mountains were faid to be in Labour, and uttered moft dreadful Groans. People came together, far and near, to fee what Birth would be produced; and after they had waited a confiderable Time in Expectation, out crept a Moufe.

The APPLICATION.

Great Cry and little Wool is the *Englifh* Proverb; the Senfe of which bears an exact Proportion to this Fable. By which are expofed, all thofe who promife fomething exceeding great, but come off with a Production ridiculoufly little. Projectors of all Kinds, who endeavour by artificial Rumours to raife the Expectations of Mankind, and then by their mean Performances defeat and difappoint them, have, Time out of Mind, been lafhed with the Recital of this Fable. How agreeably furprifing is it to fee an unpromifing Favourite, whom the Caprice of Fortune has placed at the Helm of State,

serving

ferving the Commonwealth with Juftice and Integrity, inftead of fmothering and embezzling the public Treafure to his own private and wicked Ends! And, on the contrary, how melancholy, how dreadful! or rather, how exafperating and provoking a Sight is it, to behold one, whofe conftant Declarations for Liberty and the Public Good, have raifed People's Expectations of him to the higheft Pitch, as foon as he is got into Power, exerting his whole Art and Cunning to ruin and enflave his Country! The fanguine Hopes of all thofe that wifhed well to Virtue, and flattered themfelves with a Reformation of every Thing that oppofed the Wellbeing of the Community, vanifh away in Smoke, and are loft in a dark, gloomy, uncomfortable Profpect.

FAB. XXVII. *The* Ant *and the* Fly.

ONE Day there happened fome Words between the Ant and the Fly about Precedency, and the Point was argued with great Warmth and Eagernefs on both Sides. Says the Fly, It is well known what

my Pretenſions are, and how juſtly they are ground-
ed : There is never a Sacrifice that is offered, but I
always taſte of the Entrails, even before the Gods
themſelves. I have one of the uppermoſt Seats at
Church, and frequent the Altar as often as any Body :
I have a free Admiſſion at Court; and can never
want the King's Ear, for I ſometimes ſit upon his
Shoulder. There is not a Maid of Honour, or
handſome young Creature comes in my Way, but,
if I like her, I ſettle betwixt her balmy Lips. And
then I eat and drink the beſt of every Thing, without having any Occaſion to work for my Living.
What is there that ſuch Country Puſſes as you enjoy, to be compared with a Life like this? The Ant,
who by this Time had compoſed herſelf, replied
with a great deal of Temper, and no leſs Severity :
Indeed, to be a Gueſt at an Entertainment of the
Gods, is a very great Honour, if one is invited; but
I ſhould not care to be a diſagreeable Intruder any
where. You talk of the King and the Court, and
the fine Ladies there, with great Familiarity ; but,
as I have been getting in my Harveſt in Summer, I
have ſeen a certain Perſon, under the Town-Walls,
making a hearty Meal upon ſomething that is not
ſo proper to be mentioned. As to your frequent-
ing the Altars, you are in the right to take Sanctu-
ary where you are like to meet with the leaſt Diſ-
turbance : But I have known People before now,
run to Altars, and call it Devotion, when they have
been ſhut out of all good Company, and had no
where elſe to go. You don't work for your Living,
you ſay; true : therefore when you have played
away the Summer, and Winter comes, you have nothing to live upon : and, while you are ſtarving with
Cold and Hunger, I have a good warm Houſe over
my Head, and Plenty of Proviſions about me.

D

The APPLICATION.

This Fable points out to us the different Characters of thofe that recommend themfelves in a vain-glorious Way by falfe and borrowed Lights; and of thofe whofe real Merit procures them a good Efteem wherever they go. Poverty and Folly having, at the fame Time, Poffeffion of any one Man, cannot fail of making him an Object of Pity, if not of Contempt; but, when an empty, conceited Pride happens to be joined with them, they render the Creature in whom they meet, at the fame Time defpicable and ridiculous. One who often attends at Court, not becaufe he has a Place, but becaufe he has not, fhould not value himfelf upon his Condition. They who go to Church out of Vanity and Curiofity, and not for pure Devotion, fhould not value themfelves upon their Religion, for it is not worth a Straw. They who eat at a Three-penny Ordinary, and fometimes not fo well, fhould not boaft either of their Dinner or Company. In fhort, nobody is a better Gentleman than he whofe own honeft Induftry fupplies him with a Plenty of all Neceffaries; who is fo well acquainted with Honour, as never to fay or do a mean and unjuft Thing; and who defpifes an idle Scoundrel, but knows how to efteem Men of his own Principles. Such a one is a Perfon of the firft Quality, though he has never a Title, and ought to take Place of every Man who is not fo good as himfelf.

FAB. XXVIII. *The* Old Hound.

AN old Hound, who had been an excellent good
one in his Time, and given his Master great
Sport and Satisfaction in many a Chace, at last, by
the Effect of Years, became feeble and unservice-
able. However, being in the Field one Day, when
the Stag was almost run down, he happened to be
the first that came in with him, and seized him by
one of his Haunches; but, his decayed and broken
Teeth not being able to keep their Hold, the Deer
escaped, and threw him quite out. Upon which,
his Master, being in a great Passion, and going to
strike him, the honest old Creature is said to have
barked out his Apology: Ah! do not strike your
poor old Servant; it is not my Heart and Inclination, but my Strength and Speed that fail you. If
what I now am displeases, pray don't forget what I
have been.

The

The APPLICATION:

This Fable may ferve to give us a general View of the Ingratitude of the greateſt Part of Mankind. Notwithſtanding all the Civility and Complaiſance that is uſed among People where there is a common Intercourſe of Buſineſs, yet, let the main Spring, the Probability of their being ſerviceable to each other, either in Point of Pleaſure or Profit, be but once broken, and farewel Curteſy: So far from continuing any Regard in Behalf of paſt Favours, it is very well if they forbear doing any Thing that is injurious. If the Maſter had only ceaſed to careſs and make much of the old Hound when he was paſt doing any Service, it had not been very ſtrange; but to treat a poor Creature ill, not for a Failure of Inclination, but merely a Defect of Nature, muſt, notwithſtanding the Crowd of Examples there are to countenance it, be pronounced inhuman and unreaſonable.

There are two Accounts upon which People that have been uſeful are frequently neglected. One, when they are ſo decayed, either through Age or ſome Accident, that they are no longer able to do the Services they have formerly done; the other, when the Occaſion or Emergency, which required ſuch Talents, no longer exiſts. *Phædrus*, who more than once complains of the bad Conſequences of Age, makes no other Application to this Fable, than by telling his Friend *Philetus*, with ſome Regret, that he wrote it with ſuch a View; having, it ſeems, been repaid with Neglect, or worſe Uſage, for Services done in his Youth, to thoſe who were then able to afford him a better Recompence.

FAB.

FAB. XXIX. *The* Sick Kite.

A KITE had been fick a long Time; and finding there were no Hopes of Recovery, begged
of his Mother to go to all the Churches and religious Houfes in the Country, to try what Prayers
and Promifes would effect in his Behalf. The old
Kite replied, Indeed, dear Son, I would willingly
undertake any Thing to fave your Life, but I have
great Reafon to defpair of doing you any Service in
the Way you propofe: For, with what Face can
I afk any Thing of the Gods in favour of one, whofe
whole Life has been a continual Scene of Rapine
and Injuftice, and who has not fcrupled, upon Occafion, to rob the very Altars themfelves?

The APPLICATION.

The Rehearfal of this Fable almoft unavoidably draws
our Attention to that very ferious and important Point,
the Confideration of a Death-bed Repentance. And,

to expofe the Abfurdity of relying upon fuch a weak
Foundation, we need only afk the fame Queftion with
the Kite in the Fable: How can he that has offended
the Gods all his Life-time by doing Acts of Difhonour
and Injuftice, expect that they fhould be pleafed with
him at laft, for no other Reafon but becaufe he fears he
fhall not be able to offend them any longer? when, in
Truth, fuch a Repentance can fignify nothing but a Con-
firmation of his former Impudence and Folly: For fure
no Stupidity can exceed that of the Man who expects a
future Judgement, and yet can bear to commit any Piece
of Injuftice, with a Senfe and Deliberation of the Fact.

FAB. XXX. *The* Hares *and the* Frogs.

UPON a great Storm of Wind that blew among
the Trees and Bufhes, and made a Ruftling
with the Leaves, the Hares (in a certain Park where
there happened to be a Plenty of them) were fo ter-
ribly frighted that they run like mad all over the
Place, refolving to feek out fome Retreat of more

Security, or to end their unhappy Days by doing
Violence to themselves. With this Refolution, they
found an Outlet where a Pale had been broken
down; and, bolting forth upon an adjoining Common, had not run far before their Courfe was ftopt
by that of a gentle Brook which glided acrofs the
Way they intended to take. This was fo grievous
a Difappointment, that they were not able to bear
it; and they determined rather to throw themfelves
headlong into the Water, let what would become of
it, than lead a Life fo full of Dangers and Croffes.
But upon their coming to the Brink of the River, a
Parcel of Frogs, which were fitting there, frighted
at their Approach, leapt into the Stream in great
Confufion, and dived to the very Bottom for Fear.
Which a cunning old Pufs obferving, called to the
reft and faid, Hold, have a Care what ye do: Here
are other Creatures, I perceive, which have their
Fears as well as us: Don't then let us fancy ourfelves the moft miferable of any upon Earth; but
rather, by their Example, learn to bear patiently
thofe Inconveniencies which our Nature has thrown
upon us.

The APPLICATION.

This Fable is defigned to fhew us how unreafonable
many People are, for living in fuch continual Fears and
Difquiets about the Miferablenefs of their Condition.
There is hardly any State of Life great enough to fatisfy the Wifhes of an ambitious Man; and fcarce any
fo mean, but may fupply all the Neceffities of him that
is moderate. But if People will be fo unwife as to work
themfelves up to imaginary Misfortunes, why do they
grumble at Nature and their Stars, when their own perverfe Minds are only to blame? If we are to conclude
ourfelves unhappy by as many Degrees as there are others
greater than we, why then the greateft Part of Mankind
muft be miferable, in fome Degree at leaft. But, if

they

they who repine at their own afflicted Condition, would but reckon up how many more there are with whom they would not change Cases, than whose Pleasures they envy, they would certainly rise up better satisfied from such a Calculation. But what shall we say to those who have a Way of creating themselves Panics from the Rustling of the Wind, the scratching of a Rat or Mouse behind the Hangings, the Fluttering of a Moth, or the Motion of their own Shadow by Moonlight? Their whole Life is as full of Alarms as that of a Hare, and they never think themselves so happy as when, like the timorous Folks in the Fable, they meet with a Set of Creatures as fearful as themselves.

FAB. XXXI. *The* Lion *and the* Mouse.

A LION, faint with Heat, and weary with Hunt-ing, was laid down to take his Repose under the spreading Boughs of a thick shady Oak. It happened that, while he slept, a Company of scrambling Mice ran over his Back, and waked him. Upon which, starting up, he clapped his Paw upon one

of

of them, and was juft going to put it to Death; when the little Suppliant implored his Mercy in a very moving Manner, begging him not to ftain his noble Cnaracter with the Blood of fo defpicable and fmall a Beaft. The Lion, confidering the Matter, thought proper to do as he was defired, and immediately releafed his little trembling Prifoner. Not long after, traverfing the Foreft in Purfuit of his Prey, he chanced to run into the Toils of the Hunters; from whenc, not able to difengage himfelf, he fet up a moft hideous and loud Roar. The Moufe, hearing the Voice, and knowing it to be the Lion's, immediately repaired to the Place, and bid him fear nothing, for that he was his Friend. Then ftraight he fell to work, and, with his little fharp Teeth, gnawing afunder the Knots and Faftenings of the Toils, fet the Royal Brute at Liberty.

The APPLICATION.

This Fable gives us to underftand, that there is no Perfon in the World fo little, but even the greateft may, at fome Time or other ftand in Need of his Affiftance; and confequently that it is good to ufe Clemency, where there is any Room for it, towards thofe who fall within our Power. A Generofity of this Kind is a handfome Virtue, and looks very graceful whenever it is exerted, if there were nothing elfe in it: But, as the loweft People in Life, may, upon Occafion, have it in their Power either to ferve or hurt us, that makes it our Duty, in Point of common Intereft, to behave ourfelves with Good-nature and Lenity towards all with whom we have to do. Then the Gratitude of the Moufe, and his Readinefs, not only to repay, but even to exceed the Obligation due to his Benefactor, notwithftanding his little Body, gives us the Specimen of a great Soul, which is never fo much delighted as with an Opportunity of fhewing how fenfible it is of Favours received.

FAB. XXXII. *The* Fatal Marriage.

THE Lion aforesaid, touched with the grateful Procedure of the Mouse, and, resolving not to be outdone in Generosity by any wild Beast whatsoever, desired his little Deliverer to name his own Terms, for that he might depend upon his complying with any Proposal he should make. The Mouse, fired with Ambition at this gracious Offer, did not so much consider what was proper for him to ask, as what was in the Power of his Prince to grant; and so, presumptuously demanded his princely Daughter, the young Lioness, in Marriage. The Lion consented: But, when he would have given the Royal Virgin into his Possession, she, like a giddy Thing as she was, not minding how she walked, by Chance set her Paw upon her Spouse, who was coming to meet her, and crushed her little Dear to Pieces.

The

The APPLICATION.

This Fable feems intended to fhew us, how miferable fome People make themfelves by a wrong Choice, when they have all the good Things in the World fpread before them to choofe out of. In fhort, if that one Particular of Judgment be wanting, it is not in the Power of the greateft Monarch upon Earth, nor of the repeated Smiles of Fortune to make us happy. It is the Want or Poffeffion of a good Judgment, which oftentimes makes the Prince a poor Wretch, and the poor Philofopher completely eafy. Now, the firft and chief Degree of Judgment is to know one's felf; to be able to make a tolerable Eftimate of one's own Capacity, fo as not to fpeak or undertake any Thing which may either injure or make us ridiculous: And yet (as wonderful as it is) there have been Men of allowed Goodfenfe in particular, and poffeffed of all defirable Qualifications in general, to make Life delightful and agreeable, who have unhappily contrived to match themfelves with Women of a Genius and Temper neceffarily tending to blaft their Peace. This proceeds from fome unaccountable Blindnefs: But when wealthy Plebeians of mean Extraction, and unrefined Education, as an Equivalent for their Money, demand Brides out of the Nurferies of our Peerage, their being defpifed, or at leaft overlooked, is fo unavoidable, unlefs in extraordinary Cafes, that nothing but a falfe Tafte of Glory could make them enter upon a Scheme fo inconfiftent and unpromifing.

FAB. XXXIII. *The* Wood *and the* Clown.

A Country Fellow came one Day into the Wood, and looked about him with some Concern; upon which the Trees, with a Curiofity natural to fome other Creatures, afked him what he wanted. He replied, That he wanted only a Piece of Wood to make a Handle to his Hatchet. Since that was all, it was voted unanimoufly that he fhould have a Piece of good, found, tough Afh. But he had no fooner received and fitted it for his Purpofe, than he began to lay about him unmercifully, and to hack and hew without Diftinction, felling the nobleft Trees in all the Foreft. Then the Oak is faid to have fpoke thus to the Beech, in a low Whifper, Brother, we muft take it for our Pains.

The APPLICATION.

No People are more juftly liable to fuffer, than they who furnifh their Enemies with any Kind of Affiftance.

It

It is generous to forgive; it is enjoined us by Religion to love our Enemies; but he that trusts an Enemy, much more contributes to the strengthening and arming of him, may almost depend upon repenting him for his inadvertent Benevolence: And has, moreover, this to add to his Distress, That, when he might have prevented it, he brought his Misfortune upon himself by his own Credulity.

Any Person in a Community, by what Name or Title soever distinguished, who affects a Power which may possibly hurt the People, is an Enemy to that People, and therefore they ought not to Trust him: For though he were ever so fully determined not to abuse such a Power, yet he is so far a bad Man, as he disturbs the People's Quiet, and makes them jealous and uneasy, by desiring to have it, or even retaining it, when it may prove mischievous. If we consult History, we shall find that the Thing called *Prerogative*, has been claimed and contended for chiefly by those who never intended to make a good Use of it; and as readily resigned and thrown up by just and wise Princes, who had the true Interest of their People at Heart. How like senseless Stocks do they act, who, by complimenting some capricious Mortal, from Time to Time, with Parcels of Prerogative, at last put it out of their Power to defend and maintain themselves in their just and natural Liberty!

FAB. XXXIV. *The* Horfe *and the* Stag.

THE Stag, with his fharp Horns, got the better of the Horfe, and drove him clear out of the Pafture where they ufed to feed together. So the latter craved the Affiftance of Man; and, in order to receive the Benefit of it, fuffered him to put a Bridle into his Mouth, and a Saddle upon his Back. By this Way of proceeding, he entirely defeated his Enemy; but was mightily difappointed, when upon returning Thanks, and defiring to be difmiffed, he received this Anfwer: No, I never knew before how ufeful a Drudge you were; now I have found what you are good for, you may depend upon it I will keep you to it.

The APPLICATION.

As the foregoing Fable was intended to caution us againft confenting to any Thing that might prejudice public Liberty; this may ferve to keep us upon our

Guard in the Prefervation of that which is of a private Nature. This is the Ufe and Interpretation given of it by *Horace*, the beft and moft polite Philofopher that ever wrote. After reciting the Fable, he applies it thus: This, fays he, is the Cafe of him, who, dreading Poverty, parts with that invaluable Jewel, Liberty; like a Wretch as he is, he will be always fubject to a Tyrant of fome Sort or other, and be a Slave for ever; becaufe his avaricious Spirit knew not how to be contented with that moderate Competency, which he might have poffeffed independent of all the World.

F A B. XXXV.

The Country-Moufe *and the* City-Moufe.

AN honeft, plain, fenfible Country-Moufe, is faid to have entertained at his Hole, one Day, a fine Moufe of the Town. Having formerly been Playfellows together, they were old Acquaintance, which ferved as an Apology for the Vifit. However, as Mafter of the Houfe, he thought himfelf obliged to
do

do the Honours of it, in all Respects, and to make as great a Stranger of his Guest as he possibly could. In order to this, he set before him a Reserve of delicate Grey Peas and Bacon, a Dish of fine Oatmeal, some Parings of new Cheese; and, to crown all with a Desert, a Remnant of a charming mellow Apple. In good Manners, he forbore to eat any himself, lest the Stranger should not have enough; but, that he might seem to bear the other Company, sat and nibbled a Piece of a Wheaten-Straw, very busily. At last, says the Spark of the Town, Old Crony, give me Leave to be a little free with you; How can you bear to live in this nasty, dirty, melancholy Hole here, with nothing but Woods, and Meadows, and Mountains, and Rivulets about you? Do not you prefer the Conversation of the World to the Chirping of Birds, and the Splendor of a Court to the rude Aspect of an uncultivated Desert? Come, take my Word for it you will find it a Change for the better. Never stand considering, but away this Moment. Remember, we are not immortal, and therefore have no Time to lose. Make sure of To-day, and spend it as agreeably as you can, you know not what may happen To-morrow. In short, these and such like Arguments prevailed, and his Country-Acquaintance was resolved to go to Town that Night. So they both set out upon their Journey together, proposing to sneak in after the Close of the Evening. They did so; and about Midnight made their Entry into a certain great House, where there had been an extraordinary Entertainment the Day before, and several Tit-bits, which some of the Servants had purloined, were hid under the Seat of a Window: The Country-Guest was immediately placed in the Midst of a rich *Persian* Carpet; and now it was the Courtier's Turn to entertain, who

indeed

indeed acquitted himfelf in that Capacity with the utmoft Readinefs and Addrefs, changing the Courfes as elegantly, and tafting every Thing firft as judicioufly as any Clerk of a Kitchen. The other fat and enjoyed himfelf like a delighted Epicure, tickled to the laft Degree with this new Turn of his Affairs; when, on a fudden, a Noife of fomebody opening the Door, made them ftart from their Seats, and fcuttle in Confufion about the Dining-Room. Our Country-Friend, in particular, was ready to die with Fear at the Barking of a huge Maftiff or two, which opened their Throats juft about the fame Time, and made the whole Houfe echo. At laft, recovering himfelf, Well, fays he, if this be your Town-Life, much Good may do you with it: Give me my poor quiet Hole again, with my homely, but comfortable Grey Peafe.

The APPLICATION.

A moderate Fortune, with a quiet Retirement in the Country, is preferable to the greateft Affluence which is attended with Care and the Perplexity of Bufinefs, and infeparable from the Noife and Hurry of the Town. The Practice of the Generality of People of the beft Tafte, it is to be owned, is directly againft us in this Point; but, when it is confidered that this Practice of theirs proceeds rather from a Compliance with the Fafhion of the Times, than their own private Thoughts, the Objection is of no Force. Among the great Numbers of Men who have received a learned Education, how few are there but either have their Fortunes entirely to make; or, at leaft, think they deferve to have, and ought not to lofe the Opportunity of getting fomewhat more than their Fathers have left them! The Town is the Field of Action for Volunteers of this Kind; and whatever Fondnefs they may have for the Country, yet they muft ftay till their Circumftances will admit of a Retreat thither. But fure there never was

a Man

a Man yet, who lived in a conftant Return of Trouble and Fatigue in Town, as all Men of Bufinefs do in fome Degree or other, but has formed to himfelf fome End of getting fome fufficient Competency, which may enable him to purchafe a quiet Poffeffion in the Country, where he may indulge his Genius, and give up his old Age to that eafy fmooth Life, which, in the Tempeft of Bufinefs, hé had fo often longed for. Can any Thing argue more ftrongly for a Country Life, than to obferve what a long Courfe of Labour People go through, and what Difficulties they encounter to come at it? They look upon it, at a Diftance, like a Kind of Heaven, a Place of Reft and Happinefs; and are pufhing forward through the rugged thorny Cares of the World, to make their Way towards it. If there are many, who, though born to plentiful Fortunes, yet live moft Part of their Time in the Noife, the Smoke, and Hurry of the Town; we fhall find, upon Enquiry, that neceffary indifpenfible Bufinefs is the real or pretended Plea which moft of them have to make for it. The Court and the Senate require the Attendance of fome: Law-Suits, and the proper Direction of Trade engage others; they who have a fprightly Wit and an elegant Tafte for Converfation, will refort to the Place which is frequented by People of the fame Turn, whatever Averfion they may otherwife have for it; and others, who have no fuch Pretence, have yet this to fay, that they follow the Fafhion. They who appear to have been Men of the beft Senfe amongft the Ancients, always recommended the Country as the moft proper Scene for Innocence, Eafe, and virtuous Pleafure; and, accordingly, loft no Opportunities of enjoying it: And Men of the greateft Diftinction among the Moderns, have ever thought themfelves moft happy, when they could be decently fpared from the Employments which the Excellency of their Talents neceffarily threw them into, to embrace the charming Leifure of a Country Life.

F A B.

FAB. XXXVI. *The* Mouse *and the* Weasel.

A Little, starvling, thin-gutted Rogue of a Mouse, had, with much Pushing and Application, made his Way through a small Hole in a Corn-Basket, where he stuffed and crammed so plentifully, that when he would have retired the Way he came, he found himself too plump, with all his Endeavours, to accomplish it. A Weasel, who stood at some Distance, and had been diverting himself with beholding the vain Efforts of the little fat Thing, called to him, and said: Harkee! honest Friend, if you have a Mind to make your Escape, there is but one Way for it; contrive to grow as poor and as lean as you were when you entered, and then perhaps, you may get off.

The APPLICATION.

They, who from a poor mean Condition, insinuate themselves into a good Estate, are not always the most happy. There is, many Times, a Quiet and Content
attending

attending a low Life, to which the rich Man is an utter
Stranger. Riches and Cares are almoſt inſeparable;
and whoever would get rid of the one, muſt content
himſelf to be diveſted of the other. He that hath been
acquainted with the Sweets of a Life free from the Incumbrance of Wealth, and longs to enjoy them again,
muſt ſtrip himſelf of that Incumbrance, if ever he means
to attain his Wiſhes.

Some, from creeping into the loweſt Stations of Life,
have, in Proceſs of Time, filled the greateſt Places in
it; and grown ſo bulky by purſuing their inſatiate Appetite after Money, that, when they would have retired, they found themſelves too opulent and full to get
off. There has been no Expedient for them to creep out,
till they were ſqueezed and reduced in ſome Meaſure to
their primitive Littleneſs. They that fill themſelves
with that which is the Property of others, ſhould always
be ſo ſerved before they are ſuffered to eſcape.

FAB. XXXVII. *The* Belly *and the* Members.

IN former Days, when the Belly and the other
Parts of the Body enjoyed the Faculty of Speech,
and had ſeparate Views and Deſigns of their own;
each

each Part, it feems, in particular for himſelf, and in the Name of the Whole, took Exception at the Conduct of the Belly, and were refolved to grant him Supplies no longer. They faid they thought it very hard, that he ſhould lead an idle good-for-nothing Life, fpending and fquandering away, upon his own ungodly Guts, all the Fruits of their Labour; and that, in ſhort, they were refolved for the future, to ſtrike off his Allowance, and let him ſhift for himſelf as well as he could. The Hands proteſted they would not lift up a Finger to keep him from ſtarving; and the Mouth wiſhed he might never fpeak again, if he took in the leaſt Bit of Nouriſhment for him as long as he lived; and, fay the Teeth, may we be rotten if ever we chew a Morfel for him for the future. This folemn League and Covenant was kept as long as any Thing of that Kind can be kept, which was, until each of the rebel Members pined away to the Skin and Bone, and could hold out no longer. Then they found there was no doing without the Belly, and that, as idle and infignificant as he feemed, he contributed as much to the Maintenance and Welfare of all the other Parts, as they did to his.

The APPLICATION.

This Fable was fpoken by *Menenius Agrippa,* a famous *Roman* Conful and General, when he was deputed by the Senate to appeafe a dangerous Tumult and Infurrection of the People. The many Wars that Nation was engaged in, and the frequent Supplies they were obliged to raife, had fo foured and inflamed the Minds of the Populace, that they were refolved to endure it no longer, and obſtinately refufed to pay the Taxes which were levied upon them. It is eafy to difcern how the great Man applied this Fable. For, if the Branches and Members of a Community refufe the Government that Aid which its Neceſſities require, the

Whole

Whole muſt periſh together. The Rulers of a State, as idle and inſignificant as they may ſometimes ſeem, are yet as neceſſary to be kept up and maintained in a proper and decent Grandeur, as the Family of each private Perſon is, in a Condition ſuitable to itſelf. Every Man's Enjoyment of that Little which he gains by his daily Labour, depends upon the Government's being maintained in a Condition to defend and ſecure him in it.

F A B. XXXVIII.
The Lark *and her* Young Ones.

A LARK, who had young Ones in a Field of Corn which was almoſt ripe, was under ſome Fear leſt the Reapers ſhould come to reap it before her young Brood were fledged, and able to remove from the Place. Wherefore, upon flying Abroad to look for Food, ſhe left this Charge with them: That they ſhould take Notice what they heard talked of in her Abſence, and tell her of it when ſhe came back again. When ſhe was gone, they heard the Owner of the Corn call to his Son: Well,

ſays

says he, I think this Corn is ripe enough; I would have you go early To-morrow, and desire our Friends and Neighbours to come and help us to reap it. When the old Lark came Home, the young Ones fell a quivering and chirping round her, and told her what had happened, begging her to remove them as fast as she could. The Mother bid them be easy; for, says she, if the Owner depends upon Friends and Neighbours, I am pretty sure the Corn will not be reaped To-morrow. Next Day she went out again, upon the same Occasion, and left the same Orders with them as before. The Owner came, and stayed, expecting those he had sent to: But the Sun grew hot, and nothing was done, for not a Soul came to help him. Then, says he to his Son, I perceive these Friends of ours are not to be depended upon, so that you must even go to your Uncles and Cousins, and tell them I desire they would be here betimes To-morrow Morning to help us to reap: Well, this the young Ones in a great Fright reported also to their Mother. If that be all, says she, do not be frightened, Children, for Kindred and Relations do not use to be so very forward to serve one another: But take particular Notice what you hear said the next Time, and be sure you let me know it. She went Abroad the next Day, as usual; and the Owner finding his Relations as slack as the rest of his Neighbours, said to his Son, Harkee, *George*, do you get a Couple of good Sickles ready against To-morrow Morning, and we will even reap the Corn ourselves. When the young Ones told their Mother this, Then, says she, we must be gone indeed; for, when a Man undertakes to do his Business himself, it is not so likely that he will be disappointed. So, she removed her young Ones immediately, and the Corn was reaped the next Day by the good Man and his Son.

The

The APPLICATION.

Never depend upon the Affiftance of Friends and Relations in any Thing which you are able to do yourfelf; for nothing is more fickle and uncertain. The Man who relies upon another for the Execution of any Affair of Importance, is not only kept in a wretched and flavifh Sufpence, while he expects the Iffue of the Matter, but generally meets with a Difappointment. While he who lays the chief Strefs of his Bufinefs upon himfelf, and depends upon his own Induftry and Attention for the Succefs of his Affairs, is in the faireft Way to attain his End : And, if at laft he fhould mifcarry, has this to comfort him, That it was not through his own Negligence, and a vain Expectation of the Affiftance of Friends. To ftand by ourfelves, as much as poffible, to exert our own Strength and Vigilance in the Profecution of our Affairs, is Godlike, being the Refult of a moft noble and highly exalted Reafon ; but they who procraftinate and defer the Bufinefs of Life by an idle Dependance upon others, in Things which it is in their own Power to effect, fink down into a Kind of ftupid abject Slavery, and fhew themfelves unworthy of the Talents with which human Nature is dignified.

FAB.

FAB. XXXIX. *The* Nurſe *and the* Wolf.

A Nurſe who was endeavouring to quiet a froward
bawling Child, among other Attempts, threatened to throw it out of Doors to the Wolf, if it
did not leave off Crying. A Wolf, who chanced to
be prowling near the Door juſt at that Time, heard
the Expreſſion, and believing the Woman to be in
earneſt, waited a long while about the Houſe, in
Expectation of ſeeing her Words made good. But
at laſt the Child, wearied with its own Importunities, fell aſleep, and the poor Wolf was forced to
return back to the Woods empty and ſupperleſs.
The Fox meeting him, and ſurpriſed to ſee him
going Home ſo thin and diſconſolate, aſked him
what the Matter was, and how he came to ſpeed
no better that Night? Ah! do not aſk me, ſays he;
I was ſo ſilly as to believe what the Nurſe ſaid, and
have been diſappointed.

The APPLICATION.

All the Moralifts have agreed to interpret this Fable as
a Caution to us never to truft a Woman. What Reafons
they could have for giving fo rough and uncourtly a Precept, is not eafy to be imagined: For however fickle and
unftable fome Women may be, it is well known there are
feveral who have a greater Regard for Truth in what
they affert or promife, than moft Men. There is not
Room in fo fhort a Compafs, to exprefs a due Concern
for the Honour of the Ladies upon this Occafion, nor to
fhew how much one is difpofed to vindicate them: And
tho' there is nothing bad which can be faid of them, but
may, with equal Juftice, be averred of the other Sex; yet
one would not venture to give them quite fo abfolute a
Precaution as the old Mythologifts have affixed to this
Fable, but only to advife them to confider well and thoroughly of the Matter, before they truft any Man living.

FAB. XL.　The Tortoife and the Eagle.

THE Tortoife, weary of his Condition, by which
he was confined to creep upon the Ground, and
being ambitious to have a Profpect, and look about
8　　　　　　　　　　　　　　　　　　　　him,

him, gave out, that if any Bird would take him up into the Air, and shew him the World, he would reward him with a Discovery of many precious Stones, which he knew were hidden in a certain Place of the Earth : The Eagle undertook to do as he desired ; and when he had performed his Commission, demanded the Reward. But finding the Tortoise could not make good his Words, he stuck his Talons into the softer Parts of his Body, and made him a Sacrifice to his Revenge.

The APPLICATION.

As Men of Honour ought to consider calmly how far the Things which they promise may be in their Power, before they venture to make Promises upon this Account, because the Non-performance of them will be apt to excite an Uneasiness within themselves, and tarnish their Reputation in the Eyes of other People ; so Fools and Cowards should be as little rash in this Respect as possible, lest their impudent Forgeries draw upon them the Resentment of those whom they disappoint, and that Resentment makes them undergo smart, but deserved Chastisement. The Man who is so stupid a Knave as to make a lying Promise where he is sure to be detected, receives the Punishment of his Folly unpitied by all that know him.

FAB.

FAB. XLI. *The* Wind *and the* Sun.

A Difpute once arofe betwixt the North-Wind and the Sun, about the Superiority of their Power; and they agreed to try their Strength upon a Traveller, which fhould be able to get his Cloak off firft. The North-Wind began; and blew a very cold Blaft, accompanied with a fharp driving Shower. But this, and whatever elfe he could do, inftead of making the Man quit his Cloak, obliged him to gird it about his Body as cl fe as poffible. Next came the Sun; who, breaking out from a thick watery Cloud, drove away the cold Vapours from the Sky, and darted his warm fultry Beams upon the Head of the poor Weather-beaten Travel-ler. The Man growing faint with the Heat, and unable to endure it any longer, firft throws off his heavy Cloak, and then flies for Protection to the Shade of a neighbouring Grove.

The

The APPLICATION.

There is something in the Temper of Men so averse to severe and boisterous Treatment, that he who endeavours to carry his Point that Way, instead of prevailing, generally leaves the Mind of him, whom he has thus attempted, in a more confirmed and obstinate Situation, than he found it at first. Bitter Words and hard Usage freeze the Heart into a Kind of Obduracy, which mild Persuasion and gentle Language only can dissolve and soften. Persecution has always fixed and riveted those Opinions which it was intended to dispel; and some discerning Men have attributed the quick Growth of Christianity, in a great Measure, to the rough and barbarous Reception which its first Teachers met with in the World. The same may have been observed of our Reformation: The Blood of the Martyrs was the Manure which produced that great Protestant Crop, on which the Church of *England* has subsisted ever since. Providence, which always makes Use of the most natural Means to attain its Purpose, has thought fit to establish the purest Religion by this Method: The Consideration of which may give a proper Check to those who are continually endeavouring to root out Errors by that very Management, which so infallibly fixes and implants all Opinions, as well erroneous as orthodox. When an Opinion is so violently attacked, it raises an Attention in the persecuted Party, and gives an Alarm to their Vanity, by making them think that worth defending and keeping, at the Hazard of their Lives, which, perhaps, otherwise, they would only have admired a while for the Sake of its Novelty, and afterwards resigned of their own Accord. In short, a fierce turbulent Opposition, like the North-Wind, only serves to make a Man wrap his Notions more closely about him; but we know not what a kind, warm, sun-shiny Behaviour, rightly applied, would not be able to effect.

E 3 FAB.

FAB. XLII. *The* Afs *in the* Lion's Skin.

AN Afs, finding the Skin of a Lion, put it on;
and going into the Woods and Paftures, threw
all the Flocks and Herds into a terrible Confterna-
tion. At laft, meeting his Owner, he would have
frightened him alfo; but the good Man, feeing his
long Ears ftick out, prefently knew him, and with
a good Cudgel made him fenfible, that, notwithftanding his being dreft in a Lion's Skin, he was
really no more than an Afs.

The APPLICATION.

As all Affectation is wrong, and tends to expofe and
make a Man ridiculous, fo the more diftant he is from
the Thing which he affects to appear, the ftronger will
the Ridicule be which he excites, and the greater the Inconveniencies into which he runs himfelf thereby. How
ftrangely abfurd it is for a timorous Perfon to procure a
military Poft, in order to keep himfelf out of Danger!
And to fancy a red Coat the fureft Protection for Cowardice!

ardice! Yet there have been thofe who have purchafed
a Commiffion to avoid being infulted; and have been
fo filly as to think Courage was interwoven with a Safh,
or tied up in a Cockade. But it would not be amifs
for fuch Gentlemen to confider, that it is not in the
Power of Scarlet Cloth to alter Nature; and that, as it
is expected a Soldier fhould fhew himfelf a Man of
Courage and Intrepidity upon all proper Occafions, they
may by this Means meet the Difgrace they intended to
avoid, and appear greater Affes than they need to have
done. However, it is not in Point of Fortitude only,
that People are liable to expofe themfelves, by affuming
a Character to which they are not equal; but he who
puts on a Shew of Learning, of Religion, of a fuperior
Capacity in any Refpect; or, in fhort, of any Virtue or
Knowledge to which he has no proper Claim, is, and
will always be found to be, *An Afs in a Lion's Skin.*

FAB. XLIII. *The* Frog *and the* Fox.

A Frog, leaping out of the Lake, and taking the
Advantage of a rifing Ground, made Proclamation to all the Beafts of the Foreft, that he was an

able

able Phyfician, and, for curing all Manner of Dif-
tempers, would turn his Back to no Perfon living.
This Difcourfe, uttered in a Parcel of hard, cramp
Words, which nobody underftood, made the Beafts
admire his Learning, and give Credit to every Thing
he faid. At laft, the Fox, who was prefent, with
Indignation afked him, how he could have the Impudence, with thofe thin Lantern-Jaws, that mea-
gre pale Phyz, and blotched fpotted Body, to fet
up for one who was able to cure the Infirmities of
others.

The APPLICATION.

A fickly, infirm Look, is as difadvantageous in a Phyfician, as that of a Rake in a Clergyman, or a fheepifh
one in a Soldier. If this Moral contains any Thing
further, it is, that we fhould not fet up for rectifying
Enormities in others, while we labour under the fame
ourfelves. Good Advice ought always to be followed
without our being prejudiced upon Account of the Perfon from whom it comes: But it is feldom that Men
can be brought to think us worth minding, when we
prefcribe Cures for Maladies with which ourfelves are
infected. *Phyfician, heal thyfelf,* is too Scriptural not
to be applied upon fuch an Occafion; and, if we would
avoid being the Jeft of an Audience, we muft be found,
and free from thofe Difeafes, of which we would endeavour to cure others. How fhocked muft People
have been to hear a Preacher for a whole Hour declaim
againft Drunkennefs, when his own Infirmity has been
fuch, that he could neither bear nor forbear Drinking;
and perhaps was the only Perfon in the Congregation,
who made the Doctrine at that Time neceffary! Others
too have been very zealous in exploding Crimes, for
which none were more fufpected than themfelves: But,
let fuch filly Hypocrites remember, that they whofe
Eyes want Couching, are the moft improper People in
the World to fet up for Oculifts.

FAB.

FAB. XLIV. *The* Mischievous Dog.

A Certain Man had a Dog, which was so curst and mischievous, that he was forced to fasten a heavy Clog about his Neck, to keep him from running at, and worrying People. This the vain Cur took for a Badge of honourable Distinction; and grew so insolent upon it, that he looked down with an Air of Scorn upon the neighbouring Dogs, and refused to keep them Company. But a sly old Poacher, who was one of the Gang, assured him, that he had no Reason to value himself upon the Favour he wore; since it was fixed upon him rather as a Mark of Disgrace than of Honour.

The APPLICATION.

Some People are so exceeding vain, and at the same Time, so dull of Apprehension, that they interpret every Thing by which they are distinguished from others, in their own Favour. If they betray any Weaknesses in Conversation, which are apt to excite the Laughter of their Company, they make no Scruple of ascribing it to their Superiority in Point of Wit. If Want of Sense or Breeding (one of which is always the Case) disposes them to give, or miſtake Affronts, upon which Account all diſcreet ſenſible People are obliged to ſhun their Company, they impute it to their own Valour and Magnanimity, to which they fancy the World pays an awful and reſpectful Deference. There are ſeveral decent Ways of preventing ſuch turbulent Men from doing Miſchief, which might be applied with Secrecy, and many Times paſs unregarded, if their own Arrogance did not require the Reſt of Mankind to take Notice of it.

FAB. XLV. Jupiter *and the* Camel.

THE Camel preſented a Petition to *Jupiter*, complaining of the Hardſhip of his Caſe, in not having, like Bulls and other Creatures, Horns, or any Weapons of Defence to protect himſelf from the Attacks of his Enemies; and praying that Relief might be given him in ſuch Manner as might be thought moſt expedient. *Jupiter* could not help ſmiling at the impertinent Addreſs of the great ſilly Beaſt; but however, rejected the Petition; and told him, that, ſo far from granting his unreaſonable Requeſt, henceforward he would take Care his Ears ſhould be ſhortened, as a Puniſhment for his preſumptuous Importunity.   *The*

The APPLICATION.

The Nature of Things is so fixed in every Particular, that they are very weak superstitious People, who dream it is to be altered. But, besides the Impossibility of producing a Change by Addresses of this Nature, they who employ much of their Time upon such Accounts, instead of getting, are sure to lose in the End. When any Man is so frivolous and vexatious as to make unreasonable Complaints, and to harbour undue Repinings in his Heart, his Peevishness will lessen the real Goods which he possesses, and the Sourness of his Temper shorten that Allowance of Comfort which he already thinks too scanty. Thus, in Truth, it is not Providence, but ourselves, who punish our own Importunity in soliciting for Impossibilities, with a sharp corroding Care, which abridges us of some Part of that little Pleasure which Providence has cast into our Lot.

FAB. XLVI. The Travellers and the Bear.

TWO Men being to travel through a Forest together, mutually promised to stand by each other, in any Danger they should meet upon the Way.
They

They had not gone far, before a Bear came rushing towards them out of a Thicket; upon which, one being a light nimble Fellow, got up into a Tree; the other falling flat upon his Face, and holding his Breath, lay still, while the Bear came up and smelled at him; but that Creature, supposing him to be a dead Carcase, went back again into the Wood, without doing him the least Harm. When all was over, the Spark who had climbed the Tree, came down to his Companion, and, with a pleasant Smile, asked him what the Bear said to him; for, says he, I took Notice that he clapt his Mouth very close to your Ear. Why, replies the other, he charged me to take Care for the future, not to put any Confidence in such cowardly Rascals as you are.

The A P P L I C A T I O N.

Though nothing is more common than to hear People profess Services of Friendship, where there is no Occasion for them; yet scarce any Thing is so hard to be found as a true Friend, who will assist us in Time of Danger and Difficulty. All the Declarations of Kindness which are made to an experienced Man, though accompanied by a Squeeze of the Hand, and a solemn Asseveration, should leave no greater Impression upon his Mind, than the Whistling of the hollow Breeze which brushes one's Ear with an unmeaning Salute, and is presently gone. He that succours our Necessity by a well-timed Assistance, though it were not ushered in by previous Compliments, will ever after be looked upon as our Friend and Protector; and, in so much a greater Degree, as the Favour was unasked and unpromised; as it was not extorted by Importunities on the one Side, nor led in by a numerous Attendance of Promises on the other. Words are nothing, till they are fulfilled by Actions; and therefore we should not suffer ourselves to be deluded by a vain Hope, and Reliance upon them.

FAB. XLVII. *The* Bald Knight.

A Certain Knight growing old, his Hairs fell off, and he became bald ; to hide which Imperfection, he wore a Periwig. But as he was riding out with some others a Hunting, a sudden Gust of Wind blew off the Periwig, and expofed his bald Pate. The Company could not forbear laughing at the Accident ; and he himself laughed as loud as any Body, faying, How was it to be expected that I fhould keep ftrange Hair upon my Head, when my own would not ftay there ?

The APPLICATION.

To be captious, is not more uneafy to ourfelves, than it is difagreeable to others. As no Man is entirely without Fault, a few Defects, furrounded with a Guard of good Qualities, may pafs Mufter well enough ; but he, whofe Attention is always upon the Catch for fomething to take Exception at, if he had no other bad Quality, can never be acceptable. A captious Temper, like a little Leaven, fours a whole Lump of Virtues ; and makes us difrelifh that, which might otherwife be the moft grateful Converfation. If we would live eafy to ourfelves, and agreeable to others, we fhould be fo far from feeking

Occafions

Occafions of being angry, that fometimes we fhould let them pafs unregarded when they come in our Way; or, if they are fo palpable that we cannot help taking Notice of them, we fhould do well to rally them off with a Jeft, or diffolve them in good Humour. Some People take a fecret Pleafure in nettling and fretting others; and the more practicable they find it to exercife this Quality upon any one, the more does it whet and prompt their Inclination to do it. But, as this Talent favours fomething of Ill-nature, it deferves to be baffled and defeated: Which one cannot do better, than by receiving all that is uttered at fuch a Time with a cheerful Afpect, and an ingenuous, pleafant, unaffected Reply. Nor is the Expedient of the bald Knight unworthy of our Imitation: For if by any Word or Action, we happen to raife the Laughter of thofe about us, we cannot ftifle it fooner, or better, than by a brifk Prefence of Mind to join in Mirth with the Company; and, if poffible, to anticipate the Jeft which another is ready to throw out upon the Occafion.

FAB. XLVIII. *The* Two Pots.

AN Earthen Pot, and one of Brafs, ftanding together upon the River's Brink, were both carried
away by the Flowing in of the Tide. The Earthen
Pot

Pot fhewed fome Uneafinefs, as fearing he fhould be broken; but his Companion of Brafs bid him be under no Apprehenfions, for that he would take Care of him. O, replies the other, keep as far off as ever you can, I entreat you; it is you I am moft afraid of: For, whether the Stream dafhes you againft me, or me againft you, I am fure to be the Sufferer; and therefore, I beg of you, do not let us come near one another.

The APPLICATION.

A Man of a moderate Fortune, who is contented with what he has, and finds he can live happily upon it, fhould take Care not to hazard and expofe his Felicity by conforting with the Great and the Powerful. People of equal Conditions may float down the Current of Life, without hurting each other: But, it is a Point of fome Difficulty to fteer one's Courfe in the Company of the Great, fo as to efcape without a Bulge. One would not chufe to have one's little Country-Box fituated in the Neighbourhood of a very great Man; for whether I ignorantly trefpafs upon him, or he knowingly encroaches upon me, I only am like to be the Sufferer. I can neither entertain nor play with him, upon his own Terms; for that which is Moderation and Diverfion to him, in me would be Extravagance and Ruin.

FAB.

FAB. XLIX. *The* Peacock *and the* Crane.

THE Peacock and the Crane, by Chance met together in the fame Place. The Peacock, erect-
ing his Tail, difplayed his gaudy Plumes, and looked
with Contempt upon the Crane, as fome mean ordinary Perfon. The Crane, refolving to mortify his
Infolence, took Occafion to fay, that Peacocks were
very fine Birds indeed, if fine Feathers could make
them fo; but that he thought it a much nobler Thing
to be able to rife above the Clouds, than to ftrut about
upon the Ground, and be gazed at by Children.

The APPLICATION.

It is very abfurd to flight or infult another upon his
wanting a Property which we poffefs; for he may, for
any Thing we know, have as juft Reafon to triumph
over us, by being Mafter of fome good Quality, of which
we are incapable. But, in regard to the Fable before
us, that which the Peacock values himfelf upon, the Glit-
ter and Finery of Drefs, is one of the moft trifling Con-
fiderations in Nature; and what a Man of Senfe would
be afhamed to reckon even as the leaft Part of Merit.
Indeed, Children, and thofe People who think much
about

about the fame Pitch with them, are apt to be taken with
Varnifh and Tinfel : But they who examine by the Scale
of Common-Senfe, muft find fomething of Weight and
Subftance, before they can be perfuaded to fet a Value.
The Mind, which is ftored with virtuous and rational
Sentiments; and the Behaviour, which fpeaks Complacence and Humility, ftamps an Eftimate upon the Poffeffor, which all judicious Spectators are ready to admire
and acknowledge. But if there be any Merit in an em-
broidered Coat, a Brocade Waiftcoat, a Shoe, a Stocking,
or a Sword-Knot, the Perfon who wears them has the leaft
Claim to it; let it be afcribed where it juftly belongs, to the
feveral Artifans who wrought and difpofed the Materials
of which they confift. This Moral is not intended to de-
rogate any Thing from the Magnificence of fine Clothes
and rich Equipages, which, as Times and Circumftances
require, may be ufed with Decency and Propriety enough:
But one cannot help being concerned, left any Worth fhould
be affixed to them more than their own intrinfic Value.

F A B. L.   *The* Oak *and the* Reed.

A N Oak, which hung over the Bank of a River,
was blown down by a violent Storm of Wind;
and as it was carried along by the Stream, fome of its
Boughs

Boughs bruſhed againſt a Reed, which grew near the Shore. This ſtruck the Oak with a Thought of Admiration; and he could not forbear aſking the Reed, how he came to ſtand ſo ſecure and unhurt in a Tempeſt, which had been furious enough to tear an Oak up by the Roots? Why, ſays the Reed, I ſecure myſelf by putting on a Behaviour quite contrary to what you do; inſtead of being ſtubborn and ſtiff, and confiding in my Strength, I yield and bend to the Blaſt, and let it go over me; knowing how vain and fruitleſs it would be to reſiſt it.

The APPLICATION.

Though a tame Submiſſion to Injuries which it is in our Power to redreſs, be generally eſteemed a baſe and a diſhonourable Thing; yet, to reſiſt where there is no Probability, or even Hopes of our getting the better, may alſo be looked upon as the Effect of a blind Temerity, and perhaps of a weak Underſtanding. The Strokes of Fortune are oftentimes as irreſiſtible as they are ſevere; and he, who with an impatient reluctant Spirit fights againſt her, inſtead of alleviating, does but double her Blows upon himſelf. A Perſon of a quiet ſtill Temper, whether it is given him by Nature, or acquired by Art, calmly compoſes himſelf, in the Midſt of a Storm, ſo as to elude the Shock, or receive it with the leaſt Detriment: Like a prudent experienced Sailor, who is ſwimming to the Shore from a wrecked Veſſel in a ſwelling Sea; he does not oppoſe the Fury of the Waves, but ſtoops and gives Way, that they may roll over his Head without Obſtruction. The Doctrine of abſolute Submiſſion in all Caſes, is an abſurd, dogmatical Precept, with nothing but Ignorance and Superſtition to ſupport it: But, upon particular Occaſions, and where it is impoſſible for us to overcome, to ſubmit patiently is one of the moſt reaſonable Maxims in Life.

FAB.

FAB. LI.   *The* Fox *and the* Tiger.

ASkilful Archer, coming into the Woods, directed
his Arrows so successfully, that he slew many
wild Beasts, and pursued several others.   This put
the whole Savage Kind into a fearful Consternation,
and made them fly to the most retired Thickets for
Refuge.   At last, the Tiger resumed a Courage,
and bidding them not to be afraid, said, that he
alone would engage the Enemy; telling them, they
might depend upon his Valour and Strength to revenge their Wrongs.   In the Midst of these Threats,
while he was lashing himself with his Tail, and tearing up the Ground for Anger, an Arrow pierced his
Ribs, and hung by its barbed Point in his Side.   He
set up an hideous and loud Roar, occasioned by the
Anguish which he felt, and endeavoured to draw
out the painful Dart with his Teeth; when the
Fox, approaching him, enquired with an Air of
Surprise, who it was that could have Strength and
Courage enough to wound so mighty and valorous
a Beast? Ah! says the Tiger, I was mistaken in my
Reckoning: It was that invincible Man yonder.

The

The APPLICATION.

Though Strength and Courage are very good Ingredients towards the making us secure and formidable in the World, yet, unless there be a proper Portion of Wisdom or Policy to direct them, instead of being serviceable, they often prove detrimental to their Proprietors. A rash froward Man, who depends upon the Excellence of his own Parts and Accomplishments, is likewise apt to expose a weak Side, which his Enemies might not otherwise have observed; and gives an Advantage to others, by those very Means which he fancied would have secured it to himself. Counsel and Conduct always did, and always will govern the World; and the Strong, in Spite of all their Force, can never avoid being Tools to the Crafty. Some Men are as much superior to others in Wisdom and Policy, as Man, in general, is above a Brute. Strength ill-concerted, opposed to them, is like a Quarter-Staff in the Hands of a huge, robust, but bungling Fellow, who fights against a Master of the Science. The latter, though without a Weapon, would have Skill and Address enough to disarm his Adversary, and drub him with his own Staff. In a Word, savage Fierceness and brutal Strength, must not pretend to stand in Competition with Finesse and Stratagem.

FAB. LII. *The* Lion *and the* Four Bulls.

FOUR Bulls, which had entered into a very strict Friendship, kept always near one another, and fed together. The Lion often saw them, and as often had a Mind to make one of them his Prey: But, tho' he could easily have subdued any of them singly, yet he was afraid to attack the whole Alliance, as knowing they would have been too hard for him, and therefore contented himself for the present with keeping at a Distance. At last, perceiving no Attempt was to be made upon them as long as this Combination held, he took Occasion, by Whispers and Hints, to foment Jealousies, and raise Divisions among them. This Stratagem succeeded so well, that the Bulls grew cold and reserved towards one another, which soon after ripened into a downright Hatred and Aversion; and, at last, ended in a total Separation. The Lion had now obtained his Ends; and, as impossible as it was for him to hurt them while they were united, he found no Difficulty, now they were parted, to seize and devour every Bull of them, one after another.

The

The APPLICATION.

The Moral of this Fable is so well known and allowed, that to go about to enlighten it, would be like holding a Candle to the Sun. *A Kingdom divided against itself cannot stand*; and as undisputed a Maxim as it is, was however thought necessary to be urged to the Attention of Mankind, by the best Man that ever lived. And since Friendships and Alliances are of so great Importance to our Well-being and Happiness, we cannot be too often cautioned not to let them be broken by Tale-bearers and Whisperers, or any other Contrivance of our Enemies.

F A B.LIII. *The* Crow *and the* Pitcher.

A CROW, ready to die with Thirst, flew with Joy to a Pitcher, which he beheld at some Distance. When he came, he found Water in it indeed, but so near the Bottom, that with all his Stooping and Straining, he was not able to reach it. Then he endeavoured to overturn the Pitcher, that so at least he might be able to get a little of it. But his Strength

was

was not sufficient for this. At last, seeing some Pebbles lies near the Place, he cast them one by one into the Pitcher; and thus, by Degrees, raised the Water up to the very Brim, and satisfied his Thirst.

The APPLICATION.

Many Things, which cannot be effected by Strength, or by the vulgar Way of enterprising, may yet be brought about by some new and untried Means. A Man of Sagacity and Penetration, upon encountering a Difficulty or two, does not immediately despair; but if he cannot succeed one Way, employs his Wit and Ingenuity another: and, to avoid or get over an Impediment, makes no Scruple of stepping out of the Path of his Forefathers. Since our Happiness, next to the Regulation of our Minds, depends altogether upon our having and enjoying the Conveniencies of Life, why should we stand upon Ceremony about the Methods of obtaining them, or pay any Deference to Antiquity upon that Score? If almost every Age had not exerted itself in some new Improvements of its own, we should want a thousand Arts, or, at least, many Degrees of Perfection in every Art, which at present we are in Possession of. The Invention of any Thing which is more commodious for the Mind or Body, than what they had before, ought to be embraced readily, and the Projector of it distinguished with a suitable Encouragement. Such as the Use of the Compass, for Example, from which Mankind reaps so much Benefit and Advantage, and which was not known to former Ages. When we follow the Steps of those who have gone before us in the old beaten Track of Life, how do we differ from Horses in a Team, which are linked to each other by a Chain or Harness, and move on in a dull heavy Pace, to the Tune of their Leader's Bells? But the Man who enriches the present Fund of Knowledge with some new and useful Improvement, like a happy Adventurer at Sea, discovers, as it were, an unknown Land, and imports an additional Trade into his own Country.

FAB.

FAB 54 *The* Foreſter *and the* Lion.

THE Foreſter meeting with a Lion, one Day, they diſcourſed together for a while without differing much in Opinion. At laſt, a Diſpute happening to ariſe about the Point of Superiority between a Man and a Lion; the Man, wanting a better Argument, ſhewed the Lion a marble Monument, on which was placed the Statue of a Man ſtriding over a vanquiſhed Lion. If this, ſays the Lion, is all you have to ſay for it, let Us be the Carvers, and We will make the Lion ſtriding over the Man.

The APPLICATION.

Contending Parties are very apt to appeal for the Truth to Records written by their own Side; but nothing is more unfair, and at the ſame Time inſignificant and unconvincing. Such is the Partiality of Mankind in Favour of themſelves and their own Actions, that it is almoſt impoſſible to come at any Certainty by reading the Accounts which are written on one Side only. We

have

have few or no Memoirs come down to us of what was
tranfacted in the World during the Sovereignty of ancient _Rome_, but what were written by thofe who had a
Dependency upon it; therefore it is no wonder that
they appear, upon moft Occafions, to have been fo great
and glorious a Nation. What their Contemporaries of
other Countries thought of them we cannot tell, otherwife than from their own Writers: It is not impoffible
but they might have defcribed them as a barbarous, rapacious, treacherous, unpolite People; who, upon their
Conqueft of _Greece_, for fome Time, made as great Ha-
vock-and Deftruction of the Arts and Sciences, as their
Fellow-Plunderers the _Goths_ and _Vandals_ did, afterwards, in _Italy_. What Monfters would our own Party-
zealots make of each other, if the Tranfactions of the
Times were to be handed down to Pofterity by a warm
hearty Man on either Side! And, were fuch Records to
furvive two or three Centuries, with what Perplexities
and Difficulties muft they embarrafs a young Hiftorian,
as by Turns he confulted them for the Characters of
his great Forefathers! If it fhould fo happen, it were
to be wifhed this Application might be living at the
fame Time; that young Readers, inftead of doubting
to which they fhould give their Credit, would not fail
to remember that This was the Work of a Man, That
of a Lion.

F

FAB.

FAB. LV. *The* Satyr *and the* Traveller.

A Satyr, as he was ranging the Foreſt in an exceeding cold, ſnowy Seaſon, met with a Traveller half-ſtarved with the Extremity of the Weather. He took Compaſſion on him, and kindly invited him Home, to a warm comfortable Cave he
had in the Hollow of a Rock. As ſoon as they
had entered and ſat down, notwithſtanding there
was a good Fire in the Place, the chilly Traveller
could not forbear blowing his Fingers Ends. Upon
the Satyr's aſking him, why he did ſo; he anſwered,
That he did it to warm his Hands. The honeſt
Silvan having ſeen little of the World, admired a
Man who was Maſter of ſo valuable a Quality as
that of blowing Heat, and therefore was reſolved to
entertain him in the beſt Manner he could. He
ſpread the Table before him with dried Fruits of ſeveral Sorts; and produced a Remnant of cold cordial Wine, which, as the Rigour of the Seaſons

8

made

made very proper, he mulled with fome warm Spices, infufed over the Fire, and prefented to his fhivering Gueft. But this the Traveller thought fit to blow likewife; and upon the Satyr's demanding a Reafon why he blowed again, he replied, To cool his Difh. This fecond Anfwer provoked the Satyr's Indignation, as much as the firft had kindled his Surprife: So, taking the Man by the Shoulder, he thruft him out of Doors, faying, He would have nothing to do with a Wretch who had fo vile a Quality as to blow Hot and Cold with the fame Mouth.

The APPLICATION.

Though the poor Traveller in the Fable was not guilty of any real Crime in what he did, yet one cannot help approving the honeft Simplicity of the Satyr, who could not be reconciled to fuch Double-dealing. In the moral Senfe of the Fable, nothing can be more offenfive to one of a fincere Heart, than he that blows with a different Breath from the fame Mouth; who flatters a Man to his Face, and reviles him behind his Back. Some again, juft like this Man, to ferve a prefent View, will blow nothing but what is warm, benevolent, and cherifhing; and when they have raifed the Expectations of a Dependent to a Degree which they think may prove troublefome, can, with putting on a cold Air, eafily chill and blaft all his blooming Hopes. But fuch a Temper, whether it proceeds from a defigned or natural Levity, is deteftable, and has been the Caufe of much Trouble and Mortification to many a brave deferving Man. Unlefs the Tenor of a Man's Life be always true and confiftent with itfelf, the lefs one has to do with him the better.

FAB. LVI.   Hercules *and the* Carter,

AS a clownish Fellow was driving his Cart along a deep miry Lane, the Wheels stuck so fast in the Clay, that the Horses could not draw them out. Upon this, he fell a bawling and praying to *Hercules* to come and help him. *Hercules* looking down from a Cloud, bid him not lie there, like an idle Rascal as he was, but get up and whip his Horses stoutly, and clap his Shoulder to the Wheel; adding, That this was the only Way for him to obtain his Assistance.

The APPLICATION.

This Fable shews us how vain and ill-grounded the Expectation of those People are, who imagine they can obtain whatever they want by importuning Heaven with their Prayers; for it is so agreeable to the Nature of the Divine Being, to be better pleased with virtuous Actions and an honest Industry, than idle Prayers, that it is a Sort of Blasphemy to say otherwise. These were

2   the

the Sentiments of honeft good Heathens, who were Strangers to all revealed Religion : But it is not ftrange that they fhould embrace and propagate fuch a Notion, fince it is no other than the Dictate of common Reafon. What is both ftrange in itfelf, and furprifing how it could be made fo fafhionable, is, that moft of thofe whofe Reafon fhould be enlightened by Revelation, are very apt to be guilty of this Stupidity, and by praying often for the Comforts of Life, to neglect that Bufinefs which is the proper Means of procuring them. How fuch a miftaken Devotion came to prevail, one cannot imagine, unlefs from one of thefe two Motives ; either that People, by fuch a Veil of Hypocrify, would pafs themfelves upon Mankind for better than they really are ; or are influenced by unfkilful Preachers (which is fometimes, indeed too often, the Cafe) to mind the World as little as poffible, even to the Neglect of their neceffary Callings. No Queftion but it is a great Sin for a Man to fail in his Trade or Occupation, by running often to Prayers ; it being a Demonftration in itfelf, though the Scripture had never faid it, that we pleafe God moft, when we are doing the moft Good : And how can we do more Good, than by a fober honeft Induftry, *to provide for thofe of our own Houfhold,* and to endeavour *to have to give to him that needeth.* The Man who is virtuoufly and honeftly engaged, is actually ferving God all the while ; and is more likely to have his filent Wifhes, accompanied with ftrenuous Endeavours, complied with by the Supreme Being, than he who begs with a fruitlefs Vehemence, and folicits with an empty Hand : A Hand, which would be more religious were it ufefully employed, and more devout, were it ftretched forth to do Good to thofe that want it.

FAB.

FAB. LVII. *The* Man *and his* Goose.

A Certain Man had a Goose, which laid him a golden Egg every Day. But, not contented with this, which rather increased than abated his Avarice, he was resolved to kill the Goose, and cut up her Belly, that so he might come at the inexhaustible Treasure which he fancied she had within her. He did so; and to his great Sorrow and Disappointment, found nothing.

The APPLICATION.

They who are of such craving impatient Tempers, that they cannot live contented when Fortune had blessed them with a constant and continued Sufficiency, deserve even to be deprived of what they have. And this has been the Case of many ambitious and covetous Men, who by making an Essay to grow very rich at once, have missed what they aimed at, and lost what they had before. But this comes so near the Sense of the fourth Fable, that the same Application may very well serve for both. If any Thing farther can be couched in this, it may possibly be intended to shew us the Unreasonableness and

Incon-

Inconvenience of being folicitous about what may happen hereafter, and wanting to pry into the Womb of Futurity. Which if we could do, all we fhould get for our Pains would be, to fpoil our Pleafures by Anticipation, and double our Misfortunes by a previous Senfe and Apprehenfion of them. There are fome Things that entertain and delight us very agreeably while we view them at a proper Diftance; which, perhaps, would not ftand the Teft of a too near Infpection. Beauty, being only the external Form of a Thing which ftrikes the Eye in a pleafing Manner, is a very thin gloffy Being, and like fome nice Paintings of a peculiar Compofition, will not well bear even to be breathed on : To preferve our good Opinion of it, we muft not approach too clofe; for if, like the Man in the Fable, we have a Mind to fearch for a Treafure within, we may not only fail of our Expectations there, but even lofe the conftant Relifh we enjoyed from a remoter Contemplation.

F A B. LVIII. *The* Wanton Calf.

A CALF, full of Play and Wantonnefs, feeing the Ox at Plough, could not forbear infulting him. What a forry poor Drudge art thou, fays he, to bear

that

that heavy Yoke upon your Neck, and go all Day
drawing a Plough at your Tail, to turn up the Ground
for your Mafter! But you are a wretched dull Slave,
and know no better, or elfe you would not do it.
See what a happy Life I lead; I go juft where I
pleafe; fometimes I lie down under the cool Shade;
fometimes frifk about in the open Sunfhine; and,
when I pleafe, flake my Thirft in the clear fweet
Brook; But you, if you were to perifh, have not fo
much as a little dirty Water to refrefh you. The
Ox, not at all moved with what he faid, went quietly
and calmly on with his Work; and, in the Evening, was unyoked and turned loofe. Soon after which
he faw the Calf taken out of the Field, and delivered into the Hands of a Prieft, who immediately
led him to the Altar, and prepared to facrifice him.
His Head was hung round with Fillets of Flowers,
and the fatal Knife was juft going to be applied to
his Throat, when the Ox drew near and whifpered
him to this Purpofe: Behold the End of your Infolence and Arrogance; it was for this only you
were fuffered to live at all; and pray now, Friend,
whofe Condition is beft, yours or mine?

The APPLICATION.

To infult People in Diftrefs, is the Property of a
cruel, indifcreet, and giddy Temper; for as the Proceedings of Fortune are very irregular and uncertain,
we may, the next Turn of the Wheel, be thrown down
to their Condition, and they exalted to ours. We are
likewife given to underftand by this Fable, what the
Confequence of an idle Life generally is, and how well
fatisfied laborious diligent Men are, in the End, when
they come quietly to enjoy the Fruits of their Induftry.
They who by little Tricks and Sharpings, or by open
Violence and Robbery, live in a high expenfive Way,
often in their Hearts at leaft, defpife the poor honeft Man,
who is contented with the virtuous Product of his daily
Labour, and patiently fubmits to his Deftiny. But how
often

often is the poor Man comforted, by feeing thefe wanton
Villains led in Triumph to the Altar of Juftice, while
he has many a cheerful Summer's Morning to enjoy
Abroad, and many a long Winter's Evening to indulge
himfelf in at Home, by a quiet Hearth, and under an
unenvied Roof: Bleffings, which often attend a fober,
induftrious Man, tho' the Idle and the Profligate are utter
Strangers to them. Luxury and Intemperance, befides
their being certain to fhorten a Man's Days, are very apt,
not only to engage People with their feeming Charms
into a debauched Life, utterly prejudicial to their Health,
but to make them have a Contempt for others; whofe
good Senfe and true Tafte of Happinefs infpire them
with an Averfion to Idlenefs and Effeminacy, and put them
upon hardening their Conftitution by innocent Exercife
and laudable Employment. How many do Gluttony and
Sloth tumble into an untimely Grave! while the Tem-
perate and the Active drink fober Draughts of Life, and
fpin out their Thread to the moft defirable Length.

FAB. LIX. *The* Leopard *and the* Fox.

THE Leopard, one Day, took it into his Head to
value himfelf upon the great Variety and Beauty
of his Spots, and truly he faw no Reafon why even

the

the Lion fhould take Place of him, fince he could not fhew fo beautiful a Skin. As for the Reft of the wild Beafts of the Foreft, he treated them all, without Diftinction, in the moft haughty difdainful Manner. But the Fox, being among them, went up to him with a great deal of Spirit and Refolution, and told him, That he was miftaken in the Value he was pleafed to fet upon himfelf; fince People of Judgment were not ufed to form their Opinion of Merit from an outfide Appearance, but by confidering the good Qualities and Endowments with which the Mind was ftored within.

The APPLICATION.

How much more heavenly and powerful would Beauty prove, if it were not fo frequently impaired by the Affectation and Conceitednefs of its Poffeffor! If fome Women were but as modeft and unaffuming as they are handfome, they might command the Hearts of all that behold them. But Nature feemed to forefee, and has provided againft fuch an Inconvenience, by tempering its greateft Mafter-pieces with a due Proportion of Pride and Vanity: So that their Power, depending upon the Duration of their Beauty only, is like to be but of a fhort Continuance; which, when they happen to prove Tyrants, is no fmall Comfort to us; and then, even while it lafts, will abate much of its Severity by the Allay of thofe two prevailing Ingredients. Wife Men are chiefly captivated with the Charms of the Mind; and whenever they are infatuated with a Paffion for any Thing elfe, it is generally obferved that they ceafe, during that Time at leaft, to be what they were; and are indeed looked upon to be only playing the Fool. If the Fair Ones we have been fpeaking of have a true Afcendant over them, they will oblige them to diveft themfelves of Common Senfe, and to talk and act ridiculoufly, before they can think them worthy of the leaft Regard. Should one of thefe fine Creatures be addreffed in the Words of *Juba,*

'Tis

'Tis not a Set of Features, or Complexion,
The Tincture of a Skin, that I admire.
Beauty soon grows familiar to the Lover,
Fades in his Eye, and palls upon the Sense.
The virtuous Marcia towers above her Sex.
True, she is fair, oh, how divinely fair!
But still the lovely Maid improves her Charms
With inward Greatness, unaffected Wisdom,
And Sanctity of Manners. —————

The Man that should venture the Success of a strong
Passion, upon the Construction she would put upon such
a Compliment, might have Reason to repent of his
Conduct.

F A B. LX. *The* Cat *and the* Fox.

AS the Cat and the Fox were talking Politics together, on a Time, in the Middle of a Forest,
Reynard said, let Things turn out ever so bad, he
did not care, for he had a Thousand Tricks for them
yet, before they should hurt him: But pray, says
he, Mrs. Puss, suppose there should be an Invasion,
what Course do you design to take? Nay, says the

Cat, I have but one Shift for it, and if that won't
do, I am undone. I am sorry for you, replies *Reynard*, with all my Heart, and would gladly furnish
you with one or two of mine, but indeed, Neighbour, as Times go, it is not good to trust; we must
even be every one for himself, as the Saying is, and
so your humble Servant. These Words were scarce
out of his Mouth, when they were alarmed with a
Pack of Hounds, that came upon them full Cry.
The Cat, by the Help of her single Shift, ran up a
Tree, and sat securely among the top Branches;
from whence she beheld *Reynard*, who had not been
able to get out of Sight, overtaken with his Thousand Tricks, and torn in as many Pieces by the
Dogs which had surrounded him.

The APPLICATION.

A Man that sets up for more Cunning than the rest
of his Neighbours, is generally a silly Fellow at the Bottom. Whoever is Master of a little Judgment and In-
sight into Things, let him keep them to himself, and
make Use of them as he sees Occasion; but he should
not be teizing others with an idle and impertinent Os-
tentation of them. One good discreet Expedient made
Use of upon an Emergency, will do a Man more real
Service, and make others think better of him, than to
have passed all along for a shrewd crafty Knave, and be
bubbled at last. When any one has been such a Coxcomb
as to insult his Acquaintance, by pretending to more
Policy and Stratagem than the rest of Mankind, they are
apt to wish for some Difficulty for him to shew his Skill
in; where, if he should miscarry, (as ten to one but he
does,) his Misfortune, instead of Pity, is sure to be attended with Laughter. He that sets up for a Biter, as the
Phrase is, being generally intent upon his Prey, or vain
of shewing his Art, frequently exposes himself to the
Traps of one sharper than himself, and incurs the Ridicule of those whom he designed to make ridiculous.

FAB.

FAB. LXI. *The* Partridge *and the* Cocks.

A Certain Man, having taken a Partridge, plucked
some of the Feathers out of its Wings, and turned
it into a little Yard, where he kept Game-Cocks.
The Cocks, for a while, made the poor Bird lead
a sad Life, continually pecking and driving it away
from the Meat. This Treatment was taken the
more unkindly, because offered to a Stranger; and
the Partridge could not but conclude them the most
inhospitable, uncivil People, he had ever met with.
But, at last, observing how frequently they quarrel-
led and fought with each other, he comforted himself with this Reflection; That it was no wonder
they were so cruel to him, since there was so much
Bickering and Animosity among themselves.

The APPLICATION.

This Fable comes Home to ourselves. We of this
Island having always been looked upon as cruel to Stran-
gers. Where there is any Thing in the Manner of our
Situation, as an Island, which consequently can be no
Thorough-

Thoroughfare to other Countries, and so is not made
Use of by Strangers upon that Account, which makes
us thus shy and uncivil; or, whether it be a Jealousy
upon Account of our Liberties, which puts us upon
being suspicious of, and unwilling to harbour any that
are not Members of the same Community, perhaps it
would not be easy to determine. But that it is so in Fact,
is too notorious to be denied; and probably can be accounted for no better Way, than from the natural Bent
of our Temper, as it proceeds from something peculiar
to our Air and Climate. It has been affirmed, That
there is not in the whole World besides, a Breed of Cocks
and Dogs, so fierce and uncapable of yielding as that of
ours: But that either of them, carried into foreign
Countries, would degenerate in a few Years. Why may
not the same be true of our Men? But if Strangers find
any Inconvenience in this, there is a comfortable Consideration to balance it on the other Side, which is,
That there are no People under the Sun so much given
to Division and Contention among themselves as we are.
Can a Stranger think it hard to be looked upon with
some Shyness, when he beholds how little we spare one
another? Was ever any Foreigner, merely for being a
Foreigner, treated with half that Malice and Bitterness,
which differing Parties express towards each other? One
would willingly believe that this proceeds, in the Main,
on both Sides, from a passionate Concern for our Liberties and Well-being; for there is nothing else which can
so well excuse it. But it cannot be denied that our Aversion, notwithstanding our being a Trading Nation, to
have any Intercourse with Strangers, is so great, that
when we want other Objects for our Churlishness, we
raise them up among ourselves; and there is, sometimes,
as great a Strangeness kept up between one County and
another here, as there is between two distinct Kingdoms
abroad. One cannot so much wonder at the constant
Hostilities which are observed between the Inhabitants
of South and North *Britain*, of *Wales* and *Ireland*, among
one another; when a *Yorkshire* Man shall be looked
upon as a Foreigner by a Native of *Norfolk*; and both
be taken for outlandish Intruders, by one that happens
to be born within the Bills of Mortality.

FAB. LXII. *The* Hunted Beaver.

IT is said that a Beaver (a Creature which lives chiefly in the Water) has a certain Part about him which is good in Phyfic, and that, upon this Account, he is often hunted down and killed. Once upon a Time, as one of thefe Creatures was hard purfued by the Dogs, and knew not how to efcape, recollecting with himfelf the Reafon of his being thus perfecuted, with a great Refolution and Prefence of Mind, he bit off the Part which his Hunters wanted, and throwing it towards them, by thefe Means efcaped with his Life.

The APPLICATION.

However it is among Beafts, there are few Human Creatures but what are hunted for fomething elfe, befides either their Lives, or the Pleafure of hunting them. The Inquifition would hardly be fo keen againft the *Jews*, if they had not fomething belonging to them which their Perfecutors efteem more valuable than their Souls; which
whenever

whenever that wife, but obftinate People can prevail
with themfelves to part with, there is an End of the
Chafe, for that Time. Indeed, when Life is purfued, and
in Danger, whoever values it, fhould give up every Thing
but his Honour to preferve it. And, when a difcarded
Minifter is profecuted for having damaged the Com-
mon-wealth, let him but throw down fome of the Fruits
of his Iniquity to the Hunters, and one may engage for
his coming off, in other Refpects, with a whole Skin.

FAB. LXIII. *The* Thunny *and the* Dolphin.

A Fifh, called a Thunny, being purfued by a
Dolphin, and driven with great Violence, not
minding which Way he went, was thrown by the
Force of the Waves upon a Rock, and left there.
His Death now was inevitable; but, cafting his
Eyes on one Side, and feeing the Dolphin in the
fame Condition, lie gafping by him, Well, fays he,
I muft die, it is true; but I die with Pleafure, when
I behold him who is the Caufe of it involved in
the fame Fate.

The

The APPLICATION:

Revenge, though a blind, mifchievous Paffion, is yet a very fweet Thing: So fweet, that it can even footh the Pangs, and reconcile us to the Bitternefs of Death. And indeed, it muft be a Temper highly philofophical, that could be driven out of Life by any tyrannical unjuft Procedure, and not be touched with a Senfe of Pleafure to fee the Author of it fplitting upon the fame Rock. When this is allowed, and it is farther confidered how eafily the Revenge of the meaneft Perfon may be executed upon even the higheft, it fhould, methinks, keep People upon their Guard, and prevail with them not to perfecute or be injurious to any one. The moral Turpitude of doing wrong is fufficient to influence every brave honeft Man, and to fecure him from harbouring even the leaft Thought of it in his Breaft. But the Knave and the Coward fhould weigh the prefent Argument, and before they attempt the leaft Injury, be affured of this Truth, That nothing is more fweet, nor fcarce any Thing fo eafy to compafs as Revenge.

FAB. LXIV. *The* Hawk *and the* Nightingale.

A Nightingale, fitting all alone among the fhady Branches of an Oak, fung with fo melodious and fhrill a Pipe, that fhe made the Woods echo again, and alarmed a hungry Hawk, who was at some Diſtance off, watching for his Prey; he had no ſooner diſcovered the little Muſician, but, making a Stoop at the Place, he ſeized her with his crooked Talons, and bid her prepare for Death. Ah! ſays ſhe, for Mercy's Sake, don't do ſo barbarous a Thing, and ſo unbecoming yourſelf; conſider I never did you any Wrong, and am but a poor ſmall Morſel for ſuch a Stomach as yours; rather attack ſome larger Fowl, which may bring you more Credit, and a better Meal, and let me go. Ay! ſays the Hawk, perſuade me to it if you can: I have been upon the Watch all Day long, and have not met with one Bit of any Thing, till I caught you; and now you would have me let you go, in Hopes of ſomething better, would you? Pray, who would be the Fool then?

The APPLICATION.

They who neglect the Opportunity of reaping a ſmall Advantage in Hopes they ſhall obtain a better, are far from acting upon a reaſonable and well-adviſed Foundation. The Figure of Time is always drawn with a ſingle Lock of Hair hanging over his Forehead, and the Back Part of his Head bald; to put us in Mind, that we ſhould be ſure to lay hold of an Occaſion when it preſents itſelf to us; leſt afterwards we repent us of our Omiſſion and Folly, and would recover it when it is too late. It is a very weak Reaſon to give for our Refuſal of an Offer of Kindneſs, that we do it becauſe we deſire or deſerve a better: for it is Time enough to relinquiſh the ſmall Affair, when the great one comes, if ever it does come. But, ſuppoſing it ſhould not, how can we forgive ourſelves for letting any Thing ſlip through our Hands, by vainly gaping after ſomething elſe, which we never could obtain? He who has not been guilty of any of theſe Kinds of Errors, however poorly he may come off at laſt, has only the Malice of Fortune, or of ſomebody elſe, to charge with his ill Succeſs; and may

applaud

applaud himſelf with ſome Comfort, in never having
loſt an Opportunity, though ever ſo ſmall, of bettering
and improving his Circumſtances. Unthinking People have oftentimes the Unhappineſs to fret and teize
themſelves with Retroſpects of this Kind ; which they,
who attend to the Buſineſs of Life as they ought, never
have Occaſion to make.

FAB. LXV. *The* Fox *without a* Tail.

A FOX being caught in a Steel Trap, by his
Tail, was glad to compound for his Eſcape
with the Loſs of it ; but upon coming abroad into
the World, began to be ſo ſenſible of the Diſgrace
ſuch a Defect would bring upon him, that he almoſt
wiſhed he had died, rather than left it behind him.
However, to make the beſt of a bad Matter, he
formed a Project in his Head, to call an Aſſembly
of the reſt of the Foxes, and propoſe it for their Imitation, as a Faſhion which would be very agreeable
and becoming. He did ſo ; and made a long Ha-
rangue

rangue upon the Unprofitableneſs of Tails in general, and endeavoured chiefly to ſhew the Aukward-
neſs and Inconvenience of a Fox's Tail in particular; adding, that it would be both more graceful,
and more expeditious, to be altogether without
them; and that, for his Part, what he had only imagined and conjectured before, he now found by Experience; for that he never enjoyed himſelf ſo well,
and found himſelf ſo eaſy, as he had done ſince he
cut off his Tail. He ſaid no more, but looked about
with a briſk Air, to ſee what Proſelytes he had
gained; when a ſly old Thief in the Company, who
underſtood Trap, anſwered him, with a Leer, I believe you may have found a Conveniency in parting
with your Tail, and when we are in the ſame Circumſtances, perhaps we may do ſo too.

The APPLICATION.

If Men were but generally as prudent as Foxes, they
would not ſuffer ſo many ſilly Faſhions to obtain, as
are daily brought in Vogue, for which ſcarce any Reaſon can be aſſigned beſides the Humour of ſome conceited vain Creature; unleſs, which is full as bad, they
are intended to palliate ſome Defect in the Perſon that
introduces them. The Petticoat of a whole Sex has
been ſometimes ſwelled to ſuch a prodigious Extent, to
ſcreen an Enormity, of which only one of them has been
guilty. And it is no Wonder that *Alexander the Great*
could bring a wry Neck into Faſhion in a Nation of
Slaves, when we conſider what Power of this Nature
ſome little inſignificant dapper Fellows have had among
a free People.

FAB.

FAB. LXVI. *The* Old Man *and* Death.

A Poor feeble old Man, who had crawled out into a neighbouring Wood to gather a few Sticks, had made up his Bundle, and laying it over his Shoulders, was trudging homeward with it; but, what with Age, and the Length of the Way, and the Weight of his Burden, he grew so faint and weak, that he funk under it; and, as he fat on the Ground, called upon Death to come, once for all, and eafe him of his Troubles. Death no fooner heard him, but he came and demanded of him what he wanted. The poor old Creature, who little thought Death had been fo near, and frighted almoſt out of his Senfes with his terrible Afpect, anfwered him trembling, That having by Chance let his Bundle of Sticks fall, and being too infirm to get it up himſelf, he had made bold to call upon him to help him; that indeed, this was all he wanted at prefent; and that he hoped his Worſhip was not offended with him for the Liberty he had taken in fo doing.

The

The APPLICATION.

This Fable gives us a lively Reprefentation of the general Behaviour of Mankind towards that grim King of Terrors, Death. Such Liberties do they take with him behind his Back, that upon every little crofs Accident which happens in their Way, Death is immediately called upon; and they even wifh it might be lawful for them to finifh by their own Hands a Life fo odious, fo perpetually tormenting and vexatious. When, let but Death only offer to make his Appearance, and the very Senfe of his near Approach almoft does the Bufinefs: Oh, then all they want is a little longer Life; and they would be glad to come off fo well, as to have their old Burden laid upon their Shoulders again. One may well conclude what an utter Averfion they, who are in Youth, Health, and Vigor of Body, have to Dying, when Age, Poverty, and Wretchednefs, are not fufficient to reconcile us to the Thought.

FAB. LXVII. *The* Lion *in* Love.

THE Lion, by Chance, faw a fair Maid, the Forefter's Daughter, as fhe was tripping over a Lawn, and fell in Love with her. Nay, fo violent

was

was his Paffion, that he could not live unlefs he
made her his own; fo that without any more Delay, he broke his Mind to the Father, and demanded
the Damfel for his Wife. The Man, as odd as the
Propofal feemed at firft, yet foon recollected, that
by complying, he might get the Lion into his
Power; but, by refufing him, fhould only exafpe-
rate and provoke his Rage. Therefore he confented; but told him it muft be upon thefe Conditions : That confidering the Girl was young and
tender, he muft agree to let his Teeth be plucked
out, and his Claws cut off, left he fhould hurt her,
or at leaft frighten her with the Apprehenfion of
them. The Lion was too much in Love to hefitate;
but was no fooner deprived of his Teeth and Claws,
than the treacherous Forefter attacked him with a
huge Club, and knocked his Brains out.

The APPLICATION.

Of all the ill Confequences that may attend that
blind Paffion, Love, feldom any prove fo fatal as that
one, of its drawing People into a fudden and ill-concerted Marriage. They commit a rafh Action in the
Midft of a Fit of Madnefs, of which, as foon as they
come to themfelves, they may find Reafon to repent as
long as they live. Many an unthinking young Fellow
has been treated as much like a Savage, in this Refpect,
as the Lion in the Fable. He has, perhaps, had nothing valuable belonging to him, but his Eftate, and
the Writings which made his Title to it; and if he is
fo far captivated, as to be perfuaded to part with thefe,
his Teeth and his Claws are gone, and he lies entirely
at the Mercy of Madam and her Relations. All the
Favour he is to expect after this, is from the accidental
Goodnefs of the Family he falls into; which, if it happen to be of a particular Strain, will not fail to keep
him in a diftant Subjection, after they have ftripped
him of all his Power. Nothing but a true Friendfhip,
and a mutual Intereft, can keep up reciprocal Love betwixt

twixt the conjugal Pair; and when that is wanting, and nothing but Contempt and Averſion remain to ſupply the Place, Matrimony becomes a downright State of Enmity and Hoſtility: And what a miſerable Caſe he muſt be in, who has put himſelf and his whole Power into the Hands of his Enemy, let thoſe conſider, who, while they are in their ſober Senſes, abhor the Thoughts of being betrayed into their Ruin, by following the Impulſe of a blind unheeding Paſſion.

FAB. LXVIII. *The* Lioneſs *and the* Fox.

THE Lioneſs and the Fox meeting together, fell into Diſcourſe; and the Converſation turning upon the Breeding and the Fruitfulneſs of ſome living Creatures above others, the Fox could not forbear taking the Opportunity of obſerving to the Lioneſs, that for her Part, ſhe thought Foxes were as happy in that Reſpect as almoſt any other Creatures; for that they bred conſtantly once a Year, if not oftener, and always had a good Litter of Cubs at every Birth: and yet, ſays ſhe, there are thoſe who are never delivered of more than one at a Time,

and

and that perhaps not above once or twice thro' their whole Life, who hold up their Nofes, and value themfelves fo much upon it, that they think all other Creatures beneath them, and fcarce worthy to be fpoken to. The Lionefs, who all the while perceived at whom this Reflection pointed, was fired with Refentment, and with a good deal of Vehemence, replied : What you have obferved may be true, and that not without Reafon. You produce a great many at a Litter, and often; but what are they? Foxes. I indeed have but one at a Time, but you fhould remember that this one is a Lion.

The APPLICATION.

Our Productions, of whatfoever Kind, are not to be efteemed fo much by the Quantity as the Quality of them. It is not being employed much, but well, and to the Purpofe, which makes us ufeful to the Age we live in, and celebrated by thofe which are to come. As it is a Misfortune to the Countries which are infefted with them, for Foxes, and other Vermin to multiply; fo, one cannot help throwing out a melancholy Reflection, when one fees fome Particulars of the Human Kind increafe fo faft as they do. But the moft obvious Meaning of this Fable, is the Hint it gives us in Relation to Authors. Thefe Gentlemen fhould never attempt to raife themfelves a Reputation, by enumerating a Catalogue of their Productions. Since there is more Glory in having written one tolerable Piece, than a thoufand indifferent ones. And whoever has had the good Fortune to pleafe in one Performance of this Kind, fhould be very cautious how he ventures his Reputation in a fecond.

FAB. LXIX. *The* Stag *and the* Fawn.

A Stag, grown old and mifchievous, was, according to Cuftom, ftamping with his Foot, making Offers with his Head, and bellowing fo terri-
bly, that the whole Herd quaked for Fear of him :
When, one of the little Fawns coming up, addreffed him to this Purpofe : Pray, what is the Reafon
that you, who are fo ftout and formidable at all
other Times, if you do but hear the Cry of the
Hounds, are ready to fly out of your Skin for Fear?
What you obferve is true, replied the Stag, though
I know not how to account for it : I am indeed vi-
gorous, and able enough, I think, to make my Party
good any where, and often refolve with myfelf, that
nothing fhall ever difmay my Courage for the future : But, alas ! I no fooner hear the Voice of a
Hound, but all my Spirits fail me, and I cannot help
making off as faft as ever my Legs can carry me.

The

The APPLICATION.

This is the Cafe of many a cowardly Bully in the World. He is difpofed to be imperious and tyrannical, and to infult his Companions, and takes all Opportunities of acting according to his Inclination; but yet is cautious where he makes his Haunts, and takes Care to have to do only with a Herd of rafcally People, as vile and mean as himfelf. A Man of Courage quafhes him with a Word; and he who has threatened Death in every Sentence, for a Twelvemonth together, to thofe whom he knew it would affright, at the very Frown of an intrepid Man, has leapt out of a Window. It is no unpleafant Sight, to be prefent when any of thefe Gentlemen happen to be difarmed of their Terror before the Face of their humble Admirers: There is a ftrange, boifterous Struggle, betwixt Fear, Shame, and Revenge, which blinds them with Confufion; and tho' they would fain exert a little Courage, and fhew themfelves Men, yet, they know not how, there is fomething within which will not fuffer them to do it. The Predominance of Nature will fhew itfelf upon Occafion, in its true Colours, through all the Difguifes which artful Men endeavour to throw over it. Cowardice, particularly, gives us but the more Sufpicion, when it would conceal itfelf under an affected Fiercenefs; as they, who would fmother an ill Smell by a Cloud of Perfume, are imagined to be but the more offenfive. When we have done all, Nature will remain what fhe was, and fhew herfelf whenever fhe is called upon; therefore whatever we do in Contradiction to her Laws, is fo forced and affected, that it muft needs expofe, and make us ridiculous. We talk Nonfenfe when we would argue againft it; like *Teague*, who being afked, why he fled from his Colours? faid, his Heart was as good as any in the Regiment, but protefted his cowardly Legs would run away with him, whatever he could do.

FAB.

FAB. LXX.
The Young Man *and the* Swallow.

A Prodigal young Spendthrift, who had wasted his whole Patrimony in Taverns and Gaming-Houses, among lewd, idle Company, was taking a melancholy Walk near a Brook. It was in the Month of *January*; and happened to be one of those warm sunshiny Days which sometimes smile upon us even in that winterly Season of the Year; and to make it the more flattering, a Swallow, which had made his Appearance, by Mistake, too soon, flew skimming along upon the Surface of the Water. The giddy Youth observing this, without any farther Consideration, concluded that Summer was now come, and that he should have little or no Occasion for Clothes, so went and pawned them at the Broker's, and ventured the Money for one Stake more, among his sharping Companions. When this too was gone the same Way with the Rest, he took another solitary Walk in the same Place as before.

But

But the Weather being severe and frosty, had made every Thing look with an Aspect very different from what it did before; the Brook was quite frozen over, and the poor Swallow lay dead upon the Bank of it: The very Sight of which cooled the young Spark's Brains; and coming to a Kind of Sense of his Misery, he reproached the deceased Bird, as the Author of all his Misfortunes: Ah, Wretch that thou wert! says he, thou hast undone both thyself and me, who was so credulous as to depend upon thee.

The APPLICATION.

They who frequent Taverns and Gaming-Houses, and keep bad Company, should not wonder if they are reduced, in a very small Time, to Penury and Want. The wretched young Fellows, who once addict themselves to such a scandalous Kind of Life, scarce think of, or attend to any one Thing besides. They seem to have nothing else in their Heads, but how they may squander what they have got, and where they may get more when that is gone. They do not make the same Use of their Reason that other People do; but, like the jaundiced Eye, view every Thing in that false Light in which their Distemper and Debauchery represent it. The Young Man in the Fable gives us a pretty Example of this; he sees a Swallow in the Midst of Winter, and instead of being surprised at it, as a very irregular and extraordinary Thing, concludes from thence that it is Summer, as if he had never thought before about the Season. Well, the Result of this wise Conclusion, is of a Piece with the Conclusion itself; if it is Summer, he shall not want so many Clothes, therefore he sells them: For what? More Money to squander away; as if (had his Observation been just) Summer would have lasted all the Year round. But the true Result and Conclusion of all this is: When both his Money and Clothes are irrecoverably gone, he comes to his right Senses; is ready to perish with Hunger, to starve with Cold, and to tear his own Flesh with Remorse and Vexation at his former Stupidity.

FAB. LXXI. *The* Angler *and the* Little Fiſh.

A Man was angling in a River, and caught a ſmall Pearch; which, as he was taking off the Hook, and going to put into his Baſket, opened its Mouth, and began to implore his Pity, begging that he would throw it into the River again. Upon the Man's demanding, What Reaſon he had to expect ſuch a Favour? Why, ſays the Fiſh, becauſe, at preſent, I am but young and little, and conſequently not ſo well worth your while, as I ſhall be, if you take me ſome Time hence, when I am grown larger. That may be, replies the Man; but I am not one of thoſe Fools who quit a Certainty in Expectation of an Uncertainty.

The APPLICATION.

This Fable points much the ſame Way as the Sixty-fourth, ſo that one Moral may very well ſerve for both. But the Leſſon they teach is ſo uſeful and inſtructive, that a Repetition of it is by no Means ſuperfluous. The Precept which they would inſtil into us, is, never to let ſlip the preſent Opportunity, but to ſecure to ourſelves every little Advantage, juſt in the Nick that it offers,

without

without a vain Reliance upon, and fruitless Expectation of something better in Time to come. We may cheer up our Spirits with hoping for that which we cannot at present obtain; but at the same Time, let us be sure we give no Occasion of condemning ourselves for omitting any Thing which it was in our Power to secure.

FAB. LXXII. *The* Ass *and the* Lion Hunting.

THE Lion took a Fancy to hunt in Company with the Ass; and to make him the more useful, gave him Instructions to hide himself in a Thicket, and then to bray in the most frightful Manner that he could possibly contrive. By this Means, says he, you will rouse all the Beasts within the Hearing of you; while I stand at the Outlets, and take them as they are making off. This was done; and the Stratagem took Effect accordingly. The Ass brayed most hideously; and the timorous Beasts, not knowing what to make of it, began to scour off as fast as they could; when the Lion, who was posted at a proper Avenue, seized and devoured them, as he pleased. Having got his Belly full, he called out to the Ass, and bid him leave off, telling him,

he

he had done enough. Upon this, the lop-eared Brute
came out of his Ambush, and approaching the Lion,
'asked him, with an Air of Conceit, how he liked
his Performance? Prodigiously! says he; you did it
so well, that I protest, had I not known your Nature
and Temper, I might have been frighted myself.

The APPLICATION.

A bragging cowardly Fellow may impose upon People that do not know him; but is the greatest Jest imaginable to those that do. There are many Men, who
appear very terrible and big in their Manner of expressing themselves, and, if you could be persuaded to take
their own Word for it, are perfect Lions; who, if one
takes the Pains to enquire a little into their true Nature, are as arrant Asses as ever brayed.

FAB. LXXIII. *The* Sensible Ass.

AN old Fellow was feeding an Ass in a fine green
Meadow; and being alarmed with the sudden
Approach of the Enemy, was impatient with the Ass
to put himself forward, and fly with all the Speed that
he was able. The Ass asked him, Whether or no he
thought

thought the Enemy would clap two Pair of Panniers upon his Back? The Man faid, No, there was no Fear of that. Why then, fays the Afs, I will not ftir an Inch; for what is it to me who my Mafter is, fince I fhall but carry my Panniers, as ufual.

The APPLICATION.

This Fable fhews us, how much in the Wrong the poorer Sort of People moft commonly are, when they are under any Concern about the Revolutions of a Government. All the Alteration which they can feel, is, perhaps, in the Name of their Sovereign, or fome fuch important Trifle: But they cannot well be poorer, or made to work harder than they did before. And yet how are they fometimes impofed upon, and drawn in by the Artifices of a few miftaken or defigning Men, to foment Factions, and raife Rebellions, in Cafes where they can get nothing by the Succefs; but, if they mifcarry, are in Danger of fuffering an ignominious, untimely Death.

FAB. LXXIV. *The* Boafting Traveller.

ONE who had been abroad, at his Return Home again, was giving an Account of his Travels; and, among other Places, faid he had been at *Rhodes*,

where

where he had so distinguished himself in Leaping, an Exercise that City was famous for, that not a *Rhodian* could come near him. When those who were present did not seem to credit this Relation so readily as he intended they should, he took some Pains to convince them of it by Oaths and Protestations; upon which, one of the Company rising up, told him, he need not give himself so much Trouble about it, since he would put him in a Way to demonstrate it in Fact; which was, to suppose the Place they were in to be *Rhodes*, and to perform his extraordinary Leap over again. The Boaster, not liking this Proposal, sat down quietly, and had no more to say for himself.

The APPLICATION.

It is very weak, in all Men, as well those who have travelled, as those who have not, to be solicitous with their Company to believe them, when they are relating a Matter of Fact, in which they themselves were a Party concerned. For, the more urgent a Man appears at such a Time, in order to gain Credit, the more his Audience is apt to suspect the Truth of what he relates. They perceive his Vanity is touched more than his Honour, and that it is his Ability, not his Veracity, which he cannot bear to have questioned. And, indeed, tho' a Man was ever so fully satisfied of such a Truth himself, he should consider, that he is still as far from being able to convince others, as if he were altogether ignorant of it. Therefore, in all Cases, where proper Vouchers are expected, we had better be contented to keep our Exploits to ourselves, than to appear ridiculous, by contending to have them believed. How much more then should travelled Gentlemen have a Care how they import Lyes and Inventions of their own, from foreign Parts, and attempt to vend them at Home for staple Truths. Every Time they utter a Falshood, they are liable, not only to be suspected by the Company in general, but to be detected and exposed by some particular Person, who may have been at the same Place, and, perhaps, know how to convict their Forgery even to a Demonstration.   F A B.

FAB. LXXV. *The Brother and Sister.*

A Certain Man had two Children, a Son and a
Daughter. The Boy beautiful and handsome
enough; the Girl not quite so well. They were both
very young, and happened one Day to be playing
near the Looking-Glass, which stood on their Mother's Toilet: the Boy, pleased with the Novelty of
the Thing, viewed himself for some Time, and, in
a wanton roguish Manner, took Notice to the Girl,
how handsome he was. She resented it, and could
not bear the insolent Manner in which he did it;
for she understood it (as how could she do otherwise) intended for a direct Affront to her. Therefore she ran immediately to her Father, and, with a
great deal of Aggravation, complained of her Brother; particularly for having acted so effeminate a
Part as to look in a Glass, and meddle with Things
which belonged to Women only. The Father em-
bracing them both, with much Tenderness and Affection,

G 6

fection, told them, That he fhould like to have them
both look in the Glafs every Day; to the Intent
that you, fays he to the Boy, if you think that Face
of yours handfome, may not difgrace and fpoil it
by an ugly Temper, and a foul Behaviour. You,
fays he, fpeaking to the Girl, that you may make
up for the Defects of your Perfon, if there be any,
by the Sweetnefs of your Manners, and the Agree-
ablenefs of your Converfation.

The APPLICATION.

There is fcarce any Thing we fee in the World, efpecially what belongs to, and hangs about our own Perfon, but is capable of affording us Matter for fome ferious and ufeful Confideration. And this Fable, notwithftanding the Scene of it is laid at the very Beginning and Entrance of Life, yet utters a Doctrine worthy the Attention of every Stage and Degree thereof,
from the Child to the old Man. Let each of us take
a Glafs, and view himfelf confiderately. He that is
vain and felf-conceited, will find Beauties in every Feature, and his whole Shape will be without Fault. Let
it be fo; yet, if he would be complete, he muft take
Care that the inward Man does not detract from and
difgrace the outward; that the Depravity of his Manners does not fpoil his Face, nor the Wrongnefs of his
Behaviour diftort his Limbs; or, which is the fame
Thing, make his whole Perfon odious and deteftable to
the Eye of his Beholders. Is any one modeft in this
Refpect, and deficient of himfelf? Or has he indeed
Blemifhes and Imperfections, which may depreciate him
in the Sight of Mankind? Let him ftrive to improve
the Faculties of the Mind, where perhaps Nature has
not cramped him; and to excel in the Beauties of a
good Temper and an agreeable Converfation, the Charms
of which are fo much more lafting and unalterably en-
dearing, than thofe of the other Sort. They who are
beautiful in Perfon have this peculiar Advantage, that
with a moderate Regard to Complaifance and Good
Manners,

Manners, they befpeak every one's Opinion in their Favour. But then, be the Outfide of a Man ever fo rough
and uncouth, if his acquired Accomplifhments are but
fweet and engaging, how eafily do we overlook the
reft, and value him, like an oriental Jewel, not by a
glittering Outfide, which is common to bafer Stones,
but by his intrinfic Worth, his bright Imagination, his
clear Reafon, and the tranfparent Sincerity of his honeft Heart.

FAB. LXXVI. *The* Collier *and the* Fuller.

THE Collier and the Fuller being old Acquaint-
ances, happened upon a Time to meet together;
and the latter, being ill provided with a Habitation,
was invited by the former to come and live in the fame
Houfe with him. I thank you, my dear Friend, replies the Fuller, for your kind Offer, but it cannot
be: For if I were to dwell with you, whatever I
fhould take Pains to fcour and make clean in the
Morning, the Duft of you and your Coals would
blacken and defile, as bad as ever, before Night.

The

The APPLICATION.

It is of no small Importance in Life to be cautious what Company we keep, and with whom we enter into Friendships: For though we are ever so well disposed ourselves, and happen to be ever so free from Vice and Debauchery, yet, if those with whom we frequently converse are engaged in a lewd wicked Course, it will be almost impossible for us to escape being drawn in with them. If we are truly wise, and would shun those *Siren* Rocks of Pleasure, upon which so many have split before us, we should forbid ourselves all Manner of Commerce and Correspondence with those, who are steering a Course, which Reason tells us is not only not for our Advantage, but would end in our Destruction. All the Virtue we can boast of, will not be sufficient to insure us, if we embark in bad Company: For, though our Philosophy were such, as we could preserve ourselves from being tainted and infected with their Manners, yet their Character would twist and entwine itself along with ours, in so intricate a Fold, that the World would not take the Trouble to unravel and separate them. Reputations are of a subtle insinuating Texture, like Water; that which is derived from the clearest Spring, if it chances to mix with a foul Current, runs on, undistinguished, in one muddy Stream for the future, and must for ever partake of the Colour and Condition of its Associate.

FAB.

FAB. LXXVII.
The Fox *and the* Vizor-Maſk.

A FOX, being in a Shop where Vizor-Maſks were ſold, laid his Foot upon one of them, and conſidering it awhile attentively, at laſt broke out into this Exclamation : Bleſs me ! ſays he, what a handſome goodly Figure this makes ! What Pity is it, that it ſhould want Brains !

The APPLICATION.

This is levelled at that numerous Part of Mankind, who out of their ample Fortunes, take Care to accompliſh themſelves with every Thing but Common-Senſe. In ſhort, the whole World is a Maſquerade ; and a Man of a tolerable Talent for Obſervation, may entertain himſelf as well in the mixed Aſſemblies he meets with in Life, as at the moſt magnificent and expenſive Revels provided and ordered for that Purpoſe. Many of the Faces one meets with among the gay frolick Part of our *Species,* if ſearched for Brains, would appear as arrant Vizors as that in the Fable.

FAB.

FAB. LXXVIII. *The* Two Frogs.

ONE hot fultry Summer, the Lakes and Ponds being almoft every where dried up, a Couple of Frogs agreed to travel together in Search of Water. At laft, they came to a deep Well, and fitting upon the Brink of it, began to confult, whether they fhould leap in or no. One of them was for it ; urging, that there was Plenty of clear Spring Water, and no Danger of being difturbed. Well, fays the other, all this may be true ; and yet I cannot come into your Opinion for my Life ; for, if the Water fhould happen to dry up here too, how fhould we get out again ?

The APPLICATION.

The Moral of this Fable is intended to put us in Mind *to look before we leap.* That we fhould not undertake any Action of Importance, without confidering firft, what the Event of it is like to prove, and how we fhall be able to come off, upon fuch and fuch Provifos. A good General does not think he diminifhes any Thing of his Character, when he looks forward beyond the

main

main Action, and concerts Measures, in Case there should be Occasion, for a safe Retreat. How many unfortunate Matches are struck up every Day for want of this wholesome Consideration! Profuse Living, and extravagant Gaming, both which terminate in the Ruin of those that follow them, are mostly owing to a Neglect of this Precaution. Wicked Counsellors advise, and ignorant Princes execute those Things, which afterwards they often dearly repent. Wars are begun by this blind Stupidity, from which a State is not abl extricate itself, with either Honour or Safety; and Projects are encouraged by the rash Accession of those, who never considered how they were to get out, till they had plunged themselves irrecoverebly into them.

FAB. LXXIX. *The* Covetous Man.

A Poor covetous Wretch, who had scraped together a good Parcel of Money, went and dug a Hole in one of his Fields, and hid it. The great Pleasure of his Life was to go and look upon this Treasure, once a Day, at least; which one of his Servants observing, and guessing there was something more than ordinary in the Place, came at Night, found

it,

it, and carried it off. The next Day, returning as usual to the Scene of his Delight, and perceiving it had been ravished away from him, he tore his Hair for Grief, and uttered the doleful Complaints of his Despair to the Woods and Meadows. At last, a Neighbour of his, who knew his Temper, overhearing him, and being informed of the Occasion of his Sorrow, Cheer up, Man! says he, thou hast lost nothing: There is the Hole for thee to go and ↑p at still; and if thou canst but fancy the Money there, it will do just as well.

The APPLICATION.

Of all the Appetites to which Human Nature is subject, none is so lasting, so strong, and at the same Time so unaccountable as that of Avarice. Our other Desires generally cool and slacken at the Approach of Old Age; but this flourishes under grey Hairs, and triumphs amidst Impotence and Infirmity. All our other Longings have something to be said in Excuse for them, let them be at what Time of Life soever. But it is above Reason, and therefore truly incomprehensible, why a Man should be passionately fond of Money, only for the Sake of gazing upon it. His Treasure is as useless to him as a Heap of Oyster-Shells; for though he knows how many substantial Pleasures it is able to procure, yet he dares not touch it; and is as destitute of Money, to all Intents and Purposes, as the Man who is not worth a Groat. This is the true State of a covetous Person: to which, one of that Fraternity may possibly make this Reply, that when we have said all, since Pleasure is the grand Aim of Life, if there arises a Delight to some particular Persons from the bare Possession of Riches, though they do not, nor ever intend to make Use of them, we may be puzzled how to account for it, and think it very strange, but ought not absolutely to condemn the Men who thus closely, but innocently, pursue what they esteem the greatest Happiness. True; People would be in the Wrong to paint Covetousness in such odious Colours, were it but compatible with Innocence.

cence. But here arifes the Mifchief, a truly covetous Man will ftick at nothing to attain his Ends; and, when once Avarice takes the Field, Honefty, Charity, Humanity, and, to be brief, every Virtue which oppofes it, is fure to be put to the Rout.

FAB. LXXX.
The Eagle, the Cat, and the Sow.

AN Eagle had built her Neft upon the top Branches of an old Oak. A wild Cat inhabited a Hole in the Middle; and in the hollow Part at the Bottom, was a Sow, with a whole Litter of Pigs. A happy Neighbourhood; and might long have continued fo, had it not been for the wicked Infinuations of the defigning Cat. For, firft of all, up fhe crept to the Eagle; and, good Neighbour, fays fhe, we fhall be all undone: That filthy Sow yonder, does nothing but lie routing at the Foot of a Tree, and, as I fufpect, intends to grub it up, that fhe may the more eafily come at our young Ones. For my Part, I will take Care of my own Concerns; you may do as you pleafe, but I will watch her Motions, tho' I

ftay

ſtay at Home this Month for it. When ſhe had ſaid this, which could not fail of putting the Eagle into a great Fright, down ſhe went, and made a Viſit to the Sow at the Bottom; and, putting on a ſorrowful Face, I hope, ſays ſhe, you do not intend to go abroad To-day? Why not? ſays the Sow. Nay, replies the other, you may do as you pleaſe; but I overheard the Eagle tell her young Ones, that ſhe would treat them with a Pig, the firſt Time ſhe ſaw you go out; and I am not ſure but ſhe may take up with a Kitten in the mean Time; ſo, Good-morrow to you; you will excuſe me, I muſt go and take Care of the little Folks at Home. Away ſhe went accordingly; and, by contriving to ſteal out ſoftly a-Nights for her Prey, and to ſtand watching and peeping all Day at her Hole, as under great Concern, ſhe made ſuch an Impreſſion upon the Eagle and the Sow, that neither of them dared venture abroad, for Fear of the other. The Conſequence of which was, that themſelves, and their young Ones, in a little Time, were all ſtarved, and made Prizes of, by the treacherous Cat and her Kittens.

The APPLICATION.

This ſhews us the ill Conſequence which may attend the giving Ear to a goſſiping double-tongued Neighbour. The Miſchiefs occaſioned by ſuch a Credulity are innumerable, and too notorious not to be obſerved every where. Many ſociable, well-diſpoſed Families, have been blown up into a perpetual Diſcord and Averſion to each other, by one of theſe wicked Go-betweens. So that, whoever would thoroughly acquit himſelf of the Imputation of being a bad Neighbour, ſhould guard himſelf both againſt receiving ill Impreſſions by Hearſay, and uttering his Opinion of others to thoſe inquiſitive Buſy-bodies, who, in caſe of Scandal, can magnify a Gnat to the Size of a Camel, and ſwell a Molehill up to a Mountain.

FAB.

FAB. LXXXI. *The* Goat *and the* Lion.

THE Lion feeing a Goat upon a fteep craggy Rock, where he could not come at him, afked him, what Delight he could take to fkip from one Precipice to another, all Day, and venture the breaking of his Neck every Moment: I wonder, fays he, you will not come down, and feed on the Plain here, when there is fuch Plenty of good Grafs, and fine fweet Herbs. Why, replies the Goat, I cannot but fay your Opinion is right; but you look fo very hungry and defigning, that to tell you the Truth, I do not care to venture my Perfon where you are.

The APPLICATION.

Advice, though good in itfelf, is to be fufpected, when it is given by a tricking felf-interefted Man. Perhaps we fhould take upon ourfelves, not only a very great, but an unneceffary Trouble, if we were to fufpect every Man who goes to advife us: But this, however, is neceffary, that when we have Reafon to queftion any one, in Point of Honour and Juftice, we not only confider well before we suffer ourselves to be persuaded by him, but even resolve to have nothing to do in any Affair, where such treacherous, slippery Sparks are concerned, if we can avoid it without much Inconvenience.

FAB. LXXXII. *The* Lion *and the* Frog.

THE Lion, hearing an odd Kind of a hollow Voice, and seeing nobody, started up: He listened again, and perceiving the Voice to continue, even trembled and quaked for Fear. At last, seeing a Frog crawl out of the Lake, and finding that the Noise he had heard, was nothing but the Croaking of that little Creature, he went up to it, and partly out of Anger, partly Contempt, spurned it to Pieces with his Feet.

The APPLICATION.

This Fable is a pretty Image of the vain Fears and empty Terrors, with which our weak misguided Nature is so apt to be alarmed and distracted. If we hear but ever so little Noise, which we are not able to account for immediately, nay, often before we give ourselves Time to consider about it, we are struck with Fear, and la-

bour

bour under a moft unmanly unreafonable Trepidation.
More efpecially if the Alarm happens when we are
alone, and in the Dark.   Thefe Notions are ingrafted
in our Minds very early; we fuck them in with our
Nurfe's Milk; and therefore it is the more difficult,
when we are grown up, and afhamed of them, to root
them out of our Nature.   But, in order to it, it is well
worth our while to obferve, that the moft learned, the
moft ingenious, and candid Writers in all Ages, have
ridiculed and exploded the Belief of fuch Phantoms, as
the weaker Part of Mankind are apt to be terrified with;
intimating, that Goblins, Spectres, Apparitions, Fai-
ries, Ghofts, &c. were invented by Knaves to frighten
the Fools with.   Fear is a natural Paffion; and its Ufe
is, to put us upon our Guard againft Danger, by alarm-
ing the Spirits.   Now all Paffions fhould be kept in a
State of Subjection; for tho' they are good ufeful Servants, yet, if once they get the better, they prove the
moft domineering Tyrants imaginable; nor do any of
them treat us in fo flavifh and abject a Manner, as that
of Fear.   It unnerves and enfeebles our Limbs, preci-
pitates or fetters our Underftanding; and, at the fame
Time that it reprefents a Danger near at Hand, difarms,
and makes us incapable of defending ourfelves againft
it.   This is the Cafe, even in refpect of real Dangers,
as Fire, Thieves, or violent Enemies: And, even in this
Cafe, a Man of either Senfe or Honour would be afhamed
to be detected in fuch a Weaknefs.   But when the
Caufe of our Alarm is groundlefs, and fubfifts no where
but in our own childifh Imagination, we fhould not
only take Care how we expofe ourfelves upon that Account, but refolve to man our Underftanding with Reafon and Fortitude enough to maintain it againft the Attacks of every little imaginary Phantom.   Even thofe
who have thoroughly reafoned the Point, may yet re-
tain fomething of the old Woman in their Minds,
which having taken Root too deep to be entirely plucked
out, may fometimes furprize them in an unguarded Moment, and make them ftart like the Lion in the Fable:
But then they prefently recollect themfelves, and, as he
did, treat the Caufe of their Delufion with the utmoft
Contempt.   6   F A B.

FAB. LXXXIII.
The Fir-Tree *and the* Bramble.

A Tall ſtraight Fir-Tree, that ſtood towering up in the Midſt of the Foreſt, was ſo proud of his Dignity and high Station, that he overlooked the little Shrubs which grew beneath him. A Bramble, being one of the inferior Throng, could by no Means brook this haughty Carriage, and therefore took him to taſk, and deſired to know what he meant by it. Becauſe, ſays the Fir-Tree, I look upon myſelf as the firſt Tree, for Beauty and Rank, of any in the Foreſt: My ſpring Top ſhoots up into the Clouds, and my Branches diſplay themſelves with a perpetual Beauty and Verdure; while you lie groveling upon the Ground, liable to be cruſhed by every Foot that comes near you, and impoveriſhed by the luxurious Drippings which fall from my Leaves. All this may be true, replied the Bramble. But when the Woodman has marked you out for public Uſe, and the ſounding Axe comes to be applied to your Root, I am miſtaken if you would not be glad to change Conditions with the very worſt of us.

The

The APPLICATION.

If the Great were to reckon upon the Mifchiefs to which they are expofed, and poor private Men confider the Dangers which they many Times efcape, purely by being fo, notwithftanding the feeming Difference there appears to be between them, it would be no fuch eafy Matter, as moft People think it, to determine which Condition is the more preferable.   A reafonable Man would declare in Favour of the latter, without the leaft Hefitation, as knowing upon what a fteady and fafe Security it is eftablifhed.   For the higher a Man is exalted, the fairer Mark he gives, and the more un-likely he is to efcape a Storm.   What little Founda-tion therefore has the greateft Favourite of Fortune, to behave himfelf with Infolence to thofe below him; whofe Circumftances, though he is fo elated with Pride, as to defpife them, are, in the Eye of every prudent Man, more eligible than his own, and fuch as he him-felf, when the Day of Account comes, will wifh he had never exceeded.   For, as the Riches which many over-grown Great Ones call the Goods of Fortune, are fel-dom any other than the Goods of the Public, which they have impudently and felonioufly taken, fo public Juftice generally overtakes them in the End; and, whatever their Life may have been, their Death is as ignominious and unpitied, as that of the meaneft and moft obfcure Thief.

H   F A B,

FAB. LXXXIV. *The* Bull *and the* Goat.

THE Bull, being purfued by the Lion, made towards the Cave, in which he defigned to fecure
himfelf; but was oppofed juft at the Entrance by
a Goat, who had got Poffeffion before him, and
threatening a Kind of Defiance with his Horns,
feemed refolved to difpute the Pafs with him. The
Bull, who thought he had no Time to lofe in a
Conteft of this Nature, immediately made off again;
but told the Goat, that it was not for Fear of him
or his Defiances: For, fays he, if the Lion were
not fo near, I would foon make you know the Difference between a Bull and a Goat.

The APPLICATION.

It is very inhumane to deny Succour and Comfort to
People in Tribulation; but to infult them, and add to
the Weight of their Misfortunes, is fomething fuperla-
tively brutifh and cruel. There is, however, in the
World

World a Sort of Wretches of this vile Temper, that wait for an Opportunity of aggravating their Neighbour's Affliction, and defer the Execution of their evil Inclinations until they can do it to the beſt Advantage. If any one labours under an expenſive Law-ſuit, leſt he ſhould eſcape from that, one of theſe Gentlemen will take Care to arreſt him in a ſecond Action; hoping, at leaſt, to keep him at Bay, while the more powerful Adverſary attacks him on the other Side. One cannot conſider this Temper, without obſerving ſomething remarkably cowardly in it: For theſe whiffling Antagoniſts never begin their Encounter, till they are ſure the Perſon they aim at is already over-matched.

F A B. LXXXV.
The Fowler *and the* Blackbird.

A Fowler was placing his Nets, and putting his Tackle in Order by the Side of a Copſe, when a Blackbird, who ſaw him, had the Curioſity to enquire what he was doing. Says he, I am building

a City

a City for you Birds to live in; and providing it
with Meat, and all Manner of Conveniencies for
you. Having faid this, he departed and hid himfelf; and the Blackbird, believing the Words, came
into the Nets, and was taken. But when the Man
came up to take Hold of him, If this, fays he, be
your Faith and Honefty, and thefe the Cities you
build, I am of Opinion, you will have but few Inhabitants.

The APPLICATION.

Methinks this Fowler acted a Part very like that
which fome Rulers of the People do; when they tell
them, that the Projects, which they have contrived with
a feparate View, and for their own private Interefts,
are laid for the Benefit of all that come into them. And
to fuch the Blackbird truly fpeaks, when he affirms,
that Erectors of fuch Schemes will find but few to ftick
by them at the long Run. We exclaim againft it, as
fomething very bafe and difhoneft, when thofe of a different Nation, and even our Enemies, break the Faith
which they have publicly plighted, and tricked us out
of our Properties. But what muft we call it, when Governors themfelves circumvent their own People, and
contrary to the Terms upon which they are admitted to
govern, contrive Traps and Gins to catch and infnare
them in: Such Governors may fucceed in their Plot
the firft Time, but muft not be furprifed, if thofe who
have once efcaped their Clutches, never have Opinion
enough of them to truft them for the future.

FAB.

FAB. LXXXVI. Jupiter *and* Pallas.

ONCE upon a Time the Heathen Gods had a
Mind to adopt, each a particular Tree, into their
Patronage and Tuition. *Jupiter* chofe the Oak;
Venus was pleafed to name the Myrtle; *Apollo* pitched
upon the Laurel; *Cybele* took the Pipe, and *Hercules*
the Poplar. *Pallas* being prefent, expreffed her Admiration at their Fancy, in making choice of Trees
that bore nothing. O, fays *Jupiter*, the Reafon of
that is plain enough, for we would not be thought
to difpenfe our Favours with any mercenary View.
You may do as you pleafe, fays fhe, but let the
Olive be my Tree; and I declare my Reafon for
choofing it is, becaufe it bears Plenty of noble ufeful
Fruit. Upon which, the Thunderer, putting on a
ferious compofed Gravity, fpoke thus to the Goddefs: Indeed, Daughter, it is not without Juftice
that you are fo celebrated for your Wifdom; for unlefs
fome Benefit attends your Actions, to perform them
only for the Sake of Glory, is but a filly Bufinefs.

The

The APPLICATION.

This Fable is to put us in Mind, that we fhould intend fomething ufeful and beneficial in all our Actions. To undertake Things with no other View, but that of empty Glory, whatever fome curious Dreamers may fancy, is employing our Time after a very idle, foolifh Manner. The Almighty created the World out of his infinite Goodnefs, for the Good of his Creatures, and not out of a Paffion for Glory; which is a vain, filly, mean Principle. And when we talk of glorifying the Author of our Being, if we think reafonably, we muft mean fhewing our Gratitude to him, by imitating this Goodnefs of his, as far as we are able, and endeavouring to make fome Good or other the Aim of all our Undertakings. For if empty Glory be unworthy the Purfuit of a wife Man, how vaftly improper muft it be to make an Offering of it to an All-wife Deity.

FAB.

FAB. LXXXVII. *The* Fox *and the* Bramble.

A FOX, hard preſſed by the Hounds, was getting over a Hedge, but tore his Foot upon a Bramble which grew juſt in the Midſt of it; upon which he reproached the Bramble for his inhoſpitable Cruelty, in uſing a Stranger, who had fled to him for Protection, after ſuch a barbarous Manner. Yes, ſays the Bramble, you intended to have made me ſerve your Turn, I know; but take this Piece of Advice with you for the future, Never lay hold of a Bramble again, as you tender your ſweet Perſon; for laying hold, is a Privilege that belongs to us Brambles, and we do not Care to let it go out of the Family.

The APPLICATION.

Impertinent People, who are moſt apt to take Liberties with others, are generally the moſt ſurprized, if they are retorted upon with any Severity; tho' they, of all People, have the leaſt Reaſon to expect Quarter. It cannot but be pleaſant to indifferent Spectators, when they ſee one of this Fraternity meet with his Match, and beaten at his own Weapons. He that is known to be an ill Man, may be hurt unpitied; his Misfortunes are

conferred

conferred upon him to the Satisfaction of him that occafions them; and we do not look upon him as an Object of Pity, but an Example of Juftice. This Fable has an Eye to a Moral which has been already drawn from fome others; and advifes us to be cautious whom we lay hold on, or meddle with, in too familiar a Way: For, thofe who can lay hold again, and perhaps are better qualified for it than ourfeives, are carefully to be avoided.

FAB. LXXXVIII. *The* Cat *and the* Mice.

A Certain Houfe was much infefted with Mice; but at laft they got a Cat, who catched and eat every Day fome of them. The Mice, finding their Numbers grow thin, confulted what was beft to be done for the Prefervation of the Public, from the Jaws of the devouring Cat. They debated, and came to this Refolution, That no one fhould go down below the upper Shelf. The Cat, obferving the Mice no longer came down, as ufual, hungry, and difappointed of her Prey, had Recourfe to this Stratagem; fhe hung by her hinder Legs on a Peg which ftuck in the Wall, and made as if fhe had been dead, hoping by this Lure to intice the

Mice

Mice to come down. She had not been in this
Posture long, before a cunning old Mouse peeped
over the Edge of the Shelf, and spoke thus: Aha,
my good Friend, are you there? there may you
be! I would not trust myself with you, though your
Skin were stuffed with Straw.

The APPLICATION.

Prudent Folks never trust those a second Time, who
have deceived them once. And, indeed, we cannot
well be too cautious in following this Rule; for, upon
Examination, we shall find, That most of the Misfortunes which befal us, proceed from our too great Credulity. They that know how to suspect, without ex-
posing or hurting themselves, till Honesty comes to be
more in Fashion, can never suspect too much.

FAB. LXXXIX.
The Fox and the Countryman.

A FOX being hard hunted, and having run a
long Chase, was quite tired; at last he spied a
Country Fellow in a Wood, to whom he applied

for

for Refuge, intreating that he would give him
Leave to hide himself in his Cottage, till the Hounds
were gone by. The Man confented, and the Fox
went and covered himself up clofe in a Corner of
the Hovel. Prefently the Hunters came up, and
inquired of the Man, if he had feen the Fox. No,
fays he, I have not feen him indeed : But all the
while he pointed with his Finger to the Place where
the Fox was hid. However, the Hunters did not
underftand him, but called off their Hounds, and
went another Way. Soon after, the Fox, creeping
out of his Hole, was going to fneak off; when the
Man, calling after him, afked him, if that was his
Manners, to go away without thanking his Benefactor, to whofe Fidelity he owed his Life. *Rey-*
nard, who had peeped all the while, and feen what
paffed, anfwered, I know what Obligations I have
to you well enough; and I affure you, if your
Actions had but been agreeable to your Words, I
fhould have endeavoured, however incapable of it,
to have returned you fuitable Thanks.

The APPLICATION.

Sincerity is a moft beautiful Virtue ; but there are
fome, whofe Natures are fo poor fpirited and cowardly,
that they are not capable of exerting it. Indeed, unlefs a Man be fteady and conftant in all his Actions, he
will hardly deferve the Name of fincere. An open
Enemy, though more violent and terrible, is not, however, fo odious and deteftable as a falfe Friend. To pretend to keep another's Counfel, and appear in their Intereft, while underhand we are giving Intelligence to
their Enemies, is treacherous, knavifh and bafe. There
are fome People in the World very dextrous at this Kind
of Defamation ; and can, while they feem moft vehement
in the Commendation or Defence of a Friend, throw
out a Hint which fhall ftab their Reputation deeper
than the moft malicious Weapon, brandifhed at them
in a public Manner, could have been capable of doing.

FAB.

FAB. XC. *A* Man *bit by a* Dog.

A MAN, who had been sadly torn by a Dog, was advised by some old Woman, as a Cure, to dip a Piece of Bread in the Wound, and give it the Cur that bit him. He did so; and *Æsop* happening to pass by just at the same Time, asked him, what he meant by it; the Man informed him: Why then, says *Æsop*, do it as privately as you can, I beseech you; for if the rest of the Dogs of the Town were to see you, we should all be eat up alive by them.

The APPLICATION.

Nothing contributes so much to the Increase of Roguery, as when the Undertakings of a Rogue are attended with Success. If it were not for Fear of Punishment, a great Part of Mankind, who now make a Shift to keep themselves honest, would appear great Villains: But if Criminals, instead of meeting with Punishments, were, by having been such, to attain Honour and Preferment, our natural Inclinations to Mischief would be improved, and we should be wicked out of Emulation.

FAB. XCI. Fortune *and the* Boy.

A Boy was sleeping by the Side of a Well. Fortune saw him, and came and waked him:
Saying, Prythee, good Child, do not lie sleeping
here; for if you should fall in, nobody would impute it to you, but lay all the Blame upon me
Fortune.

The APPLICATION.

Poor Fortune has a great deal thrown upon her indeed; and oftentimes very unjustly too. Those of our
Actions which are attended with Success, though often
owing to some Accident or other, we ascribe, without
any Scruple, to some particular Merit or good Quality
in ourselves; but when any of our Doings miscarry,
though probably through our own Insufficiency or Neglect, all the ill Consequence is imputed to Fortune,
and we acquit ourselves of having contributed any
Thing towards it. The silliest Part of each Sex, when
they dispose of themselves indiscreetly, or disadvan-
tageously

tageoufly in Marriage, and have nothing elfe to fay in
Excufe, cry out, O there is a Fate in every Thing, and
there is no refifting Fate, &c.   But thefe People fhould
take Notice, that, as they have a very good Proverb
on their Side, in Relation to Fortune already, it is
highly unreafonable in them to claim more than their
Share, and to afcribe the ill Succefs of their own foolifh
Negociations, to the Management of Fortune.   Probably, the firft Occafion of confining the Smiles of Fortune to People of this Stamp more particularly, might
arife from the Improbability of their fucceeding by any
Art or right Application of their own.   And, therefore,
by an oppofite Rule, the Wife and Induftrious only
fhould be intitled to ill Luck, and have it in their Power
to charge Fortune with every Lofs and Crofs which befals them : For if, when they have concerted their
Meafures judicioufly, and been vigilant and active in
their Bufinefs, Matters refufe ftill to anfwer Expectation, they muft be allowed to have very hard Fortune :
But Fools have not the leaft Right to take hold of this
Handle,

FAB. XCII. *The* Mule.

A Mule, which was well fed, and worked little, grew fat and wanton, and frisked about very notably. And why should not I run as well as the best of them? says he: It is well known, I had a Horse to my Father, and a very good Racer he was. Soon after this, his Master took him out, and being upon urgent Business, whipped and spurred the Mule, to make him put forward; who beginning to tire upon the Road, changed his Note, and said to himself, Ah! where is the Horse's Blood you boasted of but now? I am sorry to say it, Friend, but indeed your worthy Sire was an Ass, and not a Horse.

The APPLICATION.

However high their Blood may beat, one may venture to affirm those to be but Mongrels, and Asses in Reality, who make a Bustle about their Genealogy. If some in the World should be vain enough to think they can
derive

derive their Pedigree from one of the old *Roman* Families, and being otherwife deftitute of Merit, would fain
draw fome from thence; it might not be improper upon
fuch an Occafion to put them in Mind, that *Romulus,*
the firft Founder of that People, was bafe-born, and the
Body of his Subjects made up of Outlaws, Murderers,
and Felons, the Scum and Off-fcouring of the neighbouring Nations, and that they propagated their De-
fcendants by Rapes. As a Man truly great, fhines fufficiently bright of himfelf, without wanting to be em-
blazoned by a fplendid Anceftry; fo they, whofe Lives
are eclipfed by Foulnefs or Obfcurity, inftead of fhewing
to an Advantage, look but the darker for being placed
in the fame Line with their illuftrious Forefathers.

FAB. XCIII. *The* Fox *and the* Ape.

ONCE upon a Time, the Beafts were fo void of
Reafon as to chufe an Ape for their King. He
had danced, and diverted them with playing antic
Tricks, and truly nothing would ferve, but they
muft anoint him their Sovereign. Accordingly
crowned he was, and affected to look very wife and
politic.

politic. But the Fox, vexed at his Heart to fee his Fellow-Brutes act fo foolifhly, was refolved the firft Opportunity, to convince them of their forry Choice, and punifh their Jackanapes of a King for his Prefumption. Soon after, fpying a Trap in a Ditch, which was baited with a Piece of Flefh, he went and informed the Ape of it, as a Treafure, which, being found upon the Wafte, belonged to his Majefty only. The Ape, dreaming nothing of the Matter, went very brifkly to take Poffeffion; but had no fooner laid his Paws upon the Bait, than he was caught in the Trap; where, betwixt Shame and Anger, he began to reproach the Fox, calling him Rebel and Traitor, and threatening to be revenged of him: At all which *Reynard* laughed heartily; and going off, added, with a Sneer, You a King, and not underftand Trap!

The APPLICATION.

A weak Man fhould not afpire to be a King; for if he were, in the End, it would prove as inconvenient to himfelf, as difadvantageous to the Public. To be qualified for fuch an Office, an Office of the laft Importance to Mankind, the Perfon fhould be of a diftinguifhed Prudence, and moft unblemifhed Integrity; too honeft to impofe upon others, and too penetrating to be impofed upon; thoroughly acquainted with the Laws and Genius of the Realm he is to govern; brave, but not paffionate; good-natured, but not foft; afpiring at juft Efteem; defpifing vain Glory; without Superftition; without Hypocrify. When Thrones have been filled by People of a different Turn from this, Hiftories fhew what a wretched Figure they always made; what Tools they were to particular Perfons, and what Plagues to their Subjects in general. They who ftudied their Paffions and entered into their Foibles, led them by the Nofe as they pleafed; and took them off from the Guardianfhip of the Public, by fome paltry Amufement, that themfelves might have the better Opportunity to rifle and plunder it.

2 F A B.

FAB. XCIV. *The* Mole *and her* Dam.

THE young Mole fnuffed up her Nofe, and told her Dam, fhe fmelt an odd Kind of a Smell. By and by, O ftrange! fays fhe, what a Noife there is in my Ears, as if ten Thoufand Paper-Mills were going. A little after fhe was at it again. Look, look, what is that I fee yonder? it is juft like the Flame of a fiery Furnace. To whom the Dam replied, Prythee, Child, hold your idle Tongue; and if you would have us allow you any Senfe at all, do not affect to fhew more than Nature has given you.

The APPLICATION.

It is wonderful that Affectation, that odious Quality, fhould have been always fo common and epidemical; fince it is not more difagreeable to others, than hurtful to the Perfon that wears it. By Affectation, we aim at being thought to poffefs fome Accomplifhment which we have not, or at fhewing what we have, in a conceited oftentatious Manner. Now this we may be affured of, that among difcerning People at leaft, when we endeavour

vour at any Thing of this Kind, inftead of fucceeding
in the Attempt, we detract from fome real Poffeffion,
and make Qualities that would otherwife pafs well
enough, appear naufeous and fulfome: Is it not ridiculous to fee an old battered Beau put himfelf to Pain,
that he may appear to tread firm, and walk ftrong and
upright? A Man, defective in his Eyes, run againft a
Poft, rather than confefs he wants a Guide? And one
that is deaf, miftaking every Thing you fay, rather than
you fhould fufpect he cannot hear? Yet perhaps thefe
Things are done every Day; and imitated, in fome other
Affectation, by the very People that laugh at them.

FAB. XCV. *The* Fox *and the* Boar.

THE Boar ftood whetting his Tufks againft an
old Tree. The Fox, who happened to come
by at the fame Time, afked him why he made thofe
martial Preparations of whetting his Teeth, fince
there was no Enemy near, that he could perceive?
That may be, Mafter *Reynard*, fays the Boar; but
we fhould fcour up our Arms while we have Leifure, you know; for, in Time of Danger, we fhall
have fomething elfe to do.   *The*

The APPLICATION.

He that is not idle when he is at Leifure, may play with his Bufinefs. A difcreet Man fhould have a Referve of every Thing that is neceffary before-hand; that when the Time comes for him to make Ufe of them, he may not be in a Hurry and a Confufion. A wife General has not his Men to difcipline, or his Ammunition to provide, when the Trumpet founds *To Arms*; but fets apart his Times of Exercife for one, and his Magazines for the other, in the calm Seafon of Peace. We hope to live to a good old Age: Should we not then lay up a Store of Conveniencies againft that Time, when we fhall be moft in want of them, and leaft able to procure them? We muft die; nay, never ftart; we muft. Are there not fome neceffary Things for us to tranfact before we depart; at leaft, fome Trifle or other for us to bequeath, which a fudden Stroke may prevent us from doing? Sure there is. And if fo, how inexcufable fhall we be, if we defer the Execution of it, till the Alarm come upon us. *I did not think of it,* is an Expreffion unworthy a wife Man's Mouth; and was only intended for the Ufe of Fools.

FAB.

FAB. XCVI.
The Old Woman *and the* Empty Cask.

AN Old Woman faw an empty Cafk lying, from which there had been lately drawn a Piece of choice racy Palm Sack; the Spirit of which yet hung about the Veffel, and the very Lee yielded a grateful cordial Scent. She applied her Nofe to the Bung-hole, and, fnuffing very heartily for fome Time, at laft, broke out into this Exclamation: O! the delicious Smell; how good, how charming good muft you have been once? when your very Dregs are fo agreeable and refrefhing.

The APPLICATION.

Phædrus was an old Man when he wrote his Fables, and this he applies to himfelf; intimating, what we ought to judge of his Youth, when his Old Age was capable of fuch Productions. But fure this is a Piece of Vanity that diminifhes fomething of the good Savour of

an

an agreeable old Man; and it had been handfomer to have left us to make the Application for him. It is, at once, a pleafing and melancholy Idea, which is given us by the View of an old Man, or Woman, whofe Converfation is relifhing and agreeable. We cannot forbear reprefenting to ourfelves, how inexpreffibly charming thofe muft have been in the Flower of Youth, whofe Decay is capable of yielding us fo much Pleafure. Nor, at the fame Time can we help repining, that this Fountain of Delight is now almoft dried up, and going to forfake us; and that the Seafon in which it flowed in the greateft Abundance, was fo long before we were acquainted with the World. It is no difficult Matter to form a juft Notion of what the Prime of any one's Life was, from the Spirit and Flavour which remain even in the laft Dregs. Old Age, merely as fuch, can never render a Perfon either contemptible or difagreeable in the Eye of a reafonable Man: But fuch as we find People at that Time of Life, much the fame they certainly were, in thofe which they call their better Days. As they that can make themfelves agreeable, notwithftanding the Difadvantage of Old Age, muft have been highly entertaining in the Vigour of Youth; fo, whenever we meet with one in Years, whofe Humour is unpleafant, and Manners burdenfome, we may take it for granted, that, even in the Prime of Youth, fuch an one was troublefome, impertinent, and unfociable.

F A B.

FAB. XCVII. *The* Fowler *and the* Lark.

A Fowler fet Snares to catch Larks in the open Field. A Lark was caught; and finding herfelf intangled, could not forbear lamenting her hard Fate. Ah! woe is me, fays fhe, what Crime have I committed? I have taken neither Silver nor Gold, nor any Thing of Value; but muft die for only eating a poor Grain of Wheat.

The APPLICATION.

The irregular Adminiftration of Juftice in the World, is indeed a very melancholy Subject to think of. A poor Fellow fhall be hanged for ftealing a Sheep, perhaps to keep his Family from ftarving; while one, who is already great and opulent, fhall, for that very Reafon, think himfelf privileged to commit almoft any Enormities. But it is neceffary that a Shew and Form of Juftice fhould be kept up; otherwife, were People to be ever fo great, and fo fuccefsful Rogues, they would not be able to keep Poffeffion of, and enjoy their Plunder. One of our Poets, in his Defcription of a Court of Juftice, calls it a Place,

Where

Where little Villains muſt ſubmit to Fate,
That great ones may enjoy the World in State.

What a ſad Thing is it to reflect (and the more ſad,
becauſe not to be remedied) that a Man may rob the
Public of Millions, and eſcape at laſt; when he that is
taken picking a Pocket of five Shillings, unleſs he
knows how to make a Friend, is ſure to ſwing for it.

F A B. XCVIII.
The Owl *and the* Graſhopper.

AN Owl ſat ſleeping in a Tree.   But a Graſhop-
per who was ſinging beneath, would not let her
be quiet, abuſing her with very indecent and uncivil Language; telling her ſhe was a ſcandalous
Perſon, who plied a-nights to get her Living, and
ſhut herſelf up all Day in a hollow Tree.   The
Owl deſired her to hold her Tongue and be quiet:
Notwithſtanding which, ſhe was the more impertinent.   She begged of her a ſecond Time to leave
off; but all to no Purpoſe.   The Owl, vexed at
the Heart to find that all ſhe ſaid went for nothing,
caſt about to inveigle her by Stratagem.   Well, ſays
ſhe, ſince one muſt be kept awake, it is a Pleaſure,
however,

however, to be kept awake by fo agreeable a Voice;
which, I muft confefs, is no ways inferior to the
fineft Harp. And, now I think of it, I have a Bot-
tle of excellent Nectar, which my Miftrefs *Pallas*
gave me; if you have a Mind, I will give you a
Dram to whet your Whiftle. The Grafhopper,
ready to die with Thirft, and, at the fame Time,
pleafed to be fo complimented upon Account of her
Voice, fkipped up to the Place very brifkly; when
the Owl, advancing to meet her, feized, and, without much Delay, made her a Sacrifice to her Revenge; fecuring to herfelf, by the Death of her
Enemy, a Poffeffion of that Quiet, which, during
her Life-time, fhe could not enjoy.

The APPLICATION.

Humanity, or what we underftand by common Civility, is not more a neceffary Duty, than it is eafy to practife. The Man that is guilty of Ill-Manners, if he has
been bred to know what is meant by Manners, muft do
Violence to himfelf, as well as to the Perfon he offends;
and cannot be inhuman to others, without being cruel
to his own Nature. It has been obferved, in the Application to the Forty-feventh Fable, that People of
captious Tempers being generally in the wrong, in taking Things ill, which were never fo intended, are likely
to be but the more perfecuted, in order to be laughed
out of their Folly; and that, not unjuftly. But we
muft take Care to diftinguifh; and, when any Thing
truly impertinent and troublefome has been faid or done
to another, not to repeat it becaufe he takes it ill, but
immediately to defift from it; efpecially when he is fo
moderate, as to make it his Requeft two or three Times,
before he proceeds openly to take his Courfe, and do
himfelf Juftice. This Point fhould be well confidered;
for many Quarrels of very ill Confequence, have been
occafioned by a rafh unthinking Perfiftence in the impertinent Humour before-mentioned. Some young
People are fond of fhewing their Wit and Intrepidity,
and

and therefore take such Occasions to do it: And when a Friend is peevish, as one may have a private Cause for being so) they will not leave, till they have rallied him out of it; no, though he intreats them ever so gravely and earnestly. Whereas, in Truth, we have no Right to be impertinent with one another to Extremity; and tho' there is no Law to punish such Incivilities as I have been speaking of, they will scarce fail of meeting with a deserved and just Chastisement, some Way or other.

FAB. XCIX. *The* One-eyed Doe.

A Doe, that had but one Eye, used to graze near the Sea; and that she might be the more secure from Harm, she kept her blind Side towards the Water, from whence she had no Apprehension of Danger, and with the other surveyed the Country as she fed. By this Vigilance and Precaution she thought herself in the utmost Security; when a sly Fellow, with two or three of his Companions, who had been poaching after her several Days to no Purpose, at last took a Boat, and fetching a Compass upon the Sea, came gently down upon her, and shot her. The Doe, in the Agonies of Death, breathed out this

I   doleful

doleful Complaint: O hard Fate! that I fhould receive my Death's Wound from that Side whence I
expected no Ill; and be fafe in that Part where I
looked for the moft Danger.

The APPLICATION.

Life is fo full of Accidents and Uncertainties, that,
with all the Precaution we ufe, we can never be faid to
be entirely free from Danger. And tho' there is but one
Way for us to come into the World, the Paffages to let
us out of it are innumerable. So that we may guard
ourfelves againft the moft vifible and threatening Ills, as
much as we pleafe, but fhall ftill leave an unguarded
Side to a thoufand latent Mifchiefs, which lie in Ambufh
round about us. The Moral, therefore, which fuch a
Reflection fuggefts to us, is, to be neither too fecure,
nor too folicitous about the Safety of our Perfons; as it
is impoffible for us to be always out of Danger, fo would
it be unreafonable and unmanly to be always in Fear of
that which it is not in our Power to prevent.

FAB. C. *The* River Fifh *and the* Sea Fifh.

THE Waters of a River being mightily fwelled
by a great Flood, the Stream ran down with a
violent Current, and by its rapid Force carried a
huge

huge Barbel along with it into the Sea. This
Freſh-water Spark was no ſooner come into a new
Climate, but he began to give himſelf Airs, to talk
big, and look with Contempt upon the Inhabitants
of the Place. He boaſted, that he was of a better
Country and Family than any among them, for
which Reaſon they ought to give Place to him, and
pay him Reſpect accordingly. A fine large Mul-
let, that happened to ſwim near him, and heard his
inſolent Language, bid him hold his ſilly Tongue;
for, if they ſhould be taken by Fiſhermen, and carried to Market, he would ſoon be convinced who
ought to have the Preference: We, ſays he, ſhould
be brought up, at any Price, for Tables of the firſt
Quality, and you ſold to the Poor for little or
nothing.

The APPLICATION.

It proceeds from a Want either of Senſe or Breeding,
or both, when Foreigners ſpeak ſlightly of the Country
they happen to be in, and cry up their own. It is, indeed, natural to have an Affection for one's own native
Place; nor can we, perhaps, in our Mind, help preferring it before any other: But it is certainly both imprudent and unmannerly, to expreſs this in another
Country, to People whoſe Opinions it muſt needs contradict, by the ſame Rule that it pleaſes our own. But,
however, granting that there is a certain Difference between Countries, ſo as to make one greatly preferable,
in the Generality of Opinions, to another, yet what has
this to do with the Merit of particular Perſons? Or why
ſhould any one value himſelf upon an Advantage over
others, which is purely owing to Accident? It muſt be
from ſome uſeful or agreeable Talent in ourſelves, that
we are to merit the Eſteem of Mankind; and if we ſhine
in a ſuperior Degree of Virtue or Wiſdom, whatever
our native Air happened to be, virtuous and wiſe Men,
of every Nation under Heaven, will pay us the Regard
and the Acknowledgements we deſerve.

FAB.

F A B. CI.   Æfop at Play.

AN *Athenian* one Day, found *Æfop* at Play with
a Company of little Boys, at their childifh Diverfions, and began to jeer and laugh at him for it.
The old Fellow, who was too much a Wag himfelf,
to fuffer others to ridicule him, took a Bow, un-
ftrung, and laid it upon the Ground. Then calling
the cenforious *Athenian*, Now, Philofopher, fays he,
expound the Riddle if you can, and tell us what the
unftrained Bow implies.   The Man, after racking
his Brains, and fcratching his Pate about it a confiderable Time, to no Purpofe, at laft gave it up, and
declared he knew not what to make of it. Why,
fays *Æfop*, laughing, if you keep a Bow always bent,
it will break prefently ; but, if you let it go flack,
it will be the fitter for Ufe when you want it.

The A P P L I C A T I O N.

The Mind of Man is like a Bow in this Refpect ; for
if it be kept always intent upon Bufinefs, it will either
break, and be good for nothing, or lofe that Spring and
Energy, which is required in one who would acquit himfelf with Credit.   But Sports and Diverfions footh and
flacken

flacken it, and keep it in a Condition to be exerted to
the beſt Advantage, upon Occaſion. It proceeds either
from Pride, Ill-nature, or Hypocriſy, when People cen-
ſure and are offended at the Liberties which others uſe
in thus relaxing their Minds. Sloth and Idleneſs, by
which we neglect the Proſecution of our neceſſary Affairs, muſt be condemned by all Means; but thoſe who
know how to diſpatch the proper Buſineſs of Life well
and ſeaſonably enough, need be under no Apprehenſions of being ſurpriſed at their Diverſions, if they have
nothing diſhoneſt in them. As theſe Amuſements ought
to be allowed, becauſe they are proper, ſo it is no great
Matter how they are followed; we may, if we like it,
as well play with Children, as Men; and rather, if we
find they can divert us better, which is not very ſeldom
the Caſe: Some Men and Women are uſeleſs and untractable in every Circumſtance of Life; and ſome Children ſo engaging and entertaining, with an agreeable
undeſigned Mixture of Innocence and Cunning, that
the Company of the latter is, many Times, the more
preferable and diverting.

FAB. CII. *The* Jack-Daw *and the* Pigeons.

A Jack-Daw, obſerving that the Pigeons in a certain Dove-Cote lived well, and wanted for no-

thing, white-wafhed his Feathers, and endeavouring to look as much like a Dove as he could, went and lived among them. The Pigeons, not diftinguifhing him as long as he kept filent, forbore to give him any Difturbance. But at laft he forgot his Character, and began to chatter; by which the Pigeons difcovering what he was, flew upon him, and beat him away from the Meat, fo that he was obliged to fly back to the Jack-Daws again. They, not knowing him in his difcoloured Feathers, drove him away likewife: So that he who had endeavoured to be more than he had a Right to, was not permitted to be any Thing at all.

The APPLICATION.

The pretending to be of Principles which we are not, either out of Fear, or any Profpect of Advantage, is a very bafe, vile Thing; and whoever is guilty of it, deferves to meet with ill Treatment from all Sorts and Conditions of Men. But the beft of it is, there is no Fear of fuch Counterfeits impofing upon the World long, in a Difguife fo contrary to their own Nature: Let them but open their Mouths, and, like the Daw in the Fable, they immediately proclaim their Kind. If they fhould deceive for a while, by appearing in an unqueftionable Place, or hanging out falfe Colours, yet, if touched upon the right String, they would be difcovered in an Inftant: For, when People are acting a wrong Part, their very Voice betrays them; they either cannot act their Part fufficiently, or they over act it: And, which ever is the Cafe, a Man of Difcretion and Honour will be fure to diftinguifh, and to difcountenance fuch pitiful Impoftors.

FAB. CIII. *The* Sow *and the* Bitch.

A Sow and a Bitch happening to meet, a Debate arose betwixt them, concerning their Fruitfulness.   The Bitch infifted upon it, that fhe brought more at a Litter, and oftener, than any other four-legg'd Creature. Ay, fays the Sow, you do indeed, but you are always in fo much Hafte about it, that you bring your Puppies into the World blind.

The APPLICATION.

The more Hafte, the worfe Speed, is a moft excellent Proverb, and worthy to be worn upon fome confpicuous Part of our Drefs or Equipage, that it may give us a proper Check, when we go about any Thing of Importance; which otherwife we might be apt to purfue with too much Hurry and Precipitation.   It is no Wonder our Productions fhould come into the World blind, or lame, or otherwife defective, when by unnatural Methods we accelerate their Birth, and refufe to let them go their full Time. And if a hafty Publication be fuch a Crime,

I 4   what

what muſt it be to brag, and make Profeſſion of it in Prefaces and Dedications, as the Practice of ſome is? Sure ſuch Writers fancy the World will admire their Parts, when they endeavour thus to convince them how much they have wrote, and how little Time and Pains they have beſtowed upon it. But, however, the Advertiſements and Hints they give us of this Kind, may be ſo far uſeful, as to induce us to take them at their Words, and ſpare ourſelves the Trouble of peruſing a Treatiſe, which they aſſure us beforehand is incorrect and faulty, through the Idleneſs, Impatience, or wilful Neglect of the Author.

FAB. CIV. *The* Sparrow *and the* Hare.

A Hare being ſeized by an Eagle, ſqueaked out in a moſt woful Manner. A Sparrow, that ſat upon a Tree juſt by, and ſaw it, could not forbear being unſeaſonably witty, but called out, and ſaid to the Hare: So ho! what, ſit there and be killed! Prythee, up and away; I dare ſay, if you would but try, ſo ſwift a Creature as you are would eaſily eſcape from the Eagle. As he was going on with

his

his cruel Railery, down came a Hawk, and snapped him up; and notwithstanding his vain Cries and Lamentations, fell a devouring of him in an Instant. The Hare, who was just expiring, yet received Comfort from this Accident, even in the Agonies of Death; and addressing her last Words to the Sparrow, said, You, who just now insulted my Misfortune with so much Security, as you thought, may please to shew us how well you can bear the like, now it has befallen you.

The APPLICATION.

Nothing is more impertinent than for People to be giving their Opinion and Advice, in Cases, in which, were they to be the r own, themselves would be as much at a Loss what to do. But so great an Itch have most Men to be Directors in the Affairs of others, either to shew the Superiority of their Understanding, or their own Security and Exemption from the Ills they would have removed, that they forwardly and conceitedly obtrude their Counsel, even at the Hazard of their own Safety and Reputation. There have been Instances of those, who, either officiously, or for the Jest's Sake, have spent much of their Time in reading Lectures of Œconomy to the rest of the World; when, at the same Time, their own ill Husbandry has been such, that they were forced to quit their Dwellings, and take Lodgings; while their Goods were sold to make a Composition for the Debts they owed to petty Tradesmen. Without giving more Examples of this Kind, of which every one may furnish himself with enough from his own Observation, we cannot but conclude, that none are greater Objects of Ridicule, than they who thus merrily assume a Character, which at the same Time, by some Incidents of their Life, they convince us of their being so unfit for.

FAB.

FAB. CV. Cæfar *and the* Slave.

AS *Tiberius Cæfar* was upon a Progrefs to *Naples* once, he put in at a Houfe he had upon the Mountain *Mifenus*; which was built there by *Lucullus*, and commanded a near View of the *Tufcan* Sea, having a diftant Profpect even of that of *Sicily*. Here, as he was walking in the Gardens and Wilderneffes of a moft delightful Verdure, one of his domeftic Slaves, which belonged to that Houfe, putting himfelf into a moft alert Pofture and Drefs, appeared in one of the Walks where the Emperor happened to be, fprinkling the Ground with a Watering-Pot, in order to lay the Duft; and this he did fo officioufly, that he was taken Notice of, and even laughed at; for he ran through private Allies and Turnings, from one Walk to another; fo that, wherever the Emperor went, he ftill found this Fellow mighty bufy with his Watering-Pot. But at laft, his Defign being difcovered, which was, That he fancied *Cæfar* would be fo touched with this Diligence of his, as to make him free; (Part of which Ceremony confifted in giving the Slave a gentle Stroke on one

Side

Side of his Face) his Imperial Majefty, being difpofed to be merry, called him to him; and when
the Man came up, full of joyful Expectations of
his Liberty, Hark you Friend, fays he, I have obferved that you have been very bufy a great while;
but it was impertinently bufy, in officioufly med-
dling where you had nothing to do, while you might
have employed your Time better elfewhere; and
therefore I muft be fo free as to tell you, that you
have miftaken your Man; I cannot afford a Box of
the Ear, at fo low a Price as you bid for it.

The APPLICATION.

Phædrus tells us, upon his Word, that this is a true
Story; and that he wrote it for the Sake of a Set of induftrious idle Gentlemen at *Rome*, who were harraffed
and fatigued with a daily Succeffion of Care and Trouble, becaufe they had nothing to do; always in a Hurry,
but without Bufinefs; bufy, but to no Purpofe; labouring under a voluntary Neceffity; and taking Abundance of Pains to fhew they were good for nothing. But
what great Town or City is fo entirely free from this
Sect, as to render the Moral of this Fable ufelefs any
where? for it points at all thofe officious good-natured
People, who are eternally running up and down to ferve
their Friends, without doing them any good; who by a
Complaifance wrong judged, or ill-applied, difpleafe,
while they endeavour to oblige, and are never doing lefs
to the Purpofe, than when they are moft employed.
How many are there who think themfelves intitled to
good Pofts from Government, only for having been Dab-
blers in Politics all their Lives, to the Neglect and Prejudice of their proper Callings! for never failing to enquire the News of the Day of their Acquaintance, and
expreffing a hearty Satisfaction, or a deep Concern, as
the Account given has affected them! There is another
Sort, who are fo concerned left you fhould find out that
they are mere Cyphers in Life, that they over-act their
Part, and are ever in a Hurry; who appear at Coffee-
Houfes, and other public Places, looking about eagerly
for one with whom they have no Bufinefs, and wanting

-to be afked to ftay, that they may have an Opportunity
of telling you they cannot poffibly do it. People of this
Caft always fubfcribe their Letters with a *Yours, in great
Hafte*, though they write to you only becaufe they have
nothing elfe to do. In a Word, this Fable is defigned
for the Reformation of all thofe who endeavour to raife
to themfelves Merit and Applaufe from a mifapplied
Induftry. It is not our being bufy and officious that
will procure us the Efteem of Men of Senfe; but the
intending and contriving our Actions to fome noble ufeful Purpofe, and for the general Good of Mankind.

F A B. CVI.   *The* Sheep-Biter.

A Certain Shepherd had a Dog, upon whofe Fidelity he relied very much; for whenever he
had an Occafion to be abfent himfelf, he committed the Care and Tuition of his Flock to the Charge
of this Dog; and, to encourage him to do his Duty
cheerfully, he fed him conftantly with fweet Curds
and Whey; and fometimes threw him a Cruft or
two extraordinary. Yet, notwithftanding this, no
fooner was his Back turned, but the treacherous
Cur fell foul upon the Flock, and devoured the
2   Sheep

Sheep inſtead of guarding and defending them. The Shepherd, being informed of this, was reſolved to hang him; and the Dog, when the Rope was about his Neck, and he was juſt going to be tied up, began to expoſtulate with his Maſter, aſking him, Why he was ſo unmercifully bent againſt him, who was his own Servant and Creature, and had only committed one or two Crimes; and why he did not rather execute Revenge upon the Wolf, who was a conſtant, open, and declared Enemy? Nay, replies the Shepherd, it is for that very Reaſon that I think you ten Times more worthy of Death than him; from him I expeCted nothing but Hoſtilities, and therefore could guard againſt him: You I depended upon as a juſt and faithful Servant, and fed and encouraged you accordingly; and therefore your Treachery is the more notorious, and your Ingratitude the more unpardonable.

The A P P L I C A T I O N.

No Injuries are ſo bitter and ſo inexcuſable as thoſe whi:h proceed from Men whom we truſted as Friends, and in whom we placed a Confidence. An open Enemy, however inveterate, may overpower and deſtroy us, or perhaps may hurt and affliCt us only in ſome Meaſure; but, as ſuch a Treatment cannot ſurpriſe us, becauſe we expeCted no leſs, neither can it give us half the Grief and Uneaſineſs of Mind, which we are apt to feel when we find ourſelves wronged by the Treachery and Falſhood of a Friend. When the Man whom we truſted and eſteemed, proves injurious to us, it is a Calamity ſo cruelly complicated in its Circumſtances, that it involves us in Grief of many Folds, and multiplies the Sum of our Infelicity. At one and the ſame Time, we find a Foe where we leaſt expeCted, and loſe a Friend when we moſt wanted him; which muſt be as ſevere and piercing, as it is ſudden and ſurpriſing. It is natural, therefore, for our Reſentment to be in Proportion to our Senſe of ſuch an Injury; and that we ſhould wiſh the Puniſhment of ſo extraordinary a Crime may be, at leaſt, as great as that which uſually attends an ordinary one.   F A B.

F A B. CVII. *The* Thief *and the* Dog.

A Thief, coming to rob a certain House in the Night, was disturbed in his Attempts by a fierce vigilant Dog, who kept barking at him continually. Upon which the Thief, thinking to stop his Mouth, threw him a Piece of Bread: But the Dog refused it with Indignation; telling him, that before, he only suspected him to be a bad Man; but now, upon his offering to bribe him, he was confirmed in his Opinion; and that, as he was intrusted with the Guardianship of his Master's House, he should never cease barking while such a Rogue as he lay lurking about it.

The APPLICATION.

A Man who is very free in his Protestations of Friendship, or Offers of great Civility upon the first Interview, may meet with Applause and Esteem from Fools, but contrives his Schemes of that Sort to little or no Purpose, in the Company of Men of Sense. It is a common and known Maxim, to suspect an Enemy even the more, for his endeavouring to convince us of his Benevolence; because the Oddness of the Thing puts us

upon

upon our Guard, and makes us conclude, that some pernicious Design must be couched under so sudden and unexpected a Turn of Behaviour: But it is no unnecessary Caution, to be upon the Watch against even indifferent People, when we perceive them uncommonly froward in their Approaches of Civility and Kindness. The Man, who at first Sight makes us an Offer, which is due only to particular and well-acquainted Friends, must be either a Knave, and intends by such a Bait to draw us into his Net; or a Fool, with whom we ought to avoid having any Communication. Thus far the Consideration of this Fable may be useful to us in private Life; what it contains farther, in Relation to the Public, is, That a Man, truly honest, will never let his Mouth be stopped with a Bribe; but, the greater the Offer is which is designed to buy his Silence, the louder, and more constantly, will he open against the Miscreants who would practise it upon him.

FAB. CVIII. *The* Harper.

A Fellow that used to play upon his Harp, and sing to it in little Alehouses, and made a Shift, by the Help of those narrow confined Walls, to
please

pleafe the dull Sots who heard him ; from hence entertained an Ambition of fhewing his Parts upon the public Theatre, where he fancied he could not fail of raifing a great Reputation and Fortune in a very fhort Time. He was accordingly admitted upon Trial ; but the Spacioufnefs of the Place, and the Throng of the People, fo deadened and weakened both his Voice and Inftrument, that fcarce either of them could be heard ; and where they could, it founded fo poor, fo low and wretched, in the Ear of his refined Audience, that he was univerfally exploded and hiffed off the Stage.

The APPLICATION.

When we are commended for our Performances by People of much Flattery, or little Judgment, we fhould be fure not to value ourfelves upon it ; for want of which, many a vain unthinking Man has at once expofed and loft himfelf to the World. A Buffoon may be very agreeable to a Company difpofed to be mirthful over a Glafs of Wine, who would not be fit to open his Mouth in a Senate, or upon a Subject where found Senfe and a grave and ferious Behaviour are expected. It is not the diverting a little, infignificant, injudicious Audience or Society, which can gain us a proper Efteem, or infure our Succefs, in a Place which calls for a Performance of the firft Rate ; we fhould have either allowed Abilities to pleafe the moft refined Taftes, or Judgment enough to know that we want them, and to have a Care how we fubmit ourfelves to the Trial. And, if we have a Mind to purfue a juft and true Ambition, it is not fufficient that we ftudy barely to pleafe, but it is of greateft Moment whom we pleafe, and in what Refpect ; otherwife, we may not only lofe our Labour, but make ourfelves ridiculous into the Bargain.

FAB.

FAB. CIX. *The* Two Crabs.

IT is faid to be the Nature of a Crab-Fifh to go
backward: However, a Mother-Crab, one Day,
reproved her Daughter, and was in a great Paffion
with her for her untoward aukward Gait, which fhe
defired her to alter, and not to move in a Way fo
contradictory to the reft of the World. Indeed, Mother, fays the young Crab, I walk as decently as I
can, and to the beft of my Knowledge; but, if you
would have me go otherwife, I beg you would be fo
good as to practife it firft, and fhew me, by your own
Example, how you would have me behave myfelf.

The APPLICATION.

The Man, who is fo impertinent as to rebuke others
for a Mifbehaviour of which he himfelf is guilty, muft
be either a Hypocrite, a fenfelefs Creature, or an impudent Fellow. It is ftrange that Mankind, being fo apt
to act wrong in moft Particulars, fhould at the fame
Time be fo prone to Calumny and Detraction. One
would

would think that they who err so notoriously and frequently themselves, should be rather tender in concealing, than officious in carping at the Faults of their Fellow-Sinners; especially, considering that it is natural to be missed by our Passions and Appetites into some Excess or other, but unnatural and inhuman to impeach others of Miscarriages, of which ourselves are equally guilty. Granting it were ever so proper, or so much our Duty to find Fault with others, yet we must have a great Share of Impudence, if we can bear to do it while we know ourselves liable to the same Imputations. Example is a thousand Times more instructive, or at least persuasive, than Precept: For, though the Rules for Virtue were even more pressing and numerous than they are, yet let but the Fashion run upon Vice, as it most commonly does, and you see how ready and conformable the World shews itself to every Part of it.

FAB. CX. *The* Thief *and the* Boy.

A BOY sat weeping upon the Side of a Well. A Thief happening to come by, just at the same Time, asked him why he wept. The Boy, sighing and sobbing, replied, the String was broke, and a

Silver

Silver Tankard was fallen to the Bottom of the Well. Upon this the Thief pulled off his Clothes, and went down into the Well to look for it; where, having groped about a good while to no Purpose, he came up again, but found neither his Clothes nor the Boy; that little arch Diſſembler having run away with them.

The APPLICATION.

However Juſtice may be but little practiſed and purſued by particular Men in the common Courſe of their Actions, yet every one readily agrees, that it ought to be kept up and inforced by the ſeveral Penal Laws, in Reſpect to the Public in general. Many a one can ſcarce forbear robbing and defrauding another, when it is in his Power to do it with Impunity; but at the ſame Time, he dreads being robbed and defrauded again, as much as if he were the moſt innocent Man living, and is as ſevere in proſecuting the Offenders; which proves, that an unjuſt Man is deliberately wicked, and abhors the Crime in another which he dares commit himſelf. It is for this Reaſon, that the greater Part of Mankind like well enough to have Puniſhment inflicted upon thoſe who do wrong; and according ſubmit themſelves to be governed peaceably and quietly by the Laws of their Country, upon the Proſpect of ſeeing Juſtice executed upon all thoſe who do them an Injury. And, however a tender Nature may ſhrink at the Sight, and commiſerate the Condition of a ſuffering Malefactor, yet, in the main we may obſerve, that People are pleaſed and ſatisfied when the Sword of Juſtice is unſheathed; and Multitudes will even crowd to be Spectators, when the finiſhing Stroke is given. But what affords us the greateſt Pleaſure upon ſuch Occaſions, is, when we are entertained with a View of Juſtice, acting, as it were, in Perſon, and puniſhing Cheats and Trickſters, by making their own Contrivances inſtrumental in it, and by ordering, as in the Fable, that their Wickedneſs may fall upon their own Head.

FAB.

FAB. CXI. Mercury *and the* Woodman.

A Man was felling a Tree on the Bank of a River, and by Chance let his Hatchet flip out of his Hand, which dropt into the Water, and immediately funk to the Bottom. Being therefore in great Diftrefs for the Lofs of his Tool, he fat down and bemoaned himfelf moft lamentably. Upon this, *Mercury* appeared to him, and, being informed of the Caufe of his Complaint, dived to the Bottom of the River, and coming up again, fhewed the Man a golden Hatchet, demanding if that were his. He denied that it was. Upon which *Mercury* dived a fecond Time, and brought up a filver one. The Man refufed it, alledging likewife that this was not his. He dived a third Time, and fetched up the individual Hatchet the Man had loft; upon Sight of which the poor Wretch was overjoyed, and took it with all Humility and Thankfulnefs. *Mercury* was fo pleafed with the Fellow's Honefty, that he gave him the other two into the Bargain, as a Reward

ward

ward for his juſt Dealing. The Man goes to his Companions, and giving them an Account of what had happened, one of them went preſently to the River's Side, and let his Hatchet fall deſignedly into the Stream. Then ſitting down upon the Bank, he fell a weeping and lamenting, as if he had been really and ſorely afflicted. *Mercury* appeared as before, and diving, brought him up a golden Hatchet, aſking if that was the Hatchet he loſt. Tranſported at the precious Metal, he anſwered, Yes; and went to ſnatch it greedily. But the God deteſting his abominable Impudence, not only re-fuſed to give him that, but would not ſo much as let him have his own Hatchet again.

The APPLICATION.

Notwithſtanding the Proneneſs of Mankind to do Evil, and the Account which ſome find in playing the Knave, yet there cannot be invented a more true and reaſonable Maxim, than that by which we are aſſured that *Honeſty is the beſt Policy.* If we conſider it in reſpect to the other World, there never was a Religion but ſtrictly required it of its Votaries: If we examine it upon Account of this, we ſhall find that the honeſt Man, provided his other Talents are not deficient, always carries the Preference in our Eſteem, before any other, in whatever Buſineſs he thinks fit to employ himſelf.

FAB.

FAB. CXII. *The* Creaking Wheel.

THE Coachman, hearing one of the Wheels of his Coach creek, was ſurpriſed ; but more eſpe-cially when he perceived that it was the worſt Wheel of the whole Set, and which he thought had but lit-tle Pretence to take ſuch a Liberty. But, upon his demanding the Reaſon why it did ſo, the Wheel re-plied, that it was natural for People who laboured under any Affliction or Infirmity to complain.

The APPLICATION.

Though we naturally deſire to give Vent to the Ful-neſs of our Heart, when it is charged with Grief, and though by uttering our Complaints, we may happen to move the Compaſſion of thoſe that hear us, yet, every Thing conſidered, it is beſt to repreſs and keep them to ourſelves ; or, if we muſt let our Sorrow ſpeak, to take Care that it is done in Solitude and Retirement. What the Poets mention as an uſual Thing with Lovers, would not be amiſs in thoſe who are under any froward Cala-mity, which cannot be kept quiet, to utter it to the Woods and Mountains, and to call the Rocks and Ri-vers to witneſs to the Cruelty of their Deſtiny : That is, if they muſt ſhew any Weakneſs or Impatience under the Preſſure of adverſe Fortune, to do it as privately as they can : For tho' the Commiferation of a foft-hearted Perfon may be drawn forth fometimes by imparting the Bitternefs of our Condition, yet the World will be apt to think us troublefome and importunate ; and conclude, that if our Hardfhips were fo great as we would have People believe, we could not bear to talk of them fo frequently and abundantly, as fometimes we do. But befides, nothing is more generally true, than that it is much happier for us to fhare the Envy, than the Pity of Mankind. And if the firft of thefe is by no Means eligible, if we could avoid it, how much more ought we to take Care to give as little Occafion as poffible for the latter? Scarce any one is envied without poffeffing fomething valuable, or leaft defirable ; but we no fooner become Objects of Pity, than we are found out to be deficient in fome Refpect or other, and perhaps unfit and unequal for the Company and Acquaintance, with which we formerly converfed. Upon the whole, tho' we be pitied, we fhall never be the more efteemed for being miferable ; and if we can but appear happy, ten to one but we fhall be beloved in Courfe.

FAB. CXIII. *The* Man *and his* Wooden God.

A Man having a wooden God, worfhipped it every Day ; and, among other Things, prayed particularly for Wealth, becaufe his Circumftances were but low. But when he had continued to do this for many Days to no Purpose, in a Paſſion at the Diſappointment, he took the Image by the Legs, knocked it againſt the Pavement, and broke it in Pieces; upon which a great Quantity of Money, which had been incloſed within it, flew about the Room. The Man no ſooner perceived this, but addreſſing himſelf to the Idol, thou obſtinate, perverſe Deity, ſays he, who while I humbly beſought thee, hadſt no Regard to my Prayers, but now thou art uſed ill, and broken to Pieces, doſt pour forth good Things, in even a greater Abundance than I could deſire.

The APPLICATION.

This is a Fable of a very extraordinary Compoſition; if, as the ancient Mythologiſts ſay, it is deſigned to ſignify no more than, That where fair Means will not do, foul muſt be uſed. Indeed ſome Natures are ſo very rough and untractable, that gentle Uſage and moderate Treatment are thrown away upon them; they muſt be wrought upon like ſtubborn Metals, by Blows frequently and heartily applied. But what has all this to do with Religion and the Worſhip of God? The Fable is uſeleſs in that Reſpect, unleſs we conſider it in this Light, That the Adoration of Images is the moſt ſtupid Part of Religion that ever was invented. How any of the ſober ſenſible Heathen World could be induced, ſo as to give into ſuch an unreaſonable Piece of Devotion, is aſtoniſhing; or how they could ſuppoſe that a ſenſeleſs Stock or Stone, which had neither Life or Motion in it, could underſtand their Complaints, and redreſs their Grievances: Such a Suppoſition muſt be monſtrouſly abſurd and fooliſh. But what then muſt we think of thoſe Chriſtians, who blindly run into the ſame Practice, tho' they have an acknowledged and received Command from the God they worſhip, abſolutely forbidding it! What was only Stupidity in the Heathens, in them is groſs Wickedneſs, and profane impudent Impiety. But the People who can be made to believe that this is right, may be taught to ſwallow any Thing, and conſequently are the fitteſt Tools to carry on the Trade of Prieſtcraft.

F A B.

FAB. CXIV. *The* Kid *and the* Wolf.

A KID being mounted upon the Roof of a Shed, and feeing a Wolf below, loaded him with all Manner of Reproaches. Upon which, the Wolf, looking up, replied, Do not value yourfelf, vain Creature, upon thinking you mortify me; for I look upon this ill Language, not as coming from you, but from the Place which protects you.

The APPLICATION.

To rail and give ill Language, is very unbecoming, not only Gentlemen in partitular, but Men in general: Nor can we eafily determine whether Courage or Manners' are moft wanting in the Perfon who is given to ufe it. Now, when any one is fo fcreened and protected by the Place he is in, that he may commit fuch Indecencies with Impunity, however his Carcafe may efcape Scot-free, yet he is fure to pay for it in his Reputation; it being impoffible we fhould think him a Man of Honour, who endeavours to wound us from the Advantage of the Place in which he happens to be, and refufes to

K engage

engage us upon equal Terms. Whenever, therefore, we are attacked by one, whom the Company we are in, or some other Circumstance makes it improper or impracticable for us to come at, let us wisely curb our Passions of Resentment, by considering, that it is not the silly Person who speaks, but some Situation, by which he is secured, that utters the Reproach against us. The same Reflection may serve also to divert, instead of exasperating us, at the impotent Malice of those poor Spirits, who, at the same Time that they take the Advantage of a Place to brandish their infamous Tongues against us, shew how much they fear us, and that they durst not do it, unless they knew themselves to be out of the Reach of our Resentment.

F A B. CXV. *The* Judicious Lion.

A Lion having taken a young Bullock, stood over, and was just going to devour it, when a Thief stept in, and cried Halves with him. No, Friend, says the Lion, you are too apt to take what is not your Due, and therefore I shall have nothing to say to you. By Chance, a poor honest Traveller happened

pened

pened to come that Way, and feeing the Lion, modeftly and timorously withdrew, intending to go another Way : Upon which, the generous Beaft, with a courteous affable Behaviour, defired him to come forward, and partake with him in that, to which his Modefty and Humility had given him fo good a Title. Then, dividing the Prey into two equal Parts, and feafting himfelf upon one of them, he retired into the Woods, and left the Place clear for the honeft Man to come in and take his Share.

The APPLICATION.

There is not one but will readily allow this Behaviour of the Lion to have been commendable and juft ; notwithftanding which, Greedinefs and Importunity rever fail to thrive and attain their Ends, while Modefty ftarves, and is for ever poor. Nothing is more difagreeable to quiet reafonable Men, than thofe that are petulant, forward, and craving, in foliciting for their Favours : And yet Favours are feldom beftowed but upon fuch as have extorted them by thefe teafing offenfive Means. Every Patron, when he fpeaks his real Thoughts, is ready to acknowledge that the modeft Man has the beft Title to his Efteem ; yet he fuffers himfelf, too often, to be prevailed upon, merely by outrageous Noife, to give that to a fhamelefs affuming Fellow, which he knows to be juftly due to the filent, unapplying, modeft Man. It would be a laughable Thing in a Man in Power, to make a Refolution not to confer any advantageous Poft upon the Perfon that afks for it ; as it would free him from Importunity, and afford him a quiet Leifure, upon any Vacancy, either to confider with himfelf who had deferved beft of their Country, or to inquire, and be informed by thofe whom he could truft. But, as this is feldom or never praßifed, no wonder that we often find the Names of Men of little Merit, mentioned in the public Prints, as advanced to confiderable Stations, who were incapable of being known to the Public any other Way.

FAP,

FAB. CXVI. *The Wolf and Kid.*

THE Goat going abroad to feed, shut up her young Kid at Home, charging him to bolt the Door fast, and open it to nobody, till she herself should return. The Wolf, who lay lurking just by, heard this Charge given; and soon after came and knocked at the Door, counterfeiting the Voice of the Goat, and desiring to be admitted. The Kid, looking out at a Window, and finding the Cheat, bid him go about his Business; for, however he might imitate a Goat's Voice, yet he appeared too much like a Wolf to be trusted.

The APPLICATION.

As it is impossible that young People should steer their Course aright in the World, before they are acquainted with the Situation of the many Dangers which lie in their Way; it is therefore necessary, that they should be under the Government and Direction of those who are appointed to take the Charge of their Education,

whether

whether they are Parents, or Tutors by them intrusted with the Instruction of their Children. If a Child has but Reason enough to consider at all, how readily should it embrace the Counsel of his Father! how attentively listen to his Precepts! and how steadily pursue his Advice! The Father has already walked in the difficult Wilderness of Life, and has observed every Danger which lies lurking in the Paths of it, to annoy the Footsteps of those who never trod the Way before. Of these, with much Tenderness and sincere Affection, he makes a Discovery to his Son; telling him what he must avoid, and directing him how to make a safe, honourable, and advantageous Journey. When therefore the Child refuses to follow the Directions of so skilful a Guide, so faithful, so loving, and so sincere a Friend, no Wonder if he falls into many Mischiefs, which otherwise he might have escaped, unpitied and unlamented by all that know him, because he obstinately contemned the kind Admonitions of him that truly wished and intended his Happiness, and perversely followed the Examples of those who decoyed him out of the Way of Virtue, into the thorny Mazes of Vice and Error. Nor should Children take it ill, if the Commands of their Parents sometimes seem difficult and disagreeable; perhaps upon Experiment, they may prove as pleasant and diverting, as if they had followed their own Choice; this however, they may be assured of, that all such Cautions are intended out of true Love and Affection, by those who are more experienced than themselves, and therefore better Judges what their Conduct should be.

FAB.

FAB. CXVII.
The Wolf, *the* Fox, *and the* Ape.

THE Wolf indicted the Fox of Felony, before
the Ape, who upon that Occasion was appointed special Judge of the Cause. The Fox gave
in his Answer to the Wolf's Accusation, and denied the Fact. So, after a fair Hearing on both
Sides, the Ape gave Judgment to this Purpose. I am
of Opinion that you, says he to the Wolf, never
lost the Goods you sue for: And as for you, turning
to the Fox, I make no Question, said he, but you
have stolen what is laid to your Charge, at least.
And thus the Court was dismissed, with this public
Censure past upon each Party.

The APPLICATION.

A Man that has once blemished his Credit by Knavery, will not be believed for the future, even tho' he
should speak the Truth. One would think the Consideration

deration of this fhould be fome Obftruction to lying
and cheating, and a Difcouragement to the Profeffors
of that Faculty. Whoever is detected of voluntary deliberate Falfhood, altho' no Cognizance is had of it by
the Public, will yet be for ever detefted by the honeft
difcreet Part of his Aquaintance : And though he may
efcape all Manner of Penalty, from the Law of the
Land in which he lives, yet all that know him will lay
him under a tacit private Condemnation, and treat him
for ever after as an Outlaw, and an excommunicated
Perfon. Cheating and Knavery may now and then
fucceed and pafs Mufter with the moft filly undifcern-
ing Part of Mankind ; but the Contrivers of fuch villainous Plots, whatever their Advantage may be, are
fure of getting little or no Honour by their Exploits ;
and are liable to be detected and expofed, even by the
fimple Crew which they practife upon. A very Ape
knows how to diftinguifh, and pafs juft Sentence upon a
Fox or a Wolf: But the honeft juft Man, who is fair
and upright in all his Dealings, is unexceptionable to
every body, and no lefs fure of turning every Negociation
to his Profit, than to his Honour and Credit. A Knave
has a Chance, and perhaps but an indifferent one, of
fucceeding once or twice, and that with the moft foolifh
Part of Mankind ; whereas an honeft Man is fure of
being conftantly trufted, and well efteemed, and that by
all wife and good People.

FAB.

FAB. CXVIII. Jupiter *and the* Ass.

A Certain Ass which belonged to a Gardener, and was weary of carrying his heavy Burdens, prayed to *Jupiter* to give him a new Master. *Jupiter* confenting to his Petition, gave him a Tile-maker, who loaded him with Tiles, and made him carry heavier Burdens than before. Again he came, and made Supplications, befeeching the God to give him one that was more mild; or, at leaft, to let him have any other Master but this. *Jupiter* could not chufe but laugh at his Folly; however, he granted his Request this Time alfo, and made him over to a Tanner. But, as foon as the poor Ass was fenfible what a Master he had got, he could not forbear upbraiding himfelf with his great Folly and Inconftancy, which had brought him to a Master not only more cruel and exacting than any of the former, but one that would not fpare his very Hide after he was dead.

The APPLICATION.

This Fable is a lively Reprefentation of the Inftability of Mankind, who are feldom or never contented with their own Lot. But whatever Men may think, it is a thousand to one but they know less of any other Way, than of that in which they have been bred: And if Providence should comply with their humourous Request in such a Case, they would probably find themselves more at a Loss, and more uneasy in their new Station of Life, than ever they were of the old; at least, there is great Reason to suppose they would. The Vanity and Ignorance of the Men of this World are so great, that if every Man might be what he desired, few would be what they ought. So that it is not of less Importance to the Good of the Public in general, than our own particular Quiet and Happiness, that every Man should be easy and contented with the Condition which Providence and his Education have allotted him.

FAB. CXIX. *The* Boy *and his* Mother.

A Little Boy who went to School, stole one of his School-Fellow's Horn-books, and brought it Home to his Mother; who was so far from correcting and discouraging him upon Account of the Theft, that she commended and gave him an Apple for his Pains. In Process of Time, as the Child grew up to be a Man, he accustomed himself to greater

Robberies; and at laft, being apprehended and committed to Gaol, he was tried and condemned for
Felony. On the Day of his Execution, as the Of-
ficers were conducting him to the Gallows, he was
attended by a vaft Crowd of People, and among the
reft by his Mother, who came fighing and fobbing
along, and taking on extremely for her Son's unhappy Fate; which the Criminal obferving, called
to the Sheriff, and begged the Favour of him, that he
would give him leave to fpeak a Word or two to his
poor afflicted Mother. The Sheriff (as who would
deny a dying Man fo reafonable a Requeft) gave him
Permiffion; and the Felon, while as every one thought,
he was whifpering fomething of Importance to his
Mother, bit off her Ear, to the great Offence and
Surprife of the whole Affembly. What, fay they,
was not this Villain contented with the impious
Facts which he has already committed, but that he
muft increafe the Number of them, by doing this
Violence to his Mother? Good People, replied he,
I would not have ye be under a Miftake; that wicked Woman deferves this, and even worfe at my
Hands; for if fhe had chaftifed and chid, inftead of
rewarding and careffing me, when in my Infancy I
ftole the Horn-Book from the School, I had not
come to this ignominious untimely End.

The APPLICATION.

Notwithftanding the great innate Depravity of Mankind, one need not fcruple to affirm, that moft of the
Wickednefs which is fo frequent and fo pernicious in the
World, arifes from a bad Education; and that the Child
is obliged either to the Example or Connivance of its
Parents, for moft of the vicious Habits which it wears
thro' the Courfe of its future Life. The Mind of one
that is young, is like Wax, foft, and capable of any
Impreffion which is given it; but it is hardened by
Time, and the firft Signature grows fo firm and durable, that fcarce any Pains or Application can erafe it. It

is a miftaken Notion in People, when they imagine that
there is no Occafion for regulating or reftraining the
Actions of very young Children, which tho' allowed to
be fometimes very naughty in thofe in a more advanced
Age, are in them, they fuppofe, altogether innocent and
inoffenfive. But, however innocent they may be, as to
their Intention then, yet, as the Practice may grow upon
them unobferved, and root itfelf into a Habit, they
ought to be checked and difcountenanced in their firft
Efforts towards any Thing that is injurious or difhoneft;
that the Love of Virtue and the Abhorrence of Wrong
and Oppreffion, may be let into their Minds, at the fame
Time that they receive the very firft Dawn of Underftanding, and Glimmering of Reafon. Whatever Guilt arifes
from the Actions of one whofe Education has been deficient
as to this Point, no Queftion but a juft Share of it will
be laid, by the Great Judge of the World, to the Charge
of thofe who were, or fhould have been his Inftructors.

FAB. CXX. *The* Wolves *and the* Sick Afs.

AN Afs being fick, the Report of it was fpread
abroad in the Country, and fome did not ftick
to fay, that fhe would die before another Night went
over

over her Head. Upon this, feveral Wolves came
to the Stable where fhe lay, under Pretence of making her a Vifit; but rapping at the Door, and afking how fhe did, the young Afs came out, and told
them, that his Mother was much better than they
defired.

The A P P L I C A T I O N.

The charitable Vifits which are made to many fick
People, proceed from much the fame Motive with that
which prevailed upon the Wolves to pay their Duty to
the fick Afs, namely, that they may come in for fome
Share of their Remains, and feaft themfelves upon the Reverfion of their Goods and Chattels. We cannot therefore, without Pleafure, fee thefe felfish Vifitants difcovered thro' their Mafk of Charity, and treated with fuch
a Referve, as Neighbours of their Sort juftly challenge.

As a Behaviour thus grofly impertinent and officious,
muft needs be offenfive to a difcerning Man, and more
efpecially at fuch a Time, when he labours under any
Indifpofition or Pain of Body, fo it is very frequently
injurious to the Intereft of him who makes Ufe of it,
and proves to be the Means of his miffing fuch an Inhe-
ritance or Legacy, as a more diftant and modeft Deportment might have fecured to him.

F A B.

FAB. CXXI. *The* Ant *and the* Grashopper.

IN the Winter Seafon, a Commonwealth of Ants was bufily employed in the Management and Prefervation of their Corn; which they expofed to the Air, in Heaps, round about the Avenues of their little Country Habitation. A Grashopper, who had chanced to outlive the Summer, and was ready to starve with Cold and Hunger, approached them with great Humility, and begged that they would relieve his Neceffity, with one Grain of Wheat or Rye. One of the Ants afked him, how he had dif-pofed of his Time in Summer, that he had 'not taken Pains, and laid in a Stock, as they had done. Alas, Gentlemen, fays he, I paffed away the Time mer-rily and pleafantly, in Drinking, Singing, and Dancing, and never once thought of Winter. If that be the Cafe, replied the Ant, laughing, all I have to fay is, That they who drink, fing, and dance in the Summer, muft ftarve in Winter.

The

The APPLICATION.

As Summer is the Seaſon of the Year in which the induſtrious and laborious Huſbandman gathers and lays up ſuch Fruits as may ſupply his Neceſſities in Winter, ſo Youth and Manhood are the Times of Life which we ſhould employ and beſtow in laying in ſuch a Stock of all Kind of Neceſſaries, as may ſuffice for the craving Demands of helpleſs old Age. Yet notwithſtanding the Truth of this, there are many of thoſe which we call rational Creatures, who live in a Method quite oppoſite to it, and make it their Buſineſs to ſquander away in a profuſe Prodigality, whatever they get in their younger Days: As if the Infirmity of Age would require no Supplies to ſupport it; or, at leaſt, would find them adminiſtered to it in ſome miraculous Way. From this Fable we learn this admirable Leſſon, Never to loſe any preſent Opportunity of providing againſt the future Evils and Accidents of Life. While Health, and the Flower and Vigour of our Age remain firm and entire, let us lay them out to the beſt Advantage; that when the latter Days take hold of us, and ſpoil us of our Strength and Abilities, we may have a Store moderately ſufficient to ſubſiſt upon, which we laid up in the Morning of our Age.

FAB.

FAB. CXXII.

The Ass, the Lion, and the Cock.

AN Ass and a Cock happened to be feeding together in the same Place, when on a sudden they
spied a Lion approaching them. This Beast is reported, above all Things, to have an Aversion, or
rather Antipathy, to the Crowing of a Cock; so
that he no sooner heard the Voice of that Bird, but
he betook him to his Heels, and run away as fast as
ever he could. The Ass, fancying he fled for Fear
of him, in the Bravery of his Heart pursued him,
and followed him so far, that they were quite out of
the Hearing of the Cock; which the Lion no sooner
perceived, but he turned about and seized the Ass;
and just as he was ready to tear him to Pieces, the
sluggish Creature is said to have expressed himself
thus; Alas! Fool that I was, knowing the Cowardice of my own Nature, thus by an affected Courage, to throw myself into the Jaws of Death, when
I might have remained secure and unmolested!

The APPLICATION.

There are many, who, out of an Ambition to appear
considerable, affect to shew themselves Men of Fire, Spirit,

rit and Courage: But these being Qualities, of which they are not the right Owners, they generally expose themselves, and shew the little Title they have to them, by endeavouring to exert and produce them at unseasonable Times, or with improper Persons.   A Bully, for fear you should find him out to be a Coward, overacts his Part, and calls you to account for Affronts, which a Man of true Bravery would never have thought of. And a cowardly silly Fellow, observing that he may take some Liberties with Impunity, where perhaps the Place or the Company protect him, falsly concludes from thence, that the Person with whom he made free, is a greater Coward than himself; so that he not only continues his offensive Raillery and Impertinence for the present, but probably renews them in some Place not so privileged as the former, where his Insolence meets with a due Chastisement; than which nothing is more equitable in itself, or agreeable to the discreet Part of Mankind.

F A B. CXXIII. *The* Ape *and the* Fox.

THE Ape meeting the Fox one Day, humbly requested him to give him a Piece of his fine long brush Tail, to cover his poor naked Backside, which was exposed to all the Violence and Inclemency of the Weather; for says he, *Reynard*, you have already more than you have Occafion for, and a great Part of it even drags along in the Dirt. The Fox anfwered, That as to his having too much, that was more than he knew; but be it as it would, he had rather fweep the Ground with his Tail as long as he lived, than deprive himfelf of the leaft Bit to cover the Ape's nafty ftinking Pofteriors.

The APPLICATION.

One cannot help confidering the World, in the Particular of the Goods of Fortune, as a Kind of Lottery; in which fome few are intitled to Prizes of different Degrees; others, and thofe by much the greateft Part, come off with little or nothing. Some, like the Fox, have even larger Circumftances than they know what to do with, infomuch that they are rather a Charge and Incumbrance, than of any true Ufe and Pleafure to them. Others, like the poor Ape's Cafe, are all Blank; not having been fo lucky as to draw from the Wheel of Fortune, wherewith to cover their Nakednefs, and live with tolerable Decency. That thefe Things are left, in a great Meafure by Providence, to the blind uncertain Shuffle of Chance, is reafonable to conclude from the unequal Diftribution of them; for there is feldom any Regard had to true Merit upon thefe Occafions; Folly and Knavery ride in Coaches, while Good-fenfe and Honefty walk in the Dirt. The All-wife Difpofer of Events, does certainly permit thefe Things for juft and good Purpofes, which our fhallow Underftanding is not able to fathom; but, humanly thinking, if the Riches and Power of the World were to be always in the Hands of the virtuous Part of Mankind, they would be more likely to do Good with them in their Generation, than the vile fottifh Wretches who generally enjoy them. A truly good Man would direct all the fuperfluous Part of his Wealth, at leaft, for the Neceffities of his Fellow-Creatures, though there were no Religion which enjoined it: But felfifh and avaricious People, who are always great Knaves, how much foever they may have, will never think they have enough; much lefs be induced by any Confideration of Virtue and Religion, to part with the leaft Farthing for public Charity and Beneficence,

FAB. CXIV. *The* Afs *and the* Little Dog.

THE Afs, obferving how great a Favourite the little Dog was with his Mafter, how much ca-reffed and fondled, and fed with good Bits at every Meal; and for no other Reafon, as he could per-ceive, but fkipping and frifking about, wagging his Tail, and leaping up into his Mafter's Lap; he was refolved to imitate the fame, and fee whether fuch a Behaviour would not procure him the fame Favours. Accordingly, the Mafter was no fooner come Home from walking about his Fields and Gardens, and was feated in his Eafy-chair, but the Afs, who obferved him, came gamboling and braying towards him, in a very aukward Manner. The Mafter could not help laughing aloud at the odd Sight. But his Jeft was foon turned into Earneft, when he felt the rough Salute of the Afs's Fore-feet, who, raifing himfelf upon his hinder Legs, pawed againft his Breaft with a moft loving Air, and would fain have jumped into his Lap. The
good

good Man, terrified at this outrageous Behaviour, and unable to endure the Weight of so heavy a Beaft, cried out; upon which, one of his Servants running in with a good Stick; and, laying on heartily upon the Bones of the poor Afs, foon convinced him, That every one who defire it, is not qualified to be a Favourite.

The APPLICATION.

Some Men are as engaging in their Way as little Dogs. They can fawn, wheedle, cringe, or, if Occafion requires, leap backward and forward over a Stick, to the great Emolument of their Mafter, and Entertainment of thofe that behold them. But thefe are Qualifications to which every body cannot pretend; and therefore none but thofe who have a Genius for it, fhould afpire at the Employment. Many a Man envies the Happinefs of thefe Favourites, and would fain infinuate himfelf into the fame good Graces, if he did but know the Way; but, whoever has a tolerable Share of Difcretion, will diftruft his Abilities in this Refpect, and modeftly forbear the Attempt, for Fear he fhould mifcarry and look like an Afs. But, in fhort, the true Moral of this Fable is, That every one fhould confider the juft Turn and Temper of his Parts, and weigh the Talents by which he hopes to be diftinguifhed. After fuch an Examination, he may the more certainly know how to apply them to the moft proper Purpofes; at leaft, fo as not to hurt, or even mortify himfelf by any miftaken Addrefs. Since there is fuch a Variety of Tempers in the World, and a no lefs Multiplicity of Arts and Studies to fit and tally with them, how reafonable is it in general, how much would it be for the true Intereft of every one in particular, if Men would but be directed by the natural Bent of their Genius, to fuch Purfuits as are moft agreeable to their Capacities, and to the Rudiments of Education which they have moft ftrongly imbibed.

FAB.

FAB. CXXV.
The Birds, *the* Beasts, *and the* Bat.

ONCE upon a Time, there commenced a fierce
War between the Birds and the Beasts; when
the Bat, taking Advantage of his ambiguous Make,
hoped, by that Means, to live secure in a State of
Neutrality, and save his Bacon. It was not long
before the Forces on each Side met, and gave a Battle; and their Animosities running very high, a
bloody Slaughter ensued. The Bat, at the Beginning of the Day, thinking the Birds most likely to
carry it, listed himself among them; but kept fluttering at a little Distance, that he might the better
observe, and take his Measures accordingly. However, after some Time spent in the Action, the Army
of the Beasts seeming to prevail, he went entirely
over to them, and endeavoured to convince them,
by the Affinity which he had to a Mouse, that he
was by Nature a Beast, and would always continue
firm

firm and true to their Intereſt. His Plea was admitted; but, in the End, the Advantage turning completely on the Side of the Birds, under the admirable Conduct and Courage of their General, the Eagle; the Bat, to ſave his Life, and eſcape the Diſgrace of falling into the Hands of his deſerted Friends, betook himſelf to Flight; and ever ſince, ſkulking in Caves and hollow Trees all Day, as if aſhamed to ſhew himſelf, he never appears till the Duſk of the Evening, when all the feathered Inhabitants of the Air are gone to Rooſt.

The APPLICATION.

For any one to deſert the Intereſt of his Country, and turn Renegado, either out of Fear, or any Proſpect of Advantage, is ſo notoriouſly vile and low, that it is no Wonder if the Man, who is detected in it, is for ever aſhamed to ſee the Sun, and to ſhew himſelf in the Eyes of thoſe whoſe Cauſe he has betrayed. Yet, as there is ſcarce any Vice, even to be imagined, but there may be found Men who have been guilty of it, perhaps there have been as many Criminals in the Caſe before us, as in any one Particular beſides, notwithſtanding the Aggravation and extraordinary Degree of its Baſeneſs. We cannot help reflecting upon it with Horror; but, as truly deteſtable as this Vice is, and muſt be acknowledged to be by all Mankind, ſo far are thoſe that practiſe it from being treated with a juſt Reſentment by the reſt of Mankind, that, by the kind Reception they afterwards meet with, they rather ſeem to be encouraged and applauded, than deſpiſed and diſcountenanced for it.

FAB.

FAB. CXXVI. *The* Bear *and the* Bee Hives.

A BEAR, climbing over the Fence into a Place where Bees were kept, began to plunder the Hives, and rob them of their Honey. But the Bees, to revenge the Injury, attacked him in a whole Swarm together; and though they were not able to pierce his rugged Hide, yet, with their little Stings, they so annoyed his Eyes and Nostrils, that, unable to endure the smarting Pain, with Impatience he tore the Skin over his Ears with his own Claws, and suffered ample Punishment for the Injury he did the Bees, in breaking open their waxen Cells.

The APPLICATION.

Many and great are the Injuries of which some Men are guilty towards others, for the sake of gratifying some liquorish Appetite. For there are those who would not stick to bring Desolation upon their Country, and run the Hazard of their own Necks into the Bargain, rather than baulk a wicked Inclination, either of Cruelty, Ambition, or Avarice. But it were to be wished, all who are hurried by such blind Impulses, would consider

a Moa Moment, before they proceed to irrevocable Execution. Injuries and Wrongs not only call for Revenge and Reparation with the Voice of Equity itself, but oftentimes carry their Punishment along with them, and, by an unforeseen Train of Events, are retorted at the Head of the Actor of them; and not seldom, from a deep Remorse, expiated upon himself, by his own Hand.

F A B. CXXVII. *The* Cock *and the* Fox.

A COCK being perched among the Branches of a lofty Tree, crowed aloud, so that the Shrilness of his Voice echoed through the Wood, and invited a Fox to the Place, who was prowling in that Neighbourhood, in Quest of his Prey. But *Reynard*, finding the Cock was inaccessible, by Reason of the Height of his Situation, had Recourse to Stratagem, in order to decoy him down; so, approaching the Tree, Cousin, says he, I am heartily glad to see you; but at the same Time, I cannot forbear expressing my Uneasiness at the Inconvenience of the Place, which will not let me pay my Respects to you in a handsomer Manner; though I

suppose

suppose you will come down presently, and so that Difficulty is easily removed. Indeed, Cousin, says the Cock, to tell you the Truth, I do not think it safe to venture upon the Ground; for though I am convinced how much you are my Friend, yet I may have the Misfortune to fall into the Clutches of some other Beast, and what will become of me then? O dear, says *Reynard*, is it possible that you can be so ignorant, as not to know of the Peace that has been lately proclaimed between all Kind of Birds and Beasts; and that we are, for the future, to forbear Hostilities on all Sides, and to live in the utmost Love and Harmony, and that, under Penalty of suffering the severest Punishment that can be inflicted? All this while the Cock seemed to give little Attention to what was said, but stretched out his Neck, as if he saw something at a Distance. Cousin, says the Fox, what is that you look at so earnestly? Why, says the Cock, I think I see a Pack of Hounds yonder, a little Way off. O then, says the Fox, your humble Servant, I must be gone. Nay, pray Cousin, do not go, says the Cock, I am just coming down; sure you are not afraid of Dogs in these peaceable Times. No, no, says he; but ten to one whether they have heard of the Proclamation yet.

The APPLICATION.

It is a very agreeable Thing to see Craft repelled by Cunning; more especially to behold the Snares of the Wicked, broken and defeated by the discreet Management of the Innocent. The Moral of this Fable principally puts us in Mind, not to be too credulous towards the Insinuations of those, who are already distinguished by their Want of Faith and Honesty. When therefore any such would draw us into a Compliance with their destructive Measures, by a pretended Civility and extraordinary Concern for our Interest, we should consider such Proposals in their true Light, as a Bait art-

fully

fully placed to conceal the fatal Hook which is intended to draw us into Captivity and Thraldom. An
honeft Man, with a little plain Senfe, may do a thoufand advantageous Things for the Public Good, and
without being Mafter of much Addrefs or Rhetoric, as
eafily convince People that his Defigns are intended for
their Welfare : But a wicked defigning Politician, tho'
he has a Tongue as eloquent as ever fpoke, may fometimes be difappointed in his Projects, and be foiled in
his Schemes ; efpecially when their deftructive Texture
is fo coarfely fpun, and the Threads of Mifchief are fo
large in them, as to be felt even by thofe whofe Senfes
are fcarce perfect enough to fee and underftand them.

FAB. CXXVIII. *The* Cat *and the* Cock.

THE Cat, having a Mind to make a Meal of the
Cock, feized him one Morning by Surprife,
and afked him what he could fay for himfelf, why
Slaughter fhould not pafs upon him ? The Cock
replied, that he was ferviceable to Mankind, by
crowing in the Morning, and calling them up to
their daily Labour. That is true, fays the Cat, and

is the very Objection that I have against you; for you make such a shrill impertinent Noise, that People cannot sleep for you. Besides, you are an incestuous Rascal, and make no Scruple of lying with your Mother and Sisters. Well, says the Cock, this I do not deny; but I do it to procure Eggs and Chickens for my Master. Ah! Villain, says the Cat, hold your wicked Tongue; such Impieties as these declare that you are no longer fit to live.

The APPLICATION.

When a wicked Man, in Power, has a Mind to glut his Appetite in any respect, Innocence, or even Merit, is no Protection against him. The Cries of Justice, and the Voice of Reason, are of no Effect upon a Conscience hardened in Iniquity, and a Mind versed in a long Practice of Wrong and Robbery. Remonstrances, however reasonably urged, or movingly couched, have no more Influence upon the Heart of such a one, than the gentle Evening Breeze has upon the Oak, when it whispers among its Branches; or the rising Surges upon the deaf Rock, when they dash and break against its Sides. Power should never be trusted in the Hands of an impious selfish Man, and one that has more Regard to the Gratification of his own unbounded Avarice, than to public Peace and Justice. Were it not for the tacit Consent, and heartless Compliance of a great Majority of Fools, Mankind would not be ridden, as oftentimes they are, by a little Majority of Knaves, to their great Misfortune: For, whatever People may think of the Times, if they were ten Times worse than they are, it is principally owing to their own Stupidity: Why do they trust the Man a Moment longer, who has once injured and betrayed them?

FAB. CXXIX. *The* Dog *in the* Manger

A DOG was lying upon a Manger full of Hay. An Ox being hungry, came near, and offered to eat of the Hay; but the envious ill-natured Cur, getting up and fnarling at him, would not fuffer him to touch it. Upon which the Ox, in the Bitternefs of his Heart, faid, A Curfe light on thee, for a malicious Wretch, who wilt neither eat Hay thyfelf, nor fuffer others to do it.

The APPLICATION:

Envy is the moft unnatural and unaccountable of all the Paffions. There is fcarce any other Emotion of the Mind, however unreafonable, but may have fomething faid in Excufe for it; and there are many of thefe Weakneffes of the Soul, which, notwithftanding the Wrongnefs and Irregularity of them, fwell the Heart, while they laft, with Pleafure and Gladnefs. But the envious Man has no fuch Apology as this to make; the ftronger the Paffion is, the greater Torment he endures; and fubjects himfelf to a continual real Pain, by only wifh-

ing

is th Ill to others. Revenge is sweet, though cruel and
you uman; and though it sometimes thirsts even for
ple ood, yet may be glutted and satiated. Avarice is
ce mething highly monstrous and absurd; yet, as it is a
yo fire after Riches, every little Acquisition gives it
l easure; and to behold and feel the hoarded Treasure,
Cl a covetous Man is a constant uncloying Enjoyment.
C t Envy, which is an Anxiety arising in our Minds,
th on our observing Accomplishments in others, which
: want ourselves, can never receive any true Comfort,
nless in a Deluge, a Conflagration, a Plague, or some
eneral Calamity that should befal Mankind: For, as
ong as there is a Creature living, that enjoys its Being
happily within the envious Man's Sphere, it will afford Nourishment to his distempered Mind: But such
Nourishment, as will make him pine, and fret, and
emaciate himself to nothing.

FAB. CXXX. *The* Dog *and the* Sheep.

THE Dog sued the Sheep for a Debt, of which
the Kite and the Wolf were to be Judges:
They, without debating long upon the Matter, or
making

making any Scruple for Want of Evidence, gave Sentence for the Plaintiff; who immediately tore the poor Sheep in Pieces, and divided the Spoil with the unjuft Judges.

The APPLICATION.

Deplorable are the Times, when open bare-faced Villainy is protected and encouraged, when Innocence is obnoxious, Honefty contemptible, and it is reckoned criminal to efpoufe the Caufe of Virtue. Men originally entered into Covenants and civil Compacts with each other for the Promotion of their Happinefs and Well-being, for the Eftablifhment of Juftice and public Peace. How comes it then that they look ftupidly on, and tamely acquiefce when wicked Men pervert this End, and eftablifh an arbitrary Tyranny of their own, upon the Foundation of Fraud and Oppreffion? Among Beafts, who are incapable of being civilized by focial Laws, it is no ftrange Thing to fee innocent helplefs Sheep fall a Prey to Dogs, Wolves, and Kites: But it is amazing how Mankind could ever fink down to fuch a low Degree of bafe Cowardice, as to fuffer fome of the worft of their Species to ufurp a Power over them, to fuperfede the righteous Laws of good Government, and to exercife all Kinds of Injuftice and Hardfhip, in gratifying their own vicious Lufts. Wherever fuch Enormities are practifed, it is when a few rapacious Statefmen combine together to get and fecure the Power in their own Hands, and agree to divide the Spoils among themfelves. For as long as the Caufe is to be tried only among themfelves, no Queftion but they will always vouch for each other. But, at the fame Time, it is hard to determine which refemble Brutes moft, they in acting, or the People in fuffering them to act their vile felfifh Schemes.

FAB. CXXXI. *The* Hawk *and the* Farmer.

A HAWK, purfuing a Pigeon over a Corn-field
with great Eagernefs and Force, threw himfelf
into a Net, which a Hufbandman had planted there
to take the Crows; who being employed not far off,
and feeing the Hawk fluttering in the Net, came
and took him: But, juft as he was going to kill
him, the Hawk befought him to let him go, affur-
ing him, that he was only following a Pigeon, and
neither intended, nor had done any Harm to him.
To whom the Farmer replied, and what Harm had
the poor Pigeon done to you? Upon which, he
wrung his Head off immediately.

The APPLICATION.

Paffion, Prejudice, or Power, may fo far blind a Man,
as not to fuffer him juftly to diftinguifh whether he is
not acting injurioufly, at the fame Time that he fancies
he is only doing his Duty. Now the beft Way of being
convinced,

convinced, whether what we do is reasonable and fit, is to put ourselves in the Place of the Persons with whom we are concerned, and then consult our Conscience about the Rectitude of our Behaviour. For this we may be assured of, that we are acting wrong, whenever we are doing any Thing to another, which we should think unjust if it was done to us. Nothing but an habitual Inadvertency, as to this Particular, can be the Occasion that so many ingenious noble Spirits are often engaged in Courses so opposite to Virtue and Honour. He that would startle, if a little Attorney should tamper with him to forswear himself, to bring off some small Offender, some ordinary Trespasser, will, without Scruple, infringe the Constitution of his Country, for the precarious Prospect of a Place or a Pension. Which is most corrupt, he that lyes, like a Knight of the Post, for Half-a-Crown and a Dinner, or he that does it for the more substantial Consideration of a Thousand Pounds a Year? Which would be doing most Service to the Public; giving true Testimony in a Cause between two private Men, and against one little common Thief, who has stolen a Gold Watch; or voting honestly and courageously against a Rogue of State, who has gagged and bound the Laws, and stript the Nation? Let those who intend to act justly, but view Things in this Light, and all would be well. There would be no Danger of their oppressing others, or Fear of being oppressed themselves.

FAB. CXXXII. Death *and* Cupid.

CUPID, one fultry Summer's Noon, tired with Play, and faint with Heat, went into a cool Grotto to repofe himfelf, which happened to be the Cave of *Death.*   He threw himfelf carelefsly down cn the Floor, and his Quiver turning topfy-turvy, all the Arrows fell out, and mingled with thofe of *Death*, which lay fcattered up and down the Place. When he awoke, he gathered them up, as well as he could ; but they were fo intermingled, that tho' he knew the certain Number, he could not rightly diftinguifh them ; from which it happened, that he took up fome of the Arrows which belonged to *Death*, and left feveral of his own in the room of them.   This is the Caufe that we, now and then, fee the Hearts of the Old and Decrepid transfixed with the Bolts of *Love*; and with equal Grief and Surprife, behold the youthful blooming Part of our Species fmitten with the Darts of *Death.*

The

The APPLICATION.

If we allow for this Fable's being written by a Heathen, and according to the Scheme of the ancient Pagan Theology, it will appear to be a pretty probable Solution of fome Parts of the Difpenfation of Providence, which otherwife feem to be obfcure and unaccountable. For, when we fee the Young and the Old fall promifcuoufly by the Hand of *Death*, and at the fame Time confider that the World is governed by an all-wife Providence, we are puzzled how to account for fo feemingly prepofterous and unnatural a Way of working. We fhould look upon a Gardener to be mad, or at leaft very capricious, who, when his young Trees are juft arrived to a Degree of bearing, fhould cut them down for Fuel; and chufe out old, rotten, decayed, faplefs Stocks, to graft and inoculate upon: Yet the irregular Proceedings of thofe two Levellers *Love* and *Death*, appear to be every Jot as odd and unreafonable. However, we muft take it for granted, that thefe Things, though the Method of them is hidden from our Eyes, are tranfacted after the moft juft and fit Manner imaginable; but, humanly fpeaking, it is ftrange that *Death* fhould be fuffered to make fuch undiftinguifhed Havock in the World, and at the fame Time, juft as fhocking and unnatural to fee Old Age laid betwixt a Pair of Wedding-Sheets, as it is for Youth and Beauty to be locked up in the cold Embraces of the Grave.

FAB. CXXXIII. *The* Dove *and the* Ant.

THE Ant compelled by Thirst, went to drink in a clear, purling Rivulet; but the Current, with its circling Eddy, snatched her away, and carried her down the Stream. A Dove, pitying her distressed Condition, cropt a Branch from a neighbouring Tree, and let it fall into the Water, by Means of which the Ant saved herself, and got ashore. Not long after, a Fowler having a Design upon the Dove, planted his Nets in due Order, without the Bird's observing what he was about; which the Ant perceiving, just as he was going to put his Design in Execution, she bit him by the Heel, and made him give so sudden a Start, that the Dove took the Alarm, and flew away.

The APPLICATION.

One good Turn deserves another; and Gratitude is excited by so noble and natural a Spirit, that he ought to be looked upon as the vilest of Creatures, who has no Sense of it. It is, indeed, so very just and equitable

ble

ble a Thing, and so much every Man's Duty, that to
speak of it properly, one should not mention it as any
Thing meritorious, or that may claim Praise and Admiration, any more than we should say a Man ought
to be rewarded or commended for not killing his Father, or forbearing to set Fire to his Neighbour's House.
The bright and shining Piece of Morality, therefore,
which is recommended to us in this Fable, is set forth
in this Example of the Dove, who, without any Obligation or Expectation, does a voluntary Office of Charity to its Fellow-Creature in Distress. The constant
uninterrupted Practice of this Virtue, is the only
Thing in which we are capable of imitating the great
Author of our Being; whose *Beloved Son*, besides the
many Precepts he has given to enforce this Duty, used
this Expression as a common Saying, *It is more blessed
to give, than to receive.*

FAB. CXXXIV. *The* Eagle *and the* Crow.

AN Eagle flew down from the Top of a high
Rock, and settled upon the Back of a Lamb;
and then instantly flying up into the Air again,
bore his bleating Prize aloft in his Pounces. A

Crow

Crow who fat upon an Elm, and beheld this Exploit, refolved to imitate it; fo flying down upon the Back of a Ram, and intangling his Claws in the Wool, he fell a chattering and attempting to fly; by which Means he drew the Obfervation of the Shepherd upon him, who, finding his Feet hampered in the Fleece of the Ram, eafily took him, and gave him to his Boys for their Sport and Diverfion.

The APPLICATION.

Every Quality which is excellent and commendable, is not, however, always a proper Object for our Imitation. We ought to ftate our own Account honeftly and fairly, that we may fee what our Abilities are, and how our Circumftances ftand: Otherwife, we may not only become ridiculous to others, but prejudicial to ourfelves, by fome aukward and ill-judged Emulation; though it happen to be in a Qualification truly laudable and great. It behoves every Man to exert a good Share of Induftry towards the Advancement of his Intereft, or, if he pleafes, of his Reputation. But then it is highly neceffary that he does this with a true Regard to his own Capacity, and without any Danger of expofing or embarraffing himfelf in the Operation.

FAB.

FAB. CXXXV.
The Envious Man *and the* Covetous.

AN envious Man happened to be offering up his Prayers to *Jupiter*, juft in the Time and Place with a covetous miferable Fellow. *Jupiter*, not caring to be troubled with their Impertinences himfelf, fent *Apollo* to examine the Merits of their Petitions, and to give them fuch Relief as he fhould think proper. *Apollo* therefore opened his Commiffion, and withal told them, that, to make fhort of the Matter, whatever the one afked, the other fhould have it double. Upon this, the covetous Man, tho' he had a thoufand Things to requeft, yet forbore to afk firft, hoping to receive a double Quantity; for he concluded, that all Men's Wifhes fympathifed with his. By this Means, the envious Man had an Opportunity of preferring his Petition firft, which was the Thing he aimed at; fo without much Hefitation, he prayed to be relieved, by having one of his Eyes put out; knowing that, of Confequence, his Companion would be deprived of both.

The

The APPLICATION.

In this Fable, the Folly of those two Vices, Envy and Avarice, is fully exposed, and handsomely rallied. The Miser, though he has the Riches of the World, without Stint, laid open to his Choice, yet dares not name the Sum, for Fear another should be richer than himself. The Advantage of a double Quality, by receiving last, is what he cannot bear to lose, and he fares accordingly. The envious Man, though he has a Power of calling for good Things, without Measure, to himself or others, yet waves this happy Privilege, and is content to punish himself by a very great Loss, even that of an Eye, that he may bring down a double Portion of the like Calamity upon another. These are the true Tempers of the Covetous and Envious; one can scarce determine whether they are more mischievous to themselves, or to the Public; but it is manifest, that they are highly noxious to both, and should be treated accordingly.

FAB. CXXXVI. *The* Fox *and the* Lion.

THE first Time the Fox saw the Lion, he fell down at his Feet, and was ready to die with Fear. The second Time, he took Courage, and
could

could even bear being treated on him. The third
Time he had the and Repro e to come up to him, to
salute him, and t ve this to familiar Conversation
with him. m with ny

The APPLICATION.

From this Fable we may obferve the two Extremes
in which we may fail, as to a proper Behaviour towards
our Superiors: The one is a Bafhfulnefs, proceeding
either from a vicious guilty Mind, or a timorous Rufti-
city: The other, an over-bearing Impudence, which
affumes more than becomes it, and fo renders the Perfon infufferable to the Converfation of well-bred reafonable People. But there is this Difference between
the Bafhfulnefs that arifes from a Want of Education,
and the Shamefacednefs that accompanies confcious
Guilt; the firft, by a Continuance of Time and a nearer
Acquaintance, may be ripened into a proper liberal Behaviour; the other no fooner finds an eafy pra&icable
Accefs, but it throws off all Manner of Reverence, grows
every Day more and more familiar, and branches out
into the utmoft Indecency and Irregularity. Indeed,
there are many Occafions which may happen to caft an
Awe, or even a Terror upon our Minds at firft View,
without any juft and reafonable Grounds: But upon a
little Recolle&ion, or a nearer Infight, we recover ourfelves, and can appear indifferent and unconcerned,
where, before, we were ready to fink under a Load of Dif-
fidence and Fear. We fhould, upon fuch Occafions, ufe
our Endeavours to regain a due Degree of Steadinefs
and Refolution; but, at the fame Time we muft have a
Care that our Efforts in that Refpe& do not force the
Balance too much, and make it rife to an unbecoming
Freedom, and an offenfive Familiarity.

FAB.

FAB. CXXXVII. I C A ʒ e *and the* Cranes.

A Flock of Geese and a Parcel of Cranes ufed often to feed together in a Corn-field. At laft,
the Owner of the Corn, with his Servants, coming
upon them of a fudden, furprifed them in the very
Fact; and the Geefe being heavy, fat, full bodied
Creatures, were moft of them Sufferers; but the
Cranes, being thin and light, eafily flew away.

The APPLICATION.

When the Enemy comes to make a Seizure, they are
fure to fuffer moft, whofe Circumftances are the richeft
and fatteft. In any Cafe of Perfecution, Money hangs
like a dead Weight about a Man; and we never feel
Gold fo heavy, as when we endeavour to make off with
it. Therefore wife and politic Minifters of State, whenever they fee a Storm begin to gather over their Heads,
always take Care to unlade themfelves of a good Part
of their Cargo; and, by this Means, feldom find but
the Blafts of Obloquy, thro' which they are to make their
Way, are lefs deaf and inexorable than the ftormy
Waves of the Ocean. Indeed, Poverty is too frequently
the

the Occasion of Men's being treated as if they were guilty of the greateſt Crimes and Reproaches : But then, theſe Sort of Criminals have this Advantage, that no one thinks fit to treat them with any Thing worſe than Contempt : Whereas, if any Pretence can be found to fall upon the Man who is rich, it is a Miracle if he eſcapes with both Life and Money. In ſhort, Riches are like the Baggage of an Army ; very uſeful, while we lie in quiet Poſſeſſion of the Camp, or are powerful enough to defy the Enemy ; but when once we are put to the Rout, if we would get off with our Lives or Liberties, we muſt quit our Baggage as ſoon as poſſible, and leave it for Plunder to our Purſuers. Nay, however ſtrongly intrenched we may think ourſelves, as long as Money is in the Caſe, it is good to look about us for fear of a Surprize : For, after all, he that does not, upon Occaſion, make himſelf Wings with his Riches to fly off with, deſerves to be puniſhed, like a Gooſe as he is, for his Heavineſs.

FAB. CXXXVIII. *The* Horſe *and the* Aſs.

THE Horſe, adorned with his great War-Saddle, and champing his foaming Bridle, came thundering along the Way, and made the Mountains echo with his loud ſhrill Neighing. He had not
gone

gone far, before he overtook an Afs, who was labouring under a heavy Burden, and moving flowly on in the fame Track with himfelf. Immediately, he called out to him, in a haughty imperious Tone, and threatened to trample him in the Dirt, if he did not break the Way for him. The poor patient Afs, not daring to difpute the Matter, quietly got out of his Way as faft as he could, and let him go by. Not long after this, the fame Horfe, in an Engagement with the Enemy, happened to be fhot in the Eye, which made him unfit for Shew, or any military Bufinefs; fo he was ftript of his fine Ornaments, and fold to a Carrier. The Afs meeting him in this forlorn Condition, thought that now it was his Time to infult; and fo, fays he, Hey-day, Friend, is it you! Well, I always believed that Pride of your's would one Day have a Fall.

The APPLICATION.

Pride is a very unaccountable Vice: Many People fall into it unawares, and are often led into it by Motives, which if they confidered Things rightly, would make them abhor the very Thoughts of it. There is no Man that thinks well of himfelf, but defires that the reft of the World fhould think fo too. Now it is the wrong Meafures we take in endeavouring after this, that expofe us to difcerning People in that Light which they call Pride, and which is fo far from giving us any Advantage in their Efteem, that it renders us defpicable and ridiculous. It is an Affectation of appearing confiderable that puts Men upon being proud and infolent; and their very being fo, makes them, infallibly, little and inconfiderable. The Man that claims and calls for Reverence and Refpect, deferves none; he that afks for Applaufe, is fure to lofe it; the certain Way to get it is to feem to fhun it; and the humble Man, according to the Maxims even of this World, is the moft likely to be exalted. He that, in his Words or Actions, pleads for Superiority, and rather chufes to do an ill Action, than condefcend to do a good one, acts like a Horfe, and is

as

-as void of Reaſon and Underſtanding. The Rich and the Powerful want nothing but the Love and Eſteem of Mankind to complete their Felicity; and theſe they are ſure to obtain by a good-humoured, kind Conde-ſcenſion; and as certain of being every body's Aver-ſion, while the leaſt Tincture of overbearing Rudeneſs is perceptible in their Words or Actions. What bru-tal Tempers muſt they be of, who can be eaſy and in-different, while they know themſelves to be univerſally hated, tho' in the Midſt of Affluence and Power? But this is not all; for if ever the Wheel of Fortune ſhould whirl them from the Top to the Bottom, inſtead of Friendſhip or Commiſeration, they will meet with no-thing but Contempt; and that with much more Juſtice than ever they themſelves exerted it towards others.

FAB. CXXXIX.
The Huſbandman *and his* Sons.

A Certain Huſbandman lying at the Point of Death, and being deſirous his Sons ſhould purſue that innocent entertaining Courſe of Agriculture, in which himſelf had been engaged all his Life, made Uſe of this Expedient to induce them to it. He call-ed them to his Bed-ſide, and ſpoke to this Effect.

All

All the Patrimony I have to bequeath to you, Sons, is my Farm and my Vineyard, of which I make you Joint-Heirs. But I charge you not to let it go out of your own Occupation; for, if I have any Treasure besides, it lies buried somewhere in the Ground, within a Foot of the Surface. This made the Sons conclude, that he talked of Money which he had hid there: So, after their Father's Death, with unwearied Diligence and Application, they carefully dug up every Inch, both of the Farm and Vineyard. From whence it came to pass, that tho' they missed of the Treasure which they expected, the Ground, by being so well stirred and loosened, produced so plentiful a Crop of all that was sowed in it, as proved a real, and that no inconsiderable Treasure.

The APPLICATION.

Labour and Industry, well applied, seldom fail of finding a Treasure; and since something towards the Conveniencies and Pleasures of Life may be thus procured, why should we lose and throw it away, by being slothful and idle? Exercise is a great Support of Health, and Health is by far the greatest single Blessing of Life; which alone will weigh sufficiently with any considerate Man, so as to keep him from being utterly destitute of Employment. But of all the Kinds of Treasure which are sure to reward the Diligence of the active Man, none is more agreeable, either in the Pursuit or Possession, than that which arises from the Culture of the Earth. What can be more satisfactory, than to have our Hopes grow and increase every Day with the Product of the Ground; to have our Minds entertained with the wonderful Oeconomy of the vegetable World; our Nerves strengthened, and our Blood purified, by a constant Return of Exercise; and a new Relish given to every Meal from the Fragrancy of the Air, and Freshness of the Soil? Add to all these, that the Treasures and Delights of Agriculture are so various, that they are not easily to be described, and are never to be excelled. They are scarce to be conceived by one that has not felt them, nor to be truly painted by any but the greatest of Poets.

FAB. CXL. *The* Horse *and the* Lion.

A LION, feeing a fine plump Nag, had a great
Mind to eat a Bit of him, but knew not which
Way to get him into his Power. At laſt he be-
thought himſelf of this Contrivance; he gave out
that he was a Phyſician; who, h¹ᵛing gained Experience by his Travels into foreign Countries, had
made himſelf capable of curing any Sort of Malady
or Diſtemper, incident to any Kind of Beaſt; hoping by this Stratagem, to get an eaſier Admittance
among Cattle, and find an Opportunity to execute
his Deſign. The Horſe, who ſmoked the Matter,
was reſolved to be even with him; and ſo humouring the Thing, as if he ſuſpected nothing, he prayed
the Lion to give him his Advice in Relation to a
Thorn he had got in his Foot, which had quite
lamed him, and gave him great Pain and Uneaſineſs. The Lion readily agreed, and deſired he might
ſee the Foot. Upon which the Horſe lifted up one
of his hind Legs, and while the Lion pretended to
be poring earneſtly upon his Hoof, gave him ſuch a
Kick in the Face as quite ſtunned him, and left
him

him fprawling upon the Ground. In the mean
Time the Horfe trotted away, neighing, and laughing merrily at the Succefs of the Trick, by which
he had defeated the Purpofe of one who intended
to have tricked him out of his Life.

The APPLICATION.

Tho' all Manner of Fraud and Tricking is mean, and
utterly beneath a Man of Senfe and Honour, yet methinks, Equity itfelf allows us to difappoint the Deceiver,
and to repel Craft by Cunning. Treachery has fomething
fo wicked, and worthy of Punifhment in its Nature, that
it deferves to meet with a Return of its own Kind; an
open Revenge would be too liberal for it, and nothing
matches it but itfelf. However therefore abominable it is,
to be the Aggreffor in this Point, yet it cannot be inconfiftent with Virtue to counterplot, and to take all Manner
of Advantages againft the Man who is undermining us.

FAB. CLXI. *The* Lion, *the* Bear, *and the* Fox.

A Lion and a Bear fell together by the Ears, over
the Carcafe of a Fawn, which they found in
the Foreft, their Title to him being to be decided by
Force of Arms. The Battle was fevere and tough

on both Sides, and they held it out, tearing and worrying one another so long, that, what with Wounds and Fatigue, they were so faint and weary, they were not able to strike another Stroke. Thus, while they lay upon the Ground, panting and lolling out their Tongues, a Fox chanced to pass by that Way, who, perceiving how the Case stood, very impudently stept in between them, seized the Booty which they had all this while been contending for, and carried it off. The two Combatants, who lay and beheld all this, without having Strength enough to stir and prevent it, were only wise enough to make this Reflection: Behold the Fruits of our Strife and Contention! that Villain, the Fox, bears away the Prize, and we ourselves have deprived each other of the Power to recover it from him.

The APPLICATION.

When People go to Law about an uncertain Title, and have spent their whole Estate in the Contest, nothing is more common than for some little pettifogging Attorney, to step in and secure it to himself. The very Name of Law seems to imply Equity and Justice, and that is the Bait which has drawn in many to their Ruin. Others are excited by their Passions, and care not if they destroy themselves, so they do but see their Enemy perish with them. But, if we lay aside Prejudice and Folly, and think calmly of the Matter, we shall find, that going to Law is not the best Way of deciding Differences about Property; it being, generally speaking, much safer to trust to the Arbitration of two or three honest sensible Neighbours, than, at a vast Expence of Money, Time and Trouble, to run through the tedious, frivolous Forms, with which, by the Artifice of greedy Lawyers, a Court of Judicature is contrived to be attended. It has been said, that if Mankind would lead moral virtuous Lives, there would be no Occasion for Divines; if they would but live temperately and soberly, that they would never want Physicians; both which Assertions, tho' true in the main, are yet expressed in too great a
Latitude.

Latitude. But one may venture to affirm, That if Men preferved a ftrict Regard to Juftice and Honefty in their Dealings with each other, and upon any Miftake or Mifapprehenfion, were always ready to refer the Matter to difinterefted Umpires, of acknowledged Judgment and Integrity, they never could have the leaft Occafion for Lawyers. When People have gone to Law, it is rarely to be found but one or both Parties was either ftupidly obftinate, or rafhly inconfiderate. For, if the Cafe fhould happen to be fo intricate, that a Man of common Senfe could not diftinguifh who had the beft Title, how eafy would it be to have the Opinion of the beft Counfel in the Land, and agree to determine it by that? If it fhould appear dubious even after that, how much better would it be to divide the Thing in Difpute, rather than go to Law, and hazard the lofing, not only of the Whole, but Cofts and Damages into the Bargain?

FAB. CXLII. *The* Fox *and the* Sick Lion.

IT was reported that the Lion was fick, and the Beafts were made to believe that they could not make their Court better, than by going to vifit him. Upon this, they generally went; but it was particularly taken Notice of, that the Fox was not one of

the

the Number. The Lion therefore difpatched one of
his Jackalls to found him about it, and afk him why
he had fo little Charity and Refpect, as never to
come near him at a Time when he lay fo danger-
oufly ill, and every Body elfe had been to fee him.
Why, replies the Fox, pray, prefent my Duty to
his Majefty, and tell him that I have the fame Refpect for him as ever, and have been coming feveral Times to kifs his royal Hand ; but I am fo ter-
ribly frightened at the Mouth of his Cave, to fee
the Print of my Fellow-Subjects Feet, all pointing
forwards, and none backwards, that I have not Refolution enough to venture in. Now the Truth of
the Matter was, that this Sicknefs of the Lion's was
only a Sham, to draw the Beafts into his Den, the
more eafily to devour them.

The APPLICATION.

A Man fhould weigh and confider the Nature of any
Propofal well, before he gives into it : for a rafh and
hafty Compliance has been the Ruin of many a one.
And it is the Quinteffence of Prudence not to be too eafy
of Belief. Indeed the Multitude think altogether in
the fame Track, and are much upon a Foot. Their
Meditations are confined in one Channel, and they follow one another very orderly in a regular Stupidity.
Can a Man of Thought and Spirit be harneffed thus,
and trudge along like a Pack-Horfe, in a deep ftinking
muddy Road, when he may frifk it over the beauteous
Lawns, or lofe himfelf agreeably in the fhady verdant
Mazes of unreftrained Contemplation ? It is impoffible.
Vulgar Notions are fo generally attended with Error,
that wherever one traces the Footfteps of the Many
tending all one Way, it is enough to make one fufpect,
with the Fox in the Fable, that there is fome Trick in
it. The Eye of Reafon is dulled and ftupified when it
is confined, and made to gaze continually upon the
fame Thing : It rather chufes to look about it, and
amufe itfelf with Variety of Objects, as they lie fcat-

M   tered

tered up and down in the unbounded Profpect. He that goes implicitly into a Thing, may be miftaken, notwithftanding the Number of thofe who keep him Company; but he that keeps out till he fees Reafon to enter, acts upon true Maxims of Policy and Prudence. In fhort, it becomes us, as we are reafonable Creatures, to behave ourfelves as fuch, and to do as few Things as poffible, of which we may have Occafion to repent.

FAB. CXLIII. *The* Mice *in* Council.

THE Mice called a general Council; and having met, after the Doors were locked, entered into a free Confultation about Ways and Means how to render their Fortunes and Eftates more fecure from the Danger of the Cat. Many Things were offered, and much was debated, *pro* and *con,* upon the Matter. At laft a young Moufe, in a fine florid Speech, concluded upon an Expedient, and that the only one, which was to put them for the future entirely out of the Power of the Enemy; and this was, that the Cat fhould wear a Bell about her

Neck,

Neck, which, upon the leaſt Motion would give the Alarm, and be a Signal for them to retire into their Holes.   This Speech was received with great Applauſe, and it was even propoſed by ſome, that the Mouſe who made it ſhould have the Thanks of the Aſſembly.   Upon which, an old grave Mouſe, who had ſat ſilent all the while, ſtood up, and in another Speech, owned that the Contrivance was admirable, and the Author of it, without Doubt, an ingenious Mouſe ; but, he ſaid, he thought it would not be ſo proper to vote him Thanks, till he ſhould farther inform them how this Bell was to be faſtened about the Cat's Neck, and what Mouſe would undertake to do it.

The APPLICATION.

Many Things appear feaſible in Speculation, which are afterwards found to be impracticable.   And ſince the Execution of any Thing is that which is to complete and finiſh its very Exiſtence, what raw Counſellors are thoſe who adviſe, what precipitate Politicians thoſe who proceed, to the Management of Things in their Nature incapable of anſwering their own Expectations, or their Promiſes to others.   At the ſame Time, the Fable teaches us, not to expoſe ourſelves in any of our little politic Coffee-Houſe Committees, by determining what ſhould be done upon every Occurrence of Mal-Adminiſtration, when we have neither Commiſſion nor Power to execute it.   He that, upon ſuch Occaſions, adjudges, as a Preſervative for the State, that this or that ſhould be applied to the Neck of thoſe who have been Enemies to it, will appear full as ridiculous as the Mouſe in the Fable, when the Queſtion is aſked, Who ſhall put it there ?   In Reality, we do but expoſe ourſelves to the Hatred of ſome, and the Contempt of others, when we inadvertently utter our impracticable Speculations, in reſpect of the Public, either in private Company, or authorized Aſſemblies.

FAB.

FAB. CXLIV.
The Lion, *the* Ass, *and the* Fox.

THE Lion, the Ass, and the Fox, went a hunting together in the Forest; and it was agreed,
that whatever was taken should be divided amongst
them. They happened to have very good Sport,
and caught a large fat Stag, which the Lion ordered the Ass to divide. The Ass, according to the
best of his Capacity, did so, and made three pretty
equal Shares. But such levelling Doings not suit-
ing at all with the craving Temper of the greedy
Lion, without farther Delay he flew upon the Ass,
and tore him in Pieces; and then bid the Fox divide it into two Parts. *Reynard*, who seldom wanted
a Prompter, however, had his Cue given him sufficiently upon this Occasion; and so, nibbling off
one little Bit for himself, he laid forth all the rest
for the Lion's Portion. The Royal Brute was so
delighted at this dutiful and handsome Proof of his
Respect, that he could not forbear expressing the Satisfaction

tisfaction it gave him ; and asked him withal, where he cou'd possibly have learnt so proper and so courtly a Behaviour? Why, replies *Reynard*, to tell your Majesty the Truth, I was taught it by the Ass that lies dead there.

The APPLICATION.

We may learn a great deal of useful Experience from the Examples of other People, if we will but take the Pains to observe them.   And, besides the Profit of the Instructions, there is no small Pleasure in being taught any proper Science, at the Expence of somebody else. To this Purpose, the History of former Times, as well as the Transactions of the present, are very well adapted ; and so copious, as to be able to furnish us with Precedents upon almost every Occasion. The Rock upon which another has split, is a Kind of Light-House or Beacon, to warn us from the like Calamity; and by taking such an Advantage, how easily may we steer a safe Course! He that, in any Negociation with his Betters, does not well and wisely consider how to behave himself, so as not to give Offence, may very likely come off as the Ass did: But a cool thinking Man, tho' he should despair of ever making Friends of People in Power, will be cautious and prudent enough to do nothing which may provoke them to be his Enemies.

FAB.

FAB. CXLV. *The* Old Lion.

A LION, worn out with old Age, lay fetching
his laſt Gaſp, and agonizing in the convulſive
Struggles of Death. Upon which Occaſion, ſeveral of the Beaſts, who had formerly been Sufferers
by him, came and revenged themſelves upon him.
The Boar, with his mighty Tuſks, drove at him in
a Stroke that glanced like Lightning. And the
Bull gored him with his violent Horns. Which,
when the Aſs ſaw they might do without any Danger, he too came up, and threw his Heels into the
Lion's Face. Upon which, the poor old expiring
Tyrant uttered theſe Words with his laſt dying
Groan: Alas! how grievous is it to ſuffer Inſults,
even from the Brave and the Valiant! but to be ſpurned
by ſo baſe a Creature as this is, who is the Diſgrace
of Nature, is worſe than dying ten thouſand Deaths.

The APPLICATION.

He that would be reverenced and reſpected by the reſt
of Mankind, muſt lay in a Foundation for it of ſome
Kind or other; for People cannot be perſuaded to pay
Deference

Deference and Efteem for nothing. So that though we have lived in good Repute in the World, if ever we fhould happen to out-live our Stock, we muft not be furprized to find ourfelves flighted and affronted, even by the vileft Scum of the People. If therefore we would raife to ourfelves a Dignity that will continue not only to the End of our Lives, but extend itfelf far down among the Ages of Pofterity, we fhould take Care to eftablifh it upon a Foundation of Virtue and Good-nature: This will not only preferve us from the Infults of Enemies, but, upon Occafion, furround us with a trufty Guard of faithful and fincere Friends.

FAB. CXLVI. *The* Old Man *and his* Sons.

AN old Man had many Sons, who were often falling out with one another. When the Father had exerted his Authority, and ufed other Means in order to reconcile them, and all to no Purpofe, at laft he had Recourfe to this Expedient; he ordered his Sons to be called before him, and a fhort Bundle of Sticks to be brought; and then commanded them, one by one, to try if, with all their Might and Strength, they could any of them break it. They

M 4   all

all tried, but to no Purpose; for the Sticks being
closely and compactly bound up together, it was
impossible for the Force of Man to do it. After
this the Father ordered the Bundle to be untied,
and gave a single Stick to each of his Sons, at the
same Time bidding him try to break it: Which,
when each did with all imaginable Ease, the Father
addressed himself to them to this Effect. O my Sons,
behold the Power of Unity! For if you, in like
Manner, would but keep yourselves strictly conjoined
in the Bonds of Friendship, it would not be in the
Power of any Mortal to hurt you; but, when once
the Ties of brotherly Affection are dissolved, how
soon do you fall to Pieces, and are liable to be violated by every injurious Hand that assaults you!

The APPLICATION.

Nothing is more necessary towards completing and
continuing the Well-being of Mankind, than their entering into, and preserving Friendships and Alliances.
The Safety of a Government depends chiefly upon this;
and therefore it is weakened and exposed to its Enemies, in Proportion as it is divided by Parties. *A Kingdom divided against itself is brought to Desolation.* And
the same holds good among all Societies and Corporations of Men, from the Constitution of the Nation,
down to every little Parochial Vestry. But the Necessity of Friendship extends itself to all Sorts of Relations
in Life; as it conduces mightily to the Advantage of
particular Clans and Families. Those of the same Blood
and Lineage have a natural Disposition to unite together, which they ought, by all Means, to cultivate and
improve. It must be a great Comfort to People, when
they fall under any Calamity, to know that there are
many others sympathise with them; a great Load of
Grief is mightily lessened, when it is parcelled out into
many Shares. And then Joy, of all our Passions, loves
to be communicative, and generally increases, in Proportion to the Number of those who partake of it with
us. We defy the Threats and Malice of an Enemy,
when

when we are affured that he cannot attack us fingle, but muft encounter a Bundle of Allies at the fame Time. But they that behave themfelves fo as to have few or no Friends in the World, live in a perpetual Fear and Jealoufy of Mankind, becaufe they are fenfible of their own Weaknefs, and know themfelves liable to be crufhed, or broken to Pieces, by the firft Aggreffor.

FAB. CXLVII.
The Old Woman *and her* Maids.

A Certain old Woman had feveral Maids, whom fhe ufed to call up to their Work, every Morning, at the Crowing of the Cock. The Wenches, who found it grievous to have their fweet Sleep difturbed fo early, combined together, and killed the Cock, thinking that, when the Alarm was gone, they might enjoy themfelves in their warm Beds a little longer. The old Woman, grieved for the Lofs of her Cock, and having, by fome Means or other, difcovered the whole Plot, was refolved to be even with them; for, from that Time, fhe obliged them to rife conftantly at Midnight.

The

The APPLICATION.

It can never be expected that Things should be, in all Respects, agreeable to our Wishes; and if they are not very bad indeed, we ought in many Cases to be contented with them; left when, thro' Impatience, we precipitately quit our present Condition of Life, we may to our Sorrow find, with the old Saying, that seldom comes a better. Before we attempt any Alteration of Moment, we should be certain what State it will produce; for, when Things are already bad, to make them worse by trying Experiments, is an Argument of great Weakness and Folly, and is sure to be attended with a too late Repentance. Grievances, if really such, ought by all Means to be redressed, provided we can be assured of doing it with Success: But we had better, at any Time, bear with some Inconvenience, than make our Condition worse, by attempting to mend it.

F A B. CXLVIII.
The Falconer *and the* Partridge.

A Falconer having taken a Partridge in his Nets, the Bird begged hard for a Reprieve, and promised the Man, if he would let him go, to decoy

other

other Partridges into his Net. No, replies the Falconer, I was before determined not to spare you, but now you have condemned yourself by your own Words: For he who is such a Scoundrel, as to offer to betray his Friends, to save himself, deserves, if possible, worse than Death.

The APPLICATION.

However it may be convenient for us to like the Treason, yet we must be very destitute of Honour, not to hate and abominate the Traitor. And accordingly, History furnishes us with many Instances of Kings and great Men, who have punished the Actors of Treachery with Death, though the Part they acted had been so conducive to their Interests, as to give them a Victory, or perhaps the quiet Possession of a Throne. Nor can Princes pursue a more just Maxim than this; for a Traitor is a Villain of no Principles, that sticks at nothing to promote his own selfish Ends; he that betrays one Cause for a great Sum of Money, will betray another upon the same Account; and therefore it must be very impolitic in a State to suffer such Wretches to live in it. Since then this Maxim is so good, and so likely at all Times to be practised, what stupid Rogues must they be, who undertake such precarious dirty Work! If they miscarry, it generally proves fatal to them from one Side or other; if they succeed, perhaps they may have the promised Reward, but are sure to be detested, if suffered to live, by the very Person that employs them.

FAB.

FAB. CXLIX.
The Porcupine and the Snakes.

A Porcupine, wanting to shelter himself, desired a Nest of Snakes to give him Admittance into their Cave. They were prevailed upon, and let him in accordingly; but were so annoyed with his sharp prickly Quills, that they soon repented of their easy Compliance, and intreated the Porcupine to withdraw, and leave them their Hole to themselves. No, says he, let them quit the Place that don't like it; for my Part, I am well enough satisfied as I am.

The APPLICATION.

Some People are of so brutish, inhospitable Tempers, that there is no living with them, without greatly incommoding ourselves. Therefore, before we enter into any Degree of Friendship, Alliance, or Partnership, with any Person whatever, we should thoroughly consider his Nature and Qualities, his Circumstances and his Humour. There ought to be something in each of

4   these

thefe Refpects to tally and correfpond with our own
Meafures, to fuit our Genius, and adapt itfelf to the
Size and Proportion of our Defires; otherwife our Af-
fociations, of whatever Kind, may prove the greateft
Plagues of our Life. Young Men are very apt to run
into this Error; and being warm in all their Paffions,
throw open their Arms at once, and admit into the
greateft Intimacy Perfons whom they know little of,
but by falfe and uncertain Lights. Thus they fometimes receive a Viper into their Bofom, inftead of a
Friend, and take a Porcupine for a Confort, with whom
they are obliged to cohabit, though fhe may prove a
Thorn in their Sides as long as they live. A true Friend
is one of the greateft Bleffings in Life; therefore, to be
miftaken or difappointed of fuch Enjoyment, when we
hope to be in full Poffeffion of it, muft be as great a
Mortification. So that we cannot be too nice and fcru-
pulous in our Choice of thofe, who are to be our Companions for Life; for they muft have but a poor fhallow
Notion of Friendfhip, who intend to take it, like a
Leafe, for a Term of Years only. In a Word, the Doctrine which this Fable fpeaks, is to prepare us againft
being injured or deceived by a rafh Combination of any
Sort. The Manners of the Man we defire for a Friend,
of the Woman we like for a Wife, of the Perfon with
whom we would jointly manage and concert Meafures
for the Advancement of our temporal Intereft, fhould
be narrowly and cautioufly infpected, before we embark with them in the fame Veffel, left we fhould alter
our Mind when it is too late, and think of regaining
the Shore, after we have launched out of our Depth.

FAB.

FAB. CL. *The* Peacock *and the* Magpye.

THE Birds met together upon a Time, to chuse a King. And the Peacock ſtanding Candidate, diſplayed his gaudy Plumes, and catched the Eyes of the ſilly Multitude with the Richneſs of his Feathers. The Majority declared for him, and clapped their Wings with great Applauſe. But, juſt as they were going to proclaim him, the Magpye ſtept forth in the Midſt of the Aſſembly, and addreſſed himſelf thus to the new King: May it pleaſe your Majeſty Elect, to permit one of your unworthy Subjects to repreſent to you his Suſpicions and Apprehenſions, in the Face of this whole Congregation: We have choſen you for our King, we have put our Lives and Fortunes into your Hands, and our whole Hope and Dependance is upon you: If therefore the Eagle, or the Vulture, or the Kite, ſhould at any Time make a Deſcent upon us, as it is highly probable they will, may your Majeſty be ſo gracious as to diſpel our Fears, and clear our

Doubts

Doubts about that Matter, by letting us know how you intend to defend us againſt them? This pithy unanſwerable Queſtion drew the whole Audience into ſo juſt a Reflection, that they ſoon reſolved to proceed to a new Choice. But, from that Time, the Peacock has been looked upon as a vain inſignificant Pretender, and the Magpye eſteemed as eminent a Speaker as any among the whole Community of Birds.

The APPLICATION.

Form and Outſide, in the Choice of a Ruler, ſhould not be ſo much regarded, as the Qualities and Endowments of the Mind. In chuſing Heads of Corporations, from the King of the Land, down to the Maſter of a Company, upon every new Election it ſhould be inquired into, which of the Candidates is moſt capable of advancing the Good and Welfare of the Community; and upon him the Choice ſhould fall. But the Eyes of the Multitude are ſo dazzled with Pomp and Shew, Noiſe and Ceremony, that they cannot ſee Things really as they are: And from hence it comes to paſs, that ſo many Abſurdities are committed and maintained in the World. People ſhould examine and weigh the real Weight and Merit of the Perſon, and not be impoſed upon by falſe Colours, and Pretences of I know not what.

FAB.

FAB. CLI. *The* Parrot *and his* Cage.

A Parrot, which belonged to a Perſon of Quality, was fed every Day with Plenty of choice Dainties, and kept in a ſtately Cage, which was ſet abroad, upon a Marble Table in the Garden, that he might enjoy the Light of the Sky, and the Freſhneſs of the Air to the beſt Advantage. His Maſter, and all the Family, when they talked to him, uſed the moſt tender fond Expreſſions, and the Diſorder of his Feathers was ſmoothed with kindly Touches, by the fair Hand of his Lady. Yet notwithſtanding this happy Situation, he was un-eaſy, and envied the Condition of thoſe Birds who liv'd free in the Wildernſs, and hopped up and down, unconfined, from Bough to Bough. He earneſtly longed to lead the ſame Life, and ſecretly pined with Grief, becauſe his Wiſhes were denied him. After ſome Time, however, it happened that the Door of his Cage was left unfaſtened, and the long wiſhed for Oppohtunity was given him of making an Elopement. Accordingly, out he flew,
and

and conveyed himfelf among the Shades of a neighbouring Wood, where he thought to fpend the Remainder of his Days in Content. But alas! poor
Poll was miftaken; a thoufand Inconveniencies,
which he never dreamt of, attended this Elopement
of his, and he is now really that miferable Creature,
which, before, his Imagination only made him. He
is buffeted by the Savage Inhabitants of the Grove;
and his Imitation of a Human Voice, which formerly rendered him fo agreeable, does but the more
expofe him to the fierce Refentment of the feathered
Nation. The delicate Food with which he ufed to
be fed, is no more; he is unfkilled in the Ways of
providing for himfelf, and even ready to die with
Hunger. A Storm of Rain, Thunder, and Lightning, fills all the Air, and he has no Place to fcreen
or protect him; his Feathers are wetted with the
heavy Shower, and blafted with the Flafhes of
Lightning. His tender Nature, fuited to a milder
Climate, could not ftand the fevere Shock; he even
died under it. But, juft before he breathed his laft,
he is faid to have made this Reflection: Ah, poor
Poll! were you but in your Cage again, you would
never wander more.

The APPLICATION.

This Fable may be a proper Leffon to thofe who are
poffeffed with a Spirit of Rambling, and trying Experiments; who are fo infatuated with thefe airy Notions, that though they have a warm Houfe over their
Heads, and a good Table to eat at, kind indulgent Parents, or fond Hufbands, yet they cannot be contented,
but muft fally forth into the wide World, and pafs, as
it were, into a new and untried Being. People may
have felt imaginary Inconveniencies at Home; but as
they have been ufed to live in a Dependance upon
others, let them but go abroad, and try to fhift for
themfelves, and they will, in all Probability, foon feel
real

real Miferies. No Ship puts to Sea without an experienced Pilot; nor do Armies take the Field, but under a General of Conduct and Courage; yet fome Women and Children are fo perverfe and wrongheaded,
that they will leave a quiet fafe Port, and launch out
into a World of Troubles and Dangers, without the
leaft Share of Difcretion to fteer their Courfe by. How
can they hope to efcape fplitting upon every Rock, who
are thus rafh and adventurous! A fevere Repentance,
after fuch Elopement, is generally as certain, as it is
ufelefs and unregarded.

FAB. CLII. *The* Fowler *and the* Ringdove.

A Fowler took his Gun, and went into the Woods
a fhooting. He fpied a Ringdove among the
Branches of an Oak, and intended to kill it. He
clapped the Piece to his Shoulder, and took his
Aim accordingly. But, juft as he was going to
pull the Trigger, an Adder, which he had trod
upon under the Grafs, ftung him fo painfully in
the Leg, that he was forced to quit his Defign, and
threw his Gun down in a Paffion. The Poifon
immediately

immediately infected his Blood, and his whole Body
began to mortify; which, when he perceived, he
could not help owning it to be juſt. Fate, ſays he,
has brought Deſtruction upon me, while I was
contriving the Death of another.

The APPLICATION.

This is another Leſſon againſt Injuſtice; a Topic in
which our juſt Author abounds. And, if we conſider
the Matter fairly, we muſt allow it to be as reaſonable
that ſome one ſhould do Violence to us, as we ſhould
commit it upon another: When we are impartial in
our Reflections, thus we muſt always think. The unjuſt Man, with a hardened unfeeling Heart, can do a
thouſand bitter Things to others: But if a ſingle Calamity touches himſelf, Oh how tender he is! How in-
ſupportable is the Uneaſineſs it occaſions! Why ſhould
we think others born to hard Treatment, more than
ourſelves? Or imagine it can be reaſonable to do to another, what we ourſelves ſhould be unwilling to ſuffer?
In our Behaviour to all Mankind, we need only aſk
ourſelves theſe plain Queſtions, and our Conſciences
will tell us how to act. Conſcience, like a good valuable Domeſtic, plays the Remembrancer to us upon all
Occaſions, and gives us a gentle Twitch, when we are
going to do a wrong Thing. It does not, like the Adder in the Fable, bite us to Death, but only gives us
kind Cautions. However, if we neglect theſe juſt and
frequent Warnings, and continue in a Courſe of Wickedneſs and Injuſtice, do not let us be ſurprized if Providence thinks fit, at laſt, to give us a home Sting, and
to exerciſe a little Retaliation upon us.

F A B.

FAB. CLIII. *The* Sow *and the* Wolf.

A SOW had just farrowed, and lay in the Stye,
with her whole Litter of Pigs about her. A
Wolf, who longed for one of them, but knew not
how to come at it, endeavoured to infinuate himfelf
into the Sow's good Opinion. And accordingly,
coming up to her, How does the good Woman in
the Straw do? fays he. Can I be of any Service
to you, Mrs. Sow, in relation to your little Family
here? If you have a Mind to go abroad, and air
yourfelf a little, or fo, you may depend upon it I
will take as much Care of your Pigs, as you could
do yourfelf. Your humble Servant, fays the Sow,
I thoroughly underftand your Meaning; and, to
let you know I do, I muft be fo free as to tell you,
I had rather have your Room than your Company;
and therefore, if you would act like a Wolf of Honour, and oblige me, I beg I may never fee your
Face again.

The APPLICATION.

The being officiously good-natured and civil, is something so uncommon in the World, that one cannot hear a Man make Profession of it, without being surprised, or, at least, suspecting the Disinterestedness of his Intentions. Especially, when one who is a Stranger to us, or, though known, is ill esteemed by us, will be making Offers of Services, we have great Reason to look to ourselves, and exert a Shyness and Coldness towards him. We should resolve not to receive even Favours from bad Kind of People; for should it happen that some immediate Mischief was not couched in them, yet it is dangerous to have Obligations to such, or to give them an Opportunity of making a Communication with us.

F A B. CLIV.
The Husbandman *and the* Stork.

THE Husbandman pitched a Net in his Fields to take the Cranes and Geese which came to feed upon the new-sown Corn. Accordingly, he took several,

several, both Cranes and Geese; and among them, a Stork, who pleaded hard for his Life, and, among other Apologies which he made, alledged, That he was neither Goose nor Crane, but a poor harmless Stork, who performed his Duty to his Parents to all Intents and Purposes, feeding them when they were old, and, as Occasion required, carrying them from Place to Place upon his Back. All this may be true, replies the Husbandman; but, as I have taken you in bad Company, and in the same Crime, you must expect to suffer the same Punishment.

The APPLICATION.

If bad Company had nothing else to make us shun and avoid it, this, methinks, might be sufficient, that it infects and taints a Man's Reputation to as great a Degree as if he were thoroughly versed in the Wickedness of the whole Gang. What is it to me, if the Thief, who robs me of my Money, gives Part of it to build a Church? Is he ever the less a Thief? Shall a Woman's going to Prayers twice a Day, save her Reputation, if she is known to be a malicious lying Gossip? No, such Mixtures of Religion and Sin make the Offence but the more flagrant, as they convince us, that it was not committed out of Ignorance. Indeed, there is no living without being guilty of some Faults, more or less; which the World ought to be good-natured enough to overlook, in Consideration of the general Frailty of Mankind, when they are not too gross and too abundant. But, when we are so abandoned to Stupidity, and a Neglect of our Reputation, as to keep bad Company, however little we may be criminal in Reality, we must expect the same Censure and Punishment as is due to the most notorious of our Companions.

FAB.

FAB. CLV. *The* Shepherd's Boy.

A Certain Shepherd's Boy kept his Sheep upon a Common, and, in Sport and Wantonnefs, would often cry out, The Wolf! the Wolf! By this Means he feveral Times drew the Hufbandmen in an adjoining Field from their Work; who, finding themfelves deluded, refolved, for the future, to take no Notice of his Alarm. Soon after, the Wolf came indeed. The Boy cried out in Earneft. But no Heed being given to his Cries, the Sheep are devoured by the Wolf.

The APPLICATION.

He that is detected for being a notorious Liar, befides the Ignominy and Reproach of the Thing, incurs this Mifchief, That he will fcarce be able to get any one to believe him again, as long as he lives. However true our Complaint may be, or how much foever it may be for our Intereft to have it believed, yet, if we have been frequently caught tripping before, we fhall hardly be able to gain Credit to what we relate afterwards. 'Tho' Mankind are generally ftupid enough to be often impofed

pofed upon, yet few are fo fenfelefs as to believe a notorious Liar, or to truft a Cheat upon Record. Thefe
little Shams, when found out, are fufficiently prejudicial to the Intereft of every private Perfon who practifes
them. But, when we are alarmed with imaginary Dangers in Refpect of the Public, till the Cry grows quite
ftale and threadbare, how can it be expected we fhould
know when to guard ourfelves againft real ones?

FAB. CLVI. *The* Serpent *and the* Man.

A Child was playing in a Meadow, and by Chance
trod upon a Serpent. The Serpent in the Fury
of his Paffion, turned up, and bit the Child with
his poifonous Teeth, fo that he died immediately.
The Father of the Child, infpired with Grief and
Revenge, took a Weapon in his Hand, and purfuing
the Serpent, before he could get into his Hole,
ftruck at him, and lopped off a Piece of his Tail.
The next Day, hoping by this Stratagem to finifh
his Revenge, he brought to the Serpent's Hole
Honey, Meal, and Salt, and defired him to come
forth, protefting, that he only fought a Reconciliation

tion on both Sides. However, he was not able to decoy the Serpent forth, who only hiffed from within to this Purpofe: In vain you attempt a Reconciliation; for, as long as the Memory of the dead Child, and the mangled Tail fubfifts, it will be impoffible for you and I to have any Charity for each other.

The APPLICATION.

The Man who has injured you will never forgive you, is a *Spanifh* Proverb, and, after their dry Way, a very good one. It feems odd, at firft Sight, becaufe one would think the Backwardnefs to forgive fhould be on the Side of him who has received the Injury; but the Truth of the Maxim lies, with much more Certainty, on the other Side. The Confcioufnefs of having provoked the Refentment of another, will dwell fo continually upon the Mind of the Aggreffor, that he cannot reft till he has finifhed his Work, and put it as much as poffible out of his Enemy's Power to make any Return upon him. Therefore, as the Serpent wifely obferves, it is in vain for two People, who have palpably injured each other, ever to expect to live well together for the future. Morality bids us forgive our Enemies, and the Voice of Reafon confirms the fame: But neither Reafon nor Morality bids us enter into a Friendfhip with, or repofe a Confidence in, thofe who have injured us. We may refolve not to return ill Ufage; but ought never to be forgiven, if, when we can prevent it, we put ourfelves into our Enemy's Hands.

F A B.

FAB. CLVII.
The Swallow *and other* Birds.

A Farmer was fowing his Field with Flax. The
Swallow obferved it; and defired the other
Birds to affift her in picking the Seed up, and de-
ftroying it; telling them, that Flax was that pernicious Material, of which the Thread was compofed which made the Fowler's Nets, and by that
Means contributed to the Ruin of fo many innocent Birds. But the poor Swallow, not having the
good Fortune to be regarded, the Flax fprung up,
and appeared above the Ground. She then put
them in Mind once more of their impending Danger, and wifhed them to pluck it up in the Bud,
before it went any farther. They ftill neglected her
Warnings; and the Flax grew up into the high
Stalk. She yet again defired them to attack it, for
that it was not yet too late. But all that fhe could
get was, to be ridiculed and defpifed for a filly pretending

tending Prophet. The Swallow finding all her Remonstrances availed nothing, was resolved to leave the Society of such unthinking, careless Creatures, before it was too late. So quitting the Woods, she repaired to the Houses; and forsaking the Conversation of the Birds, has ever since made her Abode among the Dwellings of Men.

The APPLICATION.

As Men, we should always exercise so much Humanity, as to endeavour the Welfare of Mankind, particularly of our Acquaintance and Relations; and, if by nothing farther, at least by our good Advice. When we have done this, and, if Occasion required, continued to repeat it a second or third Time, we shall have acquitted ourselves sufficiently from any Imputation upon their Miscarriage; and having nothing more to do, but to separate ourselves from them, that we may not be involved in their Ruin, or be supposed to partake of their Error. This is an Excommunication which Reason allows. For, as it would be cruel on the one Side, to prosecute and hurt People for being mistaken; so, on the other, it would be indiscreet and over-complaisant, to keep them Company through all their wrong Notions, and act contrary to our Opinion, out of pure Civility.

FAB.

FAB. CLVIII.
The Trumpeter *taken* Prisoner.

A Trumpeter, being taken Prisoner in a Battle, begged hard for Quarter, declaring his Innocence, and protesting, that he neither had, nor could kill any Man, bearing no Arms but only his Trumpet, which he was obliged to sound at the Word of Command. For that Reason, replied his Enemies, we are determined not to spare you; for though you yourself never fight, yet, with that wicked Instrument of yours, you blow up Animosity between other People, and so become the Occasion of much Bloodshed.

The APPLICATION.

A Man may be guilty of Murder, who has never handled a Sword, or pulled a Trigger, or lifted up his Arm with any mischievous Weapon. There is a little Incendiary called the Tongue, which is more venomous than a poisoned Arrow, and more killing than a two-edged Sword. The Moral of the Fable therefore is this, that if in any civil Insurrection, the Persons taken

in

in Arms againſt the Government deſerve to die, much
more do they, whoſe deviliſh Tongues gave Birth to
the Sedition, and excited the Tumult. When wicked
Prieſts, inſtead of preaching Peace and Charity, employ
that Engine of Scandal, their Tongue, to foment Rebellions, whether they ſucceed in their Deſigns, or no,
they ought to be ſeverely puniſhed; for they have done
what in them lay, to ſet Folks together by the Ears;
they have blown the Trumpet, and ſounded the Alarm;
and if thouſands are not deſtroyed by the Sword, it is
none of their Fault.

FAB. CLIX. *The* Hare *and the* Tortoiſe.

A Hare inſulted a Tortoiſe upon Account of his
Slowneſs, and vainly boaſted of her own great
Speed in Running. Let us make a Match, replied
the Tortoiſe; I'll run with you five Miles for five
Pounds, and the Fox yonder ſhall be the Umpire
of the Race. The Hare agreed; and away they
both ſtarted together. But the Hare, by Reaſon of
her exceeding Swiftneſs, outran the Tortoiſe to ſuch
a Degree, that ſhe made a Jeſt of the Matter; and,
finding herſelf a little tired, ſquatted in a Tuft of

Fern

Fern that grew by the Way, and took a Nap; thinking, that if the Tortoise went by, she could at any Time fetch him up, with all the Ease imaginable. In the mean while the Tortoise came jogging on, with a slow, but continued Motion; and the Hare, out of a too great Security and Confidence of Victory, oversleeping herself, the Tortoise arrived at the End of the Race first.

The APPLICATION.

Industry and Application to Business makes Amends for the Want of a quick and ready Wit. Hence it is, that the Victory is not always to the Strong, nor the Race to the Swift. Men of fine Parts are apt to despise the Drudgery of Business; but, by affecting to shew the Superority of their Genius, upon many Occasions, they run into too great an Extreme the other Way; and the Administration of their Affairs is ruined through Idleness and Neglect. What Advantage has a Man from the Fertility of his Invention, and the Vivacity of his Imagination, unless his Resolutions are executed with a suitable and uninterrupted Rapidity? In short, your Men of Wit and Fire, as they are called, are oftentimes Sots, Slovens, and lazy Fellows: They are generally proud and conceited to the last Degree; and in the main, not the fittest Persons for either Conversation or Business. Such is their Vanity, they think the Sprightliness of their Humour inconsistent with a plain sober Way of Thinking and Speaking, and able to atone for all the little Neglects of their Business and Persons. But the World will not be thus imposed upon; the Man who would gain the Esteem of others, and make his own Fortune, must be one that carries his Point effectually, and finishes his Course without swerving or loitering. Men of dull Parts, and a slow Apprehension, assisted by a continued Diligence, are more likely to attain this, than your brisk Retailers of Wit, with their affected Spleen and Indolence. And if Business be but well done, no Matter whether it be done by the Sallies of a refined Wit, or the considering Head of a plain plodding Man.

FAB.

FAB. CLX. *The* Wolf *in* Sheep's Clothing.

A Wolf, clothing himself in the Skin of a Sheep, and getting in among the Flock, by this Means took the Opportunity to devour many of them. At last the Shepherd discovered him, and cunningly fastening a Rope about his Neck, tied him up to a Tree which stood hard by. Some other Shepherds happening to pass that Way, and observing what he was about, drew near, and expressed their Admiration at it. What, says one of them, Brother, do you make hanging of Sheep? No, replies the other, but I make hanging of a Wolf whenever I catch him, tho' in the Habit and Garb of a Sheep. Then he shewed them their Mistake, and they applauded the Justice of the Execution.

The APPLICATION.

'This Fable shews us, that no Regard is to be had to the mere Habit or Outside of any Person, but to undisguised Worth and intrinsic Virtue. When we place our Esteem upon the external Garb, before we inform

ourselves

ourselves of the Qualities which it covers, we may often miftake Evil for Good, and inftead of a Sheep, take a Wolf into our Protection. Therefore, however innocent or fanctified any one may appear, as to the Vefture wherewith he is clothed, we may act rafhly, becaufe we may be impofed upon, if from thence we take it for granted, that he is inwardly as good and righteous as his outward Robe would perfuade us he is. Men of Judgment and Penetration do not ufe to give an implicit Credit to a particular Habit, or a peculiar Colour, but love to make a more exact Scrutiny; for he that will not come up to the Character of an honeft, good kind of Man, when ftripped of his Sheep's Clothing, is but the more deteftable for his intended Impofture; as the Wolf was but the more obnoxious to the Shepherd's Refentment, by wearing a Habit fo little fuiting with his Manners.

FAB. CLXI. *The* Wolves *and the* Sheep.

THE Wolves and the Sheep had been a long Time in a State of War together. At laft a Ceffation of Arms was propofed, in order to a Treaty
of

of Peace, and Hoftages were to be delivered on both Sides for Security. The Wolves propofed that the Sheep fhould give up their Dogs, on the one Side; and that they would deliver up their young ones, on the other. This Propofal was agreed to; but no fooner executed, than the young Wolves began to howl for want of their Dams. The old ones took this Opportunity to cry out, The Treaty was broke; and fo falling upon the Sheep, who were deftitute of their faithful Guardians, the Dogs, they worried and devoured them without Controul.

The APPLICATION.

In all our Tranfactions with Mankind, even in the moft private and low Life, we fhould have a fpecial Regard how, and with whom we truft ourfelves. Men, in this Refpect, ought to look upon each other as Wolves, and to keep themfelves under a fecure Guard, and in a continual Pofture of Defence. Particularly upon any Treaties of Importance, the Securities on both Sides fhould be ftrictly confidered; and each fhould act with fo cautious a View to their own Intereft, as never to pledge or part with that which is the very Effence and Bafis of their Safety and Well-being. And if this be a juft and reafonable Rule for Men to govern themfelves by, in their own private Affairs, how much more fitting and neceffary is it in any Conjuncture wherein the Public is concerned: If the Enemy fhould demand our whole Army for an Hoftage, the Danger in our complying with it would be fo grofs and apparent, that we could not help obferving it; but perhaps a Country may equally expofe itfelf by parting with a particular Town or General, as its whole Army; its Safety, not feldom, depending as much upon one of the former, as upon the latter. In fhort, Hoftages and Securities may be fomething very dear to us, but ought never to be given up, if our Welfare and Prefervation have any Dependance upon them.

FAB. CXLII. *The* Young Man *and his* Cat.

A Certain young Man uſed to play with a Cat; of which he grew ſo fond, that at laſt he fell in Love with it, and to ſuch a Degree, that he could reſt neither Night nor Day for the Exceſs of his Paſſion. At laſt he prayed to *Venus*, the Goddeſs of Beauty, to pity him, and relieve his Pain. The good-natured Goddeſs was propitious, and heard his Prayers; before he roſe up from kneeling, the Cat, which he held in his Arms, was transformed into a beautiful Girl. The Youth was tranſported with Joy, and married her that very Day. At Night they went to Bed, and as the new Bride lay encircled in the Embraces of her amorous Huſband, ſhe unfortunately heard a Mouſe behind the Hangings, and ſprung from his Arms to purſue it. *Venus*, offended to ſee her ſacred Rites profaned by ſuch an indecent Behaviour; and perceiving that her new Convert, tho' a Woman in outward Appearance, was a Cat in her Heart, ſhe made her return to her old Form again, that her Manners and Perſon might be agreeable to each other. *The*

The APPLICATION.

People, as to their Manners and Behaviour, take a ftrong Bias from Cuftom and Education, but a much ftronger from Nature. Her Laws are fo ftrong, that it is in vain for us to go to oppofe them; we may refine and improve, but can never totally alter her Works.

Upon this Account it is, that we oftentimes fee filly, aukward Blockheads, difplaying their Idiotifm and Folly through all their Enfigns of Dignity; for fome Natures are fo coarfe and ruftic, that all the Embroidery of a Court cannot conceal them. Doubtlefs fuch People were intended by Nature for nothing above driving Hogs to a Fair, and laughing at the Jokes of a Country Merry-Andrew. Fortune has found them worthy of her Favours, and given them a Lift out of the Mire: But yet they do not fail to give frequent Indications of their true Compofition, by a thoufand little dirty Actions. A fine Equipage, and a great Eftate, may raife a Man to an exalted Station, and procure a Refpect to his outward Perfon; notwithftanding which, it may fo happen, that every Time he fpeaks and acts, he cannot help playing the Fool for the Blood of him.

FAB.

FAB. CLXIII. *The Afs eating Thiftles.*

AN Afs was loaded with good Provifions of feveral Sorts, which, in Time of Harveft, he was
carrying into the Field for his Mafter and the
Reapers to dine upon. By the Way, he met with a
fine large Thiftle, and, being very hungry, began
to mumble it; which, while he was doing, he entered into this Reflection: How many greedy Epicures
would think themfelves happy, amidft fuch a Variety
of delicate Viands as I now carry! But to me, this
bitter prickly Thiftle is more favory and relifhing,
than the moft exquifite and fumptuous Banquet.

The APPLICATION.

Happinefs and Mifery, and oftentimes Pleafure and
Pain, exift merely in our Opinion, and are no more to
be accounted for, than the Difference of Taftes. *That
which is one Man's Meat, is another Man's Poifon,* is a
Propofition that ought to be allowed in all Particulars,
where the Opinion is concerned, as well as in Eating
and Drinking. Our Senfes muft inform us whether a
Thing pleafes or difpleafes, before we can declare our

I   Judgment

Judgment of it; and that is to any Man Good or Evil, which his own Underſtanding ſuggeſts to him to be ſo; and not that which is agreeable to another's Fancy. And yet as reaſonable and as neceſſary as it is to grant this, how apt are we to wonder at People, for not liking This or That, or how can they think ſo and ſo! This childiſh Humour, of wondering at the different Taſtes and Opinions of others, occaſions much Uneaſineſs among the Generality of Mankind. But, if we conſidered Things rightly, Why ſhould we be more concerned at others differing from us in their Way of Thinking upon any Subject whatever, than at their liking Cheeſe, or Muſtard; one, or both of which, we may happen to diſlike? In Truth, he that expects all Mankind ſhould be of his Opinion, is much more ſtupid and unreaſonable than the Aſs in the Fable.

FAB. CLXIV. *The* Horſe *and the loaded* Aſs.

AN idle Horſe, and an Aſs labouring under a heavy Burden, were travelling the Road together; they both belonged to a Country Fellow, who trudged it on Foot by them. The Aſs, ready to

faint

faint under his heavy Load, entreated the Horſe to aſſiſt him, and lighten his Burden, by taking ſome of it upon his Back. The Horſe was ill-natured, and refuſed to do it: Upon which the poor Aſs tumbled down in the Midſt of the Highway, and expired in an Inſtant. The Countryman ungirted his Packſaddle, and tried ſeveral Ways to relieve him, but all to no Purpoſe: Which, when he perceived, he took the whole Burden, and laid it upon the Horſe, together with the Skin of the dead Aſs: So that the Horſe, by his Moroſeneſs in refuſing to do a ſmall Kindneſs, juſtly brought upon himſelf a great Inconvenience.

The APPLICATION.

Self-Love is no ſuch ill Principle, if it were but well and truly directed; for it is impoſſible that any Man ſhould love himſelf to any Purpoſe, who withdraws his Aſſiſtance from his Friends or the Public. Every Government is to be conſidered as a Body Politic; and every Man who lives in it, as a Member of that Body. Now, to carry on the Allegory, no Member can thrive better, than when they all jointly unite their Endeavours to aſſiſt and improve the Whole. If the Hand was to refuſe its Aſſiſtance in procuring Food for the Mouth, they muſt both ſtarve and periſh together. And when thoſe, who are Parties concerned in the ſame Community, deny ſuch Aſſiſtance to each other, as the Preſervation of that Community neceſſarily requires, their Self-intereſtedneſs, in that Caſe, is ill-directed, and will have a quite contrary Effect from what they intended. How many People are ſo ſenſeleſs, as to think it hard that there ſhould be any Taxes in the Nation! whereas, were there to be none indeed, thoſe very People would be undone immediately. That little Property they have would be preſently plundered by foreign or domeſtic Enemies; and then they would be glad to contribute their Quota, even without an Act of Parliament. The Charges of ſupporting a Government are neceſſary

Things,

Things, and eafily fupplied by a due and well propor-
tioned Contribution. But, in a narrower and more confined View, to be ready to affift our Friends upon all Occafions, is not only good, as it is an Act of Humanity,
but highly difcreet, as it ftrengthens our Intereft, and
gives us an Opportunity of lightening the Burden of Life.

FAB. CLXV.

The Bees, *the* Drones, *and the* Wafp.

A Parcel of Drones got into a Hive among the
Bees, and difputed the Title with them, fwearing that the Honey and the Combs were their
Goods. The Bees were obliged to go to Law with
them, and the Wafp happened to be Judge of the
Caufe; one who was well acquainted with the Nature of each, and therefore the better qualified to
decide the Controverfy between them. Accordingly, Gentlemen, fays he, (fpeaking to both Plaintiff and Defendant) the ufual Method of proceeding in thefe Courts is pretty chargeable, and flow
withal; therefore, as you are both my Friends, and

I wifh

I wifh you well, I defire you would refer the Matter to me, and I will decide betwixt you inftantly. They were both pleafed with the Offer, and returned him Thanks. Why then, fays he, that it may appear who is the juft Proprietors of thefe Honeycombs (for being both fo nearly alike, as you are, in Colour, I muft needs own the Point is fomewhat dubious) do you, addreffing himfelf to the Bees, take one Hive; you, fpeaking to the Drones, another; and go to making Honey as faft as you can, that we may know by the Tafte and Colour of it, who has the beft Title to this in Difpute. The Bees readily accepted the Propofal, but the Drones would not ftand to it. And fo Judge Wafp, without any farther Ceremony, declared in Favour of the former.

The APPLICATION.

Nothing is fo fure a Sign of a Man's being, or, at leaft, thinking himfelf in the Wrong, as his refufing to come to a Reference. And, how happy would it be for the Public, if our Judges now-a-days were empowered to difpatch Caufes in that eafy expedite Way which the Wafp in the Fable made Ufe of. But, as it is, the impudent, idle, good-for-nothing Drones of the Nation, many Times poffefs thofe Favours and Benefits, which fhould be the Rewards of Men of Parts and Induftry.

Princes may eafily be impofed upon, if they will take every little Fellow's Word for the Meafure of his own Merit. And it is indeed fcarce poffible that the Encouragements of a Court fhould always be difpenfed to the moft deferving Men; but fuch are too modeft to offer themfelves. But it highly concerns any Government, in the Difpenfation of its Favours, to diftinguifh thofe who have behaved well; and not to let Places of Profit and Advantage be run away with by Drones, who never exerted the leaft Degree of Merit.

FAB.

FAB. CLXVI. *The* Fox *in the* Well.

A FOX, having fallen into a Well, made a Shift, by sticking his Claws into the Sides, to keep his Head above Water. Soon after, a Wolf came and peeped over the Brink; to whom the Fox applied himself very earneftly for Affiftance; entreating that he would help him to a Rope, or fomething of that Kind, which might Favour his Efcape. The Wolf, moved with Compaffion at his Misfortune, could not forbear expreffing his Concern: Ah! poor *Reynard*, fays he, I am forry for you with all my Heart; how could you poffibly come into this melancholy Condition? Nay, pr'ythee, Friend, replies the Fox, if you wifh me well, do not ftand pitying of me, but lend me fome Succour as faft as you can: For Pity is but cold Comfort when one is up to the Chin in Water, and within a Hair's Breadth of Starving or Drowning.

The APPLICATION.

Pity, indeed, is of itfelf but poor Comfort at any Time; and, unlefs it produces fomething more fubftan-

tial,

tial, is rather impertinently troublesome, than any way agreeable. To stand bemoaning the Misfortunes of our Friends, without offering some Expedient to alleviate them, is only echoing to their Grief, and putting them in Mind that they are miserable. He is truly my Friend, who with a ready Presence of Mind supports me; not he who condoles with me upon my ill Success, and says he is sorry for my Loss. In short, a Favour or Obligation is doubled by being well-timed; and he is the best Benefactor, who knows our Necessities, and complies with our Wishes, even before we ask him.

FAB. CLXVII. *The Fox and the Wolf.*

THE Wolf having laid in Store of Provision, kept close at Home, and made much of himself. The Fox observed this, and thinking it something particular, went to visit him, the better to inform himself of the Truth of the Matter. The Wolf excused himself from seeing him, by pretending he was very much indisposed. All this did but confirm the Fox in his Suspicions: So away he goes to a Shepherd, and made Discovery of the Wolf, telling him,

him, he had nothing elfe to do but to come with a good Weapon, and knock him on the Head as he lay in his Cave. The Shepherd followed his Directions, and killed the Wolf. The wicked Fox enjoyed the Cave and Provifions to himfelf, but enjoyed them not long, for the fame Shepherd paffing afterwards by the fame Hole, and feeing the Fox there, difpatched him alfo.

The APPLICATION.

This Fable feems to be directed againft the odious Trade of Informing. Not that giving in Informations againft Criminals and Enemies of the Public, is in itfelf odious, for it is commendable; but the Circumftances and Manner of doing it, oftentimes make it a vile and deteftable Employment. He that accufes another, merely for the Sake of the promifed Reward, or in Hopes of getting his forfeited Eftate, or with any other fuch mercenary View, nay, even to fave his own Life, whatever he gets by the Bargain, is fure to lofe his Reputation. For, indeed, the moft innocent Company is not fafe with fuch a one in it, nor the Neighbourhood fecure in which he lives. A Villain of his Stamp, whofe only End is Getting, will as foon betray the Innocent as the Guilty: Let him but know where there is a fufpected Perfon, and propofe the Reward, and he will fcarce fail to work the Sufpicion up to High Treafon, or be at a Lofs to give fufficient Proofs of it. We have no fmall Comfort concerning this Sort of People, when we confider how improbable it is that they fhould thrive or profper long in their ill-gotten Poffeffions. For he that can betray another, for the Sake of a little Pelf, muft be a Man of fuch bad Principles, that it cannot be for the Intereft of any Community to fuffer him to live long in it. Befides, he himfelf will not be contented with one fingle Villainy; and there is no Fear but he will provoke Juftice to hurl down upon his Head, at leaft, as great a Calamity, as he, by his malicious Information, has brought upon another.

FAB.

FAB. CLXVIII. *The* Frog *and the* Mouſe.

THERE was once a great Emulation between the Frog and the Mouſe, which ſhould be Maſter of the Fen, and Wars enſued upon it. But the crafty Mouſe lurking under the Graſs in Ambuſcade, made ſudden Sallies, and often ſurprized the Enemy at a Diſadvantage. The Frog excelling in Strength, and being more able to leap abroad and take the Field, challenged the Mouſe to ſingle Combat. The Mouſe accepts the Challenge; and each of them entered the Liſts, armed with the Point of a Bulruſh, inſtead of a Spear. A Kite ſailing in the Air, beheld them afar off; and while they were eagerly bent upon each other, and preſſing on to the Duel, this fatal Enemy deſcended ſouſe upon them, and with her crooked Talons, carried off both the Champions.

The APPLICATION.

Nothing ſo much expoſes a Man's weak Side, and lays him ſo open to an Enemy, as Paſſion and Malice. He whoſe Attention is wholly fixed upon forming a Pro-ject of Revenge, is ignorant of the Miſchiefs that may be hatching againſt him from ſome other Quarter, and, upon the Attack, is unprovided with the Means of defending or fecuring himfelf. How are the Members of a Commonwealth fometimes divided amongft themfelves, and infpired with Rancour and Malice to the laft Degree; and often upon as great a Trifle, as that which was the Subject Matter of Debate between the Frog and the Moufe; not for any real Advantage, but merely, who fhall get the better in the Difpute? But fuch Animofities, as infignificant and trifling as they may be among themfelves, are yet of the laft Importance to their Enemies, by giving them many fair Opportunities of falling upon them, and reducing them to Mifery and Slavery. O *Britons*, when will ye be wife! When will ye throw away the ridiculous Diftinctions of Party, thofe Ends of Bulrufhes, and by a prudent Union fecure yourfelves in a State of Peace and Profperity! A State, of which, if it were not for your intolerably foolifh and unneceffary Divifions at Home, all the Powers upon Earth could never deprive you.

FAB. CLXIX. *The* Man *and the* Weafel.

A Man had caught a Weafel, and was juft going to kill it. The poor Creature, to efcape Death, cried out in a pitiful Manner, O pray, do not kill me,

me, for I am ufeful to you, and keep your Houfe
clear from Mice. Why truly, fays the Man, if I
thought you did it purely out of Love to me, I fhould
not only be inclined to pardon you, but think myfelf
mightily obliged to you. But whereas you not only
kill them, but yourfelf do the fame Mifchief they
would do, in eating and gnawing my Victuals, I
defire you would place your infignificant Services to
fome other Account, and not to mine. Having faid
this, he took the wicked Vermin, and ftrangled it
immediately.

The APPLICATION.

This Fable is pointed at thofe who are apt to impute
Actions, which are done with a private View of their
own, to their Zeal for the Public. This is the Cafe of
many a poor *Grub-ftreet* Writer, who perhaps is for no
Party but himfelf, and of no Principle but what is fub-
fervient to his own Intereft, yet has the Impudence to
cry himfelf up for a former Confeffor of the Caufe that
happens to flourifh, a thorough honeft Man, who durft
fhew himfelf in the worft of Times. And with this politic View, there are a hundred thoufand Men in the
Nation, well attached to which Party you pleafe ; who
are ferving the Intereft of that Side only, in their feveral Capacities. By this Way of working, they have a
doub'e Advantage ; firft, as they procure to themfelves
a good Number of conftant Cuftomers of the fame Faction ; and, fecondly, as they are entitled to fome remote
Share in the Government whenever their Faction fuc-
ceeds. But fuch a Pretence to Favours is, in Truth, little better than that of the Weafel. Both may chance to
have done the Services they boaft of ; but as they were
principally intended for the Promotion of their own private Affairs, whatever they might occafionally produce,
cannot be a fufficient Ground for them to raife any Merit
upon. A Highwayman may as well plead in his own
Behalf, that he never robbed any but thofe who were
Enemies to the Government, and Men of unfound Principles. But how abfurd would fuch a Pretence be!

FAB. CLXX.

Æſop and the Impertinent Fellow.

ÆSOP's Maſter came Home, one Day, ſomewhat earlier than uſual; and, there happening
to be no other Slave in the Houſe but _Æſop_, he was
ordered to get Supper ready as faſt as he could. So
away he runs to light a Candle, in order to kindle
his Fire; and the Weather being warm, and it
wanting a pretty deal of Night, he went up and
down to ſeveral Houſes, before he could ſpeed. At
laſt, however, he found what he wanted; and, being
in Haſte, he made no Scruple of returning directly
over the Market-Place, which was his neareſt Way
Home. But, as he went along, an impertinent Fellow among the Crowd, caught him by the Sleeve,
and would fain have been arch upon him. O rare
Æſop! ſays he; what Occaſion for a Candle, old
Boy; what, are you going to light the Sun to Bed?
Let me alone, ſays _Æſop_, I am looking for a Man.
And having ſaid this, away he ſcuttled Home, as faſt
as he could.

The

The APPLICATION:

It is not every one who calls himſelf a Man, or bears
the Appearance of one, that truly deſerves the Name.
If Man be a reaſonable Creature, and none ought to be
allowed for ſuch, but thoſe who fully come up to that
Definition, it is certain one would have Occaſion for
more Light than that of the Sun, to find them out by.
And it is plain that our old Philoſopher did not take the
impertinent Fellow in the Fable for one : Nor, indeed,
ſhould ſuch be looked upon as reaſonable Creatures,
who, with empty Nonſenſe, which they call Wit, unſeaſonably interrupt Men of Thought and Buſineſs.
When one is diſpoſed to be merry, one may bear with
any ſhallow, flaſhy Buffoonery ; as Muſic, that is not the
moſt elegant, will keep up the Spirits, when once they
are raiſed : But when the Mind happens to be in a ſerious
Caſt, and is wholly intent upon any Matter of Importance, nothing is ſo offenſive as a Fool or a Fiddle.

FAB. CLXXI. *The* Hart *and the* Vine.

A HART being purſued hard by the Hunters, hid
himſelf under the broad Leaves of a ſhady ſpread-
ing Vine. When the Hunters were gone by, and
had

had given him over for loft, he, thinking himself
very fecure, began to crop and eat the Leaves of the
Vine.   By this Means the Branches being put into
a ruftling Motion, drew the Eyes of the Hunters
that Way; who, feeing the Vine ftir, and fancying
fome wild Beaft had taken Covert there, fhot their
Arrows at a Venture, and killed the Hart; who, before he expired, uttered his dying Words to this
Purpofe: Ah! 1 fuffer juftly for my Ingratitude;
who could not forbear doing an Injury to the Vine
that fo kindly concealed me in Time of Danger.

The APPLICATION.

Ingratitude has always been efteemed the biggeft of
Crimes, and what, as it were, comprehends all other
Vices within it.   Nor can we fay, that this Eftimation
is rafhly or unadvifedly made; for he that is capable of
injuring his Benefactors, what will he fcruple towards
another? If his Confcience cannot be felt with the
Weight of an Obligation added to it, much lefs will it
have any Influence where there is none.   So that, upon
the whole, we may conclude, that the Man who has
been once guilty of Ingratitude, will not ftick at any
other Crime of an inferior Nature.   Since there are no
human Laws to punifh this infamous prevailing Mifchief,
it would be a great Piece of human Prudence to mark
and obferve this Kind of Criminals, in order to avoid all
Manner of Communication with them.   And if this
were ftrictly put in Execution, it could be looked upon
as no other than a juft and proper Punifhment.

O   FAB.

FAB. CLXXII. *The* Drunken Husband.

A Certain Woman had a drunken Husband, whom when she had endeavoured to reclaim several Ways, to no Purpose, she tried this Stratagem. When he was brought Home one Night, dead drunk, as it seems he frequently used to be, she ordered him to be carried to a Burial-place, and there laid in a Vault, as if he had been dead indeed. Thus she left him, and went away, till she thought he might be come to himself, and grown sober again. When she returned and knocked at the Door of the Vault, the Man cried out, Who's there? I am the Person, says she, in a dismal Tone, that waits upon the dead Folks, and I am come to bring you some Victuals. Ah! good Waiter, says he, let the Victuals alone, and bring me a little Drink, I beseech thee. The Woman hearing this, fell a tearing her Hair, and beating her Breast in a woeful Manner: Unhappy Wretch that I am, says she; this was the only Way that I could think of to reform the

beastly

beaſtly Sot: But inſtead of gaining my Point, I am only convinced that this Drunkenneſs is an incurable Habit, which he intends to carry with him into the other World.

The APPLICATION.

This Fable is intended to ſhew us the Prevalence of Cuſtom; and how, by uſing ourſelves much to any evil Practice, we may let it grow into ſuch a Habit as we may be never able to diveſt ourſelves of. In any Thing that we are ſenſible may be prejudicial to either our Health or Fortunes, we ſhould take Care not to let our Inclinations run up into a Habit: For though the former may be eaſily checked at our firſt ſetting out, and directed which Way we pleaſe; yet the latter, like a headſtrong unruly Horſe in his full Career, will have its own Courſe, and we are hurried impetuouſly on, without the Power of controuling it. As the Paſſions of young Men are warm, and their Imaginations lively, it would be wrong to endeavour to tie them up from the Purſuit of innocent Pleaſures. But thoſe among them, that think at all, can never form a more uſeful and happy Reſolution, than not to ſuffer themſelves to be drawn into a Habit, even in indifferent and trifling Things. He that keeps himſelf free from the Slavery of Habit, will always be at Leiſure to diſtinguiſh what is good for him, from that which is otherwiſe: And then there is no Fear, but his cool unbiaſſed Judgment will direct him to ſuch Purſuits, as will be leaſt hurtful, if not moſt uſeful to him.

F A B.

FAB. CLXXIII. The Blackamoor.

A Certain Man having bought a Blackamoor, was
so simple as to think, that the Colour of his
Skin was only Dirt and Filth, which he had con-
tracted for want of due Care, under his former Mafter. This Fault he fancied might easily be removed.
So he ordered the poor Black to be put into a Tub,
and was at a considerable Charge in providing
Ashes, Soap, and Scrubbing-Brushes for the Operation. To work they went, rubbing and scour-
ing his Skin all over, but to no Manner of Purpose : For when they had repeated their Washings
several Times, and were grown quite weary, all
they got by it was, that the wretched Blackamoor
caught Cold and died.

The APPLICATION.

Many People attempt Impossibilities, for want of considering the Nature of Things aright. For, as palpable a Blunder as this Man in the Fable committed, there
are those who are guilty of as great Mistakes ; espe-

cially when they endeavour, by fruitless Cultivations, to raise Graces from the Mind or Body, of which neither is capable. When any one went to meddle with Arts and Sciences, for which his Genius was not well and properly adapted, the *Greeks* had a Proverb to turn it into Ridicule, by saying, he was no more fit for the Business, than *an Ass to play upon the Harp*. In short, when People learn to dance without Shape and Mien, to sing, or play on Music, without a Voice or an Ear, Painting or Poetry without a Genius; it is attempting to wash the Blackamoor white. They can never attain their End, but at the same Time expose themselves to the jocose Humours of those that behold them. Instead of a Grace, they acquire a Deformity; as some Boys at School, whom the Master, by endeavouring to whip into a Memory and bright Parts, confirms stupid and invincible Blockheads for ever.

FAB. CLXXIV. *The* Travellers.

TWO Men travelling upon the Road, one of them saw an Axe lying upon the Ground, where somebody had been hewing Timber: So taking it up, says he, I have found an Axe. Do not say *I*,

says

fays the other, but *We* have found ; for, as we are Companions, we ought to fhare it betwixt us : But the firft would not confent.   However, they had not gone far, before the Owner of the Axe, hearing what was become of it, purfued them with a Warrant ; which, when the Fellow that had it, pereeived, Alas ! fays he to his Companion, We are undone.   Nay, fays the other, do not fay *We*, but *I* am undone ; for, as you would not let me fhare the Prize, neither will I fhare the Danger with you.

The A P P L I C A T I O N.

This Fable hints to us the Conveniency, if not the Neceffity, of making our Friendfhips firm and lafting. And, to this Purpofe, nothing is fo requifite as a ftrict Obfervance of the Rules of Honour and Generofity ; for the very Life and Soul of Friendfhip fubfifts upon mutual Benevolence, upon conferring and receiving Obligations on either Hand.   A ftingy referved Behaviour ftarves it ; it ought to be open, free, and communicative, without the leaft Tincture of Sufpicion or Diftruft.   For Jealoufy, in Friendfhip, is a certain Indication of a falfe Heart, though in Love it may be the diftinguifhing Mark of a true one.   Nor is there any Thing merely chimerical or romantic in this Notion ; for, if we examine, we fhall find, that Reafon will confirm the Truth, and Experience evince the Utility of it. He that hopes for Affiftance, or Accommodation in any Exigency, or Time of Misfortune, muft lay in a Provifion for it, by watching the Neceffities of his Acquaintance, and relieving the moft deferving of them in their Straits, by a ready and a willing Contribution. By this Means, Gratitude, which is never wanting to an honeft Mind, will fecure us a reafonable Fund in Reverfion ; and all the Favours we beftow, will, like the Tide of a River, in due Seafon flow back again upon us.

F A B.

FAB. CLXXV. The Fisherman.

A Certain Fisherman having laid his Nets in the River, and encompassed the whole Stream from one Side to the other, took a long Pole, and fell a beating the Water, to make the Fish strike into his Nets. One of the Neighbours that lived thereabout, seeing him do so, wondered what he meant; and going up to him, Friend, says he, what are you doing here? Do you think it is to be suffered, that you shall stand splashing and dashing the Water, and make it so muddy that it is not fit for Use? Who do you think can live at this Rate?—He was going on in a great Fury, when the other interrupted him, and replied, I do not much trouble myself how you are to live with my doing this, but I assure you, that I cannot live without it.

The APPLICATION.

This Fable is levelled at those, who, as the Proverb says, love *to fish in troubled Waters*. There are some Men of such execrable Principles, that they do not care what Mischief or what Confusion they occasion in the World, provided they may but gratify some little selfish Appetite. A Thief will set a whole Street on Fire, to get an Opportunity of

robbing

robbing one Houfe; an ill-natured Perfon will kindle the Flame of Difcord among Friends and Neighbours, purely to fatisfy his own malicious Temper. And among the Great ones, there are thofe, who, to fucceed in their ambitious Defigns, will make no Scruple of involving their Country in Divifions and Animofities at Home, and fometimes in War and Bloodfhed Abroad: Provided they do but maintain themfelves in Power, they care not what Havock and Defolation they bring upon the reft of Mankind. They fee all around them confounded with Faction and Party Rage, without the leaft Remorfe or Compaffion. The Widow's Tears, the Orphan's Cries, and the Sighs of Defpair itfelf cannot affect them. Like the Fifherman in the Fable, they boldly purfue the Sport, and only reply, It muft be fo, becaufe we cannot live, as we would do, without it. What brutifh unfociable Sentiments are thefe; fuch as a mere State of Nature would fcarce fuggeft! Thofe that have any Traces of Equity in their Breaft, or any Regard for the Rights of Mankind, fhould enter their Proteft againft fuch Notions as thefe, and oppofe the Practice of them, with all their Might and Strength.

FAB. CLXXVI. Mercury *and the* Carver.

MERCURY having a Mind to know how much he was efteemed among Men, transformed himfelf into the Shape of one of them ; and, going into a Carver's Shop, where little Images were to be fold, he faw *Jupiter*, *Juno*, himfelf, and moft of the other Gods and Goddeffes. So, pretending that he wanted to buy, fays he to the Carver, What do you afk for this ? and pointed to the Figure of *Jupiter*. A Groat, fays the other. And what for that ? meaning *Juno*. I muft have fomething more for that, fays he. Well, and what's the Price of this ? fays *Mercury*, nodding his Head at himfelf. Why, fays the Man, if you are in earneft, and will buy the other two, I will throw you that into the Bargain.

The APPLICATION.

Nothing makes a Man fo cheap and little in the Eyes of difcerning People, as his enquiring after his own Worth, and wanting to know what Value others fet upon him. He that often bufies himfelf in ftating the Account of his own Merit, will probably employ his Thoughts upon a very barren Subject ; thofe who are full of themfelves, being generally the emptieft Fellows. Some are fo vain as to hunt for Praife, and lay Traps for Commendation ; which when they do, it is Pity but they fhould meet with the fame Difappointment as *Mercury* in the Fable. He that behaves himfelf as he fhould do, need not fear procuring a good Share of Refpect, or raifing a fair flourifhing Reputation. Thefe are the infeparable Attendants of thofe that do well, and in Courfe follow the Man that acquits himfelf handfomely. But then they fhould never be the End or Motive of our Purfuits: Our principal Aim fhould be the Welfare and Happinefs of our Country, our Friends, and ourfelves ; and that fhould be directed by the Rules of Honour and Virtue. As long as we do this, we need not be concerned what the World thinks of us : For a Curiofity of that Kind does but prevent what it moft defires to obtain. Fame, in this Refpect, is like a whimfical Miftrefs ; fhe flies from thofe who purfue her moft, and follows fuch as fhew the leaft Regard to her.

FAB.

FAB. CLXXVII. *The* Thieves *and the* Cock.

SOME Thieves, entering a House with a Design to rob it, when they were got in, found nothing worth taking, but a Cock ; so they took and carried him off. But as they were about to kill him, he begged hard for his Life, putting them in Mind, how useful he was to Mankind, by crowing and calling them up betimes to their Work. You Villain, replied they, it is for that very Reason we will wring your Neck off ; for you alarm and keep People waking, so that we cannot rob at quiet for you.

The APPLICATION.

The same Thing which recommends us to the Esteem of good People, will make those that are bad have but an ill Opinion of us. It is in vain for innocent Men, under Oppression, to complain to those who are the Occasion of it ; all they can urge, will but make against them ; and even their very Innocence, tho' they should say nothing, would render them sufficiently suspected. The Advice, therefore, that this Fable brings along with it, is to inform us, that there is no trusting, nor any Hopes of living well with wicked unjust Men. When Vice flourishes and is in Power, were it possible for a good

Man

Man to live quietly in the Neighbourhood of it, and preferve his Integrity, it might be fometimes convenient for him to do fo, rather than quarrel with, and provoke it againſt him. But as it is certain that Rogues are irreconcileable Enemies to Men of Worth, if the latter would be fecure, they muſt take a Method to free themfelves from the Power and Society of the former.

FAB. CLXXVIII. _The_ Fox _and the_ Aſs.

AN Aſs, finding a Lion's Skin, difguiſed himſelf with it, and ranged about the Foreſt, putting all the Beaſts that faw him into a bodily Fear. After he had diverted himſelf thus for ſome Time, he met a Fox; and being deſirous to fright him too, as well as the reſt, he leapt at him with ſome Fierceneſs, and endeavoured to imitate the Roaring of the Lion. Your humble Servant, fays the Fox; if you had held your Tongue, I might have taken you for a Lion, as others did; but now you bray, I know who you are.

The APPLICATION.

This is ſo trite and common a Subject, that there is ſcarce any one who is ignorant of it. A Man is known by his Words, as a Tree is by the Fruit; and, if we would be apprized of the Nature and Qualities of any

O 6   one,

one, let him but difcourfe, and he himfelf will fpeak them to us, better than another can defcribe them. We may therefore perceive from this Fable, how proper it is for thofe to hold their Tongues, who would not difcover the Shallownefs of their Underftandings.

Affes and Owls, unfeen themfelves betray,
  When thefe attempt to hoot, or thofe to bray.   Garth.
The deepeft Rivers are moft filent; the greateft Noife is ever found where there is the leaft Depth of Water. And it is a true Obfervation, that thofe who are the weakeft in Underftanding, and moft flow of Apprehenfion, are generally the ftrongeft in Opinion, and moft precipitate in uttering their crude Conceptions. When, with a fecret Awe, we regard the grave Drefs and important Mien of fome Senatorian Perfon, whom we have chanced to meet in a Coffee-Houfe, what a Speaker do we often think he muft be, before we hear him fpeak! His Air breathes the Serioufnefs of a Privy Counfellor, and his erect Afpect the Dignity of an eminent Patriot: But he utters himfelf, and undeceives us; he brays, and tells the whole Company what he is.

FAB. CLXXIX. *The* Hen *and the* Swallow.

A HEN finding fome Serpents Eggs in a Dung-hill, fat upon them, with a Defign to hatch
them.

them. A Swallow perceiving it, flew towards her, and with fome Warmth and Paffion : Are you mad, fays fhe, to fit hovering over a Brood of fuch pernicious Creatures, as you do ? Be affured, the Moment you bring them to Light, you are the firft they will attack, and wreak their venomous Spite upon.

The APPLICATION.

This Fable is only to put us in Mind, once more, of what we have already, more than once, met with in the Courfe of thefe Fables, That we fhould never have any Thing to do with ill Men ; no, not even to do them Kindneffes. Men of ill Principles are a Generation of Vipers, that ought to be crufhed under our Feet, and deftroyed the firft Opportunity. Every Rogue fhould be looked upon by honeft Men as a poifonous Serpent : It is not fufficient that they avoid and keep clear of him ; but, if they have any Value for their own Safety, they fhould profecute and maul him, and render him incapable of ever doing Mifchief. The Man who is occafionally, or by Accident, one's Enemy, may be mollified by Kindnefs, and reclaimed by good Ufage : Such a Behaviour, Reafon and Morality both expect from us. But we fhould ever refolve, if not to fupprefs, at leaft to have no Dealings with thofe, whofe Blood is tinctured with hereditary, habitual Villainy, and their Nature leavened with Evil, to fuch a Degree, as to be incapable of a Reformation.

FAB.

FAB. CLXXX. *The* Dog *invited to* Supper.

A Gentleman having invited an extraordinary
Friend to fup with him, ordered a handfome
Entertainment to be prepared. His Dog, obferving
this, thought with himfelf, that now would be a
good Opportunity for him to invite another Dog,
a Friend of his, to partake of the good Cheer. Accordingly, he did fo; and the ftrange Dog was con-
ducted into the Kitchen, where he faw mighty Preparations going forward. Thought he to himfelf,
This is rare! I fhall fill my Belly charmingly by
and by, with fome of thefe Dainties! I'll eat enough
to laft me a Week; Oh! how nicely and delici-
oufly fhall I feed! While he ftood and thought thus
with himfelf, his Tail wagged, and his Chops wa-
tered exceedingly; and this drew the Obfervation
of the Cook towards him; who, feeing a ftrange
Cur, with his Eyes intent upon the Victuals, ftole
foftly behind him, and, taking him up by the two
hind Legs, threw him out of a Window into the

5   Street.

Street. The hard Stones gave him a very severe Reception, and he was almost stunned with the Fall; but recovering himself, he ran yelping and crying half the Length of a Street; the Noise of which brought several other Dogs about him; who, knowing of the Invitation, began to enquire how he had fared? O, says he, admirably well; I never was better entertained in my Life: But, in Troth, we drank a little too hard; for my Part, I was so overtaken, that I scarce know which Way I got out of the House.

The APPLICATION.

There is no depending upon a second-hand Interest; unless we know ourselves to be well with the Principal, and are assured of his Favour and Protection, we stand but upon a slippery Foundation. They are Strangers to the World, who are so vain as to think they can be well with any one by Proxy; they may, by this Means, be cajoled, bubbled, and imposed upon, but are under great Uncertainty as to gaining their Point, and may probably be treated with Scorn and Derision in the End. Yet there are not wanting, among the several Species of Fops, silly People of this Sort, who pride themselves in an imaginary Happiness, from being in the good Graces of a Great Man's Friend's Friend. Alas! the Great Men themselves are but too apt to deceive and fail in making good their Promises; how then can we expect any Good from those who do but promise and vow in their Names! To place a Confidence in such Sparks, is indeed so false a Reliance, that we should be ashamed to be detected in it; and, like the Cur in the Fable, rather own we had been well treated, than let the World see how justly we had been punished for our ridiculous Credulity.

FAB.

FAB. CLXXXI. Jupiter *and the* Herdſman.

A Herdſman miſſing a young Heifer that belonged to his Herd, went up and down the Foreſt to ſeek it. And having walked a great deal of Ground to no Purpoſe, he fell a praying to *Jupiter* for Relief; promiſing to ſacrifice a Kid to him, if he would help him to a Diſcovery of the Thief. After this, he went on a little farther, and came near a Grove of Oaks, where he found the Carcaſe of his Heifer, and a Lion grumbling over it, and feeding upon it. This Sight almoſt ſcared him out of his Wits; ſo down he fell upon his Knees once more, and addreſſing himſelf to *Jupiter*; *O Jupiter!* ſays he, I promiſed thee a Kid to ſhew me the Thief, but now I promiſe thee a Bull, if thou wilt be ſo merciful as to deliver me out of his Clutches.

The APPLICATION.

How ignorant and ſtupid are ſome People, who form their Notions of the Supreme Being from their own poor ſhallow Conceptions; and then, like froward Children with their Nurſes, think it conſiſtent with infinite Wiſdom, and unerring Juſtice, to comply with all their whimſical Petitions. Let Men but live as juſtly as they

can,

can, and juft Providence will give them what they ought
to have. Of all the involuntary Sins which Men commit, fcarce any are more frequent, than that of their
praying abfurdly and improperly, as well as unfeafon-
ably, when their Time might have been employed fo
much better. The many private Collections fold up and
down the Nation, do not a little contribute to this injudicious' Practice : Which is the more to be condemned,
in that we have fo incomparable a public Liturgy ; one
fingle Addrefs whereof (except the Lord's Prayer) may
be pronounced to be the beft that ever was compiled ;
and alone preferable to all the various Manuals of Oc-
cafional Devotion, which are vended by Hawkers and
Pedlars about our Streets. It is as follows :

*Almighty God, the Fountain of all Wifdom, who knoweft
our Neceffities before we afk, and our Ignorance in afking ;
we befeech thee to have Compaffion upon our Infirmities ;
and thofe Things, which for our Unworthinefs we dare
not, and for our Blindnefs we cannot afk, vouchfafe to give
us, for the Worthinefs of thy Son* Jefus Chrift our Lord.

FAB. CLXXXII. *The* Fighting Cocks.

TWO Cocks were fighting for the Sovereignty
of the Dunghill. And one of them having got
the

the better of the other, he that was vanquished crept into a Hole, and hid himself for some Time; but the Victor flew up to an eminent Place, clapt his Wings, and crowed out *Victory*. An Eagle who was watching for his Prey near the Place, saw him, and making a Stoop, trussed him in his Talons, and carried him off. The Cock that had been beaten perceiving this, soon quitted his Hole, and shaking off all Remembrance of his late Disgrace, gallanted the Hens with all the Intrepidity imaginable.

The APPLICATION.

This Fable shews the Impropriety and Inconvenience of running into Extremes. Much of our Happiness depends upon keeping an even Balance in our Words and Actions; in not suffering the Scale of our Reason to mount us too high in Time of Prosperity, nor to sink us too low with the Weight of adverse Fortune.

It is a Question, Which shews People in the most contemptible Light, exulting immoderately upon a fresh Accession of Good, or being too abjectly cast down at the sudden Approach of Evil. We are apt to form our Notions of the Man from the Stability of his Temper, in this Respect; and account him a brave or a wise Man, according to the Proportion of Equanimity, which he exerts upon any Change of his Condition. But tho' our Reputation were no Ways concerned in the Case, and a Man were not to be reckoned a Coxcomb for being elated, or a Coward for being dejected with the Vicissitudes of Life, yet the true Regard of our own private Satisfaction should incline us to play the Philosopher, and learn to keep our Spirits calm and even; because Life would be a Labyrinth of Perplexities without it. One sudden Turn would come so thick upon the Back of another, that we should be bewildered in the quick Succession of Joys and Terrors, without having so much as a quiet Moment to ourselves.

FAB.

FAB. CLXXXIII.
The Young Men *and the* Cook.

TWO young Men went into a Cook's Shop, under Pretence of buying Meat ; and while the
Cook's Back was turned, one of them snatched up a
Piece of Beef, and gave it to his Companions, who
presently clapt it under his Cloak. The Cook turning about again, and missing his Beef, began to
charge them with it; upon which he that first took
it swore bitterly he had none of it. He that had it,
swore as heartily that he had taken up none of his
Meat. Why, look ye, Gentlemen, says the Cook, I
see your Equivocation ; and tho' I cannot tell which
of you has taken my Meat, I am sure between you
both, there is a Thief, and a Couple of Rascals.

The APPLICATION.

An honest Man's Word is as good as his Oath; and so
is a Rogue's too ; for he that will cheat and lye, why should
he scruple to forswear himself? Is the latter more criminal than either of the former ? An honest Man needs no
Oath to oblige him ; and a Rogue only deceives you the
more certainly by it ; because you think you have tied him
up, and he is sure you have not. In Truth, it is not easy

with the Eye of Reason, to difcern, that there is any Good in Swearing at all. We need not fcruple to take an honeft Man's bare Affeveration; and we fhall do wrong if we believe a Rogue, though he fwears by the moft folemn Oaths that can be invented. There are, befides, a Sort of People who are Rogues, and yet do not know that they are fuch; who, when they have taken an Oath, make a Scruple of breaking it; but rack their Invention to evade it by fome Equivocation or other; by which, if they can but fatisfy their Acquaintance, and ferve their own Scheme, they think all is well, and never once confider the black and heinous Guilt which muft attend fuch a Behaviour. They folemnly call the Supreme Being to witnefs; to what? To a Sham, an Evafion, a Lye. Thus thefe unthinking prevaricating Wretches, at the fame Time that they believe there is a God, act as if there were none; or, what is worfe, dare affront him in the higheft Degree. They, who by fwearing would clear themfelves of a Crime, of which they are really guilty, need not be at much Pains about wording their Oath; for, exprefs themfelves how they will, they are fure to be forfworn.

FAB. CLXXXIV. *The* Jackdaw *and the* Sheep.

A Jackdaw fat chattering upon the Back of a Sheep.
Peace, you noify Thing, fays the Sheep; if I were a
Dog,

Dog, you durſt not ſerve me ſo. That is true enough, replies the Jackdaw, I know very well who I have to do with : I never meddle with the ſurly and revenge-ful : but I love to plague ſuch poor helpleſs Creatures as you are, that cannot do me any Harm again.

The APPLICATION.

Many People in the World are of the Temper of this Jackdaw in the Fable, who do Miſchief for Miſchief's Sake ; and, at the ſame Time, are never ſo well pleaſed, as when they do it to the Innocent and Undeſerving. They love themſelves too well to offer an Injury to one of their own malicious Principles, for Fear of a ſuitable Return ; but deſire no better Grounds, at any Time, for being hurt-ful, than the Proſpect of being ſo with Impunity. How inconſiſtent are ſuch Proceedings as theſe, with Honour and Generoſity ! How oppoſite to the Character of a great and a good Man ! and how directly contrary to the Rules preſcribed for the Behaviour of noble and heroic Spirits.

FAB. CLXXXV. The Plowman and Fortune.

THE Plowman, as he was plowing the Ground, found a Treaſure. Tranſported with Joy, he
immediately

immediately began to return Thanks to the Ground, which had been so liberal and kind to him. *Fortune* observed what he did, and could not forbear discovering her Resentment of it. She instantly appeared to him, and, You Fool, says she, what a Blockhead are you to lie thanking the Ground thus, and take no Notice of Me! You Sot, you! if you had lost such a Treasure, instead of finding it, I should have been the first you would have laid the Blame upon.

The APPLICATION.

If our Affairs succeed and go well, we ought to let them have the Credit of it, to whose Interest it is chiefly owing, and whom, upon any Miscarriage, or ill Management, we should have found Fault with. That just Rule of Equity, *to do as we would be done unto*, should, as near as we can, be observed in every Action of our Lives. But Vanity and Peevishness dispose us too often to break it; one makes us ascribe that to our own good Address, which perhaps is owing to some Accident; the other puts us upon charging *Fortune*, or somebody besides ourselves, with that ill Success, for which we may probably be indebted to our own Stupidity and Negligence only. What Titles of Honour, what Stations of Dignity, what Places of Profit in Church and State, are now and then possessed by dull useless Wretches! who never once dreamt that they were obliged to *Fortune* alone for their Happiness in obtaining them. Yet, if the Case were quite otherwise, if those Places had been filled with Men of known Abilities, and these Creatures left low and undistinguished as their own Merit, it is ten to one but they would have cursed their Stars, fretted at their ill Luck, and stormed at the barbarous Treatment of their capricious *Fortune*.

FAB.

FAB. CLXXXVI.
The Ape *and her two* Young Ones.

AN Ape, having two Young Ones, was dotingly
fond of one, but difregarded and flighted the
other. One Day fhe chanced to be furprifed by the
Hunters, and had much ado to get off. However, fhe
did not forget her favourite Young One, which fhe
took up in her Arms, that it might be the more
fecure : The other, which fhe neglected, by natural
Inftinct, leapt upon her Back, and fo away they
fcampered together. But it unluckily fell out, that
the Dam, in her precipitate Flight, blinded with
Hafte, dafhed her Favourite's Head againft a Stone,
and killed it. The hated one, clinging clofe to her
rough Back, efcaped all the Danger of the Purfuit.

The APPLICATION.

This Fable is defigned to expofe the Folly of fome
Parents, who by indulging and humouring their favourite Children, fpoil and ruin them ; while thofe, of
whom they have been the leaft fond, have done very
well. The Child that knows it can command its Parents Affections, will hardly be brought to know how
to obey. The Fondnefs of indifcreet Parents to fa-

vourite Children, is blind as Love itſelf; they are ſo far from ſeeing any Blemiſhes or Imperfections in them, that their very Deformity is Beauty, and all their ugly Tricks Graces. Thus, without ever being checked and corrected for their Faults, but rather applauded and careſſed for them, when they come Abroad upon the Theatre of the World, what Rock will they not ſplit upon? While the Child who is ſo happy as to eſcape theſe very tender Regards, theſe pernicious Indulgences is obliged to be good and honeſt in its own Defence. The Parent looks upon it with an Eye clear from the Miſts of Fondneſs. He has no Regard to its Diſlike or Approbation; but for his own Credit, puts it into ſuch a Way of Education as Reaſon dictates; and forces it to be as accompliſhed, as its Capacity will admit.

F A B. CLXXXVII.
The Shepherd *turned* Merchant.

A Shepherd that kept his Sheep near the Sea, one clear Summer's Day, drove them cloſe to the Shore, and ſat down upon a Piece of a Rock to enjoy the cool Breeze that came from the Water. The green Element appeared calm and ſmooth; and *Thetis* with her Train of ſmiling beautiful Nymphs, ſeemed

to

to dance upon the floating Surface of the Deep.
The Shepherd's Heart thrilled with fecret Pleafure,
and he began to wifh for the Life of a Merchant.
O how happy, fays he, fhould I be, to plow this
liquid Plain, in a pretty, tight Veffel of my own !
and to vifit the remote Parts of the World, inftead
of fitting idly here, to look upon a Parcel of fenfelefs Sheep, while they are grazing ! then what ample Returns fhould I make in the Way of Traffick !
and what a fhort and certain Path would this be to
Riches and Honour ! In fhort, this Thought was
improved into a Refolution ; away he pofted with all
Expedition, fold his Flock, and all that he had ;
then he bought a Bark, and fitted it out for a
Voyage ; he loaded it with a Cargo of Dates, and
fet Sail for a Mart that was held upon the Coaft of
Afia, five hundred Leagues off. He had not long
been at Sea, before the Wind began to blow tem-
peftuoufly, and the Waves to rage and fwell ; the Violence of the Weather increafed upon him, his Ship
was in Danger of finking, and he was obliged to
lighten her, by throwing all his Dates overboard :
After this, his Veffel was driven upon a Rock near
the Shore, and fplit to Pieces ; he himfelf hardly ef-
caping with Life. Poor, and deftitute of Subfiftence,
he applied himfelf to the Man who had bought his
Flock, and was admitted to tend it as a Hireling. He
fat in the fame Place as before, and the Ocean again
looked calm and fmooth. Ah ! fays he, deceitful, tempt-
ing Element, in vain you try to engage me a fecond
Time ; my Misfortunes have left me too poor to be
again deluded the fame Way ; and Experience has
made me fo wife as to refolve, whatever my Condition
may be, never to truft thy faithlefs Bofom more.

The APPLICATION.

Bought Wit is beft : And the more Variety of Difap-
pointments we meet with, the greater will be our Expe-
P   rience,

rience, and the better we fhall be qualified to rub thro'
the World. Mankind has a ftrange Propenfity for Things
that are new and untried: and fo ftrong a Bias inclines
them to fhifting and changing, that every one difre-
lifhes his own Profeffion, and wifhes he had been of fome
other Employment. The young Academic, defigned
to the moft grave of all Profeffions, hates to think of his
peculiar Habit, of that formal referved Deportment by
which he is to feparate himfelf from what he counts the
Pleafures of the World, and bid adieu to that Irregularity which Youth fo much delights in. He longs for
a Commiffion in the Army, that he may be fafhionably
licentious, and indulge himfelf unqueftioned in the
wanton Sallies of a brifk youthful Appetite. In the
mean Time, the old Soldier, harraffed out with laborious Campaigns abroad, and vexed with the flow Returns of his Half-pay at Home, repines at the happy
Condition of the Ecclefiaftic, battening in Eafe and
Plenty, and fleeping unmolefted in one of the upper
Stalls of a Cathedral. With Remorfe he calls to Mind
his former Perverfenefs in quitting a College Life, and
defeating the Purpofe of his Relations, who had purchafed the next Reverfion of a fat Benefice for him. He
fhakes his Head, and reflects, that, if it had not been
for his Folly, inftead of aching Limbs, and an empty
Purfe, he might have enjoyed as much Leifure and
Luxury, as any Prieft in the Land.

Thus, fometimes with, fometimes without Reafon, we
are difgufted at our Station, and even thofe who are
embarked in another Way: Which, however it may
feem to be a Misfortune intailed upon us, yet carries
this Advantage with it, that, as we are almoft fure of
being difappointed by a Change, we are as certain likewife of gaining fome Experience by the Bargain, and
being wifer for the future.

FAB.

FAB. CLXXXVIII.
The Young Man and the Lion.

THERE was a certain old Man, who was Lord of a very great Estate; and had one only Child, a Son, of whom he was exceeding tender and fond; he was likewise one very apt to be influenced by Omens, Dreams, and Prognostics. The young Man, his Son, was mightily addicted to Hunting, and used to be up early every Morning to follow the Chace. But the Father happening to dream, one Night, that his Son was killed by a Lion, took it so to Heart, that he would not suffer him to go into the Forest any more. He built a fine Castle for his Reception, in which he kept him close confined, lest he should step out privately a hunting, and meet his Fate. Yet, as this was purely the Effect of his Love and Fondness for him, he studied to make his Confinement as agreeable to him as possible; and, in order to it, furnished the Castle with Variety of fine Pictures, in which were all Sorts of wild Beasts, such as the Son used to take Delight in hunting; and, among the rest, the Portrait of a Lion. This the young Man viewed one Day more attentively

than ordinary; and being vexed in his Mind at the
un eafonable Confinement which his Father's Dream
had occafioned, he broke out into a violent Paffion,
and looking fternly at the Lion, Thou cruel Savage,
fays he, it is to thy grim and terrible Form that I
owe my Imprifonment; if I had a Sword in my
Hand, I would thus run it thro' thy Heart. Saying
this, he ftruck his Fift at the Lion's Breaft, and unfortunately tore his Hand with a Point of a Nail
which ftuck in the Wainfcot, and was hid under the
Canvas. The Wound feftered, and turned to a Gan-
grene; this threw the young Man into a Fever, and
he died. So that the Father's Dream was fulfilled
by the very Caution that he took to prevent it.

The APPLICATION.

This Fable, though it may feem to favour and encourage the Notion of Dreams, and fuch fancied Difco-
veries of future Events, is however intended to ridicule
and explode them. What can be more abfurd than the
Practice of thofe credulous Fools, who, having Faith
enough to believe the Veracity of Oracles, had the Impudence or Stupidity to try to defeat them afterwards?
This was making a God with one Hand, and throwing
him away with the other. Firft they afk the Almighty
what he intends to do? When he has told them, they
believe him and tremble, but are refolved to difappoint
him if they can : Nay, they think they can, and fet about
it accordingly. Thefe low inconfiftent Notions of God,
gave the firft Birth to Atheifm : And were they not too
common in the World ftill, that pernicious Principle,
if there be any fuch Principle in Reality, would be either entirely rooted out, or grow fo thin, as not to hinder the Increafe of Virtue. When the Deity, which
the Generality of the World acknowledge, is ufed as if
he were a Deity of Irrefolution, Inftability, Mutability
and Paffion, Men of any Difcernment immediately re-
nounce fuch a Deity as that; and, for Want of due
Confideration, remain Atheifts. It being indeed lefs abfurd of the two, not to believe a Supreme Being at all,
than to believe he is fubject to the Frailties of us wretched
Mortals, and governed by Whim and Fancy.

FAB. CLXXXIX. *The* Hen *and the* Fox.

A FOX having crept into an Out-houfe, looked up and down, feeking what he might devour; and at laft fpied a Hen fitting upon the uppermoft Perch, fo high, that he could by no Means come at her. He then had Recourfe to his old Stratagem; Dear Coufin, fays he, addreffing himfelf to the Hen, how do you do? I heard that you were ill, and kept within; at which I was fo concerned, that I could not reft till I came to fee you. Pray how is it with you now? Let me feel your Pulfe a little; indeed you do not look well at all. He was running on after this impudent fulfome Manner, when the Hen anfwered him from the Rooft, Truly, Coufin *Reynard*, you are in the right on't; I never was in more Pain in my Life: I muft beg your Pardon for being fo free as to tell you, that I fee no Company; and you muft excufe me too for not coming down to you; for, to fay the Truth, my Condition is fuch, that I fear I fhould catch my Death, if I fhould do it.

The APPLICATION.

There are fome People in the World, whofe Addrefs

and Converfation are fo impertinent, fo fhocking, and
difagreeable, that it is doing Penance, and fuffering a
Kind of bodily Pain, to be in their Company. When
thefe familiar Fools with their repeated Officioufnefs, afk
us how we do, no Wonder if we are really fick; for how
can we be well when they are near us ? They either mean
nothing, and are vain, filly Impertinents, whom we abhor;
or cover fome evil Purpofe under a Difguife of naufeous
palpable Flattery, and therefore are to be treated with
Referve and Caution. A Man who fees thro' Flattery, is
indeed free from the Danger of it. But he fhould not be
fatisfied with that. If he is a public-fpirited Man, he ought
to difcountenance and expofe the Perfon that practifes it,
to prevent it from flourifhing abroad, and hurting thofe
who may not be wary enough to difcern, or ftaunch enough
to refift its Attacks. The Men of Flattery, as they are, in
fome Degree or other, a common Mifchief, ought to be
treated as common Enemies : And, as it is generally their
Defign to delude and impofe upon others, if we can be
before-hand with, and difappoint them, we fhall act, if
not generoufly, yet, however, fairly and difcreetly.

FAB. CXC. *The* Man *and the* Gnat.

AS a clownifh Fellow was fitting upon a Bank, a
Gnat fettled upon his Leg, and ftung it. He
clapped

clapped his Hand with great Vehemence upon the Place, with Intention to kill the Gnat; but the little nimble Infect, fkipping lightly between his Fingers, efcaped; and every Time he ftruck, he gave himfelf a fmart Blow upon the Leg, without being in the leaft able to touch the Gnat. This provoked him very much, fo that in the Height of his Paffion, he fell to invoking *Hercules*. O mighty *Hercules*, fays he, fince nothing can withftand thy Power, aid me, I befeech thee, againft this pernicious Gnat, and with thy invincible Strength, fubdue him, in Compaffion to me, miferable Creature, who am tormented with his venomous Sting.

The APPLICATION.

Many People, like the Clown in the Fable, are apt to invoke the Almighty upon every little trifling Accident that befals them. Not in an habitual unmeaning Exclamation, fuch as Children and childifh Folks ufe, but in a ferious deliberate Meditation, conceived in a Fit of Rapture, and delivered from the Clofet or Cabinet, in the ufual Seafon of Devotion. How many Things are prayed for with much Earneftnefs, which, if we were to enquire into them, are mere Vanities, and fuch as we ought to be afhamed of having! Not that the Supreme Being, who is all knowing and prefent every where, can be fuppofed to be ignorant of every little Thought of our Souls, or unable to comply with the Multiplicity of our Wifhes: But it is contrary to his exalted Nature to condefcend to our paltry felfifh Schemes, or to grant any of thofe Petitions, which we ourfelves, if we confidered, fhould be afhamed to put up.

FAB.

FAB. CXCI. *The* Deer *and the* Lion.

A Deer being hard pursued by the Hounds, found a Cave, into which he rushed for Security. But he was no sooner got in, than he saw himself in the Power of a Lion, who lay couched at the farther End of the Cave, and sprung upon him in an Instant. Being at the Point of Death, he complained thus: Unhappy Creature that I am! I entered this Cave to escape the Pursuit of Men and Dogs, and am fallen into the Jaws of the most cruel and rapacious of all wild Beasts.

The APPLICATION.

Some are so unfortunate, as to be ever running into Troubles and Difficulties; their ill Luck seems to ride them through a Series of Misfortunes, and, in the mean Time, like stumbling Horses, the oftener they are spurred, the more they flounce along in the Dirt, and the more Trips they make. But as much of this may be attributed to Fear and Hurry, which, wherever they take Place, indispose and hinder us from acquitting ourselves as we should do; it is therefore highly necessary for such as would be thought to behave themselves like Men, never to let Fear have any Share in their Words or Actions. This Passion blinds us from discern-

ing.

ing our true Intereſt: It no ſooner points out an Evil to
us, but it throws us into the utmoſt Confuſion, in our
Manner and Method of flying from it. We ſtart from
the preſent Miſchief, before we have pitched upon a
Place of Refuge; and, in the Hurry, fall into a thouſand worſe Accidents, which we have not Time to obſerve and avoid. But all this is far below the Character
of a great and a good Man. He dreads nothing more
than Shame; nor is aſhamed of any Thing ſo much as
Fear. Not all the Terrors of this, or any other World, can
blind the Eyes of his Reaſon, or diſarm his Underſtanding. Honeſty dictates to his Conſcience, and his Conſcience is the Rule of his Actions. And in this happy Situation of his Mind, tho' the World were to be cruſhed,
and thunder in Pieces about his Ears, he would be found
without Surpriſe amidſt the Ruins of it. It is peculiar to
Knaves or Fools to be hurried, through a Senſe of their
own Guilt or Shame; and to be always labouring under
Jealouſies, Doubts, Diſtruſts, and Diſappointments.

FAB. CXCII. *The* Gardener *and his* Dog.

A Gardener's Dog, friſking about the Brink of a
Well in the Garden, happened to fall into it.
The Gardener very readily ran to his Aſſiſtance; but

as

as he was endeavouring to help him out, the Cur bit him by the Hand. The Man took this ungrateful Treatment so unkindly, that he left him to shift for himself, with this Expostulation: Wicked Wretch, quoth he, are you so unreasonable as to injure the Hand that comes to save your Life! the Hand of me, your Master, who have hitherto fed and taken Care of you! Die, as you deserve; for so mischievous and ill-natured a Creature is not fit to live.

The APPLICATION.

All the Obligations you lay upon an ungrateful Person are thrown away. And therefore they who would be esteemed wise, as well as good, should use some Exactness in the Direction of their Favours, as well as Generosity in the Disposal of them. For there are some of such malevolent Tempers, that they are not only improper Objects of our Good-nature, as to themselves, in being undeserving; but of such vile Dispositions in respect to us, that we cannot approach them, though to do them a Kindness, without endangering our own Safety. Our Good-nature, therefore, as good a Quality as it is, will not excuse us, if we fall into the Hands of these Kind of People; something must be imputed to our Easiness and Want of Attention; and if we are so free as to bestow our Favours, without considering where we place them, the discerning Part of Mankind will rank us in the Class of Fools or Madmen, instead of giving us the Applause that is due to Actions truly liberal.

FAB.

FAB. CXCIII. *The* Cock *and the* Fox.

THE Fox, paffing early one Summer's Morning near a Farm-Yard, was caught in a Spring, which the Farmer had planted there for that End. The Cock, at a Diftance, faw what happened; and, hardly yet daring to truft himfelf too near fo dangerous a Foe, approached him cautioufly, and peeped at him, not without fome Horror and Dread of Mind. *Reynard* no fooner perceived it, but he addreffed himfelf to him, with all the defigning Artifice imaginable. Dear Coufin, fays he, you fee what an unfortunate Accident has befallen me here, and all upon your Account. For, as I was creeping through yonder Hedge, in my Way homeward, I heard you crow, and was refolved to afk you how you did before I went any further: But by the Way I met with this Difafter; and therefore now I muft become an humble Suitor to you for a Knife to cut this plaguy String; or, at leaft, that you would conceal my Misfortune; till I have gnawed it afunder with my Teeth. The Cock, feeing how

P 6　　　　　　　the

the Cafe ftood, made no Reply, but pofted away as faft as he could, and gave the Farmer an Account of the whole Matter; who, taking a good Weapon along with him, came and did the Fox's Bufinefs, before he could have Time to contrive his Efcape.

The APPLICATION.

Tho' there is no Quality of the Mind more graceful in itfelf, or that renders it more amiable to others, than the having a tender Regard to thofe who are in Diftrefs; yet we may err, even in this Point, unlefs we take Care to let our Compaffion flow out upon proper Objects only. When the Innocent fall into Misfortune, it is the Part of a generous brave Spirit to contribute to their Redemption; or, if that be impoffible, to adminifter fomething to their Comfort and Support. But when wicked Men, who have been Enemies to their Fellow-Subjects, are entrapped in their own pernicious Schemes, he that labours to deliver them, makes himfelf an Affo-ciate in their Crimes, and becomes as great an Enemy to the Public, as thofe whom he would fcreen and protect.

When Highwaymen and Houfebreakers are taken, condemned, and going to fatisfy Juftice, at the Expence of their vile paltry Lives; who are they that grieve for them, and would be glad to refcue them from the Rope? Not honeft Men, we may be fure. The reft of the thieving Fraternity would perhaps commiferate their Condition, and be ready to mutiny in their Favour: Nay, the rafcally Solicitor, who had been employed upon their Account, would be vexed that his Negocia-tions had fucceeded no better, and be afraid of lofing his Reputation among other Delinquents for the future. But every Friend to Juftice would have no Reafon to be diffatisfied at any Thing but a mournful Reflection which he could not forbear making, That, while thefe little Criminals fwing for fome trifling inconfiderable Rapine, others, fo tranfcendently their Superiors in Fraud and Plunder, efcape with a whole Skin.

FAB.

FAB. CXCIV. *The* Raven *and the* Serpent.

A Hungry Raven flying about in Queſt of his Prey, ſaw a Serpent baſking himſelf upon the Side of a ſunny Bank: Down he ſouſed upon him, and ſeized him with his horny Beak, in order to devour him: But the Serpent, writhing to and fro with the Pain, bit the Raven again with his venomous Teeth, to ſuch a Degree, that he could not ſurvive it. The Raven, in the Agonies of Death, is ſaid to have confeſſed that this Judgment happened to him juſtly; ſince he had attempted to ſatisfy his craving Appetite, at the Expence of another's Welfare.

The APPLICATION.

They who are of a ravenous greedy Temper, and for ſwallowing all that comes in their Way, may chance to meet with a Sting in the End. When People are actuated by an inſatiable Avarice, they ſtick at nothing; without conſidering the Lawfulneſs, or even the real Emolument of ſnapping at all; right or wrong, down it goes; and, if it has but the Appearance of Gain, they are for making a Seiſure, let the Conſequence be what it will.

'Thus the Covetous, whom God and Man abhor, puniſhes himſelf for his own Iniquity. Being deaf to the

Voice of Conscience, and the Dictates of Natural Reason, and blind to every Thing but his own vile selfish Views, throws himself after Getting, with a precipitate Violence, and often dashes himself to Pieces upon an unseen Rock.

FAB. CXCV. *The* Fox *and the* Hedgehog.

A Fox was swimming across a River; and, when he came to the other Side, he found the Bank so steep and slippery, that he could not get up it. But this was not all his Misfortune; for while he stood in the Water, deliberating what to do, he was attacked by a Swarm of Flies, who settling upon his Head and Eyes, stung and plagued him grievously. A Hedgehog, who stood upon the Shore, beheld and pitied his Condition, and, withal, offered to drive away the Flies, which molested and teazed him in that sad Manner. Friend, replies the Fox, I thank you for your kind Offer, but must desire you by no Means to disturb these honest Bloodsuckers that are now quartered upon me, and whose Bellies are, I fancy, pretty well filled; for if they should leave me, a fresh Swarm would take their Places, and I should not have a Drop of Blood left in my whole Body.

The APPLICATION.

This Fable is recorded by *Ariſtotle*; who tells us, that *Æſop* ſpoke it to the *Samians*, as an Argument to diſ-ſuade them from depoſing their great Miniſter of State. And a ſhrewd and weighty one it is too. For a Miniſter of State is either an honeſt public-ſpirited Man, and la-bours for the Good of the Commonwealth, or he is chiefly intent, by all Ways and Means, upon filling his own Coffers, and upon aggrandizing and enriching his Re-lations. Now, where the firſt happens, one need not ſay how much it behoves every particular Man, and all in general, to wiſh for the Continuance of ſo wiſe and good a Patriot: Neither ſhould they part with him merely for being one of the other Stamp; for, however crimi-nal he may be, in having robbed and plundered the Pub'ic, we ſhould conſider, that, like the Flies in the Fa-ble, he is pretty near full; and if he were to be re-moved, would only make Way for ſome other more hungry, who ſhould ſqueeze out of the poor People the Remainder of their Property.

FAB. CXCVI. *The* Maſter *and his* Scholar.

AS a Schoolmaſter was walking upon the Bank of a River, not far from his School, he heard a

Cry as of one in Diftrefs; advancing a few Paces farther, he faw one of his Scholars in the Water, hanging by the Bough of a Willow. The Boy had, it feems, been learning to fwim with Corks; and now, thinking himfelf fufficiently experienced, had thrown thofe Implements afide, and ventured into the Water without them; but the Force of the Stream having hurried him out of his Depth, he had certainly been drowned, had not the Branch of a Willow, which grew on the Bank, providentially hung in his Way. The Mafter took up the Corks, which lay upon the Ground, and throwing them to his Scholar, made ufe of this Opportunity to read a Lecture to him upon the inconfiderate Rafhnefs of Youth. Let this be an Example to you, fays he, in the Conduct of your future Life; never to throw away your Corks till Time has given you Strength and Experience enough to fwim without them.

The APPLICATION:

Some People are fo vain and felf-conceited, that they will run themfelves into a thoufand Inconveniencies, rather than be thought to want Affiftance in any one Refpect. Now there are many little Helps and Accommodations in Life, which they who launch out into the wide Ocean of the World, ought to make Ufe of as Supporters to raife and buoy them up till they are grown ftrong in the Knowledge of Men, and fufficiently verfed in Bufinefs, to ftem the Tide by themfelves. Yet many, like the Child in the Fable, through an Affectation of being thought able and experienced, undertake Affairs which are too big for them, and venture out of their Depth, before they find their own Weaknefs and Inability.

Few are above being advifed: Nor are we ever too old to learn any Thing which we may be the better for. But young Men above all, fhould not difdain to open their Eyes to Example, and their Ears to Admonition. They fhould not be afhamed to furnifh themfelves with Rules for their Behaviour in the World. However

mean

mean it may feem to ufe fuch Helps, yet it is really dangerous to be without them. As a Man who is lame with the Gout, had better draw the Obfervations of People upon him, by walking with a Crutch, than expofe himfelf to their Ridicule by tumbling down in the Dirt. It is as unnatural to fee a young Man throw himfelf out in Converfation with an affuming Air, upon a Subject which he knows nothing of, as for a Child of three Months old to be left to go without its Leading-ftrings: They are equally fhocking and painful to the Spectator. Let them have but Patience till Time and Experience ftrengthen the Mind of the one, and the Limbs of the other, and they may both make fuch Excurfions as may not be difagreeable or offenfive to the Eye of the Beholder.

And here it may not be improper to fay fomething by Way of Application to the Whole. It is not expected that they who are verfed and hackneyed in the Paths of Life, fhould trouble themfelves to perufe thefe little loofe Sketches of Morality; fuch may do well enough without them. They are written for the Benefit of the Young, and the Unexperienced; if they do but relifh the Contents of this Book, fo as to think it worth reading over two or three Times, it will have attained its End; and fhould it meet with fuch a Reception, the feveral Authors originally concerned in thefe Fables, and the prefent Compiler of the Whole, may be allowed not altogether to have mifemployed their Time, in preparing fuch a Collation for their Entertainment.

THE END.

INDEX.

I N D E X.

A.

ADVICE, when to be rejected, *Page* 141. Who are unfit to give it, 177. Confider who gives it, before you take it, 44.

Affectation, the Inconveniencies of it, 78. It is the Bane of Beauty, 106. Other Inconveniencies of it, 161.

Agriculture recommended, 236.

Athenians enflaved by *Pififtratus*, 6.

Attorney draws the 'Squire into a Mortgage, 45.

Avarice, and Ambition, frequently difappointed, 102. Unaccountable, 138. That and Envy expofed and enquired into, 229. That and Ambition ought to fuffer, 9. The Inconveniencies of it, 325.

Authors Merit, not by writing much, but well, 121.

B.

Beauty, that of the Mind preferable to that of the Body, 106.

Biter bit, 187.

Brave Men, above being provoked by Cowards, 26.

Bribe, cannot tempt an honeft Man, 182.

Britons, jealous of Strangers, 109.

Bullies, generally Cowards, 122. Overact their Part, 207.

C.

Captious, not good to be fo, 83.

Change, feldom makes Things better, 250.

Changeling Plumftock, Sir, vieswith Lord *Caftlebuilder*, 21.

Children ought to take their Parents Advice, 196.

Church, thofe that frequent it out of Vanity, their Re'igion not worth a Straw, 49.

Civility,

INDEX.

Fashions,

INDEX.

F.

Fashions, oddly introduced, 116.

Fault, not to be found with others, if guilty ourselves, 185.

Favourite, every one not fit to be so, 211. Surprising when honest, 47.

Fear, the Inconveniencies of it, 320. It is unreasonable, 55. Vain and insignificant, 142.

Flattery, mischievous, but hard to be avoided, 17.

Foreigners should not slight the Country they are in, 171.

Fortune, often blamed wrongfully, 156. Ought to have her Due, 310.

Forwardness should be discouraged, 195.

Foul Means, sometimes best, 192.

Friend, false one, a detestable Thing, 154. Them and Relations not to be depended on, 72. We should be nice in our Choice of them, 252.

Friendship, necessary to our Well-being, 94, 248, 294. Insecure till tried, 84.

G.

Gaming-Houses, those stupid that frequent them, 125.

Genealogy, foolish to insist upon it, 158.

Generosity, a handsome Virtue, 57.

Glass, a Reason why we should often consult it, 132.

Glory, nothing should be undertaken for the Sake of it, 150.

God, served better another Way than by Prayer, 100.

Good-nature, our Interest to exercise it, 57.

Government, necessary to be supported, 69.

Greatness, exposed to Storms, 145.

Great Cry and little Wool, 47.

Great Men, bad Neighbours, 87.

H.

Habit, the Inconvenience of it, 291.

Haste, the more, the worse Speed, 175.

Honest Man, his Word as good as his Oath, 307.

Honesty the best Policy, 189. Dangerous in bad Times, 4.

Humanity, how far it ought to go, 267. Is a great Virtue, 168.

Idle

INDEX.

I.

K.

L.

7

INDEX.

INDEX.

Self,

INDEX.

S.

Self, every Man should exert himself, and not trust others, 72.
Self-love, no ill Principle, 278.
Servants neglect their Masters' Affairs, 34.
Slavery, Rogues and Villains who consent to bear it, 36.
Spectres, &c. when they flourish most, 142.
Spendthrifts repent too late, 125.
Suspicion, an useful Quality, 153.

T.

Times deplorable, when Villainy is protected, 221.
Traitors, hated by those that employ them, 251.
Travellers, given to Lying, 130.
Trust, have a Care whom, 273.
Trust, no Injuries so bitter as from those we trust, 181.
Turn, one good, deserves another, 226.

V.

Very pretty Fellows, Strangers to Virtue and Knowledge, 2.
Virtue, troublesome to a young Lady, 15.
Visits, which appear charitable, not always so, 10.
Vulgar, not to be followed, 52.

W.

Weakness in Conversation, what happens upon it, 82.
Wicked Men, in Power, easily find Pretences, 218. Hate those that are otherwise, 298. We should avoid them, 301.
Wife, that loves her Husband, what she should do, 32.
Wit, dangerous for Fools to attempt it, 24. Hurtful to him that uses it to hurt others, 21.
Words, Men known by them, 299.
Worth, a Man lessens his own by enquiring after it, 297.

Y.

Young Lady practising at her Glass, 14.
Young Men, a Piece of Advice to them, 328.

F I N I S.